Woodland Academy

MAËVA DEBEAUQUENNE

First paperback edition 2022

Book cover by Yuliya Horobets
Book design by Jennie Lyne Hiott @bookcoverit.com
Book design edited by Dylan Crosbie
Illustrations by Valentyna Petyurenko
Edited by Christine Baker

ISBN: 978-988-76458-0-1 (paperback)

www.maevadraws.com

FOR EWAN & ULYSSE, WHO INSPIRED THIS BOOK.
FOR GREG, WHO'S BEEN MY ROCK THROUGH
EVERYTHING.
Je vous aime

Contents

Before You Start...

The story you're about to read is filled with animals but I took some small liberties with some species (mostly with their nocturnal habits and lifespans).

I hope you enjoy this trip to Woodland Forest as much as I enjoyed creating it!

Maëva

Chapter 1

Can you guess what I am?

Every story starts with "once upon a time", so let's not do that! I want to begin this book with a simple "hello!" Hello, how are you? My name is Applesauce and I'm here to talk about myself. Well, myself and my best friend Buttercup. But I can't talk about Buttercup without also talking about his sister Almond. And of course I will have to mention Apricot, Tulip, and Violet. And I'm sure to talk about Hazelnut, too, at some point, plus my parents, our neighbours... Ok, you know what? Let's just say it's going to be a story about my friends and I. Oh ... but what if I also want to talk about Sunny? She's not really my friend but I'll probably need to mention her too. I know, let's start this again!

Pretend you haven't read those first few lines. Can you do that? Just to be sure, close your eyes and shake your head to forget this terrible beginning. I can't see you, so I'll have to trust you on this.

I'll start again and we can all pretend that the next sentence is the first one in this book. Are you ready? Argh no, I didn't mean to add the "are you ready?" part. Now you're going to think that was the first (well, second first) sentence of this book but no no no, it's not!

Ok let's try this one last time and if it doesn't work I'll just go and eat a big chocolate cake covered with whipped cream (with a scoop of vanilla ice-cream on the side because life is always better with ice-cream) and I'll let you write this book! So the real story starts ... now!

Hello, how are you? My name is Applesauce and I'm here to talk about myself. Well, all the wonderful creatures (minus Sunny) that live in Woodland Forest and me. Do you know Woodland Forest? I don't imagine you do, because most humans don't know the name of our beloved forest. Oh, did I forget to mention that I'm not human? Sorry, my bad! I would start again from the beginning but let's be honest, I'm too tired for that. Plus, someone mentioned something about a chocolate cake, whipped cream (and ice cream!) earlier so now I'm starving too!

So yes, I am not human.

Let's see if you can guess what I am.

First, I will say that I am NOT a scary three-eyed monster with a bad smell and a tongue that never stays in its mouth.

Second, I will also say that I am NOT a giant shiny green alien slobbering slime everywhere it goes and trying to hug everyone in the street, thank you very much!

So, do you know what I am yet? No? Oh yeah, maybe I should give you some clues about what I am instead of telling you the things I am not.

Well, just one last hint about what I am not because I think it's a silly thing to say in a book (and I love silly things): I am NOT a giant carrot with long blue hair and a purple hat. I told you it was a silly one.

Ok, so what am I?

I'm an animal. Can you guess what kind yet? What do you mean, it's not enough information? Alright, alright, I'll stop teasing you. Let's see...

I live in the woods. Now that I think about it, maybe you've already guessed this since the title of this book has the word woodland in it. Unless it's the kind of book that likes to trick readers. You think it's going to talk about a forest but it ends up being a book about the history of umbrellas or about how many colours of pencils exist in the world. But no, this is not a book that tricks people. I really am a woodland animal. Let's see, how can I describe myself? I don't have a mirror so I'll cover the basics.

I am quite small, I have a tail and four legs. I can use all four at once, or I can use only two if needed. I can also tell you that I have claws but not the scary type. And I can run in trees. Run in them, climb them, jumping from branches to branches. Oh yeah that's a good clue for you: I spend a lot of time in trees!

My last clue: I am fluffy! Well, not my whole body (except after my bath but I don't want to talk about it and please don't ask my mum to show you those embarrassing pictures). The truth is, it's really my tail that's fluffy. In fact, I'm so fluffy some of my friends call me The Fluffy King or sometimes Orange Fluff. Yes, I'm orange, good job on spotting the last clue!

So have you guessed? I am a ... rat! No, I'm kidding, I'm a squirrel!

Oh, and by the way, no one really calls me The Fluffy King, which is a pity because I think it would be a fun nickname! My real name is Applesauce. I still don't know why my parents called me this but I admit, my own name always makes me hungry. With two parents who love to cook as much as mine do, I guess it's not surprising I have such a tasty name.

My mum and dad own a bakery. Well, it's not just any bakery, it's the only bakery in Woodland to be precise. It's called Sweet Treat and it sells all kinds of pies: apple, chocolate, peach, caramel - you name it, we have it. Plus all the flavors of cupcakes, pastries, brioches, and the most delicious bread. They love to try new things like making their own chocolates, testing new recipes and serving homemade hot chocolate for the customers to drink with their food. They even created cookies shaped like the animals of our forest. So you can say, "Hello! I would like a fox cookie today!"

Everyone loves those cookies and their bakery is always busy. And, if you're looking for their biggest fan, don't look further, I'm right here! I could eat their pastries all day. If you want to find me among the other squirrels of our forest, it's easy: I'm the chubby one with yummy food always stuck in his cheeks. If it fits, I take it! You never know when you're going to be hungry again. I love being a squirrel because we can use our cheeks as bags. Bags filled with delicious chocolate-y food ...

Anyway, sorry, I'm starting to daydream about food again (I tend to do that) and I forgot to tell you all about Woodland. After all, this book is not all about me (but don't worry I'm the one telling the story so my fans won't be disappointed)!

Are you ready to learn more about my friends and our magical forest? Yeah? Let's go!

Chapter 2
What's a Buttercup?

I'll start with myself because it's easier.

We haven't met but maybe you can imagine what I look like. Have you ever seen a squirrel? I don't mean a picture in a book but a real squirrel? Maybe in your garden or a forest? It's easy to think all squirrels look the same but that's absolutely not true. Just like no two humans are the same. Even twins have tiny differences that help you tell them apart.

My body is bright orange with tiny black spots, especially on my face. I like to think this makes me look older and I like that, even though my friend Almond insists that it does not. (I won't tell you how old I am because it's very rude to ask a squirrel his age.) My ears are covered with soft orange hairs, my whiskers are thin and black, and my belly is all white. My favourite part of my body is my tail, of course. Did I mention that it is very fluffy? I did? Several times? Oops, sorry!

Well, my magnificently soft and majestic tail also has something peculiar: it's bright orange with a silver-y grey stripe down the middle. Don't worry, I'm not sick. I'm actually really proud of my grey stripe because it's the sign that I'm part of Woodland Forest. Every animal here is born with this grey mark somewhere on its body. For some it's on the face, for others it's on their hooves or on their paws.

I love that we all share the same mark even though we're all so different. My stripe is on my tail but on my best friend Buttercup it's on the inside of his left ear. Yes, inside!

But that's not the only thing that makes him and I different.

First of all I'm a squirrel and Buttercup is a ...

Actually, no I won't tell you, I want you to guess again (maybe I should write the whole book with riddles!) Ready? Go!

He's small.

Can you guess yet? No? Well, you're not really good at guessing games, are you?!

I'm kidding, I know I haven't given you enough clues! I'm going to make this second round super duper really really hard and I bet you'll never guess what animal Buttercup is.

He is ... drum roll please ... covered with spines that can be really painful to touch! Ah ah I know it's a very difficult game and you - what do you mean you guessed it already?! You think Buttercup is a hedgehog? Oh!

Yeah, you're right. I don't know how you managed to guess so easily. Was it the painful spines? Ok, I guess it was a bit of a giveaway. Maybe the hedgehog on the cover helped you too? Well, I think I'm the one who's not really so good at guessing games after all.

Actually, did you know the hedgehog is not the only animal with spines or quills? Can you think of another one? You know what? I'll go grab something to eat while you're thinking about it, ok?

I'm going into the kitchen...

... opening every cupboard ...

... no, I don't want fruit, no nuts either ...

... going to check near the fridge ...

... oh! I see the cookie jar ...

... praying it's filled with Dad's delicious chocolate cookies ...

.... opening the jar ...

... yes! There are some cookies left! I'll take one ...

... heading back toward you ...

I'm back! What? How many cookies did I eat? I don't see how that's relevant to our story but fine, I'll tell you! I ate one. And then maybe one more because the first was so small it barely counted. Ok, you got me, I grabbed two more on the way out to eat while I'm talking to you! (Sorry in advance if you find cookie crumbs in this book!)

Anyway, back to my question. Have you guessed the other animals with spines? If you did, here's a cookie. If you didn't, it's ok. I'll help you by sharing what I know.

So ... I give to you my "super long list of animals with quills or spines":

The hedgehog, of course!

The sea urchin.

The porcupinefish, also known as the blowfish. You know, it's this funny round yellow fish covered with sharp spines that can inflate its body by swallowing water. If you don't know what I'm talking about, look it up in a book or online, you'll see!

The echidna. I know what you're thinking but no, an echidna is not the same as a hedgehog. They are bigger and they live in a different country.

The porcupine. Also bigger than a hedgehog, with longer spines and a different body shape but most importantly they always look like they are just coming out of the hairdresser. They look so funny and trendy!

The thorny devil. I think the name alone is proof that it belongs on this list. This Australian lizard looks so peculiar that it's sometimes called a thorny dragon despite being so small.

Sorry, in the end, that wasn't really a long list but I hope it will inspire you to look for more information about our spiny friends.

Anyway, where was I before I tried to make you guess that Buttercup is a hedgehog? Oh yes, our differences.

So he's a hedgehog, I'm a squirrel. That's one difference.

What else?

I could eat all day. Buttercup is a small eater.

I love everything with chocolate or lots of sugar. He's the healthiest animal I know. Buttercup mainly eats grains and fruit, and he absolutely loves carrots. I'm not kidding. When I'm snacking on a chocolate muffin, he's nibbling at his carrot sticks. The only exceptions he allows to his diet are the delicious orange pastries my parents make at the bakery. They're his favourite.

Buttercup is a very chatty animal. He goes around and talks easily to everyone all the time. He stops to say hello to our neighbours on our way to the supermarket and loves it when they share their stories with him.

Personally, I'm a more quiet boy. I don't dislike talking to other animals and I do say "hello", "please" and "thank you" when I should. But I don't know how to chat as easily as he does. Also, I really do enjoy being alone, in a quiet place. Give me a good book, a nice cup of hot chocolate, an empty tree hole and I'm in heaven!

I'm an only child. Buttercup has four sisters.

Buttercup loves to wake up early, I could easily sleep all day. And I really mean it: all day!

That's our friendship. Despite all our differences, we are best friends and always have been. We don't see what's different, we celebrate what we love in each other. I'm a quiet squirrel but I admire how he always manages to talk so easily with everyone and make friends so quickly. In return I'm sure he appreciates being friends with the fluffiest animal in the forest.

Chapter 3

Do you believe in magic?

Today is a very special day for me because it's my first day of school. My first day at Woodland Academy. Oh, didn't I mention that I was a young wizard? (If you're wondering what to call a squirrel wizard, it's simple: a squizard! No, I'm kidding! But don't you think it's a great name?)

You're probably wondering why you've never heard of Woodland Academy and all its squizards. Well you see, humans used to know about us and practice magic too but unfortunately over time they have closed themselves to it. So, in order to protect ourselves, we had to hide our world. Our forest is still visible to humans but our magic is not. So next time you see a little bird in a tree, think twice before thinking it's just a bird innocently singing because it may actually be practicing spells. Although there are some birds who really do enjoy singing, like my friends, Breeze and Echo. They are twins and they are always singing. They sing when they fly, when they are resting on their branches, even when they are queueing at the supermarket with their mum. I'm not even sure they know how to talk. They sing about everything!

So yes, even if most people can't see it anymore, we are doing magic in our forest and there's more going on than what your eyes show you. The truth is, people who look carefully and who believe in magic can still see us.

Not all of us practice magic though. I chose to enrol at Woodland Academy but not all the animals in Woodland Forest do. Yes, you read it correctly: I was not born a wizard, I chose to be one! I know that you've probably read other books about wizards and witches born from magic blood. Nah, it's just a lie.

Those stories were written by grown ups just to make sure you won't bug them with, "Mum, can I go to the magic school? My school is so boring I want to learn how to fly on a broomstick ..."

But I, Applesauce, am an honest squizard so I will tell you the truth.

Truth number one: anyone can learn magic. No matter your age, your size or where you're from!

Sadly, here's truth number two: humans stopped teaching magic a long time ago and closed all of their schools. Here, we call them academies, but I heard that human wizards called them schools. No idea why! I heard a rumour that there's still one big school hidden somewhere in England with a very famous boy but I don't know if it's true or if it's just another made up story.

And now, I think I can predict your two next questions.

1. Why did humans close the magic schools?

Answer: They closed them because some human wizards were becoming too powerful and were using their magic to do bad things. People got really scared and, after a long war to fight this dark magic, they decided to end it all. Close the schools and pretend it was all fairy tales and children's stories. Hopefully, some families still pass stories of this magic past down from one generation to the next, so some people still know about it even though no human practices magic anymore.

2. Do my parents know about this?

Answer: Well, I don't know your parents personally but this is how I see it.

Some adults don't know anything about it at all because they didn't grow up believing in magic. In fact, I'm pretty sure some grown ups went directly from newborn babies to boring adults with no imagination, no sparkle in their eyes and no dreams in their head. I've even heard that some adults don't read. I'm shivering just thinking of a life without books. A life where you don't discover new friends and new worlds every time you open a book? How dreadful! I feel sad for those people because I love dreaming. (Maybe too much according to my parents.) And then there are some humans who used to believe in a world where magic exists but who got too scared of it when they grew up and now they prefer to think it's not real. Actually I'm sure I can picture a conversation between you and your parents if they fall in this second category.

Your mum/dad, "Hello darling, how was your day?"

They give you a quick kiss on the cheek before handing you your after school snack.

You: "Good, good but I..."

Your mum/dad, "What? What is it sweetie?"

They ask with their eyes focused on their phones.

You, "I decided I want to change my school!"

Your mum/dad, suddenly looking up from their screen, "What? Why? What's wrong with _____ (insert the name of your human school here)?

You: "Well, it's good, I like it and I love my friends but ..."

Your mum/dad, "But what? Come on, tell me, I don't have all day!"

(Why are parents always so busy? Do you think you have to be a grown up to be busy like them all the time? Because it doesn't seem very fun, does it?)

You, "I want to go to a school where they teach you magic!"

Your mum/dad, laughing a little bit, "Oh you mean you want to learn magic tricks like they do on TV?"

You, "No, I mean real magic!!"

Your mum/dad, raised eyebrows, "What? What are you talking about ____ (insert your name here)?"

You, "You know, a real magic school for witches and wizards, like Applesauce told me about." (Ok, I'll stop you right there. Please

11

don't use my name, I don't want trouble with your parents. Just use a fake name for me. Let's just say I'm called Sebastian!)

You, "A real magic school for witches and wizards, like Sebastian told me about."

Your mum/dad, "Honey, there are no such things as wizards and witches, you know that! They are only stories in books and movies. Now, come on and eat your snack."

Then they get so nervous about this conversation that they ignore your answer and pretend to get a sudden phone call, even though you're sure you didn't hear the phone ring and that the screen is still black.

So here it is, the sad truth. With time, the adults forgot all about real magic, they got scared and now they prefer to pretend they don't know anything about it.

That's why, before I begin telling you all about my Academy, you must promise me that YOU do believe in magic and that you won't make fun of us. Well I allow you to laugh if, at some point in this book I get my nose stuck in a cookie jar or if Almond tells a good joke for example. But you are not allowed to say that magic is not real. Otherwise this book will bite you. No, I'm kidding! Or am I?

Chapter 4
Woodland forest

There are magic academies in lots of places: rainforests, deserts and even mountains but our story takes place in England, in Woodland Forest. It's not much but it's home. It's cosy, friendly (most of the time) and we all love it. Well, except Sunny the frog but she likes to complain all the time for no reason. For someone with a name like that, let me tell you she's really not a ray of sunshine. More like a big grey cloud ready to burst on your good day with all her negativity. She's always complaining about Woodland Forest: the winter is too cold, the neighbours too noisy, the dirt too brown or the water too wet! And she's a frog! Can you believe it? Anyway, apart from Grumpy Sunny, everyone here loves our forest!

I have never travelled to other forests so I can't really compare but our village is really a wonderful place to live in. Depending on their size, some animals think Woodland is a small forest while others say it's so big they can't see the end of it.One thing is sure though: it's a happy forest! There's space for everyone and you'll find a nice variety of species, from tiny worms to small river otters, from deer to wolves and big furry bears.

It's also a happy place because, as I've already told you, you can find the best bakery in the world here! I honestly don't know why my parents named it Sweet Treat instead of The Best Bakery in the World. Dad told me that you can't declare yourself the best, it's not humble. Well *humble mumble,* I think it's the best and that's that!

We also have a small hospital (technically called Care Centre for Wounded and Sick Animals but we all call it The Hospital), as well as a small post office (run by birds of course), a police station, some shops (for food, books, clothes and other stuff) and of course, our Academy.

This year the Academy is located in the north part of the forest between the hospital and the supermarket. Our forest is small but my parents explained to me that we like to move the school around regularly to help the forest renew itself. I love that: it's good for the forest and it means that it's never boring!

A long time ago, one of the Headmasters thought it would be a good idea to have the Academy set up in a tree but, as you can imagine, it didn't work very well with bears and other big students. You won't be surprised to learn that this Headmaster didn't stay in charge of the Academy very long.

I'm not sure if all magic schools are the same but ours is divided into two campuses. A dry one and an underwater one, called the Wats campus, for the pond animals. Of course I will be going to the dry one. Both campuses have three different classes and unlike your human schools, we are not grouped by age but by level. Basically it goes like this:

The Seed Class for beginners like me, with zero knowledge of magic.

The Flower Class for the upper level.

And finally, the advanced level, which I like to call the "I know so much magic I can rule the forest and the world if I want to" level. But everyone just refers to it as The Tree Class. Less fun if you ask me!

So you see, everyone going to the Academy has to start at The Seed Class, no matter how old they are or what they think they know about magic. That way we all start equal. Some animals only start school when they are adults, so sometimes the students are older than their teachers! It also means each class is filled with a lovely mix of different animals of all ages and species. Doesn't that sound fun?

I'm starting school today but I already know some of the animals who will join me in the beginner class, like Dean the deer, and Breeze and Echo, the blue bird twins, as bright as they are loud. Buttercup and Almond will also start with me today and I have to say it's so fun to begin a new adventure with my two best friends. Don't get me wrong, I'm really excited to join the Academy but to be honest, I'm also a tiny bit nervous. I keep wondering if I'll be a good wizard and I'm nervous about meeting my classmates. Having Buttercup and Almond with me, learning magic together, makes it less scary. That's what I love about friendship. Friends can be there to play with you but they can also help you through difficult moments. Sometimes they don't even need to do anything to help you. Just being there at your side is enough. You feel strong and confident just because they're here. It's almost like magic, isn't it?

Speaking of magic, it's time to get ready for school! It's breakfast time and I'm starving!

The oak tree I live in with my parents is quite big for a small family of three squirrels but obviously, it's not big enough for my parents to bake their delicious pastries and cook in there, so they built a kind of extension to our house on the ground, at the bottom of our tree. They use it as a kitchen to keep our food and to cook in a little wooden oven that they made, with a hole at the top to let the smoke escape. Apart from the delicious food in it, the thing I love most about this extra room is that my parents turned it into a community kitchen to share with our neighbours. They built it to be quite big right from the beginning to allow Almond and other animals bigger than us to use it too.

Oh yes, I told you that Almond was Buttercup's sister but I think I forgot to mention that she's not a hedgehog, she's actually a fox! How is that possible? How can they be brother and sister if they're not the same species? It's easy: because families don't need an explanation. To form a family, you just need love. You see, some time ago Almond lost both her parents in a terrible hunting accident outside of Woodland and even though Buttercup's parents already had four children they knew they couldn't leave this little fox all alone, so they adopted her. So now we all live next to each other: my family, the Softpaws, up in our tree, and the Dreamcreek family in the ground next to our tree's roots. Almond sleeps in her den with the hedgehogs' nest just next to her, and we all meet in our common area on the ground. We have a big wooden table outside, next to our kitchen, where we often eat all together. I love eating and I love it even more when I get to share meals with my friends.

Chapter 5

Breakfast is the most important meal of the day! (But let's be honest, every meal is important to me!)

So, as I was saying, it's Breakfast time (and no, those cookies I just had don't count)!

Nervous or not, I'm always a hungry squirrel, so I go quickly down our tree to explore our kitchen cupboards in search of the perfect "first day of school breakfast". Not surprisingly my mum is already there, with a tray full of all my favourite food ready for me on the kitchen table!

Like a lot of the furniture in Woodland, this table comes in two sizes to ensure it's the right fit for every animal. Most of the time you'll find a big piece of furniture with a smaller version next to it. Sometimes the smaller animals will put their own chairs on top of the big table so we can all chat and enjoy our lunch together. Most of the time we use our small inside table for cooking and for our two families to dine on. But if we have some of our bigger neighbours over for tea (like the bears or the deers), we'll use the big table outside since they wouldn't be able to fit on the inside table.

My mum has her back turned to me and is humming her favourite song when I enter so she's a bit startled when I say, "Good morning Mum!"

She jumps a bit before turning around to answer me in one big breath,

"Hello honey! How are you? Did you sleep well? Are you ready for your first day? Do you want to eat? What am I saying, of course you want to eat ... You're always hungry. Look I made you your favourite bread, and I have some honey and raspberry jam, or you can have some chocolate buns, and there's some juice and lots of fruits ... and some milk of course! You want milk, Applesauce?"

My mum must have superpowers because she managed to say all this while smiling, pouring me the juice and twirling a bit before handing me the glass! Yeah, I have a very joyful mum! She's always dancing, humming and smiling, even when she's cooking. She speaks a lot in a very speedy fashion but it's only because she's a very passionate squirrel! It's a wonder I'm such a quiet squirrel in comparison!

I smile at her welcoming words and at all the food she has prepared for me before going to kiss her near her right ear. Her grey mark covers the outside of both her ears, it's so funny! She kisses me back and smiles at me.

"Everything looks delicious, it's perfect! Thank you for all this, Mum!"

"Did you have a good night?" She asks again while I sit down.

"Yes! I slept like a bear! But I had a funny dream that Buttercup was suddenly a big elephant with two tails and Almond and I were chasing him ... And just as we all transformed into giraffes, I woke up!"

My mum laughs very loudly at this. "Oh I'm imagining Buttercup and Almond as giraffes but still covered in prickles and Almond still with her orange tail!"

Just as I start to picture it, Buttercup arrives quietly in the kitchen.

"Good morning! Why are you both laughing so much? And why did I hear my name? Were you making fun of me?" He asks this last one to me while sitting down on my right.

We tell him about my funny dream and how my mum pictured it as she pours him some almond milk and hands him a plate of nuts.

"Oh my favourite! Thank you, Auntie Rose!!"

My mum isn't really Buttercup's aunt but our two families are like one big family, so he calls my parents Auntie and Uncle and I do the same with his!

"Oh and there's also a box of dried berries on the table if you want Buttercup." She gestures to a little container with a lid and he smiles at it.

"Oh thanks, that's perfect!"

I love nuts and berries too but I start my breakfast with two chocolate buns and one slice of Mum's bread. Buttercup raises his eyes at me when he sees how full my plate is.

"Do you think you'll have enough food until lunch?"

"Oh no, this is just to warm up my stomach! I'll have some apricot pie and a croissant before we leave!"

He laughs at this.

"Your appetite never ceases to impress me, Applesauce! Especially for such a small animal!"

"What? I don't want to start school on an empty stomach!"

"But I've seen you eat big breakfasts like this even on a normal day!"

I blush a bit at this but it doesn't stop me from looking for the apricot pie farther away on the table.

"So, are you boys excited to start school?" My mum asks us while sitting down with us.

I nod, my mouth too full to speak. Buttercup answers her nicely, without any food in his mouth, like the polite hedgehog he is.

"Yes I'm really happy! I hope the teacher will be nice."

"Oh yeah, don't worry about that! This year the teacher for the Seed Class is Mrs Winter and she's lovely! She's always stopping by the bakery to get her daily brioche after school."

I'm trying to see which one of our regular clients Mum is talking about when it finally hits me.

"Oh, the wolf with her grey mark right in the middle of her back?"

"Yes. A very charming lady!"

I'm still not convinced that, on top of being a great fan of our brioches, Mrs Winter is a good teacher when Mum adds, "Well, I heard she can be a bit strict but it's fine, a bit of authority won't hurt you Applesauce."

She winks at me with a mischievous smile on her face so I'm not sure she's really serious about the authority part. Buttercup catches my worried expression and tries to reassure me.

"I'm sure she'll be perfect! Don't worry Applesauce!"

Almond arrives just before we leave and as always she's rushing, her big orange tail tickling me when she passes by me. She only stops to say hello to my mum and quickly grabs some food to eat on the way. My dad is already at the bakery, and the rest of the Dreamcreek family is either still sleeping or at work, so there's only Mum to wish us a good first day. I hug her tightly and the three of us are off.

The Academy is on the other side of the forest so the three of us have some time together before we meet our new friends and teacher. As soon as Almond has swallowed her bread, she starts to ask us a million questions about how we are feeling. Buttercup and I look at each other and smile.

"You know that you're doing a great imitation of my mum, babbling non stop like this?" I ask her, with a small laugh.

"Oh, it's only because I'm so excited to start school! We're finally going to learn magic, learn spells and, oh, the best part is that we're going to meet new animals! Yeah! I love new animals!"

"We know you do," Buttercup smiles at his sister.

"Mum said that our teacher will be Mrs Winter. She's a wolf-"

I can't even finish my sentence because Almond literally jumps into the air at this announcement.

"A wolf? Really? Oh it's going to be so much fun!"

She's skipping to school, I've never seen such a happy fox!

"Do we know who the other teachers are?"

"I heard that there's a hen but I don't know what class she takes care of." Buttercup answers.

I laugh with him at the idea of a hen teaching woodland animals but Almond seems to love the idea.

"I like it. I don't find it stranger than a fox being adopted by a hedgehog family."

I think about this and nod. "It's true."

Almond is such a warm-hearted fox. She always sees the good in others and doesn't let the fact that she lost her parents define who she is. Of course she misses them but she's always looking forward to meeting new animals and finding new things to like. I'm glad she ended up in Buttercup's family because they share this attitude, and they are all so kind and caring.

Since he and I are both smaller than her in size, Almond always offers us a ride on her back when we walk together. Of course, both Buttercup and I can walk, but we tend to slow her down when we walk with her. Almond's not just fast because she's bigger than us, she's also always jumping around, skipping, hopping. I don't think she knows how to walk, she runs all the time. She says life is too exciting and she can't slow down! So this morning, as usual, we ended our journey to school on her back.

Since I don't have to focus on walking I love to daydream and enjoy the view. To be honest, I daydream even when I am walking and should be looking where I'm going. This usually ends up with me tripping over some roots but I can't help it, I love to think and imagine many things at the same time!

After a nice ride on Almond's back, exchanging theories about what's waiting for us today, we finally arrive at the Academy. There's no wall, no big scary doors and no castle tower. Our campus is very simple but I already know I'm going to love it!

Chapter 6
First day, yay!

Almond stops at the entrance and Buttercup and I jump on the ground next to her. Instead of a door, there is a big arch to indicate the location of the Academy. It's made of several thin tree trunks on each side linked on the top with a mix of twigs and branches and it's decorated with colourful leaves and pinecones. The big wooden sign on top says "Woodland Academy for Wizards of all Ages and Sizes."

"Wooooah that's a long name!" I cry after reading the big sign.

"Yes! Wouldn't it have been easier to put "Woodland Academy" though?" Buttercup asks with a small chuckle.

"Oh I love it!! At least we know it's open to everyone, youhou!!!" Almond says, jumping up and down. "Come on, let's gooooo! What are you waiting for?"

Ok, now she's even singing to ask us to follow her!

Buttercup and I laugh at Almond's amazing enthusiasm and follow her. As Buttercup runs after her, she's already talking with a small rabbit arriving at the same time. I, on the other hand, slow down a bit to take it all in, to really grasp the idea that this is it! Today is my first day of school and I'm on my way to become a great squizard! I mean I don't know if I'll be a great one but I have to believe that at least I'll be the best I can be. And I'll make new friends so that's definitely a new adventure. I hope they will be nice to me.

I tend to take some time to warm up to new animals and I know that not everyone understands this kind of behaviour. Most people prefer you to be all chatty right away but it's a bit hard for me. I don't know how to be as social as Buttercup and I'll never be like Almond because no one can be as energetic and full of positive energy as she is! (Even my mum comes a close second compared to her.) I prefer to observe my new friends a bit before committing too much to a conversation. I like to see how their minds work first. But once I sense that I really like them, then I'm all in and I'll talk very easily when I see them. I just need some time to start. And this morning sure is a new beginning! I try to stay calm and remind myself that I won't be alone, I'll have my two best friends with me so everything will be fine. As I take all my new surroundings in, watching the tree tops and listening to the lively background noises of all the animals around us, I suddenly stop dead in my tracks as I smash into ... a concrete wall! The shock is so powerful that I stumble and fall backward. Just as I'm starting to think it's all my fault for not paying attention I hear a confused deep voice repeating "Sorry, oh I'm so sorry" again and again. When I look up I finally understand the cause of my accident and the owner of those apologies. I didn't run into a wall, but into a brown bear!

Of course I've seen bears around Woodland before, but I've never been knocked over by one! Still lying on the ground, I start to tell this apologetic bear that it's ok, there's no harm done, but quickly he grabs me to help me back on my paws.

"Oh my oh my, I'm so sorry, so sorry!! Are you ok? I was not looking where I was going and I didn't see you, you're so small..."

I laugh at this.

"Oh no, I didn't mean it as an insult, I ... Oh I'm such a clumsy bear, argh ..."

I can barely answer him because he's so agitated and talking so fast but as soon as he pauses to draw a breath, I jump in to reassure him once more.

"It's ok, don't worry, I'm fine! And it's also my fault I was too busy looking at the Academy and I didn't see you."

He's standing before me, fidgeting with a twig between his two massive paws, his eyes moving constantly. He seems much older than me but I don't think he's an adult bear yet either. He's so big I could have sworn he was a teacher if it wasn't for his agitation. And suddenly it hits me: he was going in the opposite direction from me when we smashed into each other. He wasn't entering the Academy, he was leaving it! Already? Before school has even started? I don't want to stress him out too much though, so I decide to introduce myself before asking him if he was trying to ditch school on the first day.

"Hi, I'm Applesauce!"

He stops fidgeting and looks down at me. It seems to help him calm down so I keep talking.

"It's my first day today. What about you?"

I see him getting nervous again as soon as I ask, so I follow right away and ask him his name. It works! He calms down a bit and answers in a quiet voice (well, as quiet as possible for an animal that big!).

"Hi, sorry I am forgetting my manners. My name is Wind."

"Oh, what a nice name!"

"You think so? It was my great grandfather's name and it comes with a lot of responsibilities, so I'm not really sure how I feel about it."

I'm not sure what to say to that but I can see he needs someone to comfort him so I do my best to reply to him.

"Oh ... Well you know, I think a name is what you make of it. I think the only responsibility you have is to live up to your own name!"

"What do you mean?" He asks me intrigued.

"Make sure you make this name yours. You're your own unique bear so make others think of you as such and not as 'grandson of Wind the First'."

I add the last bit as a joke to make him smile and it works. He laughs a bit, before adding, "great-grandson, actually".

"Even more reason to make sure everyone knows who YOU are! Who cares whether your great-grandpa had the same name?" I tease. "Soon the animals of Woodland will think he was lucky to share the same name as you and not the other way around."

Another smile from him so I continue. "What did this Wind make that was so great anyway? I'm sure no one remembers him-"

"He built the Woodland hospital," he mumbles and his smile disappears.

"Oh! Ok ... well that's something, yes, but it doesn't mean you won't do great things yourself!"

"What if I never do something big like him?"

"Well most people don't, so I don't think you should worry about that. Just be you and I'm sure it will be great!"

He seems to think this over and finally looks at me with a shy smile back on his face. Just then, we hear a bell ring to announce that class will start soon.

"We should head in," I say.

"But I'm so nervous ..."

"Yes, I guessed that when I saw you try to run away!" I laugh softly.

Thankfully he doesn't take it the wrong way and laughs too.

"But don't worry, it's my first day too so we can stay together and I'll introduce you to my friends."

He nods and we follow the path indicated for the Seed class with a little wooden arrow attached to a tree. As we draw closer to our class, we see other students arriving on the same path and chatting together. Wind looks around and says, "Oh I thought there would be way more students in the Academy!"

"This is only the Seed class. The Flower and Tree classes are in other parts of the campus. You didn't see the arrows at the entrance showing the way to each class?"

He shakes his head no. "I guess I was too busy panicking."

"Don't worry, it'll be fine! Here, let's go sit down with Buttercup."

The Seed class is a big open space, slightly closed by bushes and small trees in a circular shape. The teacher, Mrs Winter, is standing in front of a tall chestnut tree beside a big wooden table covered with a white cloth to hide what's under it. She's gesturing to everyone to come and sit down, and waiting patiently while we do. It's hard to see in just one look if she'll be a strict teacher.

In front of her, arranged in a semi-circle, are big benches for us to sit on. There's quite a lot of space between each bench to accommodate the bigger animals and there are two sizes to choose from. Naturally, the smaller students all start to sit down in the front rows. Except for Buttercup who is near the back, which will be perfect for Wind. It will be more comfortable for someone his size and it will make it easier for him to listen without being too much in the spotlight today. I sit down next to Buttercup, with Wind on my right side. After introducing my new friend to my best friend, I ask quietly where Almond is. Buttercup simply smiles and says, "Where do you think?"

Of course, his sister is in the first row, near the teacher's desk, barely containing her excitement. I don't even have time to look around me to see who my new classmates are when Mrs Winter starts talking.

"Hello everyone and welcome to Woodland Academy!" I chuckle at the fact that she didn't use the full name of the school and as I look briefly at Buttercup I can see that he's thinking the exact same thing! Best friend's super powers!!

"Since it's your first day, let's start by-"

But before the teacher can finish her sentence, a loud and piercing noise suddenly interrupts her!

Chapter 7
Introductions

The piercing noise comes from above us and sounds like "sorry sorry sorry" sung very fast, by two very high pitched voices. We all look up to see Echo and Breeze flying at a fast pace in the class (too fast for such a small space if you ask me!) and landing in front of our teacher, on her desk. They bow to her to apologise again and sing to her, "We're so very sorry that we're late, we were so excited that we lost track of time and got lost on our way. Sorry, it won't happen again!"

"Mmmm..."

Mrs Winter looks at them with a doubtful expression, like she doesn't really believe the "it won't happen again" part.

"No need to ask you two for your names, your reputation precedes you. The singing twins."

Her slightly annoyed expression indicates that she didn't mean this as a compliment on their singing skills but Breeze and Echo only nod as an answer, before our teacher tells them to find a seat on a bench or a branch. They fly to the lowest tree branch and Mrs Winter clears her throat to start her introduction again.

"So, as I was saying before we were interrupted, since it is your first day we will start the hour by introducing each other. But first, let me tell you a bit about what you can expect this year."

She starts walking among us between the benches, at a slow pace as if she wants to observe us all one by one as she talks. I feel scrutinised and it makes me a bit nervous, so I reached for my tail to stroke it. It always calms my nerves.

"I'm Mrs Winter and I will be your Seed class teacher for this first year. Some of you will learn quickly and others may need more than a year to master the spells and potions from this level I class and that is totally fine. This is not a competition and you are all here to learn. Always remember to do it at your own pace and to take pleasure in learning. Magic can't be born within an unhappy witch or wizard."

As she walks by Buttercup, Wind and I, she smiles at us three. This little smile helps me calm down but I notice that Wind seems very flustered by her speech so I give him a little pat on the paw to reassure him. Unfortunately, our size difference is so big that I don't think he even felt my tiny paw on his.

"I want you to feel welcome here at Woodland Academy," she continues, "and to share with your friends and I if you don't understand a spell or a recipe. There's no shame in not understanding something so don't be afraid to ask for help. It took me some time to learn the basic 'Lifty Leafy' spell when I was in my first year. And I could tell you stories about some of your parents' own troubles during their school days that would surprise you all!"

That gets a laugh from the whole class and it helps everybody finally relax.

She smiles at us and starts to think out loud.

"Now ... What shall we do? Start with the students' introductions or the Choosing Ceremony?"

As soon as she says the last two words, a loud murmur starts to spread among us all. Everyone has an opinion on what we should do first and the majority of my classmates seem to want to start with the Ceremony. I have no idea what the Ceremony could be but as long as it delays the moment I have to talk in front of everyone to introduce myself, I'm in!

"What's the Ceremony?" I whisper to Buttercup, leaning toward him, with my eyes still on the teacher.

"You don't know? Your parents never told you about it?"

He seems so surprised that I turn around to face him, worried.

"No, they always said they wanted me to get a surprise and experience the Academy with brand new eyes."

Right now I wish they hadn't felt this way because I feel like I'm the only student who doesn't have the faintest idea what the Ceremony is and I don't like this. Even Wind seems to know, and he seems very calm about it!

"You already know what you're going to choose?" Wind asks Buttercup, who nods with total confidence.

Choose? Choose what? What are they all talking about?

Before I can ask any of my friends to explain all this to me, Mrs Winter finally makes her decision and says something. I have no idea what she said though, because everyone is so loud that I can't hear her voice. I'm starting to get impatient and I squirm on my seat, overwhelmed by all the sudden noise. Just as I start to cover my ears with my paws, I notice that Mrs Winter seems to be focusing on something. She says a word that I can't hear (again!) and suddenly we can all hear her voice very clearly and very loudly.

"Silence please!"

Oh! That was an amplifying spell to make her voice louder. I've heard about them but I've never seen anyone use one. Our tree is too small for us to need this kind of spell. She certainly has everyone's attention now.

"I know that you are all very excited about the Ceremony but I've decided that we'll start with the students' introductions. So you are to come here one by one to tell us a bit about yourself and then we will have the Ceremony. Stay seated while your friends are talking. We'll go in order of seating, starting from the front left row to the right, then the rows behind, and we'll finish with the students in the trees. When it's your turn please tell us your name, something you love and something you're good at. Is that clear?" She asks us with a warm smile.

We all nod in agreement and she gestures to the first student to stand up and go over to her desk.

As soon as the first animal stands up, I start to panic. I hate

31

talking in front of animals I don't know. I stroke my fluffy orange tail again but Buttercup notices it right away and tries his best to help me calm down.

"Don't worry, it'll be fine. Do you know what you're going to say?" He asks in a quiet voice.

Apart from my name, I have no idea what to say. I'm so nervous my mind is suddenly all blank.

"Does eating count for something I'm good at?" I joke.

He laughs with his funny tiny hedgehog laugh that I love. It's a very special kind of laugh, almost like the sound a chime makes. You know those little bells that you can hang up in trees or at your windows? It's such a relaxing sound and it's one of my favourite things in the world. So just like that, thanks to my best friend, I feel better, and I don't worry so much anymore. Super Buttercup to the rescue! I manage to relax and to listen to my classmates introduce themselves. I love hearing about their stories.

I get to meet:

Sidney, a small worm who likes to go on hikes and who doesn't like to be told that she's a bit small for that kind of activity. She's small but I wouldn't want to mess up with her because she seems quite fierce. Oh, and she adds that she's also good at martial arts! Yep, I'm definitely going to make sure I never fight with her.

Smore, a brown bear who's good at building things with wood and who loves to play with his dad in the lake.

Plum, a wolf who loves to run with her brothers and who can cook nice pies. Oh, a fellow pie lover!

Almond introduces herself by saying she's good at making her friends feel better when they're sad. I totally agree with this! Buttercup explains to the class that he loves spending time with his friends and that he's good at making crafts. Wind tells us that he loves to draw but struggles to find something he's good at. I know it'll be my turn next and I'm still wondering what I'll say so I don't hear what his final answer is.

"Next!" Mrs Winter calls.

I walk toward my teacher and stop next to her. I take a deep breath, think of a tasty apple tart and I turn to face my classmates.

"Hello." Ok, so far so good! Good job Applesauce! But I think the teacher wants us to say more than a simple hello so I keep going.

"My name is Applesauce. I love ... books." I smile at this and I add, "A lot!" to make sure everyone understands how much I love reading.

Some animals laugh a bit at this but not to make fun of me so that's nice! You know, like they're laughing at my joke but not at me. So that's fine, I can handle this.

"And I really, really love to eat too."

As soon as I start talking about food, I forget that I am afraid to talk and add, "I especially love the treats from my parents' bakery and I wish I could sleep inside because the smell is incredible!"

Mrs Winter chuckles, "I can confirm! And if your parents decide to open a hotel inside their bakery let me know, I'll be their first customer to spend the night in!"

Everybody laughs and I start to imagine what a bakery/hotel would look like. Maybe we could sleep in a loaf of brioche or have a room covered with chocolate. I'd totally eat the whole room! But then Mrs Winter's voice brings me back to the real world.

"What else? Can you tell us something that you're good at Applesauce?"

"Making up stories," I answer, without hesitation.

"Oh really? Do you tell them to yourself or do you share them with others?"

"Most of the time it's just for me but at night I share some with my best friends Buttercup and Almond."

"Ok, great, thanks for telling us! And maybe someday you'll want to share one with us too?"

I mumble a "maybe" but I'm not sure I could ever have the courage to do that.

Those stories live in my head, I don't even write them down. The idea that other people could actually hear them and tell me how bad they are is terrifying. I don't know how writers do that. How do they dare to actually write down their own made up story on paper for the world to see? In my head, I picture all writers with a cape, braver than the most famous superheroes!

After that, the rest of the introductions seem to go by in a flash and the last two students to introduce themselves are our friends Breeze and Echo who, without surprise, explain that they love to sing. And I'll let you guess what their "I'm good at" thing is ... Yes, that's right, singing!

Chapter 8
The Ceremony

After Breeze and Echo are done with their introductions, everyone starts talking with everyone and it's quickly becoming very noisy again. A bit too noisy for me. I want to make new friends and hear what they have to say but I can't hear a thing. I can barely hear myself think, so I can't imagine chatting with someone I've never met before in these conditions!

Thankfully Mrs Winter stops the chatter quickly by asking us to go back to our seats before we begin the Ceremony. The word "Ceremony" is enough to have everybody quiet in an instant! Mrs Winter settles back beside the big table that's covered with a white cloth and I'm dying to see what's under it. Food maybe? I wouldn't say no to a second breakfast. In my opinion, there's always room for more if the food is good!

"The Ceremony is an important moment in the life of every wizard and witch. As you probably all know already, you will need to select the magic object that will allow you to perform magic. This magic object, called Magicol, will be yours for life, so choose carefully."

Choose? How are we supposed to know what's best for us? I'm

confused and a bit worried about this process. It seems that I'm not the only one because I see a female badger raise her paw to ask the question that is burning in my mind.

"Excuse me, professor, but how do we choose?" She's an adult badger but has a tiny shrill voice.

"Well, some animals feel a certain connection to their magic object and say they are drawn to it. Some animals say they choose solely on practicality because of the kind of animal they are. Even if you won't need to hold it, it's important to think about your size and whether you have a beak or paws."

I'm relieved to see that I'm not the only one with questions and doubts about our Magicol because I hear a lot of murmurs going around the class. Thankfully Mrs Winter continues her explanation.

"It's also very important to know that you don't have to hold your Magicol to cast spells. The basis of spell casting is saying it out loud for it to work."

"Then we don't need the Magicol?" asks Plum.

"Yes you still do, to draw magic from it. If you try casting a spell just by wording it without your magical object, the only thing that will happen is that you may get surprised looks from those around you."

She winks at this and we all laugh.

"You don't have to hold it but it has to be on you for the connection to work. Always remember that a spell without a Magicol is useless and that you will need it at all times."

I hear students mumbling around me but before I can worry myself with new questions, Mrs Winter continues.

"Once you have chosen your Magicol, it will be marked with the Woodland mark and it will only recognise you. Make sure you never lose it! With time you will learn to pour magic into new objects so they can be used by the Woodland Forest residents who don't practise magic, the Non-Magicals. It's important to put your magic to good use and to help others.

She approaches the massive table and grabs the cloth with her teeth. Once it's gone we can see it's covered with different objects of various sizes. I think we all recognise what they are but she still explains.

"Today is your first day as a Magical and you'll have to choose between these three objects: a wand, a stone or an acorn. Right now they are nothing more than twigs and bits that humans could pick up in the woods without paying much attention. But once they are filled with our magic, it will be impossible for a human to take any of these objects away from Woodland Forest."

I hear some of my classmates let out a very surprised, "Ohhh!"

Mrs Winter smiles at this before being very serious again.

"For the Ceremony, we have already filled these objects with a pinch of magic. Just enough to create a reaction between you and your future Magicol. But once it has been chosen, it will have to be properly activated for you. It is a big responsibility to fill an object with magic, so please welcome the Great Wizard of Woodland!"

I have heard the Great Wizard is a very powerful wizard, the most powerful one actually. I heard that his magic alone could protect the whole forest against a wildfire but I've never seen him. There are many rumours about him and a lot of mysteries. I don't even know what kind of animal he is. Probably a big bear or another wolf. I'm really excited to finally see him and as I look at my best friend next to me I can see that Buttercup is sharing my excitement. Everyone seems to be. The whole class is silent and we all wait patiently.

We hear some sounds coming from behind the trees and suddenly an animal appears! And ... the Great Wizard is a racoon! A female one! I love this forest, it's always full of surprises! From the stories I heard I was expecting a massive male animal, old and very serious with a cane and a big hat but instead we got a joyful raccoon.

She joins Mrs Winter, waving and singing to us, "Hello everyone, hello, hello hello! How are you?" like she's here to entertain us.

She quickly climbs on the big table where I can see that she's dressed with a very colourful robe made of different pieces of fabric like patchwork. She's also wearing a big chunky necklace with a blue feather and some thin bracelets around her paws. She shakes her cane around her and I wonder if it's part of her process or if she's just chasing a fly away.

"Hello Seed class! I'm the Great Wizard of Woodland and I'm here to make this day magical! Or should I say Magicol?"

She laughs briefly at her own joke and gets on with the

explanations.

"So you'll come here one by one, have a look and select your Magicol! Easy Peasy Sweet Honey Bee!"

She smiles a lot and we're all surprised by the difference of tones between her and Mrs Winter. She makes the Ceremony sound like a piece of cake, like it's not a big deal at all to choose the magical object that we'll use for the rest of our lives! She's funny and not at all what I imagined! I don't know if she's really that happy or if she's trying to make us less nervous but if that's the case, it works! Mrs Winter tells us to come choose in the same order as before so Buttercup, Wind and I have some time before it's our turn.

"Hey guys, do you know what you're going to choose?" Wind asks us softly.

Buttercup answers right away that he'll probably get an acorn.

"Oh yeah? Me too!" Wind sounds really excited by this and I can't blame him. It is exciting! To know we are so close to choosing our Magicol!!

"What about you, Applesauce?"

I don't have time to answer because it's already Almond's turn and we are all watching her.

"What do you think she's going to take?" Buttercup asks me. "She could get a wand but ..."

He seems all nervous at this idea and I understand why. I finish his sentence for him.

"But she'll probably hurt herself with all the jumping and running she does?"

He looks at me, not surprised that I guessed his thoughts again (Best Friends' Superpowers!) and nods with a small smile. We watch as Almond is practically jumping around the table, trying to decide. Finally she goes for the acorn and I hear Buttercup let out a sigh of relief.

Everyone around us goes to the table one by one and selects a wand, a stone or an acorn. Usually you wear them around your neck: the stones in a little pouch, the acorns have a little hole to be worn like a necklace, and the wands can be carried in a wand holder like a satchel across your body.

Finally it's our turn to go choose! Wind stands up (which lifts the bench we're sitting on a bit) and comes back a few minutes later with a wand.

"I thought you wanted an acorn?" I ask as Buttercup leaves his seat too.

"I did! But then I realised it made more sense for me to have a wand. I'm not sure I'd be able to wear the acorn. I'm so big and it's so small, I'm afraid I'd lose it or break it ... Besides, look how cool my wand looks!"

He shows it to me and it sure is cool! It's made of two long pieces of walnut wood intertwined together. It's so pretty, with different shades of brown.

"And look at my Woodland mark."

"Oh, it's so nice!"

The Woodland mark is grey, just like the one we all have on us. I've watched all my classmates choose their Magicol, so I have had time to observe the process. The mark appears once the Great Wizard has powered the Magicol with magic. Every mark is unique so it represents the owner. Wind's mark looks like a splash of paint. I wonder what mine will be.

Chapter 9

Wand, acorn or stone?

Buttercup returns to his seat with an acorn around his neck but I don't have time to stop to look at it because Mrs Winter is calling my name! Woah, it feels so official, like something I'll remember all my life.

Come on, Applesauce, deep breath and let's go! I walk toward the table where all the remaining Magicols lay and use the special stairs installed for small animals like me to reach the top. I wait for instructions but the Great Wizard doesn't seem to notice me at all, she's just humming a song to herself next to me and even dancing a bit! I don't see Mrs Winter nearby, I think she's gone to the back of the class to look at the Ceremony. I don't dare to look for her, I'm afraid I'll see my classmates looking at me, wondering what's wrong with me. I'm confused, I don't know what to do, how to start. I didn't see how everyone else started their process. I mostly watched when they were picking up their objects. Maybe I should remind the Great Wizard that I'm here.

"Mmm ... excuse me. Miss ... I mean Great Wizard?"

She stops singing and looks down at me a bit surprised. Has she forgotten why she's here?

"Yes?" She asks with a wide smile.

"What am I supposed to do?" I ask, my voice barely audible. Oh gosh, I'm so nervous.

"Oh! Well, you're supposed to choose my dear!" She answers simply, like it's the most obvious and easiest thing in the world. Well, of course I knew I was supposed to pick one but I thought maybe there was a special way to do it. I haven't even looked at the Magicols available yet, afraid to do it wrong. What am I talking about? A special way to look at objects?

OK, maybe I'm getting too nervous about all of this but I admit I thought the process would be a bit more official. With the Great Wizard dancing with herself and telling me to "just pick one" I feel like I'm simply choosing which tart flavour I'll get today (and even this always takes time with me!).

So here I go! I finally look at all the objects available for me on the desk and I'm surprised by how wide the choice is. I was a bit afraid that all the good Magicol would be gone but there's still plenty of wands, acorns and stones to choose from. I guess it makes sense, they need to have a large selection of each. They are all organised by type to make it easier for the animals to see what's best for them according to their size. Everything is so beautiful, with different shapes, colours and styles. Now I understand why some of my friends were taking so long to decide. I look at some of the acorns and see some interesting ones, carved with little details all around. Some are lighter and others seem to reflect the natural light. I have a look at the stones just to be sure but I don't feel like they are for me. Then, just as my eyes start to glance over the wands section, I see it! That's it, that's my wand, I just know it! It's the last one of its row, at the far end of the desk and it's perfectly imperfect.

I take it in my paw to observe it closely. It's not very big and the whole wand is made from orange wood, so needless to say, this is perfect for me! I don't know if there's a tree that made this wood or if it was coloured by magic but I love it! The wood on the handle is not polished like the other wands available, it feels all rough, like it just fell down from a tree this morning. It is covered with needles, like the ones you see on a pine tree and they remind me of Buttercup's spines! They are all in the same direction so it doesn't hurt when you handle the wand. I turn it over and see that the main part of the wand is still bare, just orange wood, probably to leave space for the Woodland mark. And at the extremity of the wand there's one really cute and tiny pinecone, the perfect size to fit in there. It looks like a great way to symbolise our forest. The whole wand is fantastic, really unique and I don't see any other one like it. I love it!

I don't even look at the rest of the Magicol closely, I have already made my choice. I look up at the Great Wizard and say, "This one!"

Strangely my choice seems to make her really excited and she starts jumping around from one paw to the other. Ok ... That's odd, I'm not sure why my choice makes her so happy but why not! She gestures to me to follow her on to the ground and indicates to me the Circle (marked with a blue powder) where the magic happens. I'm so excited I don't take the stairs this time and jump from the table to join her, where she tells me to stand right in front of her with my wand and my tail inside the Circle. She suddenly becomes very serious and asks me, her voice sounding so different now, "Applesauce, you have now chosen your Magical Object! Are you sure about your choice?"

I don't hesitate and nod "Yes your..." I stop myself before calling her your majesty. Your majesty? What's wrong with me today?

"Yes." I repeat calmly this time.

Another strange smile from her but she just says, "Very well. Once this wand is filled with Woodland Magic, it will be yours forever. It will be your responsibility but it will also be your guide and your friend when you need one."

My friend? What is she talking about?

She must be able to read minds because she tells me in a lower voice. "Sometimes a magical object can bring comfort to its owner by helping him or her make a decision or by guiding them where they need to go."

I nod, not sure if she means this literally or as a metaphor.

"Hold your wand in front of you please."

I obey, laying my wand in my open palm between her and me and, after a dramatic pause, she raises her paws over it. Immediately, I see a circle of yellow light glow around us two. It starts small around her paws, then it expands around mine and my wand, and

43

finally it becomes a big ball protecting us and the Circle. All the sounds around us disappear. I keep my eyes on my wand and I can see the magic flow from the ball of light to my wand, filling it in. It feels warm and reassuring. And as soon as I feel my new Magicol hot with magic, the light around us disappears and I can hear the murmur of my classmates again.

I take a deep breath and look up at the Great Wizard, who winks at me. She comes closer to me and whispers in my ear, "I'm glad you chose this wand. I'm the one who made it!"

Even though she's whispering, her voice sounds very excited and happy.

I raise my eyebrow surprised, "Really?"

She nods, "Yes! That, right there, is the only wand ever made by me! I made it ten years ago but it has never been chosen because everyone thinks it's too peculiar, too different from the rest. I think it was just waiting for its rightful owner. I'm glad it's you."

She winks again and tells me to go back to my seat before calling the next student.

I go back to my bench, happy to finally have my wand, surprised by its origin and relieved that the Ceremony is finally over for me! As I sit down next to Buttercup, he asks to see it and as I show it to him I realise I haven't seen my Woodland mark yet. It must have appeared after my wand became hot with its magic but I was so focused on the Great Wizard's revelation that I forgot to check for it. I turn the wand around and it's here, in the back, covering the whole length. And just like the rest of the wand, the mark is perfect: it shows three grey paws, of different shapes and sizes. Three paws that look strangely similar to Buttercup's, Almond's and mine!

Chapter 10

No book today?

I'm still looking at my brand new and one of a kind wand when the last student goes back to her seat (well, to her branch since we finish the Ceremony with the birds.) Mrs Winter tells us that we can have a ten minute break to chat and run around before our first class starts. That's it, we have our magical objects, now we're going to learn.

Oh it's so exciting, I love learning! I like the idea that one minute you have no clue about a subject and the next you have this new knowledge inside your head! It's magic, no? Of course, the hardest part is to keep this to reuse later but still, I think it's great! And learning means reading so I'm even more excited about our first class. I wonder what books we will learn from, how big they will be, and what subjects they will teach me.

Since we have some free time, everybody tries to talk with the friends they already know or the ones they made this morning. Some, like Buttercup, are even braver and are talking to animals they don't know at all! He's so brave! I can't do that, I'm too scared. But I remind myself that I actually already made a new friend today, even if it was by accident, so I should be proud of myself!

Speaking of Wind, I try to find him but I can't see him anywhere.

How can a bear become invisible? He's the biggest animal in the class, it shouldn't be possible. Wait a minute … unless … unless he ran away again? Oh no! Quick I need to find him! I try to locate Buttercup quickly to let him know the situation but I can't find him either, so there's no time to lose. I have to go for it and find Wind before he leaves the Academy. I turn around, get ready to run and … run directly into Wind himself! (For the second time today, is it turning into a habit?) Oh I see: the reason I couldn't see him was because he was right behind me, with Buttercup and Almond. Silly me, I really need to get better at controlling my emotions. I got all worked up when he was actually standing just behind me.

Hopefully no one saw me so I don't have to be embarrassed. I join my two best friends and our new friend and just when I'm about to ask them to show me their Magicols, we are joined by some classmates that I don't know. A rabbit and a mouse. I think Almond knows them already because she's calling them by their names and they are laughing together. How did she do that? When did she have time to make new friends? I feel like we just arrived at the Academy.

She even remembers to introduce them all to our group.

"Everyone, this is Honeysuckle and Caramel," She gestures to the girl rabbit first, and then to the adult male mouse.

We all say hi (mine sounds more like a murmur than an exclamation) and she introduces us to them.

"Meet my best friend Applesauce and my brother Buttercup."

Introducing Buttercup the small hedgehog as her brother always gets some funny looks and surprised reactions but Almond never notices. She just smiles at them and then looks at me with a strange expression. I think she's trying to tell me something but I don't understand what. I only hear, "Applesauce, I don't know … mumble mumble, so you should … mumble mumble."

I really don't get it. I'm about to ask her directly when Buttercup nudges me really softly (he knows how to do it without hurting me with his prickles, don't worry) and says to the whole group, "and this," gesturing to Wind, "is our new friend Wind."

He introduces him like it's easy, no big deal, when I was still trying to understand Almond's cryptic message. Ohhh now I get it! She meant, "Applesauce, I don't know your new friend's name, so you should be the one introducing him."

It's a relief Buttercup was here to save me! (Once more.)

Quickly, we all show our Magicol to each other with excitement, the six of us gathered in a small circle. It's not that many animals but since I don't know half of them, it's enough to scare me and make me silent. So I do what I do best: I stay quiet, a bit on the edge of the group and only say a few words here and there, mostly to my friends. Honeysuckle picked a stone and Caramel an acorn. We compare our objects' sizes and grey marks, all happy with our choices, and thankfully, before I have to say much, it's already time to go back to class for our first lesson! Yeah!!

"Ok Seed class, please go back to your seat and settle down."

No one seems to know if we're supposed to go back to the exact spots we were in before or if we can choose new ones, but Mrs Winter says, "You can sit down anywhere, it doesn't matter. As long as you're comfortable and not bothering your classmates behind you, it's fine. We'll be standing up soon anyway."

We all go back to our previous seats with a few changes here and there. Honeysuckle joins Almond in the first row and Wind moves to the last one so our classmates behind can see properly now that the class is starting. Buttercup and I stay where we were. I'd like to go forward one row to be closer to the teacher and to be sure we both see her well but at the same time, I'm afraid that if I'm too close to her desk, I'll feel too visible. I am eager to learn but not to be seen. I'm a shy squirrel.

The Great Wizard is gone, the unchosen magical objects have been cleared away from the big table, packed in small cloth bags and stored in a box for next year and Mrs Winter is standing in front of us. She looks at us silently, her dark eyes stopping on me a bit longer than the rest of the class and I try to act as normal as possible. Am I supposed to do something? Smile back? Wave to her? Who knows, I've never been to school before.

After having a good look at everybody, she clears her throat and starts.

"So, as I said before the Ceremony, this is the Seed class and I will be your teacher this year. I'll do my best to help you when you don't understand and to show you the best way to practise spells. I can't say the proper way to practise magic because ... well, there's no proper way to do it. Magic is very specific to each individual and has to come from the heart. If your heart is not really into it you may be able to produce some basic magic spells but you won't go further than that I'm afraid. I'm willing to help any students in need but," and she insists on this last part,"I don't tolerate nonsense."

She pauses and looks at the class from right to left, all the way to the top branches where Echo and Wind are. I have a feeling those last words are for them.

"If you are here to be silly or if you're only here because your parents told you to, I can give you one piece of advice right now: don't come. It's simple. Magic is a serious subject and it has to be wanted. Are we clear?"

We all nod and mumble, "yes Mrs Winter."

Strangely, I don't feel embarrassed by this because, even though I have no idea if I'll be a good wizard, I already know I'll try my best.

"Good!" she continues. "There will be no book in this first lesson!"

Oh no, what a disappointment for me!

Many of the students seem happy about this but then Mrs Winter explains with a smile. "Oh, don't worry, there will be books later. Today is just an exception since it's your first day and the point of this morning's class is more about us meeting and, most importantly, about you getting used to your Magical Object. If you don't know how to work with it, learning spells from a book will be absolutely useless. So the first thing you'll do is to try connecting with your Magicol."

Connect with it? What does it mean? How am I supposed to connect with my wand or Buttercup with his acorn? Do we just need to touch them? Lick them? I'm glad to see that we all seem confused by this. Our teacher explains with a little smile.

"There's no tutorial on how to connect with a new Magicol. And I admit, it's a bit hard to explain. It will come easily for some and take a bit longer for others."

"Please let me be in the first category!" I repeat to myself in my head. But I wonder if I really thought this in my head or if I said it out loud because Buttercup is nudging me softly as if to tell me, "Don't worry, you'll be great!" with a little smile.

"So..." Mrs Winter goes on, "start by finding a quiet spot in the class or in the open area around us. Make sure you're alone, because no matter how great they are, it's not something your friends or siblings can help you with."

I'm pretty sure she just gave a warning look at the twin birds.

"Find a comfortable spot. Whether you prefer to be on the floor, on a branch, sitting or standing up, it doesn't matter as long as you're feeling comfortable. If you want to lie down, go for it, we won't judge you."

This gets a few giggles and now I wonder if she's serious or if it was only a joke to help us relax.

"For those who can, it helps if you touch your Magicol, hold it in your paw. Then simply close your eyes and connect!"

She says this last word with lots of joy and for a second I'm afraid she's going to stop her explanation there. I can imagine her telling us, "You connect. That's it. Bye bye!"

Thankfully she adds some explanations, "Now that the objects are filled with magic, you need to create a long lasting connection between you two. It's like signalling to your Magicol, 'hello it's me!' And then, over the next few days, you'll have to make sure you keep working on this bonding exercise to have the best connection possible. Once you have your eyes closed and you're in contact with your object, just relax, take a deep breath and close your mind to anything around you. Focus only on your Magicol and try to call it to you."

"We have to name it?" interrupts a yellow bird on a branch next to me.

Mrs Winter smiles a bit but she doesn't seem to think it's a stupid question. That makes me feel better because I was actually wondering the same thing.

"No, you don't have to give it a name. But you can if it helps you!"

Most of the students seem surprised by this.

"But don't worry, you don't have to choose a name today. This morning the important bit is to open a connection. Once it's done you'll have time to name it and make your link stronger later. The more you connect with your Magicol, the stronger your magic will be."

We all nod.

"So, with your eyes closed, think about your Magicol. Visualise it and try to open your mind. And if you don't feel anything happening immediately, you can send it little messages."

"Messages? What kind of messages? Like our coordinates? Our address?" asks a student in the front row that I can't see. Some giggle a bit at this question but Mrs Winter reminds us kindly that there are no stupid questions and that it is always a good idea to ask. I'm starting to like her more and more.

"Simple messages like ... 'I'm here' or 'Hey, it's me!' You can tell it your name. You can even send it a joke if you think it'd help." We all laugh at this. "As long as it's something that comes from inside you, it will help you connect."

"And what if... what if it still doesn't work?" This time I recognise the nervous voice. It's Wind, with his loud but timid voice coming from the back of the class.

"Well if you still don't feel a connection, I'll suggest you open your mind and your heart one hundred percent to it. Don't try to be shy or hide who you are. Show yourself with your fears and your best qualities. Your Magicol will be your most powerful companion in life so you need to be honest with it. Don't pretend to be ok if you're actually very nervous, for example."

I nod and stroke my fluffy tail quickly.

"OK, so there you go. Stand up and find your quiet space. You can move the benches around if there's not enough space or you can go a bit further. It's time to connect!"

Chapter 11
Connection

O k, this is it! Deep breath, it's time to connect with
my Magicol and not feel scared or intimidated or
nervous or scared...Wait, did I say scared twice? Oh,
I guess that's not the best way to prove to you that I
am not afraid, is't it? Maybe if I say it in big capital
letters you'll believe me more? Let's try: I, APPLESAUCE, AM
CERTAINLY NOT SCARED! Nope, not scared, not at all.

Why would I be scared of a piece of wood? There's no reason my
wand and I won't be able to connect. Mrs Winter said it could take
time but she never said anything about not being able to connect at
all. What if I become the first wizard that can't create a connection
with his Magicol? Then I'll always be known as the Non Magical
wizard. Actually, now that I think about it, if I can't connect with
it I won't be able to do magic so I won't even be called a wizard. I'll
just be Applesauce, who failed wizard school on his first day. What
would my parents say? Would they ban me from the bakery? A
whole life without eating their cakes, that's not a life ...

"Applesauce are you coming?"

I'm so lost in my crazy and nonsensical thoughts that I barely
hear Buttercup call me. I snap out of it and see him gesture to me
to follow him. I realise that all our classmates have already made

their way to the back of our classroom. The grounds where our class will be held are divided in two: the main part has big benches set in front of the chestnut tree, where Mrs Winter stands. And behind, a more lush and open space with some flowers dotted here and there. I imagine this is where we will relax between classes and practise some of our spells. The whole classroom is surrounded by bushes that must have been arranged like this by magic, to act like walls. They also hide our classroom from any curious humans who might walk through our forest. From their point of view it might even look as if the class area doesn't exist and there's just one giant bush here. I don't know what they see from the outside. I should ask the teacher. I wonder if she knows the story of the school and-

"Applesauce!"

Oops I did it again!

"You were daydreaming again, weren't you?" Buttercup asks. I nod and he laughs a little at my bad habit. What I love about him is that he's never mean. He never makes fun of others or thinks you're stupid if you don't know something.

"Sorry," I mumble, "I'm so nervous that I started to think about the story of the school ..."

"Don't be nervous, it will be fine. Remember what the teacher said. It's ok if it takes some time, just be yourself, ok?"

I nod, feeling more confident. It's funny how he never needs to say a lot to make me feel better.

"Ok I think I'll go this way," he tells me, gesturing toward an empty corner.

I wave my paw at him, "Ok see you in a bit then."

Then I look for the best spot to work on my own connection. Where do I want to go? The ground is too crowded with the biggest animals. There are bears, wild boars, deers, raccoons, badgers and wolves all around me. Even though I'm sure I'll get used to so many classmates around me at once, for now I need some peace. I need to be able to focus so I look up at the nearest tree, making sure this one is empty. I quickly climb toward a high branch, one that is so leafy that it will hide me from everyone still on the ground. It's perfect up here: quiet and lonely, with just enough space for me and my wand. I still have it in my left paw (yes, I'm a left pawed squirrel!) and I start to wonder if the teacher will give us our wand holders after this. I picture how it might look, the colour, the fabric and who else picked a wand in the class ... No, no, I have to stop thinking about anything else and focus on my wand. Not my wand holder, not my classmates, or how green the leaves are around me, just my wand. Ok take a deep breath Applesauce, you can do it!

I sit down on the branch and try to relax. I close my eyes and take a deep breath. For a moment that's all I do, I just stay there, breathing in and out with my eyes closed, closing myself from the surrounding noise. Once I'm so calm I can't hear anything around me, I visualise my one of a kind wand and I just think, "hello, it's me."

I smile at this. I thought it would feel ridiculous to talk to my wand like this because it just seems like talking to myself but it doesn't. I talk to myself all the time and it doesn't feel the same. This feels like calling a friend, asking him if he wants to come play with me. I stay focused and repeat in my head, "hello, it's me."

With my eyes still closed, I feel a tiny shiver coming from my left paw. Well not directly from my paw at first, but from somewhere close. It gives me hope so I keep going.

"I'm Applesauce, your new ... friend," I say because I think it seems like the best word to describe the relationship I want to have with my Magicol. I don't want to be its master or its owner, I want to feel like we're friends. As I think those words I immediately feel another shiver, this time directly coming from my paw. I resist the urge to open my eyes and peek at my wand to check if it's really moving. I focus on the feeling only. I realise that it's not really the wand that is vibrating in my hand. It feels more like my paw is surrounded by a bubble of energy, I can feel it around me. I keep going.

"I'm a squirrel and I hope we're going to be great friends."

Another vibration, like my wand is telling me to go on.

"To be honest, I'm not sure if I'll be very good at magic but I hope so. I really want to do well and to use my magic to help animals in need of assistance or to do something for our forest."

The vibrations are now coming constantly when I'm talking and I even start to feel a nice warmth streaking towards my paw as well. I hope it's a good sign and not a warning that my wand is going to explode. I don't know how I know this but I feel very reassured by this warmth. It doesn't feel like a threat at all, so I keep talking to my new friend.

I tell it about my family, my parents and their delicious bakery, about my best friends, and how I was both scared and happy to start school this morning. I talk about how my mum loves to sing in the kitchen and how my dad gives the best cuddles. And the more I talk (I'm not talking out loud but it feels like it now), the more I feel this little ball of warmth around me coming directly to my paw, spreading itself around, and making me feel heard and loved. With every word I say, I feel my wand connect to me more and more, until finally there's almost like a click between us. I can hear it in my head, like when you connect two jigsaw puzzle pieces together and you're happy to see that it fits.

My wand and I fit together and I'm so happy to realise that, despite all my earlier fears it was easy. I think I spent more time worrying about whether the connection will work than I spent on working on the actual connection. It's like Buttercup always says: there's no need to worry in advance. Something might give you some trouble but until it does: if there's nothing you can do about it, then it's useless to worry.

Chapter 12
Berry

After I'm done connecting with my wand, I stay up in the tree and try to think if I want to give it a name. Mrs Winter said it's not mandatory but I feel like I would feel better if it had a name, it would feel more personal.

Ok, think Applesauce, what kind of name could be good for a Magicol? Should I choose a regular name? Or a human name? That would be funny. I hear some from time to time when humans come through our woods. Let's see ... Martin? Steve? No, I don't think my wand wants to be called Steve. Maybe Martha? Or Sophie? Ruth? No, all those are too ... human ... and they don't really go with my world.

I need something more personal. What kind of name could be related to my magic world? I'm thinking of words that fit the vocabulary of a wizard, turning them in my head over and over but nothing sounds personal to me either. My mind is blank and I'm starting to feel discouraged. Or am I feeling hungry? Sometimes it's hard to see the difference with me.

I'm getting distracted by the thought that our lunch time is approaching and that we're supposed to have a picnic with the school for our first day. What am I going to eat? I hope my parents packed some pies for me. Of course they did, it wouldn't be a real meal without pie! Everyone knows that! And just like that, when I'm about to think about my favourite pie flavour, I have my answer! I know what I'm going to call my wand: Berry! It's sweet, it's a unique name and it's very personal. I close my eyes again, focus on my wand, on the energy that's still palpable since we connected and I send a new message towards it.

"Hey, it's me again. You remember me?" I don't know why I'm trying to joke with a magic wand but it already feels very natural to talk to it like I usually do with my friends. I mean the ones that can answer back. Actually, it does answer me! As soon as I ask my question, I feel it vibrate slightly in my paw again. Oh it feels so nice to have it react like this!

"I have found you a name. I'm calling to call you ... Berry!"

I don't have time to wonder whether it likes this name because straight away I feel a warmth that tells me the wand thinks it's great! Berry it is then!

I suddenly feel really happy, proud of myself and relaxed. I'm done with my task and I finally go down the tree to meet my classmates and teacher again. Once on the ground I look around to see how everyone is doing and I'm surprised to see that I'm among the first ones to be done. There are still a lot of wizards and witches scattered everywhere, in trees, behind bushes, or even standing on benches, trying to connect with their Magicol. I see a lot of them struggle, shaking their Magicol above their heads like they are trying to connect it to some invisible magic network instead of to themselves, or jumping up and down with their Magicol around their neck. I'm not sure if they are doing this because our teacher told them to or because they saw someone else do it and thought they should do the same. Judging by Mrs Winter's expression, I'd say it's the latter. She goes to each group of struggling students with a warm smile and explains everything to them again. I think Mum was right, we're lucky to have her as a teacher for our first year. She may look stern but she also seems patient and kind.

I look around for Buttercup and Almond, but can only spot the latter coming out of a very colourful shrub. She sees me right away and runs toward me, as usual.

"Hey Applesauce!" She almost sings my name and I have to hush her and remind her to speak quietly when we're at school, especially right now when everyone around us is trying hard to focus.

"Oops, sorry!" She looks a bit ashamed, I know she doesn't like to cause trouble, but it doesn't take her smile from her face.

"How did it go?" She asks in a low voice. "Did you manage to connect with yours?"

I nod with a big smile. I'm proud of myself and I want the world to know it!

"Yes! I did it quickly, I'm so happy! I was so afraid I wouldn't manage to connect at all, but I think my wand likes me!"

Almond rejoices with me, and just as I'm wondering if I should tell her the name I chose for my wand, she starts her own story quickly, almost in one breath.

"I did it too! It was not easy though ... I'm not sure if I did it right or if my acorn was not in the mood but all I felt was sparkles between us. Do you think it's normal? Should I exchange my Magicol? No of course not, I can't do that ... But what if I picked a broken one? Do you think Mrs Winter would let me change it? Or do we have to see this with the Great Wizard?"

"Almond, calm down and relax. You know I can't understand you when you talk so fast!"

The good thing is that we've been friends for so long, she doesn't get mad at me for saying that. We both laugh and she relaxes a bit.

"You're right, I got too excited ... again!" She is trying to joke about it but I know my friend and I can see that she's actually really upset about this. I need to help her feel better.

"Ok, so you said that you did manage to connect properly?"

She nods and answers, slowly this time.

"Yes. Right away I did feel a sort of snap between us but that didn't seem to be very powerful. Nothing else happened after that. I waited for a while but I guess I'll have to try again later to make it stronger."

"Maybe if ..."

"What? Maybe what? Do you have an idea?" She is speaking loudly again, and jumping up and down, all excited that I may have a solution. I laugh but I give her that look again, to remind her that we're still supposed to be quiet. She looks sheepish for a second but gives me a little push with her front paw (almost knocking me down, she's very strong when she gets excited).

"Go on, tell me."

"Well, I don't know but from what I saw with Ber..." Oops, I almost say Berry's name and I realise that I don't think I'm ready to share that yet! Especially when my friend is so miserable. I don't want to make it worse by showing her that I connected so well with mine that I even gave it a name! So I correct myself and go on. "...with mine, I think it helps if you stay quiet and empty your head. If you were jumping up and down, it may explain why it was so hard."

She's silent for a bit, thinking about it, maybe trying to remember how she acted during her Connection time and she nods.

"Yep, I think you're right. I'll try again and stay calm this time."

She's smiling again so I'm happy! I love helping my friends.

Unfortunately Almond doesn't have time to try again because Mrs Winter calls us all.

"Ok Seed class, gather around. Everyone seems to be done with their Connection so I can congratulate you all. Take a seat while I explain to you the next step."

I look around while everyone is sitting down and I see some unhappy faces so I guess Almond was not the only one who had a hard time connecting. Buttercup, Almond and Wind are all next to me on the bench now. Mrs Winter stands in her spot in front of us. As soon as we are all settled down, she starts her explanations.

"So, all of you managed their Connection on their first day and that's already a success. Not everybody can do this, you know? Most of the time, there's a wizard or two who can't connect the first time and it's totally fine. It's a lot of pressure."

I feel Wind fidgeting next to me on the bench but I try to focus on the teacher's words.

"I'm actually surprised by this class. Well done, everyone, well done! You're all off to a good start, I can feel it! And for those of you who only felt a small connection, don't worry, as I told you all that's perfectly normal. It can take time but you will get there. I advise you to keep your Magicol with you at all times from now on to help your connection grow. You can always try again to have a quiet moment with it at home later. Being in a familiar environment can really make a difference. I hope you're all happy with the Magicol you picked and that you will work well with it. Don't forget that your wand, stone or acorn will be your best friend when it comes to magic. My door is always open to those who have questions about the connection, or anything else -"

"Door? What door?" interrupts my curious new furry friend next to me. I hear some laughs behind us and I have to say I would laugh too but I don't want to hurt Wind's feelings. I think the others thought he was making a joke but I don't think he was. I guess he's just so nervous that he doesn't realise that our classroom doesn't have a real door.

"It's an expression Wind," our teacher answers with a smile.

"Oh!"

"Anyway, as I was saying, I'm always available if you need help. But, in the meantime ..." She pauses to make sure she has everyone's attention. "In the meantime, it's lunch time!!!" Everybody cheers at this and so does my tummy.

"We will start the proper lessons tomorrow. Today we feast and meet our new friends!"

Chapter 13
New friends

Since we will have the picnic with the whole school, it must be held outside the Academy grounds or there won't be enough space. We can only celebrate with the dry campus since there's not enough room around the pond to gather with the wet campus students.

"Oh, what a shame! It would have been nice to be with everyone," Buttercup says when he learns this.

I nod silently as we start walking toward the picnic area, before answering so softly that he's the only one who can hear me, "Mmmm, meeting the students from our class plus the Flower and Tree classes is already a big step for me. I think I won't mind not meeting the water animals today."

He smiles at me to reassure me and adds, "Oh but you're doing great, you already made a friend today! And you connected with your wand, didn't you?"

I smile again thanks to him and I tell him how I loved connecting with my Magicol. I'll probably tell him and Almond the name I chose for it later tonight, when it's just us three.

"What about you? How did it go?"

"I managed to do it, yes. It took some time at first but once I realised I could just treat it like any of my friends, it worked quickly."

"I know, me too!" We laugh at this, happy to know that we both came to the same conclusion. Although, I guess it must have been easier for Buttercup because he's such a friendly animal. He could make friends with a rock or even some moss on a tree! I envy how easily he can talk to others.

"Do you know if Almond managed all right?" he asks, concerned for his sister. "I wanted to check on her but she left the bench so quickly to run to the picnic place that I don't know."

"Yeah, I saw her after I finished. She connected with hers but she said she didn't feel a deep connection yet."

"Oh! I'm sure it will come."

"Yes, of course!"

I'm feeling very confident about her success. It's funny how I always have more faith in my friends than myself.

"I told her to try again when she's calmer. You know how she is, she was jumping up and down so much so ..."

Buttercup agrees and we are soon joined by Wind, walking on the path next to us. Oh, if you're wondering how Buttercup and I can hear Wind talking, even though he's so much bigger than us, it's easy. When they are with smaller animals, the big ones try their best to get down to our level. So instead of standing up, Wind is walking next to us on his four paws. He's still bigger than us but at least we can have a conversation more easily. Or we travel on their backs like we did this morning with Almond. There's always a solution when you are willing to try to make it work!

"Hey, do you know a lot of the students in the other classes?" I ask Wind.

He nods and says that he does know some but his mind seems to be very far away and he looks very nervous. Well, more nervous than before.

"Are you okay?" Buttercup asks him quietly. I love the way he noticed that Wind was not well so quickly, even though he's only just met him.

Wind stops walking and mumbles a soft, "No, not really."

We stop walking too and Buttercup invites us to the side of the road so we can talk easily without bothering anyone.

"What's the matter?"

Wind sits down on the ground between two small bushes and his sad expression breaks my heart. He stays quiet for a bit and starts to play with a fallen branch before finally confessing, "I lied!"

We both look at him surprised. Lied? About what?

"I didn't connect with my Magicol."

"Oh, it's ok you'll get a better connection with time..." Buttercup starts.

"No, I didn't connect with it. At all." He adds, hiding his face behind his big paws.

Oh yeah, that's bad indeed! But I guess I can't say that out loud. I look at Buttercup, hoping he'll know what to say and as usual he does.

"It's ok! Don't worry, I'm sure it will come soon."

"How can you be sure if I didn't manage it today after trying for so long?" He doesn't sound angry, just miserable and that's somehow worse. I hate seeing my friend like this.

"Well ... it's true, I don't know for sure," Buttercup admits and just hearing him being honest seems to get Wind's attention. He looks down at my best friend, waiting for an explanation.

"What I mean is ... no one can know for sure if you'll succeed, not even the teachers. But," and he says this second part with a big smile and a very confident tone, "I have faith in you! It's not a matter of knowing but a matter of trusting. I trust you but most importantly, you need to trust yourself, Wind!"

"How? I'm so bad at this magic thing ..."

"Of course you're bad, it's your first day! No one can be good before learning a new skill. Do you think Mrs Winter was born with all her great magical techniques or knowing all the spells and potions? She's no more special than us."

This last bit gets a giggle from me and a nervous hush from Wind, who is afraid she will hear us and get mad. But it doesn't stop Buttercup. On the contrary, he keeps speaking with enthusiasm!

"I'm serious! She knew nothing more than you when she started to learn magic! Same for the Great Wizard. She didn't go to her first class thinking, 'Great! That's it, I nailed it, I'm going to become the next Great Wizard one day, bam!' No, they all had to learn and make mistakes. And you heard Mrs Winter, she said that there's always a student who can't connect the first time. So you see that happens a lot, you're not the only one! I'm sure you'll be fine!"

"You really think so?" Wind asks with a small smile.

"I know so! Go talk to Mrs Winter, I'm sure she'll have some advice and you can try again at home where you're more relaxed."

I'm mesmerised by my best friend's encouraging words and I'm happy to see Wind smile again!

"Thank you, Buttercup. You're right, I'll try again and maybe it will work this time ..."

"No, no, no! Not maybe! I know it will work! Trust me!"

And with that, Wind sounds like a new bear! Well not really a new bear, he's still physically the same size with the same chocolate brown fur, but he is more confident and he's smiling again! SuperButtercup to the rescue! I should make him a cape! We stand up and try to catch up with the rest of the students who are already ahead and by the time we finally reach the picnic place most of the students are there.

Thanks to our little chat and Buttercup's enthusiasm, I am now less anxious to meet the rest of the Academy and to be around strangers. The picnic takes place at Kappa meadow, at one end of our forest. There's a lot of space for everyone, including the deers, the wolves and the bears (Wind is quite a small bear compared to some other students, so the space is not a luxury!). But it's probably a good thing we don't have any elephants in Woodland because I don't know where they would fit. Although, as I told you at the beginning of this story, there are academies for wizards and witches all around the world, so there must be some in the desert and the jungle. I'd love to visit other schools with animals so different to ours. Can you imagine one with elephants, giraffes, and zebras ...? Oh I would love to see a wizphant (a wizard elephant of course) holding a wand, or a giraffe with an acorn.

Anyway, back to our picnic! The biggest animals in Woodland are the bears but once you assemble all of the classes and teachers together in one space, there really are quite a lot of animals. All the chattering makes it quite noisy but this time I don't find it overwhelming. It's nice actually. It seems like we were among the last to arrive because once we're there, one of the teachers that I don't know signals to the headmaster that we can begin.

The headmaster is a big brown bear, with thick black glasses and a stern expression always on his face. His grey mark runs all along his back, it's quite impressive. Especially when he's standing on his two rear paws like he is now. He's so massive that Wind and Smore look like cubs compared to him. I haven't met him properly but I've seen him many times before in the forest. He doesn't look very funny if you ask me. His face seems to say, "I'm sure someone near me misbehaved in the last hour and I'm going to find out who it is!"

I think I'm not the only one being scared of him because everyone stopped talking as soon as he stood up tall. He didn't even have to ask for silence. It's quite impressive to see! Even though everyone is looking at him, he still clears his throat to make sure he has our attention. I don't dare to move, in case the leaves under my paws make too much noise.

"Welcome, welcome everyone! I am Mr Pinecone, the current headmaster of Woodland Academy and I welcome all of you: our new students, our returning wizards and witches, and of course our valuable teachers."

He pauses and it seems to be a signal for "please clap now". Everyone claps but as usual I'm so bad at reading social situations that I only start clapping along once everyone else is silent again. Hopefully my paws are so small that my clap is too soft for anyone to notice my mistake.

"I hope you all had a wonderful morning and that you will have an amazing year full of knowledge and new spells. Thank you to the families who brought some food for the picnic earlier today."

Oh yeah, that's why my dad was been baking extra pies yesterday and that's why my mum was packing food last night. They told me about the picnic but I was too focused on the extra pies to really listen to anything they were saying. They had to hide them to make sure I didn't eat them and now I realise I'll finally get to eat them! Where are the pies? I look around, stretching my neck to see them but all I see is a big walnut wooden table in the middle of the crowd. I mean a really giant table. It's really huge but there are some steps leading to it and some smaller tables on it for us, the smaller bunch! I want to look at all the food laid there but Buttercup nudges me gently and reminds me with a smile, "Stay focussed. You'll get to eat soon, don't worry!"

Oh yes, Mr Pinecone is still talking. I hope he didn't say anything too important. Let's try to ignore the food and listen.

"... of course, your teachers will explain all this in detail later. Don't worry!"

Oh no, I guess it was important! What did I miss? At least he said not to worry so I'll trust him on that. Worst case, I'll ask Buttercup. That's what best friends are for, right?

"Your time at the Academy will define who you are as a wizard and I ..."

I hear someone add, with a small whisper "or as a witch!" and as I turn around I see that this remark came from Honeysuckle, the girl rabbit I met earlier. I smile at this and think she's right. Why did he say wizard and not witch? That's not really nice.

"... I expect you all to give your best and to make the school proud of its wizards ..."

This time I'm the one who adds "and witches" but unlike Honeysuckle, I forget to whisper, so Mr Pinecone hears me. Oops!

"I'm sorry, what did you say? I didn't hear you!" he asks, his eyes looking for the animal who was crazy enough to interrupt him. Me. Oh no, what is he going to do to me? Expel me? Ban me from the forest? No, no, no, he can't do that, he's the headmaster of the school, not the chief of Woodland forest or the king of the world. And now I'm wondering if there is such a thing as the king of the world? Or queen? I don't have time to ask myself any more questions because I realise that everyone is staring at me and I need to talk. I look up at him, panicking.

"Yes, you! What were you saying over there?"

Ok, let's be brave, he won't hurt me! Or if he does, at least there will be witnesses.

"Mmmm ... I said, 'and witches'."

"I don't understand," His eyes are still fixed on me, oh he's so scary!

"Because ... because you were saying something about making the Academy proud of its wizards, so I just added 'and witches' to make sure everyone was included in your speech."

I feel a bit hot and short of breath from talking to this big bear who scares me so badly, but I feel confident that I'm right to defend the witches' right to be seen, so I don't let these physical details stress me out.

Mr Pinecone looks at me a bit confused and simply adds a murmured, "Yes, yes of course. Wizards and Witches."

He finally takes his piercing stare away from me and continues his speech. Waouh I can't believe I survived that. So far no harm done and he didn't kick me out of the school. Unless he plans on doing it later in private? No, I'm just imagining too many things now.

"So, anyway, what I meant to say was ... enjoy this picnic and take the time to get to know your classmates and teachers today."

And he finishes with a loud, "Let the feast begin!"

I expect a giant firework or a magical dust cloud bursting over our heads to go with this big declaration, but no, nothing. He just stops talking abruptly and awkwardly gestures to everyone to help themselves to the food on the table.

As soon as he finishes his speech, I feel a little tap on my shoulder. I turn around and see Honeysuckle congratulating me with a big smile, "Great job!"

"Who? Me?"

"Yes! That was impressive! Talking to the headmaster like that, I was so happy to see someone say something to stand up for witches."

"Oh thanks ..." I mumble. I'm not used to having so much attention on me or having people congratulate me like this. "Well actually it's because I heard you the first time, that I said it."

"Yeah but you were brave enough to say it louder than me." Mmm, should I tell her that I only said it out loud by accident. "And you even had the guts to reply to him when he asked you what you'd said. I'm not very courageous, I think I would have lied ..."

I laugh at this and explain to her that I'm not very brave either.

Buttercup says "Oh, I think you're braver than you think!" before asking us if we're hungry. Judging by how fast we all rush towards the food, I'd say we are but I bet none of them is as hungry as me. I know I ate a lot this morning but breakfast seems like a lifetime ago now and I'm starving!!

Chapter 14
Honeysuckle

O nce I reach the table, I see dishes from all the families and I'm drooling: mushroom stew, mashed potatoes, every kind of salad you could imagine (with carrot, corn, cucumber, green pepper, lettuce ...), crispy toasts topped with tomatoes and herbs, chocolate cakes, walnut bread, tasty little energy balls with nuts and dried fruits, blueberry muffins, carrot cake, banana bread, and an assortment of the best pies in the world.

I recognise dishes from my parents' bakery, as well as some made by Buttercup and Almond's family. I also see new ones I've never tried before. While I'm trying to decide what to choose, I notice a framed note on the table telling us to do our best to eat with someone new today and to use this opportunity to get to know them better. Then the note lists ideas for topics to discuss with our new friends. What a great idea! I'm so bad at getting to know new people because I never know what to say. I never dare to ask any questions that could be too personal and in the end I just stay silent. Ok, so what are the topics suggested?

How many brothers and sisters do you have?

Oh this one will be easy for me to answer. I'm an only squirrel!

What is your favourite sport?

Does sleeping count as a sport?

Do you prefer winter or summer?

Summer!

What is your favourite food?

Easy, all of them!

Do you like to read?

Is it even a question? Of course I love to read!

The list goes on like this and I try my best to remember a few to ask around. I realise that, out of habit I was just going to sit with Almond and Buttercup. I didn't even think about using this picnic to meet my new classmates, when that's obviously the point of this event! Once my bowl is full of food (well, my first bowl. I intend to have a second helping later of course), I stop and look around, wondering who to eat this with. I really find it scary to go talk to someone I don't know. I always imagine I'll be rejected, made fun of or even ignored. But so far, my classmates have been nice, so I tell myself to be a brave squizard and to find a new friend to eat lunch with.

I look around and notice Honeysuckle eating alone in a corner. I take a deep breath and start to walk towards her when I see that she has a book in her paws. And just like that, I'm not scared anymore! Books make everything easier for me. They are the easiest way to break the ice. I approach her slowly so I don't scare her. I know that when I'm reading I'm so lost in the story that I don't see anyone around me and can get scared if someone talks to me.

"Hi, can I eat with you?"

She looks up from her book and nods with her small bunny smile. I sit down with my bowl of food in front of me.

"I'm Applesauce by the way." I think introducing myself is a good start.

"I know, we met earlier. With your friend's sister, remember?"

"Oh yeah I know. I just wasn't sure if you remembered my name. Sometimes if you meet a lot of animals at the same time, you end up forgetting their names and then it's very embarrassing ..."

She laughs and cuts in with her story. "Oh I know! When we moved here, my parents introduced us to the neighbours and there were so many of them I couldn't remember who was who. Then I started to play with this racoon boy every day but I still couldn't remember his name. And it was so awkward because the days went by and I didn't know how to ask him his name without sounding like a weirdo, you know?"

I'm laughing with her now. "So what did you do?"

"Well," and she tries to put on a very serious expression but I can see her smiling, "I developed a plan, a very clever plan!"

"Oh what was it?"

"Well, you see, I knew the names of the animals I had met the first day but I just didn't know who was who. So one day I saw him and went to hide behind a tree to call his name."

"What name? Did you make one up?"

"No, I just tried them all."

"What?"

"Yeah, I just went and yelled, 'Mika?' There was no response so I tried the next one on my list. 'Miles?' Nope. I tried the next one."

I'm laughing at her funny plan. "So how many did you try?"

"Quite a few before he answered to one!"

"What was it?"

"Lenon."

"And he didn't find it weird that you were calling him different names like this?"

"Oh no, I was hiding and I disguised my voice so he didn't know it was me! But you want to know the funniest part?"

I nod, wondering what could be funnier than Honeysuckle changing her voice just to learn the name of her new friend!

"His name wasn't even Lenon, it was Lemon!!"

"Did he ever learn what you did?"

"Oh no, he moved out the following week," she announces,

deadpan.

"You're kidding?" I'm now laughing so much my belly hurts.

"No, I'm serious. His family moved to another forest! Such a waste! All this great detective work for nothing!"

And she starts eating her salad like she just told me the most serious story.

"Oh, that was so funny! You're really good at telling stories!"

"You think so? Thanks! My parents always say I talk too much."

"Oh mine too!"

"They also say that I read too much and that I should be a more sensible girl, helping with my brothers and sisters instead of reading all the time!"

"Read too much? That's crazy!"

I take a bite of the bread with tomato from my bowl (so yummy!) and ask her "What are you reading by the way?"

Her face lights up at those words and she quickly grabs the book she put away when I arrived.

"Oh it's this great story about a bear that comes from Peru and ends up living with a human family."

"Oh, does he have magical powers? Is he a wizard too?"

"Mmm, I don't think so. I haven't finished it yet so maybe he'll realise later that he has special abilities. But so far, he's mostly really good at making a mess wherever he goes, so that's really funny."

"Oh I can relate to him then. I'm kind of a daydreamer and tend to fall over a lot ..."

"I can lend it to you when I'm done if you want?"

"Really? Oh thanks, I'd love this!"

"No problem."

"And maybe I have books that you'd like to borrow too. We can swap!"

We talk about our favourite books for a few minutes before I see Almond run toward us.

"Hey guys! Can we join you?"

I nod before realising that by "we", she means her and the whole Seed class. I laugh because it's just her style to do something like this. She probably started thinking she'll collect a few friends to eat with and ended up with the whole class. She sits down on the grass facing me and everyone starts to spread around us in a sort of circle.

"I thought it would be nice if we could get the whole class together!" She explains with a big smile and I see that her positive energy is reaching everyone because they all seem happy with her decision. Everyone is gathered together and introducing themselves to each other again. Honeysuckle whispers to me, "Pss ... If I forget a name, I counting on you to remind me before I have to use my trick again, ok?"

"Deal!" I smile. "But only if you do the same for me?"

She winks at me and I see Buttercup look at us with curiosity.

And just like that, thanks to the friendly, thoughtful Almond, we are all getting to know each other, without the stress of the classroom. I count quietly and see that we have sixteen students in the beginner class. We take turns answering the same round of questions (Buttercup's idea!). Some are from the list of ideas suggested on the table and some are our own.

Every time we finish a turn, the last person to answer gets to pick the next question. This way we discover who has siblings (Honeysuckle wins with a total of twelve), who has lived in Woodland Forest their whole lives (some of us have moved here recently and some have been here for generations), who lives where in the forest, and who picked what as a Magicol (I notice a large majority of wands and acorns, but not a lot of stones).

When it's my turn to ask the question, I hesitate between "favourite book" and "favourite pie flavour" but I go for the first one. Some answers are quite funny. For example, Sidney, the worm who loves hiking and martial arts simply answers by saying that she doesn't like to read. And when Bean, an adult male badger remarks that it's kind of funny for a worm not to be a bookworm, she gets a bit mad and explains that this bookworm name is just a ridiculous stereotype.

"There's no reason why we should love books more than wolves or deers."

Ok, so I'll have to remember never to talk about books with her. On the other hand, I try to remember the names of the favourite books of my classmates who do like to read so I can look them up later. So far I've noticed that Rain (an adult wild boar,) Nutmeg (a young raccoon), and Bloom (an adult badger) are the ones who read the most along with Honeysuckle and me. Maybe we'll all become good friends over this shared love of books.

Time goes by like this and it's so nice to realise that my classmates don't feel like strangers anymore. Maybe I won't be friends with all of them but I'll sure do my best to be friendly with them. I'm sure Almond will quickly be friends with each and everyone of them but I'm fine with a smaller circle of friends. After all, we all know that small things are the best. Right?

Chapter 15
Home

J ust as we are all tidying up our bowls and scraps of leftover food (that we keep as compost to help nourish our forest), Mrs Winter comes to see our little group to say how happy she is that we had our first lunch all together and that she hopes to see us well and rested tomorrow morning for our first class!

"And remember to keep practising your connection at home."

We say goodbye to Wind and Honeysuckle as they live closer to the school than us three, and I start my walk home with my two best friends. I had originally planned for us to stop by "Sweet treats" on our way home but I think we are all too full from the picnic. Almond kindly offers to carry us on her back for the ride home but she adds, "I won't go fast though, I feel like my belly is going to explode with all the food I ate!"

It's a rare sight to see Almond walk slowly but I can totally relate with her.

"Oh I know, I'm the same, my belly is going to burst any second but I couldn't help myself, everything was so good!" I say while trying to find a comfortable position on my friend's back. Buttercup laughs at this.

"What? It's true, everything was delicious, no?" I ask him.

"Oh yes I agree! I'm just laughing because I didn't think it was possible for you to be full. I was expecting you to ask us to stop by the bakery on our way back!"

"Me too!"adds Almond.

"Actually that was my plan but no, I'm too full. I can't eat anything anymore ..."

They both laugh at how well they know me.

"Oh but I'm sure you'll be hungry again in an hour."

Yes they do know me really well! I may be full now but I'm already thinking of what I'll eat later for dinner!

We're all too sleepy from the picnic so the ride home is really quiet but we agree to meet up after dinner as usual. Once home, I stop by our kitchen to get myself a nice cup of tea and I take it up in our tree to relax with my book and my wand. Mrs Winter told us that the best way to get used to our Magicol is to take it with us everywhere. It will help us get used to it but it will also help our object to get to know us if we keep it on us while doing the things we love the most. She assured us it will strengthen our connection.

"Remember to treat it like a friend and not a tool," she said before we finished our class. I hope Wind will manage to connect with his Magicol tonight.

I settle in my favourite nook, high in our tree. It's well hidden from the outside but still lets in a lot of natural light and my mum helped decorate it with comfy blankets and cushions. I put Berry and my tea next to me, and as soon as I open my book, I get lost in the story and I don't notice time passing by. This is the story of a witch who is so small she can't scare anyone. Either people don't see her at all, or they just laugh at her for being so small. But she thinks it's her duty as a witch to scare everyone, so she goes on a quest, determined to solve her problem.

She meets an ancient sorcerer who tells her to find the lost book of the darkest spells. She walks for weeks and weeks through dark forests and humid caves, and along the way she meets some friends that help her find this mysterious book.

Once she finally finds it, she gets the ability to grow bigger than any of the humans in her village. She comes back triumphant, excited to finally be able to frighten everyone. But she soon realises that it's actually not that funny to be the scary witch, especially when even her new friends are afraid of her. She finishes her adventure back to her regular size but happier than ever. I love this book so much that I've read it several times already. I even know the last sentence by heart, "I'd rather be small and surrounded by my friends than giant but all alone."

I get so lost in my book that I forget to go down to eat my snack. I am surprised when I hear that my mum and dad are already back from the bakery.

"Applesauce? You're here?" My dad calls from the bottom of our tree.

"Yes, I'm here, I'm coming, Dad!"

I put down my book with a sigh. Not a sigh of frustration, but one of satisfaction after such a great time spent with a story I love so much. I slide my bookmark in (it's made by Buttercup) and go down to join my parents with Berry.

"Oh are we eating out tonight?"

"Yes, we thought the weather was just perfect for that, so we brought some food from the bakery and we have some leftovers, so we'll just put everything here and have a little feast."

Oh I love it when we have feasts. They are not really feasts, we just call them that but it's the best. It's basically a bit of everything: some veggie sticks, some nuts, bread, fruits, and the rest of the pies of the day. Always pies.

"Great! I'll get the drinks."

I kiss my dad and go into the kitchen to greet my mum with a kiss and a hug. As I get a pitcher of homemade lemonade from the fridge I ask her, "Are we eating with Buttercup and Almond?"

She seems tired and I even see her yawn before answering me.

"Ohhh ... no, I'm sorry. I wanted to invite them over but I admit I'm pretty tired. Sorry love."

"It's ok, Mum. I just wanted to know. It's fine, I'll see them after anyway."

I don't want my mum to feel guilty for not hosting for our friends, she already works a lot for our community.

"Ok, let's get everything on the table and you can tell us all about your first day!"

Once the food is on the table, we all sit down on the outside bench with my dad next to me and we start to eat. My mum looks a bit refreshed after a glass of fresh lemonade and is excited to hear what I have to say.

"So tell us everything Applesauce! How was your first day? Was the teacher nice? What Magicol did you pick? Did you make friends?"

I laugh at the thousands of questions my mum already has for me.

"It was great! Our teacher seemed a bit stern at first but actually she's really nice. She gave us some good advice for connecting with our Magicol."

"That's great, that's very important! She came to the bakery after school but I was too busy to ask her anything. I'll give her a free wolf cookie tomorrow for being so nice to you!"

"Mum, no, she'll think you're buying her to give me better grades!"

My mum giggles, "Ah, don't worry, you won't get graded so I can't buy her! I just want to be nice!"

That sums up my mum pretty well, always trying to be nice without wanting anything in return. At one point she was giving away so many free samples at the bakery, my dad had to remind her that they were supposed to make some money and not to hand over all their stock for free.

"So we had the Ceremony with the Great Wizard. It was a bit intimidating at first but then when my turn came, I found my wand quite quickly. I saw it and I just knew!"

"Oh, you got a wand too? Show me!" says my dad, who also has a wand. My mum has an acorn.

I show them Berry, they look at it carefully and I explain to them what the Great Wizard told me about it.

"Oh you've got a special one! Not a lot of Magicol are made by Great Wizards you know. It's really an honour," my dad explains.

"Did you make new friends at the picnic?"

My mum always wants to know if I have made friends, no matter the situation. Even when I run an errand to the supermarket she imagines I'm going to make ten friends in thirty minutes. So you can imagine how excited she is that I have started school.

"Yes! I even made one just as we were arriving at the Academy!"

"Really? Oh that's wonderful honey!"

"Yeah. Well, I sort of bumped into him when I was walking ..."

So I tell them all about how I met Wind by accident, about the other students in my class, the Connection and I finish with the picnic.

"Oh it's so nice that you've made new friends honey! This Honeysuckle seems to be funny, I'm happy you met someone who loves to read like you do!" my dad says.

"Yes we already talked about lending each other books and -" I look at the clock hanging from a tree branch and see that it's already eight. Our usual meeting time with Applesauce and Buttercup!

"Oh, it's time! Can I go now?"

"Of course! Just bring your glass and plate back to the kitchen and go."

"Do you want some help to clear the table before I go?"

My dad shakes his head sleepily. "No, don't worry about it, we'll magic everything back to the kitchen. But can you turn the kettle on while you're up?"

And then he tells my mum, "I'll make us a nice cup of chamomile tea before we go to bed, what do you think Rose?"

"I think this makes me more in love with you, Sprout!"

My parents are so cute. They have been mates for a long time and are still very much in love. I go back to the kitchen with my plate and cup, pour some water in the kettle, turn it on and leave to see my best friends for our daily appointment.

Chapter 16

The fort under the stars

Every night, Buttercup, Almond and I meet in a little meadow not far from our tree, on the other side of a close-by hill. We go there to look at the stars and talk about our day. Sometimes I even share with them the stories that I made up in my head that day. We have been doing this for as long as I can remember, but just as I'm about to leave, my mum asks me if I haven't forgotten anything.

"Oh! Sorry!"

I go over to the table and kiss her goodbye.

She laughs quietly, with the kind of laugh she only has at the end of the day when she's tired.

"Not that you silly sausage! I meant your evening drinks!"

"Oh yeah!!

Every night we meet around some tea and hot cocoa. Sometimes we also have some treats to go with them. I'm generally the one bringing them but occasionally Buttercup and Almond's mum bakes a cake or some cookies for us to share. Usually I make hot cocoa and tea so we all have a choice but tonight there's no time to lose if I don't want to be late, so I quickly go back to the kitchen and make us a nice warm thermos of cocoa. As my dad joins me in the kitchen to make their tea, he hands me the biscuit tin that's on the counter with a little wink.

"Thanks Dad!" I grab my usual basket from under the table, stack the thermos, the tin, and our three mugs in it and I'm off!

I start to run out of the kitchen but my mum reminds me that my friends will still be there even if I'm a bit late and that they won't disappear.

"I know, I'm just happy to see them!"

"You know you've already spent the day with them, right?" she teases me with a smile.

"Well, I haven't seen Almond much, she was so busy chatting with everyone else and anyway, I still have so much to tell them ..."

She laughs again and just waves at me to go.

I wait until I'm out of view to walk faster toward our meeting point. We call it "the Fort under the stars". It's like a little secret hideout: it's very similar in shape to an igloo, but instead of ice we used wood planks (since it's easier to get our paws on wood than on ice!) and there's no roof so we have a great view of the night sky. It's well hidden with branches and leaves to shield us from the rest of the world. We even have some blankets and soft pillows stored in a wooden trunk that always stays there in the fort. It's perfect!

I arrive and ... I can't see them outside! Where are they? Maybe they really waited too long and disappeared? I start to look around before approaching our fort. Maybe they're already inside? And just as I'm about to peek my head inside, I get the fright of my life (ok maybe not that big!) as a big leafy monster jumps on me and yells, "Booooo!!!"

I yell a loud "arghhhh!", close my eyes out of fright and almost drop our basket on the ground. But as soon as I reopen my eyes I see my two best friends giggling and I quickly realise that the "leafy monster" was just Almond and Buttercup wearing face masks made of big colourful leaves.

"Oh that was so funny!" laughs Almond, rolling on the ground from laughter. "You should have seen your face!"

Buttercup is laughing too, and I'm torn between joining him and turning back home with the treats just to teach them a lesson.

"Oh you two! I almost dropped the basket with our mugs in it!"

We've had those three mugs for a while and they are very special since Buttercup made them for us.

"Sorry," they both say a bit sheepishly.

"But admit it was funny though?" Almond asks.

I put the basket on the ground and, even though I'm trying hard not to smile, I can't hold it long and end up laughing with them. I can't help it, just looking at Almond's mischievous face is enough to make me crack!

"It was, yes! What are those anyway?" I ask, gesturing toward the masks.

"Oh, Buttercup made them for us this afternoon after school."

"Just to scare me?"

"No, of course no! I was bored so I started to play with some leaves and before I knew it, I had a mask. My sisters saw me, so they all asked me for one too, so in the end it took me most of the afternoon."

He smiles and hands me one.

"Here, I made one for you too, Applesauce! I didn't put the band on yet because I need to adjust it to your size."

It's really pretty with the perfect mix of green and orange leaves, some darker, some lighter. All different sizes. He even glued everything on soft orange fabric so it won't be itchy to wear. I love how creative Buttercup is.

"Thanks! I love it!"

Almond offers to test the masks on our school friends and teachers but we quickly convince her that it's a terrible idea.

"You think so?"

"I'm sure! Poor Wind will have a heart attack if you jump on him like that!"

"But he's a bear, he won't be frightened by us, we're so small compared to him!"

"He may be a bear but I think he gets scared easily."

Almond sighs. "Oh yeah you may be right."

But, as usual she gets excited very quickly again.

"What about Mrs Winter? Do you think she will like it?"

Buttercup and I both laugh loudly at that.

"What? Don't you think she'll like the masks?"

"Are you crazy? She won't find this funny at all Almond! She may find the masks pretty but I don't think she will love being scared by them!" Buttercup explains to his sister.

"Ok let's settle down. So, I didn't bring any tea tonight, only cocoa because I was a bit late. But look, my dad gave me some biscuits."

"Oh chocolate chips and pecan! My favourite!"

Almond grabs our hidden blankets and pillows from the trunk and we unpack the drinks and the food.

"By the way, where were you this afternoon and at dinner? I didn't see you come back to eat ..." I ask them.

"Oh, well, we were home for a while when we made the masks. Then we went to play near the pond with Raven. We would have asked you to tag along but we knew you were reading so we thought you'd rather stay home."

Raven is a turtle who also goes to the Academy but she is already in class II and in the water campus. I know what you're thinking, Raven is a funny name for a turtle, right? I think her parents chose this name because her shell is so dark.

"And just as we were heading home, we met Mum and Dad, who told us we were eating out tonight to celebrate our first day."

"Oh really? That's nice!"

"Yeah it was really fun to eat out all together."

"What did you do for dinner? We would have asked you but we were not very close to home ..."

"Oh no, don't worry, we had a feast so it was great too! And I think my mum and dad were quite tired anyway."

Like every night, once we finally settle down on the blanket with our biscuits and mugs of cocoa, we start talking about our day. We usually chat about everything but tonight, obviously it's all about our first day. It's a nice mix of comments and questions from the three of us.

"Oh, it was such a great first day, wasn't it?"

"I love my Magicol!"

"What did you think of the teacher?"

"The picnic was a really great way to meet everyone!"

"I was so surprised when it turned out the Great Wizard was a racoon!"

"She seems so fun, though! Not at all scary like I thought!"

And then Buttercup says something really nice to me. "Applesauce, I was so proud of you for making friends today. I know it's a bit scary for you to meet new animals but I was so impressed when you came into class with Wind!"

"I know, I impressed myself too!" We all laugh at this. "And I met Honeysuckle too, two friends in a day! Can you believe it?"

"She seems really nice!"

We talk some more about our new friends, then we talk about our magical objects. Two acorns and one wand.

"So have you named your Magicol yet?"

"Yes, I named mine Berry!" I finally tell them.

"Oh it's such a cute and perfect name for you, Applesauce!"

"I'm not sure if I'm going to name mine," confesses Buttercup.

"What about you, Almond?"

And the evening goes on like this, with the stars, three now empty mugs, some laughter and just this peaceful feeling that we had a great day!

One of our rituals is that we always end our evening by saying something that made us happy today or something that we are grateful for. Tonight it's Buttercup's turn to choose the question and he picks, "So what made you happy today?"

Almond goes first with, "Making masks with you Buttercup! Well, I mostly watched you make them to be honest but it was great!"

I love that she picked an activity so simple, instead of something that happened at the Academy. She loves her siblings so much.

"I'm happy that I made new friends and that I have found Berry," I answer with my wand in my paw, feeling its heat radiate through me.

"And you Buttercup?"

"I'm happy that our teacher is so nice."

What about you? Yes, you, reading this! What made you happy today? I'm sure there has to be something. We all have days that are better than others, but even on the days when you feel grumpy, mad or sad, it's always nice to try to think of something good that happened before going to bed. It will erase some of the bad things from your day and I'm sure you'll feel better after, even if it's only a little bit! And you know what the best thing is? It's totally free and you can practice this anytime, anywhere! You can even do it with friends or family!

"Ok, time to go home!" I say to conclude our evening. As we all stand up and start packing up everything, I think to myself that it was a great day but all those emotions really made me feel tired. I'm really going to enjoy getting into bed tonight and having a nice sleep until tomorrow!

Chapter 17
Books and potions

A s soon as I wake up the next day, I think about the fact that today we're going to start learning magic for real! Proper magic yeah!! I can feel Berry getting all excited next to me as I think about all the spells I'm going to learn soon. It's funny how in less than a day, I have so quickly become used to carrying it everywhere with me, even though I'm not using it yet. The school gave me a simple wand holder made of thick fabric that goes across my body like a bag, so it's easy to keep it with me anywhere I go.

My friends and I grab our breakfast together in the kitchen before going to school like yesterday, on Almond's back. It's so much fun to have a friend who can carry you like this! We would have reached the Academy sooner but we had to turn back home because she realised after five minutes that she had forgotten her acorn. Buttercup and I wait for her on the side of the path and we smile at how absent minded she is.

"One day she'll forget her own head!" I tell him as we see her rush back toward us.

"I'm back, I have my acorn! Let's go!"

"You know you can just leave it on you all the time since it's a necklace. It's easy!"

"I know, I know, I just need time to get used to it."

We finally reach school and we even have some time left to chat with our new friends before class starts. I spot Honeysuckle sitting alone against a tree and go see how she's going.

"I'm fine, thanks. And you?" I sit down next to her. "What did you do yesterday after school?"

I tell her about the hours spent reading in my tree and our evening feast with my parents.

"Oh you're so lucky! I have twelve siblings so it's hard for me to find the time to read in peace when I'm home. I have to help my parents and when I do have some free time it's hard to find a quiet place with all of them around me."

"Oh no, that's so bad indeed!"

"Yeah. I even came to school early today just so I could read! I'm happy that my brothers and sisters are still too young to be in class with me so at least I can get some peace here."

Poor Honeysuckle! I'm so lucky that my family and my best friends know me so well that they leave me to read in peace. They understand that I need some alone time everyday. I love being with them but I need to be with my books too. It's a way for me to recharge my batteries. Well if I had batteries. Suddenly I have an idea.

"Oh! Do you know Dreams?"

"Dreams? What is it? A book?"

"No, it's a bookshop here in Woodland. Well, a bookshop and a library at the same time."

She looks at me confused. "How can it be a bookshop and a library at the same time?"

"Well the owners, the Moon sisters, have this amazing place where you can either borrow books or buy them."

"What kind of books do they have?"

"Oh, a lot of them. Picture books for children, novels, biographies, graphic novels, history books about the forest ..."

"Really?"

"Yeah, they even have fascinating books about human history. I love borrowing them to learn about their world and imagine what their lives are like."

"That's great that they offer both options."

I nod and offer to bring her there after school.

"Oh that would be great, thank you!"

"And you'll see, the Moon sisters are really nice!"

We keep chatting for a few minutes, then Mrs Winter arrives and asks us all to take a seat. Today the class is also filled with tables for us to work on. Each table has two benches facing each other and, as usual, there are different sizes to accommodate everyone. Without talking, I join Buttercup on a bench and Honeysuckle joins us on the bench opposite us. Next to us is Bean, a male badger that we met yesterday. He's the only adult at the table but he doesn't seem to mind and greets us with a lot of enthusiasm! Wind waved hello to me when he arrived but due to his size it's easier if he sits at another table. I turn around to check that he's ok and see that he's not alone. He's seated next to another bear (Smore I think his name was) and they are talking while settling down. Good. I wouldn't want him to feel all alone in the back. I'll make sure to check on him after the class.

"Good morning everyone! I'm glad to see that you are all back today to learn magic with me. It means I haven't frightened anyone yet."

There are some giggles in the class and I think everyone is a bit more relaxed than yesterday. We're past the stress of the first day and now we're all excited to see what the first hours of class will bring us. From what I know, Mrs Winter is our only teacher and will be the one teaching us everything.

"As you can see, you will find your books on your table. Each set is yours now so you can write your name down inside to avoid confusion later."

I look and indeed, we all have two books each: "The Book of Spells" and "Potions and Concoctions". Mrs Winter gives us a minute to write our name inside and as I take a quick peek inside I can see that both books cover the three class levels of the Academy.

"So today we will start with one simple potion and two basic spells. We will start slow because some of you still need to strengthen your link with your magical object. And even if you did manage to create a good link yesterday, they will be your first spells, so they will require some strength from you and your Magicol. Not physical strength of course but magical strength. You may quickly get tired of me saying this but magic is something that you have to nurture and look after. I'll repeat it all year long if I have to, but you really can't go far if you don't understand this basic idea."

We all agree quietly.

"So we will start with these two spells for the first few days: Lifty Leafy and The Easy Lift spells. You will never have a deadline to learn a spell because, like I told you yesterday, everyone learns magic at a different pace. We usually teach two at the same time so that the students who can conjure the first spell can start on the second one. Also, it gives you an opportunity to switch back and forth if you get stuck on one of them. Instead of spending one hour nonstop on the first spell and getting angry, you can try the second one. You don't need to master the first spell to succeed with the second one."

Oh, that's good to know and less scary indeed.

"Always remember that: don't get frustrated with your magic. Sometimes, simply trying another spell will help you unlock something in you and you'll come back to the first one and realise you can now do it! Since it's not possible for every animal to write, we teach spells orally without the need to write and read runes. However, for those who are interested, I do have an afternoon class to teach rune reading on Thursdays. Of course, those of you who can write and prefer to take notes, feel free to write them down. For the other ones, pay close attention. But don't worry, everything will make more sense as time passes by.

"Anyway, the best way to learn your spells is to practise them again and again. You'll learn here in the morning with me but you will be able to practise at home and I advise you to do it whenever you get the chance. For example, you can try lifting leaves or twigs on your way back home. You can also practise your potions with your family if you want to share this with them."

She starts to move toward her own desk but remembers, "Oh and before we start our lesson, I just want to let you know that you can also take some extra classes in the afternoon if you're interested in other subjects. So, like I said I'll be teaching runes but you can also learn History of Wizards and Witches, Locals and Internationals with Miss Pamplemousse, Magical Properties of

Aquatic Plants with Mr Fawn and Herbology with Mr Wells if you wish to learn more about plants."

Oh I'll definitely take the history class, I'm sure it's fascinating! And we'll probably have to do a lot of reading!

"Due to the nature of our first potion, today we will start with this first and work on our spells after."

She settles down behind her desk to read from her own book and starts to explain.

"Potions are enchanted infusions that can be drunk or used directly on someone or something. Without the magic they would only be drinks. The recipe is important but if you don't end it with the final magic Whisper it won't work. They are usually made of herbs and flowers with a base of liquid like water or juice. With time you will also learn how to make powders and ointments. Those are mostly used to heal. So, today our first potion will be the 'Peace and Calming' one. It is a simple potion that will help you relax. It's perfect to get a clear mind before getting started on your spells. It's the easiest one and requires the least magic so don't worry if you don't have a strong connection with your Magicol yet."

Mrs Winter tells us the recipe out loud and asks us to come pick up the ingredients from the big table where she's standing. I write down the quantities in my notebook to be sure I won't forget.

"Once you have everything, return to your table and I will demonstrate it once for everyone to see. If it's not a hundred percent clear, do not hesitate to ask me. I can show it again or give more explanations."

We all go one table after another and I do my best to collect everything necessary. I need 5 branches of verbena, two of hibiscus, two spoons of lavender, a spoon of honey and a bowl of water. Mrs Winter explains that we have to use the water from the forest pond since it's filled with Woodland's magic. Technically you can do your potion with any water in the world but since we're beginners, it helps to have the forest's magic in it."

I come back slowly with my ingredients, making sure not to fall on my way back to the table. I see the bigger animals helping the smaller ones carrying their bowl of water. That's so nice! Once everyone is back at their tables, Mrs Winter explains, "Make sure to start by pouring the water in your cauldron and to wait until it's bubbling before adding the rest."

While waiting for my cauldron to heat up, I spread all my ingredients on our table and cut the herbs as instructed. I make sure I don't mix them up on the table, keeping the verbena and the lavender apart. Once the water is hot, I add my spoons of lavender first and the rest of the ingredients according to the recipe.

"Once you have added everything in your cauldron and in the correct order, make sure you have your Magicol in your paws, around your neck or against you in their holder. And then you simply have to say the magic Whisper,

"Calm mind
Clear mind
Serenity is mine"

At our table Bean raises his paw to ask, "How will we know if the potion is ready?"

"Good question! It's easy: once the magic has been activated, your potion will start to sparkle."

"Waouh! Really? That's so cool!" someone says behind me. "Is it always like that, Mrs Winter?"

"Yes, all your potions will sparkle once they are magically filled with magic."

Ok, I have done everything so now it's time to connect with Berry and do some magic.

I look at my cauldron in front of me, take my wand in my paw and immediately feel Berry come to life, as if it's asking me, "What can I do for you today?"

I smile at this nice feeling and think of the Whisper one time for her before saying it out loud, "Calm mind, Clear mind, Serenity is mine!"

I feel my wand answer to me with a sort of, "Yeah ok, no problem I can do this!" and suddenly, very simply, I feel the magic happening. I feel the now familiar warmth tickle my paw and travel from my wand to the cauldron. The potion is now sparkling! I can't believe it, I did it! I did magic!

Chapter 18
Spells

Mrs Winter was right: the potion was easy to make and everyone managed it without any trouble. After checking our potions, she invites us to drink a glass of it and gives us five minutes to tidy up our table and feel the effects of the potion sink in. Everyone is cleaning their remaining bits of branches and looking at each other wondering if we are going to see a physical change in each other. But no, for with this potion, the magic only happens inside us. I am back in my seat and putting Berry back into my wand carrier when I suddenly feel its effect on me. I can't really describe it but I feel like I'm on a cloud, all calm and at peace. I feel light and sure of myself. I smile and look around me to see Honeysuckle all happy too. Actually the whole class seems to be smiling and radiating with confidence. Mrs Winter is walking among the rows and seems happy with our results.

"Well, I see that your potion has worked its magic on you all so we're ready to start working on your first spells! I will show you the Lifty Leafy and The Easy Lift and you can choose which one you want to try first. Remember to move on if you don't see progress on one spell. Magic is a living thing, and it needs time to develop in each of us. It's a constant work in progress between you and your

Magicol but also between you and ... well, you."

"What does it mean?" Someone whispers behind me.

I just shrug, hoping Mrs Winter will explain but Buttercup raises his tiny paw and asks for clarification.

"It means that as much as you need your magical object to help you perform magic, you also need to believe in yourself to succeed. If you're confident and feel good about yourself, your magic will come more easily than if you're having a bad day. But don't feel bad, even those who are trained face this problem, it does not only apply to first year students. When I am tired or angry I feel it in my magic. You can easily visualise your spells incorrectly if you don't focus. And I'm sure you have witnessed it with wizards and witches around you."

Oh yes, I have heard my mum say that her magic was off because she was too tired, so I think I understand what Mrs Winter means.

"So be kind with yourself, it will help you perform well and it will help deepen your link with your Magicol."

She moves back near her desk and clears her throat once.

"Spells can seem very easy to perform on the surface but they can be tricky too. Never think that casting spells is too easy for you. You can master one very well but take weeks to see results with another one. Spells work thanks to three things. First, of course your Magicol. It has to be in contact with you to give you the magic you'll need. Then, the Whisper that you say out loud. No need to shout it, just say it in a normal speaking voice. And finally the Visualisation. No matter the spell, you will need to visualise what you want from it. If you picture it too big or too windy, your results will be very different. Magic is not a game, you have to stay focused at all times."

I find her words fascinating and stressful at the same time and I hear some worried whispers all around me in the class.

"But don't worry it will get easier with practice. You will learn how to visualise correctly with time."

I take notes of everything she's telling us as fast as I can as I don't want to forget anything.

"So remember the MWV: Magicol, Whisper and Visualisation. Don't forget that you will need to be in contact with your Magicol, you can't simply have it near you in the room. It seems obvious but for some reason, I have to remind this to new students every year. Those who have a wand will need to hold them and those with an acorn or a stone will need to make sure it's around their necks. Don't worry, you will quickly get so used to them that you won't even have to think and you will carry them with you at all times without realising it. So, are you ready to try?"

We all answer with an enthusiastic "yes" and I straighten myself up in my seat. I'm two hundred percent focused!

"The Lifty Leafy is used to lift small and light objects up in the air. Something as light as leaves, feathers, twigs, nuts. Its Whisper is..."

Nuts? Did she say nuts? I'm more of a chocolate lover but now that she has talked about food, I'm hungry! No, focus Applesauce, stay focused!

"And you have to visualise the object floating around."

I didn't hear the Whisper but she demonstrates the spell right away with a leaf lying on her desk.

"UP UP UP" she says loudly for all of us to hear and as we see some light going from her stone (well, from the pouch where her stone is) to the leaf, it starts flying upward in front of her. Her gaze is focused on the leaf and it stays in front of her eyes for a bit before falling down nicely back on the wooden surface.

"I know it seems easy from an outsider point of view but as I told you yesterday it took me a while to master this when I learned magic, so don't feel bad if you can't do it right away."

Next she moves slightly to stand in front of her spells book on the right side of her desk.

"And The Easy Lift will allow you to make an object lighter than it really is, which is ideal to carry your books for example. It is a favourite of smaller animals but is also used by bigger ones to perform heavy work like moving tree trunks around. The Whisper to cast for this one is 'LIGHT AS A FEATHER'. For this spell you will have to imagine that the object you want to carry around is very light which can be tricky. I'll show you."

She says the Whisper, her eyes on the book and we see some light go from her Magicol to the book in front of her.

"Would anyone like to volunteer to carry this and check if I did well?"

A few animals volunteer and in the end it's Sidney the worm who goes to the table to carry the book. We are all on the edge of our seats, sure that she's too small to carry such a big object but she lifts it up so easily, we all look at each other shocked. Mrs Winter laughs at our surprised faces.

"So, as you can see the spell did work. Didn't it, Sidney?"

Sidney nods and confirms that the book feels very light to her.

"Thank you. You can put it down and go back to your seat. Now if there's no questions, you can all start practising!"

I was expecting a lot of noise but as soon as she gives us the signal to start practising the whole class is silent.

"Come on, don't be shy, start practising!" She encourages us with a smile. "Is there any question? Something you didn't understand?"

I think we all understood but we're just a bit afraid to start. Everyone is just looking at their table in silence.

"Ok I'll show you once more."

And she does. She takes her time and demonstrates the spells to us one more time, making sure we can all see properly. Then, like yesterday, we all head to a corner of the big open classroom and we practice. Some stay near the benches while others prefer to hide in the bushes or trees.

At first I can't seem to focus at all because I'm too busy watching what everyone else is doing. I see my classmates getting agitated, trying to move or jump with the feather they are trying to lift up. I'm hearing too much noise, feeling too much of their stress and I'm starting to panic. It reminds me of yesterday all over again. The difference is that today I'm not alone. While my mind is going in every direction, I feel Berry calling me, its magic pulling me toward it. Its warmth reminds me that it's here to help, like a friend saying, "I'm here, don't worry."

So I take Berry out of my wand holder and I focus only on it. I forget about my classmates and I set the twig I chose for my first spell on the ground in front of me. Let's do this! I visualise the twig flying up in the air and I say "UP, UP!"

Nothing.

What? What did I do wrong? I'm trying to remember

everything Mrs Winter told us until I realise that I need to say "UP" three times not two! I start again, making sure I use the correct Whisper this time. I feel Berry vibrate a bit and ... nothing else happens! The twig just stays on the ground! Ok, let's try again then! After spending ten minutes working on this over and over, focusing only on Berry and my twig, I finally see it move a tiny bit! Oh it's so exciting! I try again and again until I can see the twig move every time, and finally, after a few more times, the twig goes up in the air, just like it's supposed to! I can't believe it, my first spell! What an amazing feeling to make something fly, even if it's only a tiny twig.

Chapter 19
By the lake

The rest of the morning goes on like this, with the whole class working hard on their first spells in a happy hubbub of noise with small objects flying around. I see some practising on making their books lighter too. I don't know if it's because they have already managed the first spell or if it's because they just wanted to try the second spell. I try not to worry and not to think about it too much. Like Mrs Winter said, this is not a competition, this is only about learning for us. I spent my time working on my Lifty Leafy spell because I wanted to really focus on it and perform it well rather than do a mediocre job of both spells. I will have a lot of time to work on *The Easy Lift* tomorrow and the rest of the week.

"Well done class! I think you have all progressed nicely and deserve to go have lunch now!"

Is it already lunch time? It must be the first time in my life that I reach lunch without thinking about eating ahead. I guess it's easier to forget you're hungry when you're focused on something that interests you so much.

"I'll stay here a bit longer for anyone who wants to ask me questions. Don't hesitate, there are no stupid questions! The rest of you, I'll see you all tomorrow!"

I go back to my table to pack my stuff and wait for my friends.

"Is Almond eating with us?" I ask Buttercup as soon as he's back.

He shakes his head. "No, she said she'll eat with some new friends she made. I think she also wants to stay behind and ask the teacher a million questions, so I think we can go without her."

I have some questions too but for now I prefer to write them down at home and see if I can find the answers in my books. I know I could ask Mrs Winter but I find it so exciting to explore a new book. I can't wait to have a proper look at the ones we got today. Although, since it's our first week and we haven't mastered the The Easy Lift spell yet, we are allowed to leave them at school if they're too heavy for us to take home. So I guess I'll need to be patient or borrow my parents' copy if I want to study at home tonight.

"I told Honeysuckle I'll take her to Dreams today. Shall we eat together by the lake before going there?"

"Perfect!" Buttercup says with his usual friendly smile.

We wait for Honeysuckle and tell her our plan.

"Really? You don't mind if I eat with you guys?"

"No, of course not! And we know a nice place to go eat our lunch, you'll see!"

We wave goodbye to our classmates and on our way to Woodland Lake we compare the lunches we brought. My mum packed me a small chocolate cookie to celebrate my first day and I'm pretty sure I saw her put a mix of his favourite nuts in Buttercup's lunch bag. Honeysuckle is a bit upset because neither of her parents had time to prepare her something sweet to mark the occasion.

"They were too busy with my siblings I guess, "she explains sadly.

It breaks my heart to see her like that.

"Oh! Don't worry, we know the perfect place to boost your mood after lunch."

Buttercup agrees, "Oh yes, you'll have your choice of treats there!"

"Really? Thanks. You guys really do know all the good places then?"

"We sure do! And speaking of perfect places, here we are, our lunch spot!"

We reach the big lake located on the east side of Woodland Forest and Honeysuckle seems really impressed with it.

"Waouh, I've never seen that much water! It's so pretty, we can see the light reflected on the surface. I love it! Oh, it makes me think of this book I love, Anne of Green Gables. Anne loves to give names to places so for example she names a pond the Lake of Shining Waters."

"Oh that's a pretty name, I love it!" I say. "I don't know this book. Is it good?"

"Oh Applesauce, it's so good, it's one of my favourites! Anne is a very talkative girl with a big imagination, and this always gets her into trouble. You should read it."

"I'll check at Dreams if they have it!"

We explain to Honeysuckle that the lake actually marks the end of Woodland Forest.

"If you walk all the way around it, you'll reach Blackpool Meadow and then I think there's another forest before a small city. I'm not sure, we've never left Woodland. I've been to Blackpool Meadow once or twice with my dad but never any farther."

"A city? Really?"

"Yes. That's why we have some humans coming over here sometimes. Especially on weekends."

"Real humans? You've seen them? Can we go there?"

Buttercup and I both laugh at her excitement.

"Not today, but maybe we'll show you the meadow some day."

"Wicked! I hope I'll get to see real humans too. Where we used to live there were never any, we were too far in the woods."

"Oh yeah you'll see some, don't worry."

"Here, we'll show you our favourite spot."

We walk a bit farther along the lake and stop under a big Weeping Willow tree. Whatever the time of the day, it's so massive that once you sit under it, it provides a lot of shade. Its long thin branches fall all around us like a curtain, hiding the rest of the forest from us. I love how the tip of the branches reach the water, like they're too hot and looking for some freshness. I like imagining the tree branches dancing in the wind like they have a mind of their own.

"Oh it's so pretty. I love it! Thanks for bringing me here! I can see myself reading here all afternoon."

"It is a nice reading spot, unless Sunny is here," Buttercup tells her while we all sit down and unpack our lunches.

"Who's Sunny?"

"Argh, Grumpy Sunny is the moodiest animal in Woodland," I explain.

Buttercup agrees while offering some of his food to us.

Honeysuckle chuckles and wants to know why he got this nickname but there's no need to explain because just then, guess who arrives? Yep, Sunny himself! A big dark green frog with some black spots jumps out of the water and comes to our spot to bark at us (well frogs can't technically bark but you get my point).

"Are you talking about me? What are you saying? Mmmm? Who's that?"

Sunny is always like that, jumping on you without saying hello and asking several questions at once without really waiting for an answer. He just likes to complain and mumble. ALL THE TIME! Buttercup manages to stay civil with him, but honestly I don't know how he does it.

"Oh hello Sunny," he says, like he's our dearest friend. "Yes we were explaining to our new friend that you live here. How are you today?"

Sunny simply groans that it's too hot for him today and comes jumping around us to look at our food.

"Why do you have so many carrots?" he asks Honeysuckle aggressively when he spots her box full of carrot sticks. "Are you a rabbit or something?"

Thankfully she seems to find it funny so she simply answers that yes she is indeed a rabbit while trying to contain her giggling to a minimum. Sunny simply glares at her and just like that, without a word, jumps back in the water and disappears again. Not a single goodbye. Nothing.

"So ... that was Sunny."

"Is he always like this?"

"Always. Today he was actually quite cheerful compared to other days."

"Really?" Honeysuckle laughs.

"Oh yes, you should see him on the days when he complains that the water is too wet, it's ridiculous!"

We all explode in laughter as we tell her more about Grumpy

Sunny and we spend the rest of the lunch like that, chatting, comparing our first day doing magic, and getting to know Honeysuckle better. She tells us how happy she was to make lots of light objects fly. She tells us how she experimented with twigs, feathers and leaves just to have fun. She also tried The Easy Lift spell without any luck.

"I'm sure you'll manage tomorrow, don't worry!" Buttercup tells her.

We digest by lying down and practising The Lifty Leafy with some of the fallen leaves around us. It really is so fun to know that now we can do this!

"Ok, who's ready for some snacks?" Buttercup asks us after we've rested enough.

No one says no to that (obviously not me) and Honeysuckle admits to being very excited to discover what we want to show her.

"You'll see, it's not far."

Chapter 20
Sweet treat

We walk west for ten minutes in a part of the forest that's more densely forested to get to Sweet Treat. We have fun making the leaves on our path fly but as the smells from the bakery get stronger we stop doing magic and start walking faster. Honeysuckle is suddenly really excited and as we arrive I finally tell her (proudly, of course!) that this is my family's bakery.

"Waouh really? That's amazing! If it's as good as it smells you're so lucky because it smells incredible!"

We see the wooden sign propped against three old barrels announcing the name of the bakery, and painted under it you can read *Bread and Pastries by Rose & Sprout Softpaw*.

"Come on in, I'll introduce you to my parents."

The bakery is so old that all the wooden walls outside are covered with moss and mushrooms. The whole roof is actually made up of ground covered in grass because the bakery was built directly under a small hill. I have never asked my parents, but I'm pretty sure magic was involved to get this result. The big door and the small windows are all round to fit with this peculiar architecture and there are flowers everywhere: growing from the roof and in pots at the entrance, on windowsills or on the floor. There are even vines with flowers growing on the blue mailbox by the door. The inside has just as many flowers as the outside; in pots, in vases and in planters hanging from the ceiling. But my favourite bit (apart from the food of course) is one wall of the bakery that's totally covered with glass to let the natural light shine in. My mum has hung a bunch of suncatchers around it to catch the light and project colours all over the walls, making our bakery look truly magical.

The kitchen is in the back but has a large window so customers can see my parents at work and my parents, in return, don't get lonely all the way back there. All the walls are painted yellow and orange, which makes the green of the plants stand out even more and the right wall is covered with some gorgeous watercolour paintings of the pastries that my parents make. They also have a wall where they post all the little notes and postcards they've received from customers all over the years. Cards announcing the birth of a new baby, drawings from children who love coming here and notes simply saying thank you for the great food they offer. There's also a bookshelf with a selection of books available to enjoy with your food and even some board games for people to play with friends or family. And there's always some kind of music playing in the background. I'm sure you won't find another bakery like ours!

As we walk in, the little squirrel shaped chime at the door lets my parents know there's someone in the shop. I love this little sound. When I'm in there with them I always feel so happy knowing someone just arrived to try their delicious food! I love to try to guess who it is just by their voice or the sound they make. For example lighter animals with tiny paws like Buttercup make cute sounds when they walk in on the wooden floor. And the bigger ones - like the bears, the boars or wolves - make big vibrations on the floor that give their presence away.

"Mum? Dad? It's me!"

My mum is lost in thought, taking notes behind the counter and talking to herself. What started as a simple counter is now covered with a colourful tile mosaic. It was a project to keep Buttercup and I busy last year during a rainy month and now I'm glad it rained so much because the result is really nice. It's another one of the things that make Sweet Treat truly unique.

"Ok, so, two pies and three cakes, that'll make three hundred Woodcoins, plus the loaf of bread and the croissants ..."

Mum lifts her head and stops reading her notes when she sees us.

"Oh Applesauce, Buttercup, come on in! How was your second day? Not too tiring I hope? Did you manage to do some magic? Did you eat? Oh I'm sorry, I'm being rude, who's your new friend?"

Honeysuckle laughs quietly at all the questions my mum just asked us. I don't blame her. So many questions in just one breath, I don't know how she does it.

"Hi Mum!" I go behind the counter to kiss her. "This is our new friend Honeysuckle. She's in the Seed class with us."

"Hello dear! I haven't seen you around before. Are you new here?"

"Yes, my family moved to Woodland just before school started."

"Oh that's interesting. New faces! Where were you before?"

"A bit far, I don't know if you know it. It doesn't really have a name actually, it was a small place a bit farther than Woodbury Forest, near the Greenlands. But it was a bit too far from other families for my mum's taste so we moved here."

"Oh yes, it is far indeed! I haven't been there since I was a young squirrel myself! Do you like Woodland?"

"Yes, I love it! And your son and Buttercup are showing me around."

"That's nice!"

"What's nice?" my dad asks, emerging from the kitchen, his glasses so covered with flour that he doesn't see us. (There's a water repelling spell but nothing for flour yet!) Even though I'm used to seeing him like that, I still giggle at the sight of him blinded like this. He takes them off and finally realises we're here.

"Oh hello! I didn't hear you come! I'm sorry I'm all so messy, covered in flour like this, I was making the next load of bread."

"Dad, this is Honeysuckle."

"She just moved here from Woodbury Forest," my mum tells him.

"Oh, that's far!" He goes to the sink to clean his paws and glasses.

"Sit down, sit down, we'll bring you something to eat. You all deserve something nice after your big day!"

We all smile and settle down at the nearest table. Each table is covered with a colourful tablecloth and every chair is unique, with different colours and materials. There are vases of fresh flowers on each table: ours has a small bouquet of primroses and common bluebells.

The bakery is empty right now, except for an old badger in a far corner who likes to come every afternoon to take his tea with a piece of cake. Same order every day and he always comes with his book. He spends two hours here: eats, drinks, reads his book, and leaves without a word. A simple badger, I like him.

"Did you all have a good day?" my mum asks as she gathers some cups to give us hot cocoa while my dad is putting a selection of pastries in a small basket.

"Yes it was great!"

"We learned one potion and two spells. I haven't tried the second spell yet but it was so nice to start doing magic."

"Yes! And the teacher really explained everything well. I like her."

"Oh yes, Mrs Winter is a nice teacher, I'm sure you'll be in good paws with her," my dad says as he makes two little trays carrying our drinks and food fly to our table.

"You do like cocoa Honeysuckle, don't you? If not, I can bring you something else. And if you don't like those pastries I can bring you some pies, we have lots of choices: pumpkin pie, apricot, strawberry. Or we have some salty food too-"

"It's perfect, don't worry Mr Softpaw. And yes, I love chocolate!" she tells him.

"Mr Softpaw! Please, call me Sprout. Applesauce's friends can't go around calling me Mr Softpaw. It makes me sound so old," he tells her with a funny wink. My dad can't wink but somehow he's convinced that he's great at it, it's hilarious!

He sits down with us to chat a bit while my mum is still busy scribbling notes on paper behind the counter.

"What is Mum doing?" I ask him.

"Planning an event for the hospital for next week. They want pastries, pies and bread for a big party, so she is calculating how many of each we need to make."

While she's busy, we enjoy our snacks, chatting with my dad, telling him about our first spells and about our plan to go to

Dreams next. We go there so often that my dad isn't even surprised by this. He knows it's like a second home (well, third after the bakery) for Buttercup and I.

"Well, have fun kids! I need to go back, the ovens are calling me!"

"And the books are calling us!" I joke once we're done eating. "Come on, it's time we show you Dreams!" I tell Honeysuckle, all excited to show her my favourite place.

Chapter 21
Dreams

The distance between Sweet Treat and Dreams is very short and the path simple: you just have to follow a dirt path for five minutes. It's easy to know when you get close because all around the shop the forest is decorated with all sorts of things: small colourful lanterns hanging from trees, large sculptures made of wood, flower arrangements in handmade clay vases and statues of important Woodland animals. The path is also decorated with tiles of different colours and sizes, and lit up with some fairy lights in nearby bushes and trees. It's enchanting!

As we arrive, I jump around excitedly and point the place out to Honeysuckle.

"So, this is Dreams, aka the best place in the world!"

Buttercup looks at me curiously with a funny smile.

"The best place? Really? You must have seen so much of the world to be able to know which places are the best ones."

"Oh I don't need to see the whole world, I just know nothing can be as good as Dreams, for the simple fact that no other place has the Moon sisters in charge."

He nods in agreement but they still laugh at my enthusiasm. Honeysuckle looks at the decorations in the shop window and asks us.

"So, what is it exactly? Because now that I'm here, I admit I'm a bit confused."

"Well," Buttercup starts to explain, "this is an art centre ..."

"An art centre? I thought you said it was a bookshop?" she asks me.

"...and a bookshop!" I continue.

"And a library," Buttercup finishes with a smile.

"Ok, it still doesn't make any sense but I trust you."

We all laugh at this weird explanation and Honeysuckle looks up to see the white wooden sign on top of the door. It shows a pile of books and a paintbrush, with the name Dreams in gold paint, surrounded by paint stains. The shop window is filled with dozens of book pages and small decorative firefly shaped lights flying up and down. The Moon sisters love to use magic to make the shop more lively and they like to change it regularly, depending on the season and their mood.

"Waouh! I've never seen a place that combines art and books like this. And it's a great idea to have a bookshop and a library. Like this, those who don't have too much money can still read. I love this!"

"Yes! And there are some books that you want to read once but you don't necessarily want at home all the time. Plus, many of us don't have the space to store a lot of books here in Woodland. I couldn't keep all the books I've read in our tree, but with this library it's fine, I can just come here and not worry about space."

"Where I used to live there was no shop at all, so I had to wait until my dad was going to the nearest big forest to go get me some books. So I really don't have a lot. I mostly reread the same books. A lot."

This makes me sad for a bit but then I decide to focus on the fact that now Honeysuckle lives here so she will have access to "Dreams" too!

We let her observe the shop window when suddenly she asks, "Wait, I have a question! You say humans often come here in Woodland. But how come they don't see the shops or the hospital? How about the Academy? It's quite big, they can't possibly miss it."

I let Buttercup explain it to her.

"Well, it's simple: it's Woodland magic! Unless they believe in magic, humans only see chunks of wood, piles of leaves, tree trunks on the ground. All our buildings are protected by runes that make them invisible to the human eye."

"Waouh, that's so clever!"

"OK, let's go in!"

We open the door to find a relatively empty shop. A few animals are here looking at books to buy and there's a small group of rabbits studying in the library corner. I see Hazelnut, one of the Moon sisters, organising new books to put up for sale. She insists on being called Hazelnut instead of Miss Moon.

"First, I'm still very young, so it would be ridiculous to call me Miss. And second, how would we know who you really want to talk to if everyone calls both my sister and I Miss Moon?"

In the end, both sisters are really kind and love Dreams so much. Oh, and they are both badgers. I often forget to mention that kind of detail, sorry! Don't hesitate to ask me if you're lost or you don't know who's who, ok?

"Hello Hazelnut!" I say.

"Oh hello, and ... who's that new face? Are you bringing us a new bookworm?" she asks, with a big cheery smile for Honeysuckle.

"Hello! Yes, I'm new here. Applesauce and Buttercup told me I should come and check out this place. This is a great shop, I really love it!" Honeysuckle tells her, still looking around.

Since every wall is covered with bookshelves, most of the light comes through the big round glass ceiling. There are several tables (small and big) if you need to study and different reading corners to snuggle in comfortably with a book. There are nice armchairs and lots of cushions and it always smells nice because of the natural oils the two Miss Moons love to diffuse. Today it smells like lemongrass!

"Oh thank you." Hazelnut replies, blushing a bit. "My sister and I worked hard on it to make sure it's the best place we can offer."

"So how does it work?" our new friend asks her.

"Oh let's see ... So if you're going to come here often you're going to need a card. The Dream card. Here, I'll show you."

She gestures to us to take a seat while she goes behind the counter to get an empty member card from a box and hands it to Honeysuckle. The card is light blue and decorated with a cloud on one side and a space for the personal information on the other. There are some empty lines and a place for the member's picture. Honeysuckle is surprised by this.

"Oh I didn't bring a picture of me, I didn't know..."

"Oh no no no, don't worry, you won't need one. We don't ask for pictures. We draw them."

"What? I have to draw myself?"

"No, don't be silly, sweetie. Not you. One of your friends will draw you. Or if they don't want to, I will."

Honeysuckle seems to wonder if this is a joke but then she smiles and looks at us.

"I can do it if you want!" Buttercup suggests.

Oh yeah, you see that's the reason my best friend and I both love Dreams so much. I love books and he loves crafts and anything art related. He likes to paint but he also loves to upcycle anything he can to make accessories, little gifts, or great cardboard costumes for our pretend games. He's a very creative hedgehog. That's why I always feel like Dreams was made for our friendship!

Honeysuckle agrees to let Buttercup draw her. Despite his tiny paws, he's really good at drawing and once he's done, Honeysuckle fills in her name and details on the card.

If you're ever in the need of a Dreams member card, let me tell you what informations you'd need to put on it:

- Name
- Favourite thing to do
- Favourite book
- Favourite colour

I don't know if all library cards work like this but I suspect not. These questions make Honeysuckle giggle and I have a look to see what her answers are.

- Honeysuckle
- Read and talk about books
- *Charlie and the Chocolate Factory* and *Anne of Green Gables*
Purple

"Great, you're all ready to go now!" says Hazelnut. She applies the Dreams stamp to Honeysuckle's card and shows her around.

"So, as you can see, the right wall is for the library books and the left wall is for the books we sell. And the art centre is upstairs. We have some art supplies for sale and we often organise workshops to make fun projects. If you're interested-"

Just as he starts to explain how this works, Honeysuckle shyly interrupts to say that she doesn't think she will be able to participate in the workshops.

"Oh!" Hazelnut says, realising what she means. "Don't worry, we actually have a free workshop once a month and for Dreams members who can't pay, we also offer some workshops in exchange for help."

"Help?"

"Yes. Basically you come and work here a bit every now and then instead of paying for the workshop. What do you think about that? Do you think you'll be interested?"

Honeysuckle seems so happily surprised by this offer that she only answers a very low "Yes I would love that!"

"Great! Now that you have your member card, you can borrow five books at once for a week. You can renew them if you're not done and if there's a book you're looking for don't hesitate to ask us! Ok?"

"Ok! Thank you very much Miss Hazelnut!"

We all laugh at this.

"There's no Miss Hazelnut, it's just Hazelnut silly!"

Honeysuckle giggles at her own mistake but I can see that she looks very happy and she doesn't lose a second before exploring the library. Like most things in Woodland, all books are offered in a standard medium size and can be adjusted to your needs when you check them out. They also make them lighter for animals who can't perform magic. Or who can't perform magic yet. I can't wait to be able to surprise Miss Moon and Hazelnut by doing the spell on the books myself.

"Is Miss Moon upstairs?" we ask Hazelnut.

"Yep! She's unpacking the new supplies we just received. You should go have a look Bee, I think you're going to like the new stock!"

Hazelnut loves to call us by different names. Buttercup is Bee, and I'm Arnold. Why Arnold? Because the first time I came here

I was so shy that I said my name quietly and she misheard it for Arnold. And of course it stuck, she's been calling me Arnold ever since! I don't mind, it's like a secret code name just between us, it's fun! I wonder what Honeysuckle's new name will be.

Buttercup lets me know that he's going upstairs and I ask Hazelnut if they have the book Honeysuckle told me about, with this Anne girl who dreams a lot.

"Oh yes, Anne of Green Gables! Let me see ... It's over there in the M section. And if you love it there are seven more books after that."

"Really? Great! Thanks Hazelnut!"

Once I find the book and borrow it, I settle down in one of my favourite armchairs. I see Honeysuckle going over every row of books and she seems thrilled. When she finally comes to see me, she has her paws full of books and a big smile on her face.

"I can't believe this place exists! I love it! Thank you so much for bringing me here Applesauce!"

I smile and think how glad I am that I made my new friend so happy.

Chapter 22
Apricot, Tulip and Violet

The days pass and our first weekend arrives quickly. Even though we only have class in the morning, the days still seem very full and time goes by really fast. There are so many things to learn that I don't see the hours at the Academy pass. We learn at school in the morning, I have lunch with my friends and we often stop by Dreams together after school to read, study or relax. Honeysuckle loves the fact that she can have this quiet space away from her many siblings where she can finally read new books.

"I love my books but it's so nice to be able to read new ones too," she says.

She says she only has ten books at her house, so I can imagine her happiness when she discovered the library. Since this is the weekend I ask her if I can borrow her copy of this Charlie and the Chocolate Factory book she wrote about on her Dreams card. It's her favourite book and it talks about chocolate, so it must be really great! I know what I'll be doing today.

I'd love to take advantage of the weekend and sleep in but on Saturdays we make sure we all eat breakfast together. And I mean all together: my parents, me, and the whole Dreamcreek family (Buttercup, his parents and all his sisters). Buttercup is really surrounded by girls, as he has four sisters: Apricot, Tulip, Violet and Almond. It's such a fun family because the girls are all quite different from each other!

Apricot, the eldest, is very adventurous, always exploring every part of our forest, finding treasures ... She goes to the Academy too but is already in the level III class. So yes, soon she should be able to perform magic so well that she could rule the world.

Tulip has already graduated from Woodland Academy and is crazy about fashion. She loves to accessorise her spines with bows or colourful bits of leaves and twigs when she can't find anything else. So, like her brother, she loves going to Dreams to find supplies and fabric for her creations. She dreams of opening a clothes shop in our forest. What do you mean animals don't need clothes? We might not need them but a lot of us love to wear them and there are so many accessories that we can use that I think it would be great if she had her own boutique. We already have a tailor but his style is quite old fashioned while Tulip's is more colourful. She loves to knit scarves, sew bags, make hats, headbands ... She's never out of ideas.

Violet has no interest in magic and spends most of her time at my parent's bakery! Not to eat, but to work there. She loves to give them a hand (well, a paw) and learn from them. She loves to bake but she prefers to cook and would love to open her own restaurant. My parents always help her whenever they can, showing her some dishes and asking for her help to collect fresh ingredients in the forest (we have our own vegetable patch at home for our daily needs but it doesn't have everything.)

Don't tell the Dreamcreek sisters but out of all the older girls I like her the best because she always makes me taste her food when she's cooking. Anyone who puts food in my squirrel tummy is a favourite of mine!

And of course you already know Almond! Energetic and full of life, our one and only Almond!

This morning, as I climb down from our tree, I see everyone is already here, setting plates, bowls, drinks and food on the big table we have outside. I say hello to everyone, kiss my mum and dad, and ask how I can help.

"Can you grab the tray of blueberry muffins in the kitchen

please? Thanks dear. I think that's the last thing missing."

As I enter the kitchen I see Tulip cleaning the floor with the broom. Well she enchanted the broom with a spell because it's quite hard for hedgehogs to hold a broomstick. Oh, and before you ask, no we don't use those to fly on. That's something you only see in stories. Here in Woodland we only use them to sweep our floors. Same for hats. We don't need them to recognise wizards or witches, we just wear them to look nice or to protect our ears from the sun.

"Hey Tulip! How are you?"

"Hi Applesauce! I haven't seen you all week. It's so strange. How are you? How was your first week?"

"It was great. I already learned to do a few spells."

I grab the muffins, she breaks the spell on the broom, then takes a jug of apple juice from the fridge and we head back outside to our families.

"And Mum told me you're making friends. That's really nice to see!"

"Yes. Honeysuckle and Wind are really great! And Honeysuckle seems to love books as much as I do so I finally have someone to swap books with."

"I bet you took her to Dreams?"

She knows me so well.

"Of course!"

"I hope Hazelnut didn't scare her?"

"No, no. She surprised her but Honeysuckle fell in love with Dreams right away."

"And how's class? You have Mrs Winter right? I had her too, she seems scary at first but she's really sweet."

We sit down side by side and exchange opinions about the Academy and stories from this week. Before I started school I used to see Tulip in the morning so it's been so strange not to see her like that this week.

"Have you started the afternoon classes?"

"No, not yet. We start on Monday. I can't wait!"

"What are you going to take?"

"All the classes seem interesting but Dad said it's better not to take too many at first so I'll just start with *History of Wizards and Witches, Locals and Internationals.*"

"Good choice! A lot of reading, it's perfect for you!"

"Ah ah yes I guessed so. How about you? What did you do this week? Any new projects?" I ask her as I get the maple syrup for my pancakes. She suddenly remembers something.

"Oh yes! Oh I'm so silly, I forgot! Stay here I have something for you! I'll be right back!"

She leaves the table in a rush and runs back inside the kitchen to grab something but I can't see what it is. She comes back to her seat next to me and hands me something soft. At first I think it's some sort of bag but then I realise what it is.

"A wand holder? Oh thank you, that's perfect Tulip!"

"Do you like it? I kind of had to rush to make it because I had to wait until your Ceremony."

"Are you kidding? I love it! It's so pretty!"

For my first few days I had to use the basic one provided by the Academy, made of plain grey fabric but this one is handmade just for me. She chose a soft black fabric and she embroidered small designs on it with an orange thread. And in the middle she even put an A.

"I wanted to write your whole name but there was not enough space. Hopefully it should be enough for you to know that it's yours."

"Oh it's perfect like this, you always make the most unique gifts! I really love it when I know it's one of a kind. You should offer a personalisation service like this once you open your shop."

"You think so?"

"Absolutely! You could offer your own basic model of wand holder with the option to add details if customers want. I'm sure they would sell well."

"I'll think about it!" she replies with a small smile.

"Everyone, look what Tulip made me!"

I show my new wand holder to our families and they all take turns looking at it and congratulating Tulip on her work. She then gives Almond and Buttercup their own gift: a necklace for their acorns.

"Sorry, acorns leave less room for personalisation so I did my best."

And indeed she did! For Almond, she braided several cords together and then dyed the whole thing into a rainbow of gently changing colours. One end is dark red, which gradually morphs into orange, then yellow, and so on...

"I didn't add beads on yours, Almond, because you run so much I thought they might break or fall."

Almond giggles a bit and thanks her sister for making something so pretty for her.

"Oh, it's nothing, it was really simple-" Tulip starts to say.

"It's not nothing, because you made it for me!"

For Buttercup, Tulip strung a necklace with beads of different shades of blue, with just enough space for him to add his acorn in the middle.

"I chose your favourite colour."

"Thank you, I love it!"

"That was very thoughtful of you, Tulip!" says their mum, Dahlia from the other side of the table. Dahlia is a quieter mum than mine but she always has kind words for her children. This kindness runs in the Dreamcreek family so I'm not surprised by Tulip's generosity. She's always been like this, making little gifts for us and all of her friends without a special occasion. She always jokes that it's just a way for her to test future products on us but I know she really does all this out of kindness.

Chapter 23
Saturday with Charlie

Breakfast is over, everyone tidies up the big table while the adults get ready for work. Dahlia works at the post office and her husband, Basil is a manager at the supermarket. Violet works with my parents today and she's helping my dad pack some food for their lunch when my mum comes to give me a kiss.

"What are you going to do today? Will you stop by later?"

"Honeysuckle lent me her favourite book so I'm planning on ..."

"Staying in your little corner and reading all day?" Mum finishes for me with a wink.

"Yes! But I'll probably stop by to see you later too."

"Ok, I'll keep a slice of pie or something on the side for you then."

"Could you keep -"

"Yes, I'll keep one for Buttercup too, don't worry."

"Thanks! Have a good day Mum!"

"You too, honey!" She starts to leave but returns in a flash.

"Oh I forgot to ask you if you want to invite your new friends to tomorrow's lunch?"

"Oh! Wind and Honeysuckle? Yes that would be a nice idea but ... actually I don't know where they live."

"Ah yes. Well, I'm sure you won't have any trouble finding Honeysuckle, she'll probably go to Dreams today? Anyway it's just an idea, let me know if they can come. Bye sweetie."

Just as we make sure we have breakfast together every Saturday morning, every Sunday we have a nice potluck lunch with our immediate neighbours. My parents started this tradition a long time ago and we all love it. Everyone brings some food, we chat, we laugh, we play games, and sometimes the adults start to sing while talking about "the old days". It's a nice way to spend our Sunday. I'll have to see if I can contact Wind and Honeysuckle today. Otherwise I'll invite them for next Sunday.

Before heading up in my tree to get lost in my new book for hours, I check with my best friends what their plans are. I'm not surprised to learn that Almond wants to go for a run.

"And you?" I ask Buttercup.

"Well first I have to check my craft supplies box, go to Dreams to get what I need and I'll probably stay there to work on something. I want to make a thank you card for Tulip and a scrapbook about our first week of school."

"Ok, I'll see you later there."

Buttercup knows I'll stop by Dreams in the afternoon. I always do. Even if I have enough books at home, I'll stop by just to be surrounded by books. They feel like friends to me.

I spend my morning in my tree, all snuggled up in my reading corner discovering the world of Willy Wonka and his incredible factory, meeting Charlie Bucket, the Oompa Loompas, and all the naughty children. From time to time I hear noises coming from downstairs: Basil cleaning their house (he usually goes to work a bit later than everyone else), Tulip working on a new hat at the outdoor table, and just all the simple life of Woodland around me. Birds flying around, and the wind blowing through the branches and making the fallen leaves twirl above the ground.

Once I'm halfway through the book, I realise that I'm thirsty so I go down to the kitchen to get myself a glass of the fresh lemonade we made yesterday with Almond. And since I'm in the kitchen, I might as well grab something to eat just so I don't have to come down again too soon. Let me see ... What should I take? I look around the kitchen cabinets and see a small box on the table and a note with my name and a heart on it. I recognise my dad's style of drawing a heart. He must have left this for me before going to work. I check inside and smile when I see one cookie. The last cookie that he brought back from the bakery last night. He kept it for me. Maybe I'll join Buttercup later on at Dreams to make him a thank you card too. He really is the best Dad any hungry squirrel could ask for.

And so the rest of my morning goes on like this. I eat my cookie, finish my book, make myself a sandwich and take a quick nap before going out to meet my best friend at the store. On my way to Dreams I take Berry out of my new wand holder and have fun practising the spells I've learned so far. Simply lifting some fallen leaves does not seem like much but is so much fun when you just started using magic. I'm having so much fun that I even reach the bookshop quicker than I expected.

Miss Moon welcomes me as soon as I enter. She wears glasses and likes to have a light scarf on her (my mum says it's not a scarf but a shawl whatever that means).

"Hello Applesauce! How are you?"

"Hello Miss Moon! I'm great, thanks! And you?"

"I'm good, I'm good. What are you reading at the moment? I've been so busy with the new stock of books and craft supplies that I haven't seen you a lot this week, so I don't know what you borrowed."

"Oh today I read a book Honeysuckle lent me, Charlie and the Chocolate Factory. It was really great. I understand why she loves it so much. And I borrowed Anne of Green Gables here this week. I'm going to see if you have the sequel. Hazelnut said there were several books in this series."

"Great! Mmm, I think I've seen them in stock recently so you should be able to borrow the second one at least. Ok, help yourself, I'll be upstairs, I have to organise some new paint brushes that we just got."

I quickly find Anne of Avonlea on the shelves and take it upstairs to check on Buttercup. The first floor is not as big as the ground floor but there's enough space for the art supplies shop and the tables where the two sisters organise their workshops. It's also less luminous since it's more like an attic but I personally like how cosy it feels.

I spot Buttercup easily, working at one of the craft tables, focused on the card he's making.

"Hey, how are you?" I ask him as I sit down next to him. "What did you make?"

"Oh hi!" He's so lost in what he's doing that he didn't see me coming. Just like me when I'm reading. "Well not much. After I finished my card for Tulip, I helped Hazelnut plan an art exhibition for next month, then we reorganised some of the supplies cabinets, I had a light lunch with Miss Moon, chatted with some friends that were passing by and I only just started on this new card."

I laugh at his notion of "not much" but I know he's not kidding. He's used to doing a lot.

"Indeed you haven't done anything!" I tease him. "Show me the card you made."

He grabs a folded card decorated on the outside with a small watercolour painting of a bunch of flowers. The flowers are so delicate and light, I love how he can make something so beautiful with just a few strokes of his paint brush. And when I open the card there's a 3D flower made of paper that pops up.

"Waouh! You made this? It's amazing!"

"Oh it's nothing. Hazelnut showed me how at one of her workshops so I thought I'd finally try it."

"What? That was your first try?" I ask, shocked.

"Yes. Does it show? Do you think Tulip will mind that I gave her my first try?"

Did I mention how modest Buttercup is? He has a hard time recognising that he did something great.

"Stop it. Buttercup, it's amazing! Of course she's going to love it!"

"Thanks!" He finally takes my word for it but blushes a bit. Well, as much as a hedgehog can blush.

"And who is this one for?" I ask, pointing to the one he's working on.

"For Mrs Winter. I want to thank her for being a nice teacher with us."

"Can you help me make one for my dad?"

I'm good at reading (and eating) but I don't have many creative ideas in my head. I need some help.

"I just need some ideas, don't stop yours for me."

He helps me with the choice of colours, shows me his technique and gives me some ideas of what to draw on it. We both work on our cards while talking about the weekend. I also ask him about the art exhibition he mentioned.

"Hazelnut wants to show the paintings her students made recently and invite their families to come and see."

Just then, Hazelnut arrives from downstairs and joins us at the table. I tell her how much I love this exhibition idea. I'm not good at painting but I do love watching what others have made.

"I'll definitely come!"

"Oh by the way, HoneyBee just arrived!"

"HoneyBee?" Buttercup asks.

"Oh you mean Honeysuckle?"

"Yes! But HoneyBee is better don't you think?"she asks us with a funny wink. Ok, so I guess she didn't need long to find Honeysuckle a nickname.

"Thanks, I'll go see her, I need to ask her something."

I tidy up all the mess I created while making my "thank you dad for being amazing" card and place it in my library book. As soon as I arrive downstairs I spot Honeysuckle in her usual corner. I prefer to read in the armchairs but she seems to prefer the cushions on the floor.

"Hi! I was hoping to see you there. How are you?" I ask her quietly. (Because of course the number one rule of any library is to speak quietly!)

"Good! But I'm not staying long. I only have an hour and then I have to go back home to help my parents with some chores."

"Oh ok. My parents wanted to ask if you and your family want to join us tomorrow for lunch? We usually have a potluck with all our neighbours on Sundays. You can meet my parents, Buttercup and Almond's other sisters, and the Baileys, who live next door."

"Oh thanks, it's so nice to invite us! I think we'll be free, yes. What do we need to bring?"

"Any food you like!"

We chat (quietly) a bit more, I show her my new wand holder

and then I have an idea.

"Stay here, I'll be right back!"

I leave my book in Dreams and go next door to see my parents. Violet is at the cashier when I rush inside the bakery.

"Hey! Your mum left you some food in the kitchen," she says right away.

"Thanks!"

I head directly to the kitchen where both my parents are busy finishing a new batch of cookies.

"Hey honey, your food is there!" my mum tells me as soon as she sees me, gesturing toward the corner table.

I check inside the tin box and find an orange pastry for Buttercup and an apricot one for me.

"Thanks! Mum, can I take some more food?"

She laughs at this and tells my dad, "You know sometimes I wonder if we have a squirrel or a big lion. Our son is always hungry."

I laugh too. "No, it's not for me!" (Although, between you and me, I would never say no to more food.) "I want to take some tea and food to Dreams for my friends and the Misses Moon."

"Oh that's so sweet of you. Help yourself to more pastries then. I'll bring some tea over."

"Thanks Mum!" I give her a kiss and end up with some of the flour that was on her on my snout.

I wish I was experienced enough to bring the tea myself but I can't magically lift heavy objects like a teapot yet. I'm still in my first week of school, so at best I would be able to carry the tea leaves by magic! Not very useful, don't you agree?

I go back into the shop to select some pastries for Honeysuckle and the Moon sisters, and I pack everything on a nice tray. I wait for my mum to be ready so we can arrive at Dreams together. She knows a spell to boil water quickly, so the tea is ready to go in no time! Luckily enough, when we enter Buttercup and Hazelnut are back downstairs. Mum and I put the tea and the food on the big table.

"I thought we could have tea time together," I tell everyone as they gather around the table.

"Oh that's so sweet of you, Applesauce!" Hazelnut says as she looks around for her sister. "I'll go fetch Miss Moon."

Mum helps me set everything on the table and leaves in a flash. "Back to work! Enjoy, kids!"

When Hazelnut comes back with her sister, Mum is gone and they both ask where she went.

"She's not staying for tea?"

"No. You know her, always working."

Miss Moon nods at that. "Well, anyway, thank her for us. And thank you Applesauce for this idea. It's so sweet. I needed a break, I'm starting to get tired. All the new stock that arrived this week is killing me."

We spend a lovely time over the food and tea, chatting about books and the upcoming exhibition until Honeysuckle has to leave. Miss Moon helps us take everything back to the bakery, then Buttercup and I go home to help Auntie Dahlia and Apricot cook dinner.

Chapter 24
Food & friends

The next day starts quietly because everyone sleeps in. Almond likes to wake up early no matter the day to go for her morning run. Buttercup is quite an early riser too, but their sisters are more like me and like to take things easy on Sunday. Even my parents like to sleep longer when they are not working. We cooked everything for the potluck last night with Apricot and Auntie Dahlia, so there are no big chores to do before lunch.

Often on Sundays I take my breakfast and a book in a little crossbody bag and eat it alone by the lake. I love my friends and family but on days when I know I'll be with a lot of people after, I like to plan some alone time ahead. It's my way of charging my batteries. No one takes offence or thinks that it's bad for me to be alone. They know that even though I do need this time alone, I also love being with them. I think that's the best proof of love, when you understand others without trying to change them. And I know that my parents love their quiet breakfast time too, with my mum doing her crosswords and my dad reading his book.

Today for breakfast I made myself some strawberry jam sandwiches with some homemade brioche and I packed a thermos of chocolate milk. I don't want to run into Grumpy Sunny today so I settle down a bit farther from our usual tree, not so close to the lake bank. I spend my morning there, reading the second book of the Anne of Green Gables series, enjoying the quiet around me and the sight of the lake. It's so peaceful here. I see some animals come and go from time to time but no one disturbs me. Sunny must be on the other side of the lake for once and I won't complain about that!

As lunch time approaches I notice the sky getting darker and I hurry home before it starts pouring. I don't want my book to get wet. There's a spell to repel water from objects but I don't know it yet. I should suggest to Miss Moon to enchant all the library books with it just to be sure. It seems that I'm lucky though because it only starts to rain once I've been home for a few minutes. I quickly go up to my room to tidy up my books and protect them from the rain. As I'm coming down I see Dahlia and my mum casting the spell to repel the rain from ... well everything. It's called the Rain Rain Go Away spell and it works as an invisible umbrella. You can protect objects individually to make them waterproof but we would still be wet during our lunch. My mum told me once that this spell is very hard to master. It's a level III spell and it's quite impressive to watch. Since we will need a lot of space for our two families, our neighbours and the friends we invited, they're casting the spell over a large area and need to focus a lot. I have seen them do it before but it impresses me every time.

Once it's done and we can all walk around without risking a shower, Dad and Basil conjure some extra tables to accommodate everyone. We use some nice tablecloths that Tulip made especially for these kinds of occasions. She even enchanted them with the waterproof and the No Stain spells. Like this, they stay in perfect condition and no one has to clean them afterwards. How great is magic!

Then we all get to work to set everything up. We bring the food, the plates, the bowls, the napkins and place some drinks on the tables while singing a funny song Basil made up when his girls were small and didn't want to do chores. With time it has became a joke for us all to sing it together when we have to set the table or do house chores.

Our neighbours, the Denver family, arrive early as usual. They are wild boars: two parents and their girl Jasmine. She has already graduated from Woodland and she's really good at magic. They have brought their usual mushroom stew. It's a recipe they had for a long time and we all love it! Then the Baileys arrive not long after. They are a racoon couple from a bit farther away in the woods, with no children. They don't practise magic at all. They say they are too afraid to set the forest on fire because they are so clumsy and, from having known them all my life, I'd say it's probably a good thing. They are quite prone to accidents so giving them access to magic may be dangerous. But Magicals or not, they are really nice neighbours and they always lend me a lot of their books when they get new ones. They love to travel around and bring books from other places. I love going to their house: they built a big bookshelf between two dead trees and asked some friends to protect it all from the rain with magic. They always have new stories to tell and new books to show me. As soon as they arrive I run to say hi to them and we jump right away into what books we've been reading since I last saw them.

"Do you still have time to read now that you've started school?" Mango asks me. I love how original his name is!

"Well, I do read a bit less during the day but I still manage to find time after school and during the weekend. And I need to read for class! Isn't that great?"

"Oh yes, I remember my school days, reading and learning so much through books ..." he says dreamily.

"But I thought you never went to magic school?" I ask, surprised.

"Oh no, I never did. But before we came to Woodland, Maple and I used to sneak into the Human world a lot and we followed some of their classes. They call it 'university'. They had lots of classes about language, history and science. Even music class! It was great."

"Oh but literature was my favourite," adds Maple.

"Really? You studied at a Human school? How did you do it?" I'm so impressed by that. "That's so brave!"

They both giggle at my excitement.

"Well it may have been brave but it was also dangerous. We were following those classes from the very back, hiding in a dark corner so the humans couldn't see us. The classroom we were going to was in an old building under the roof and we had to sneak in through a hole in the window. The old rooftops of Paris were perfect for this!"

"You used to live in Paris?" I've heard about France in books. I know it's not far from us but I know there's some water between

Woodland Forest and this whole other country, so I'm really amazed that they managed to move from our country to France. And with no magic? Waouh!

"Yes we did." They both smile at the memory and explain to me how they did this for a while, sneaking in and stealing a book here and there to read about the course at home too.

"It was going great until one day we were spotted-"

"- by humans?" I ask, unable to stop myself from interrupting him.

"By humans, yes, in the middle of a history class," Mango finishes half laughing at the memory.

"Well, he's laughing at this now, but believe me Applesauce, we didn't laugh much that day," Maple continues their story. "The teacher spotted us and the whole class went mad, yelling, running away or throwing stuff at us to make us leave. We were so scared. We ran out through our usual spot and escaped on the rooftop. I don't think they would have been able to follow us there but we were so afraid, we just ran and ran for a long time. After walking on the rooftops of Paris for hours, we went back to our small home, packed our bags and left for England."

"How did you manage to cross the water?" I ask, still puzzled by this fact.

"We hid in a truck travelling through the tunnel under the sea."

"I wish we could have travelled by boat and seen the view but going through the tunnel was safer."

"What do you mean? A tunnel under the sea?"

They both laugh and explain to me that you can travel between France and England by a very big boat, bigger than anything we'll ever see here in our forest, or that you can take the tunnel under the Channel.

"Waouh, humans are amazing! How did they build this without magic?"

They're busy explaining to me a bit more about this tunnel when I see Honeysuckle arrive with her family. She waves at me when she spots me and I gesture to her to come over.

"Oh this is my new friend from school. You're going to like her, she loves to read too!" I tell the Baileys.

"Hey Honeysuckle! How are you?"

"Good, sorry we're late, my mum couldn't find one of my baby brothers. He was hiding in a bush."

"Don't worry!"

After I introduce her to Maple and Mango, we quickly start talking about books and she's impressed to hear them talk about their book collection.

"You're welcome to borrow some if you want. Any friend of Applesauce is a friend of ours too!"

"Oh thank you!"

After meeting Honeysuckle's parents and two of her little sisters, we all make our way to the food table. I start with some stew and Honeysuckle takes some carrot cake that Dahlia made.

As the afternoon progresses all the children present sit down to have their desert together on a blanket on the ground. There's me, Buttercup, Violet, Honeysuckle, Tulip, Almond, Apricot and Jasmine, plus the three Rumble children, Peach, Parsnip and Paprika. The three Ps. They are a deer family who live near Mum and Dad's bakery. They are really good friends with them. And yes, as you can imagine, their parents really love food! They are really close to Almond because they love to run in the woods together, no matter the weather.

The rain is still raging on top of us but no one is paying any attention to it (thanks magic!). We're all too busy chatting, exchanging stories, playing guessing games and singing silly songs. Friends and food make everything better, I think. Next time, I'll manage to invite Wind too and it will be absolutely perfect!

Chapter 25

Missing tail and lost ears

The months go by and without us even noticing, our first year at the Academy progresses really fast. It's not always easy or free from mistakes but I think we're all having a great time. We've all now connected deeply with our Magical Objects and are using magic whenever we can to make the most of our bonds. The only one who still seems to struggle is Wind. He can master the spells but his potions are always lacking a little something. They work but never one hundred percent. For example, when we practise the potion that makes an object change colour, his objects always have a small portion that doesn't change or the colour is still very light compared to the teacher's demonstration. I don't know what to do to help him. I've seen a new potion in our book to help with confidence, I might try making it and mixing it in a juice for him.

Everyone in the class became friends quite quickly and even though we all have our little groups of best friends, we all get along easily with each other. And since we all take different afternoon classes (they are optional but everyone takes at least one), we also get to be with a different group, which makes for a nice change. The extra classes last all afternoon but since there are less animals in them, they feel a bit more relaxed, like a summer camp. I'm taking the history class with Miss Pamplemousse, Almond and Honeysuckle are learning about runes and Buttercup is focusing on herbology with Mr Wells. It gives us something else to talk about when we meet and I love to have a look at their runes and herbology books whenever I can. Next year, I think I'll take astronomy.

We have learned so much in the last few months, it makes me giddy! So far Mrs Winter has taught us to: make something hot (very useful for reheating my drink when I'm reading!), make objects change sizes, create wind and water, make things lighter, and lift light and heavy objects in the air. We won't learn to lift very heavy objects like trees or to make fire until the level III class.

We've also learned lots of potions to relax, heal stomach aches, get rid of a cold, focus, make objects change colour (not something we'll need a lot in our daily life but Mrs Winter told us it's a good way to practice magic in the beginning). We won't learn the ones to transform our appearance until class II and III. From what I've seen in the book, there are some advanced potions that will give you claws or fangs for a few hours, and others to make you shrink or grow as much as you want. Can you imagine me with fangs or Buttercup being the size of a bear?

I'm fine waiting to learn those advanced potions because we've been learning the coolest potion EVER! It's a very light blue potion that sparkles with bubbles and that makes you invisible for a short time! Did you read that? INVISIBLE!!!!! It's absolutely insane how great this is! Why do we learn this you ask? Well, apart from the obvious fact that you can play pranks on others and have some quiet time anytime you want, Mrs Winter told us that it's actually a very important potion to help us protect ourselves.

"Being able to make yourself invisible could save your life one day if you get lost outside Woodland Forest. That's why it's the only transforming potion that we teach in the first year. If you're in danger of being attacked by another animal or being hunted by humans, you can just make yourself invisible for a while."

Someone asks Mrs Winter, "Attacked by another animal? But we're all friends here. Who would attack us?"

"I know you all see the animals around you as friends here, but outside our forest the world is a more dangerous place than you imagine. Animals chase each other and humans hunt us too."

I think of how Almond's parents were killed by hunters and my heart breaks for her once more.

"That's why you have to be careful when you step outside our woods. Once you've mastered this potion I advise you to never leave the forest without a vial of it on you. With time, once your magic is stronger, you will learn other ways to defend yourself, but for now this one is a very easy way to hide yourself from danger."

Since this is a tricky potion we've been working on it for a few weeks now. Mrs Winter said it's worth putting a lot of time into this one since it's so important.

"And no one wants to be half invisible, don't they?" she says.

We all laughed at this when she said it, but we quickly saw that she was not joking. I think we've all had a case of missing body parts since we started working on this potion. The first one to half disappear was Wind so, I admit, I thought it was because his skills still needed improving. But no, everyone else had the same problem. So far in our class we've had: animals turning invisible on one side of their body only, others had their whole body affected by the potion but only incompletely, so they were just transparent. Some disappeared for only two seconds and many of us have had bits of our bodies missing at some point.

Wind lost his ears like this for a while, Rain a leg, Caramel his whiskers, Plum the tip of her snout, and we had a lot of invisible paws. A lot! But the worst was when my fluffy tail went missing! Well, it didn't go missing, it was still attached to my body but no one could see it anymore. I stayed like this for an hour and it was heartbreaking. Buttercup said it was quite funny to watch: since I was stroking my invisible tail to calm myself, it just looked like I was patting a non-existent cat.

Thankfully everyone's bits came back fully visible, and with time and perseverance we've now all managed to master this potion properly. Well, except for Wind, who still goes around with a visible nose while the rest of his body is completely invisible. It's a bit funny to see only his nose wandering about but of course we don't tell him that and do our best to support him. He ends today's class like this again and I hear Mrs Winter tell him to meet her after class so they can keep practising it.

Now that we're done for the day Mrs Winter is facing what looks like an empty classroom but then she casts the *Reveal your True Colours!* spell to end the lesson and make us all visible again. "Ok everyone, gather around please."

We all go back to our seats and, as usual, many of us are checking that we have reappeared fully. I admit, I check too. I trust Mrs Winter's skills to make my tail reappear but better safe than sorry!

"Well done everyone! You've all worked hard on the invisibility potion over the last few weeks and you all deserve the well-earned holidays that start today."

We all cheer at this, even Wind (fully visible again), who was looking so down a minute ago. Some start to pack their books away but Mrs Winter is not done.

"But before you all go and enjoy time with your families, I have an announcement to make."

Chapter 26
Special projects

An announcement? I wonder what it is? Could it be a test? No, she told us at the beginning of the year that there are no tests at the Academy. Oh I know, maybe she's going to assign us some books to read during the holidays! Lots of books! That would be awesome!

"We're now well advanced in your first school year and, even though there are no proper tests during the year, you will have to prove that you have mastered everything that you've learned before you can graduate to the level II class, the flower class. To do that, you'll have to show your skills to the school with the Level I Special Project. The LISP, or SP for short."

The name gets some laughs and Mrs Winter comments on it too.

"I know, it's not very original. I've been telling our Headmaster to spice up the names of those projects for years but he won't listen ... Anyway, that's not the point."

At least it made the class laugh and the students who were nervous have relaxed a bit.

"So, this special project, what is it? I'm sure you all want to know what you will need to do, right?"

Yes, I'm dying to know what this is all about.

"Well, I'll tell you all about it after the holidays. See you in two weeks!"

What? The whole class gasps in surprise. She can't leave us like this, not knowing for two whole weeks, that would be plain cruel.

"I'm kidding, I'm kidding, don't worry!" Mrs Winter adds quickly, with a funny smile on her face.

She's a great teacher but we rarely hear her joke like this. She knows she surprised us because she adds, "Oh yes I can joke too, you know. I thought it would be funny to end the term with a bit of humour but I can see that I've shocked you."

She laughs some more at our surprised faces.

"So it's a joke? There's no special project?" Wind asks with his paw raised in the air and a very relieved grin on his face.

Mrs Winter becomes serious again and explains, "Oh no, the project is real, I was just messing with you about not explaining it to you before your break, that's all."

"Oh!" Wind's disappointment is written all over his face.

"So, this special project! I can already see some panicked faces but don't worry, this is not an impossible task. The beauty of the SP is that it can be whatever you choose it to be."

"What do you mean?" Echo asks from a low branch where he follows the class with his sister.

"I mean that you'll have to present something but you get to pick what it will be. The point is for you to show that you can use your magic for the community. Show us what you can do with all the things I've taught you."

"All of it?" asks Bloom.

"No, no, no, don't worry. The point is not to mix all the spells and potions for one project. Can you imagine? It would be useless and very messy."

She smiles at this thought.

"No, the point is to put what you learned to good use. Make something that you can use in your daily life or, even better, that can be used by others. It's like a circle: the school taught you magic and you give back by doing something for Woodland Forest. Do you see what I mean?"

Some of us nod but I think we're still very confused by the details.

"Can you give us some examples?" asks Buttercup.

"Of course! A good example is the project made by Mr Nook, who is now the teacher for the tree class. He enchanted an acorn to amplify teachers' voices. It was a simple idea but it really helped the smaller teachers. Once his spell was inside the acorn, the animal just had to carry it around their neck to be heard properly by their class. He couldn't have known when he created his project that a few years later, he would be using it as a teacher himself. The most impressive thing is that he actually had to invent his own spell for this but he was a rare case so don't worry about that. Work with what you know and I'm sure it will be great. Also, we encourage students to give their projects a name. For example Mr Nook named his Can you EAR me? He spelled it "ear" instead of "hear" to play with the idea that this acorn was like an extra ear for students."

We all laugh at the pun in the project's name. Hear me, ear. That's funny. I would have never guessed that Mr Nook could be so witty. I've seen him around the school and the woods, and he always looks so serious.

"What was your project Mrs Winter?" Honeysuckle asks.

"My own project when I was in my first year was ..."

She seems to hesitate a bit before saying, "Well I used different spells and potions to make a set of medicines to help the animals who don't practise magic. I was inspired by my parents, actually. They never learned magic and as they were getting older, they got sick more often so I wanted to use my magic to help them and other animals like them."

Wait a minute, is she telling us that she's the one behind the Winter's line of medicines we all know and have at home and at the hospital? Those medicines are different from the basic healing potions we've learned so far because they have a longer shelf life. A simple potion can only be kept for a day but hers can last a year. It also means that you don't need to waste time making a potion when you're in pain. And she added a fruity taste so most animals prefer them to homemade potions.

I think we're all realising the same thing because I hear several of my friends say "Oh so she invented the Winter's Cold Remedy?

And the Winter's Painkiller? And ..."

As we're all thinking the same thing, I realise something else and raise my paw to ask her.

"But how did you manage to create all those medicines with just the knowledge you learned in your first year? We've all had your medicines and I don't see how you managed to create them using only the potions we've learned so far! They even work faster than the potions we know."

"Yes! It's amazing!" I hear Honeysuckle whisper in admiration next to me.

"Well," Mrs Winter blushes at this but explains to us anyway "I told you I struggled a bit with some of my spells in my first year but I was quite good with my potions. In fact, I loved working on them so much that I was already studying from the class II part of the book."

"Waouh!" some students say. I've had a peek at the more advanced magic in our book too and it's impressive that she managed to do those potions properly! She must have been really good.

"But don't compare yourself to me because I am not necessarily a good example."

"What do you mean?" Almond asks her.

"Well you see, by the end of my first year, yes, I was very good at potions and I did become really good at spells too, but I had no friends. I was so busy practising and reading every book I could find on magic that I never took the time to make friends with my classmates."

"Weren't you lonely?" someone asks softly.

"Well, yes and no. Of course I must have been but I think I was too busy to see it. I didn't realise it until the day to show our project came along and it hit me that I had no friend to cheer for me when my turn came. All the other students were supporting each other and clapping once they were done but I had no one."

"That's so sad. Were the other kids mean?"

"Oh no, not at all. You see, the truth is that no one cared about me because I didn't take the time to care for them either. I thought magic was all that mattered. So I don't blame them. It was my fault, I got lost in my books and my ambition. But there's a lesson in my story for you," she continues with a smile, "don't be like me, be a good student but be a good friend too. Doing magic really well is less fun if you have no one to share it with. I know you've all made friends so far but it's still something to keep in mind for the future. Don't let your desire to be a skilled witch or wizard be more important than the people around you."

We all nod and smile at the classmates at our table.

"And, don't worry, I didn't stay lonely for a long time. Once I realised my mistake I reduced the time I spent studying and tried my best to learn about my classmates. I apologised to them for being so silent before and they all accepted me into their circle. I even learned a lot by being around them. I watched how they were doing magic, the way they were using their Magicol, the ideas they had for their projects and it taught me things I couldn't have learned in my books.

"Remember that magic is not only learned at school and by reading, but also by the experiences you have and what you learn by watching others. You'll find inspiration to develop your magic into something more personal everywhere around you. And the same goes for your project. Don't worry if you don't have an idea right now at this very moment. Your project idea will probably come to you when you least expect it. Maybe you'll be in need of something or you'll observe someone needing your help. Don't overthink it, let the magic and your Magicol speak to you and guide you. Your SP can have a lot of spells and potions, or just a few. This won't mean that it's better or worse than your classmates'. Every year I love watching the students show their projects because it's so interesting to see the world through their eyes."

She goes around her desk and starts packing her things before finishing the class.

"Anyway, use these holidays to start thinking about it. You don't have to come back with a fully formed project yet, don't worry you have plenty of time. But think about it, ask yourself what could be better? For yourself or for others. And," she pauses and looks at Wind a bit longer than the rest of us, "use those two weeks to rest and relax, ok? Practise your magic everyday, read your spells and potions book now and then, but don't overdo it. Having fun can actually make your magic stronger. Like I've said before, a clear mind is better prepared to do magic. Oh! And don't forget to tell someone if you practise your invisibility potion during the break so they can help you afterwards. Especially if it doesn't work properly."

I definitely see her wink at Wind for this last bit.

"Make sure you don't forget your Magicol in class and enjoy your Grateday holidays! I'll see you all in two weeks."

Chapter 27

Pear

We all pack our things and say goodbye to the teacher on our way out. It's so strange to think I won't be coming to class for two whole weeks. I wait for Almond, Buttercup and Wind to see what they have planned for this afternoon. Honeysuckle is busy talking with the teacher but we've already made plans earlier to eat together. Almond says she's going to check on the Rumbles in class III to see if they want to go for a run.

"I'm so excited about this project, I need to burn out some energy!" she explains to us.

"Ok, say hi to Peach, Paprika and Parsnip!" says Buttercup.

Wind is used to Almond's energy by now but he still comments, "Waouh she really never stops, doesn't she?"

"No, she doesn't." Buttercup laughs. "I love it!"

"What about you guys?" I ask. "What are your plans?"

"Mmm, I'm going home with Smore. He's leaving tomorrow to visit his family for the holidays so we want to spend some time working on our craft before he goes."

"Great, have fun! Wind? What are you doing?"

"Nothing special. I have to go home anyway, I forgot my lunch." He mumbles, a bit ashamed of himself and I think he's still feeling bad about not mastering the invisibility potion.

"Oh you can come and eat with Honeysuckle and me then! We're going to eat at my parent's bakery, they have some great sandwiches."

"Really? You don't mind?"

"Of course not!"

"But is it big enough for me to sit there?"

"Oh yes don't worry, there are big tables outside too."

"Oh great!" He smiles at this and as soon as Honeysuckle joins us, I let her know that Wind will be joining us for lunch!

"Awesome, the more the merrier! Have you ever been there before?" she asks him.

"No, I don't think so."

"Really? I never took you there?" I'm so surprised and a bit ashamed too. "Well you'll see, they have great food and my parents don't bite!"

Honeysuckle laughs at this. "Well, it would be kind of funny, tiny squirrels biting a big bear like him, wouldn't it?"

We all laugh at this and I start picturing it in my head. A couple of squirrels that look really nice and friendly in their small bakery but then suddenly reach up to bite the big bear with their tiny fangs. Maybe I'll write a story about it and read it to Almond and Buttercup at our nocturnal meeting. I'm daydreaming, already writing it in my head and I bump into Honeysuckle.

"Sorry, I was ..."

"Dreaming, yeah I know!" She giggles. "It's a good thing you're small and light. Imagine if Wind was like you, always bumping into others because he was daydreaming. It would be more painful for us!"

"Well, actually that's how Applesauce and I met!" Winds explains to her.

"Really? Oh tell me!"

I smile at the memory and let Wind tell the story of our first day at school.

"Mmm, it was our first day at school and I was really nervous about it so I didn't look where I was going and I bumped into Applesauce ..." He pauses like he just realised something. "I never asked you how come you didn't see me come. What were you doing that day?"

I blush a bit at the memory but explain anyway.

"Well, when I arrived I was very anxious about making friends so I was trying to calm myself by looking at the school and the trees around us."

"Really? You, nervous about making friends? But you were so great with me that day, you helped me relax and you took me to class without me realising. It was very clever," he tells Honeysuckle.

She smiles and adds her opinion. "Yeah and when I met you at the picnic after, you were very social too! Why were you worried?"

"Argh sometimes it seems like I'm good at talking and making friends but it's not as easy for me as it is for Almond and Buttercup. Those two are naturals, they could talk to rocks and still befriend them!" I joke. "I don't know, it just takes more time with me, I prefer to observe people before talking to them. I feel better if I can think ahead about what I'll say to them and prepare little things to talk about. I guess it was easy with you guys because well, Wind, you didn't let me any time to prepare anything. I couldn't worry ahead and I immediately wanted to help you feel better so that helped me too. And Honeysuckle, I think it was easy because I saw you reading. Talking about books is the one thing that can help me relax instantly."

"And food!" Wind adds with a big smile.

"Yes! You could wear a sign saying 'talk to me about food or books if you want to be my friend'!" Honeysuckle suggests.

I laugh at her idea. "If you had come to me talking about food with a book in your hand it would have been easy peasy!"

"That was a great story, meeting and becoming friends by bumping into each other," Honeysuckle says.

"Oh you know, he came crashing into me so hard that I even fell backward on the ground," I tell her. Wind winces at the memory.

"Sorry! I was too busy panicking and you seemed so small that day."

"You forgot to say that you ran into me because you were trying to run away from school!" I tease him.

"What?" Honeysuckle cries. "You were really running away?"

"Not really ... I was just hiding ... Oh ok, I was trying to run away. I was so nervous, I was leaving the school and didn't look where I was going. But in a way I'm glad I did because it means I bumped into you and we became friends. It really helped me relax, meeting you right away, you know? So thank you for being a small squirrel that daydreams a lot," he says with a wink.

" Ah ah, you're welcome!"

As we walk towards my parents' bakery, we chit chat about our plans for the holidays and how weird it'll be not to go to school for so long. We are all so used to the Academy now.

"I wonder what the teacher will be doing." Honeysuckle says.

"I don't know what her plans are but I'm sure she'll be happy not to have to fix my messed up potions, that's for sure," Wind says sadly.

"Oh come on, you're getting better! And she said that resting can help your magic so I'm sure you'll be better when we come back! What are your plans?"

"Oh I know what I'm going to do! I'm going to sleep. A lot!" Wind tells us with so much emphasis on those last words that we all laugh. "What about you guys?"

"I'll probably have to help my parents with my siblings but if I can escape a bit I want to read a lot and ... let me see ... oh yeah, read some more!"

We laugh as she goes on.

"Oh, you think I'm joking but it's true! There's so many books I want to read: between the books you recommended to me, the ones at the library and the ones that Mango and Maple lent to me, I feel like I'll never have enough time to read everything."

She smiles and adds, "But it's fun like that, isn't it?"

"Yes it is," I love being a bookworm, there's always a new book waiting for you to be read somewhere.

"What about you, Applesauce?"

"Let's see," I pause for comedic effect, "sleep, read, eat and think about my project I guess."

"Do you have any ideas of what you'll do?" Wind asks.

"No, not yet. But I'm hoping I can do something related to books, you know. And you?"

Honeysuckle says she may have an idea but she's not telling us anything yet, she needs to think about it first. She seems very secretive about it, I wonder what it can be.

We're almost at the bakery when I spot Pear, an old beaver resting by the lake. He's not a student anymore but we know him because of all the times we've spent here.

"Oh look! Pear is there," I tell my friends. "Let's go and ask him what his first year's project was."

"Great idea!"

He's just finishing eating some plants from the lake and tidying up something when he sees us arrive at his level. He seems to have a big strangely shaped bag next to him.

"Hey Pear! How are you?"

He quickly hides something behind his back (a bottle I think) before turning around to say hello to us.

"Hey guys, I'm good and you? Enjoying your first hours of the holidays, aren't you?" His voice is deep and rough like he's always sick with a bad cold.

"Yes!" we all reply enthusiastically.

"Eh, can you help us with something?" I ask him.

"Sure. What can I do for you? Do you need a special kind of seaweed? Some pumpkin juice bottles? The latest bestseller? Some imported cheese from France? What do you need?"

I'm confused by all his suggestions and I hear Honeysuckle ask him, "Are you ... Are you running a black market or something?"

A black market? The place where you can buy illegal goods?

"No ... Yeah ... maybe, why do you ask? It depends who's asking ..." There's a silence and when he sees our confused faces he changes his answer to, "No, of course not. I'm not selling anything that I obtained illegally, of course not. I can assure you that I definitely don't steal from humans to resell here later."

Another silence from all of us. I'm too surprised to say anything, so Honeysuckle moves on and explains what we want.

"We just learned about the special project we have to do for the end of our first year and ..."

"-and you were hoping I could do yours for you? Sure, no problem!" He says this like it's the most normal thing in the world to ask for and immediately starts counting on his front paws.

"I charge five hundred Woodcoins for a project idea and two thousand for the execution. Let me get my list of ideas." And he starts rummaging through his bag full of odd bits. I spot some bottles, some loose pieces of paper, some packaged food that definitely didn't come from our forest, some string...

"What? Do the project for us? No! No, no, no, of course not!" I finally reply.

"Oh, sorry, my bad!" He coughs like he's trying to change the subject or make us forget what he just said.

"No" I say again, "we just wanted to ask you what was your project when you were in our class? What did you do?" Honestly, after all the strange things he just told us now, I'm not sure I want to know.

"Oh, ok." He stops to think for a bit and makes a funny face like it's physically hard for him to remember something from that long ago and then he finally says, "Oh yes I remember! I made this!"

He shows us his wand holder.

"You're the one who invented the wand holder? Waouh!" Wind asks him all in awe.

"No of course not, I'm not that old thank you!"

We laugh at this but Wind looks a bit sheepish.

"I didn't invent the wand holder, I made mine waterproof."

"Ohhh!" Wind simply says this time. Still an interesting project but not as impressive in Wind's opinion, I think.

"Wait, how come you have a wand? I thought aquatic animals had magic stones instead of wooden magic objects?"

"Yeah, we usually do. But I don't like to do things like anyone else so I thought it would be funny to be the only one with a wand in my class. I didn't think of the fact that there was a reason the Wats campus students don't use wands or acorns. Honestly, I blame the teachers for even giving us the option. What's the point?"

He's grumpy and reaching for his bottle of apple cider. He takes a swig and continues.

"Until I came up with the project it was such a nightmare. My teacher had to put a spell on it every day before class to make it waterproof but it didn't last long enough for me to keep the wand with me all the time so I had to find a place to keep it dry and safe on the ground before going home every day. I had to make sure nosy humans couldn't see it so I hid it in the trees."

"But humans can't take away your Magicol. We learned that on our first day," Honeysuckle explains like it's the most obvious thing. He's fidgeting, putting his bottle back in his already full bag.

"Well, I didn't know that. No one told us ... or maybe I didn't listen enough, it's possible," He admits. I can see that he's getting grumpier a bit more every time we ask him a question. "So, anyway, for my project I made a water repellent potion for my wand holder and I enchanted my wand so that it would always repel water. It created a sort of protective field a few centimetres around it at all times and I made the spell repeat itself everyday. So now I can use it all the time underwater."

Once he sees that we all look impressed he grabs his bag, mumbles a quick "ok, gotta go, bye kids" and jumps back in the water. We all look at each other, wondering why he left so quickly.

"Did we say something? Why did he leave so suddenly?" Wind asks, worried.

"Honestly I don't think we did anything wrong, I think it just goes with his ... personality." Honeysuckle explains.

I agree and add, "Ok, so Pear is a bit unusual but I have to admit I'm impressed that he managed a spell like that during his first year."

"Do you think he was always this grumpy?"

"I don't know but maybe he is in a club with Grumpy Sunny! They probably meet every week to complain about everything!" I suggest.

"Who's Grumpy Sunny?" Wind asks.

"Oh, she's a frog that lives here and she's annoyed about everything."

"Everything? Really?"

"I've heard her say that the sun was too sunny and the water too wet so, yes, everything!"

"Waouh!"

"Anyway, who's hungry?"

Chapter 28

A happy place

We arrive at "Sweet treat" and I tell Wind to get us a table outside. Technically he can fit inside the bakery but I prefer not to risk him knocking anything over since he tends to be clumsy when nervous. As he sits down at one of the bigger tables I enter the bakery with Honeysuckle to get us some food.

My mum is behind the counter serving a few customers waiting in line. There's a mouse, a wolf and a skunk waiting in line while two birds and a cub are at the table drinking their tea and reading their books.

"Here's your change. Have a good day Miss Palmer!" my mum tells the mouse. "And let me know about your tea party so we can plan how many cakes you'll need!"

"I will! Thank you dear!"

As we wait in line, I think of what I want to eat today.

"Do you already know what you're going to take today?"

"Mmm, my usual I think," Honeysuckle replies with a smile.

"Carrot pie?"

"You know me!"

"And I'll take some rabbit cookies to bring back to my family! They loved the ones you gave me last time."

When it's our turn my mum greets us behind the counter with her usual cheerfulness.

"Oh hey honey! Hello Honeysuckle!"

"Hello Rose!" My Mum insists on being called Rose, not just by our friends but by everyone she knows. Even the customers know my parents as Rose and Sprout. Just like Hazelnut, she thinks being called Mrs is boring.

"What can I get you? The usual?"

"Yes! A carrot pie for me. And a box of rabbit cookies to bring back to my-"

She doesn't have time to finish her sentence that my mum hands her a box already wrapped up with a bow.

"I already prepared one for your family. A little gift to celebrate the holidays!" She winks at her.

"Oh really? That's really nice of you! Thank you so much!"

"My pleasure, sweetie!"

I smile at her kindness and wonder once more how my parents manage to make any profits with all the gifts they're always giving to everyone. But I guess I can't complain about having parents that are too nice. I don't think you can be too generous, can't you? And if you can, at least it's a nice flaw.

As I place the orders for Wind and I, my mum is excited to learn that we brought our friend with us today. Well, it's true, she is excited about almost everything but, again, we can't blame her for being too positive, can we?

"Ok, go sit outside, and I'll bring you everything in a minute."

"Are you sure you don't want our help carrying anything?" Honeysuckle asks her.

She tuts at her, "No, no, no. Don't worry, I'll manage easily. What would be the point of doing magic otherwise?"

She starts to hum her favourite song while Honeysuckle and I join Wind outside. We find him looking around and seeming relaxed for once.

"Waouh this place is so pretty! I can't believe I've never been here before."

We chat for a few minutes before my mum comes with our food and drinks floating in the air in front of her, while she's carrying another box of cookies in her paws.

"Hello Mrs Applesauce! It's a nice place you have there."

We all laugh at this name for her. He's so nervous he called her by my name!

"Hello, Wind, nice to see you again! This is for you." She hands him a box of bear cookies and adds right away, "Oh, and please call me Rose!"

Poor Wind is so surprised by her generosity and her request that he can't manage to say anything other than thank you. She makes the trays hover next to her and sets our food on the table before adding, "and here's some nice iced tea for you all. Don't hesitate to come inside if you need anything else!"

Once everything is on the table, she quickly dashes back into the bakery with a little dance.

We chit chat for a bit while eating our pies and sandwiches. Then suddenly Wind tells us "I think I know what project I'm going to do!" before grabbing his first bear shaped cookie out of his box.

"Really? Waouh you're so quick! What is it?"

"I'm thinking of creating a kind of device to help students stay awake during class."

"A device?" Honeysuckle and I look at each other dubiously. "What kind of device?"

"Well," he starts but stops to take his first cookie bite and says "Oh these are so good!"

He swallows and continues his explanation.

"Well, I don't know exactly ... Maybe something that could send some kind of electric shock at regular intervals, or when it feels like you might fall asleep..."

Electric shocks? What is he talking about?

"... or maybe I can use something with spikes or sharp bits on it to make sure you don't fall asleep. Or that, if you do, the pain will wake you up! I'm not sure yet."

"What?" Honeysuckle just asks. She seems as baffled as me by Wind's strange plan.

He grabs a second cookie and keeps explaining like it's a totally sane plan. A plan with spikes and electric shocks. Normal, right?

"You know, like a small rock with spikes and when it feels you're falling asleep bam it hurts you, keeps you awake and you can keep on listening to the teacher!"

He doesn't wait for us to respond and goes on with his crazy idea. "I even have some name ideas for it. I was thinking of Sleepy Head or Snooze Not or, my favourite," and he's really excited about this last one, "You Snooze you Lose! But of course I'll need to find other students with the same problem to work on the details."

"Mmmm ... I don't think I know anyone else with this kind of problem." Honeysuckle tries to say gently. But he's not listening. He's so excited about his idea that he doesn't notice our lack of enthusiasm.

"Oh I know! What about Pippin? She sleeps a lot."

"She's a bat!"

"So?" He asks, clueless about the situation.

"Well, it's in her nature to sleep that much, that's all."

"Oh!" He finally seems to understand our point.

"And she doesn't even go to school! She just lives near it."

"Besides," I add, "your project is about falling asleep in class, so I don't think the teachers will be pleased about that."

"Why not? It's a great idea!"

Honeysuckle and I look at each other again. I let her explain this part to him.

"You're thinking of a project to help you stay awake during their class."

"Yeah and they should be grateful about such a great project," Wind explains like it's obvious and he's doing the school a service.

"But, don't you see, it means that you find the classes so boring and so hard to go through that you're falling asleep during them. Not sure they'd love this."

He finally gets our point. "Oh ... I see!"

I've often wondered why Wind joined our school if he doesn't like it since an education at the Academy is not compulsory.

"Wind, why are you at the Academy if you find the classes so boring?"

"My parents forced me. They want me to be a great wizard like my grandfather."

"Oh, I see." I remember him telling me that his grandpa was the one who built the Woodland Hospital. I can see how it must be hard to follow his steps. But still, it's not right, he shouldn't feel so much pressure just because of who his grandfather was.

"But you love learning at the Academy, I've seen you have fun ..."

"I do."

"So how come you fall asleep so much?"

"I spend so much time stressing about how great I should be in class that I don't sleep well, or I don't sleep enough, and then I'm tired at school."

I'm trying to think of a way to make him less nervous about it but Honeysuckle seems to have some kind of inspiration before me.

"OK, let's just pretend there's no school, no spells to learn, no pressure ... What would YOU like to do? What would you like to learn? How would you spend your day?"

He thinks about it for a bit and then shyly tells us, "Well, I'm not any good at it but I really love to make stuff. Even if it doesn't make any sense to others, I love to paint and create portraits with anything I can find. Bits of wood, fabric, tiles, acorns, flowers ..."

"Well that's great!"

"I used to make many things when I was a cub but when I grew up my parents forbid me to do anything like this anymore."

"Forbid you? Why?"

"They said that it's useless and that I should focus all my attention on learning magic and making something great for our community instead."

"That's ridiculous!" Honeysuckle cries out. "You know what I think? If you were allowed to do what you like and be your true self, then you would be way happier."

"But my parents won't see it like this ..."

"Well they will if I have something to say about it!"

I smile at my friend's enthusiasm.

"You'd be less stressed so you'd succeed more at school. Don't you think?"

"I guess it makes sense, yes. But they threw away all my craft supplies."

Honeysuckle looks at me with a knowing smile.

"Don't worry, we know the perfect place for you!"

"Really?" Wind asks, suddenly all hopeful.

"Yes, just wait and see." I gather all our glasses on our tray and cast the spell to make all of this lighter. I love magic and how convenient it is!

"I'll bring this back inside and we'll bring you there."

I enter the bakery with my arms full and a big smile, thinking that we're about to make our friend's day better. I put the tray down in the designated area and see my dad cleaning some of the indoor tables.

"Hey darling! How was your lunch? Everything ok?"

"Yes, thanks! Everything was delicious. Wind loved the cookies by the way!"

He smiles at that, always so happy when we compliment their baking. As I see him I think of Wind's parents and I feel the sudden urge to hug my dad. He hugs me back naturally and I love that he always smells of sugar from all the baking he does.

"What was that for? "he asks with a gentle smile.

"I'm just so happy to have amazing parents like you two, that's all."

I tell him quickly what Wind told us about his parents and he doesn't look surprised by their harsh treatment.

"Oh yes, I know them, they're not really fun. The dad thinks very highly of himself because of who his dad was. He has some nerve putting all this pressure on his son when he hasn't done anything for the community himself. And he never even went to the Academy. He started the first day with your mum and I, and left because, apparently, he was better than all of us and didn't need to learn any of this."

"Really?"

"Mmm. He left school and I think he travelled for a while. That's how he met his wife. He brought her back here, they had their son but they mostly keep to themselves with some other bears in the far end of the forest. His dad may have done great things but he hasn't done anything and should be ashamed of treating his son like this."

I tell him we're taking Wind to Dreams and he hands me an extra bag of little honey cakes to give to him. Really, their bakery should be called, "Free food for all!"

"Thanks Dad!"

I go back outside, hand the new cakes to Wind and we walk the short distance to Dreams.

"Tada!!!!!" Honeysuckles says in a very dramatic way. "Here's the place that you needed without even knowing it!"

"What is this place? I've never been this far in the forest," Wind confesses.

"This is a bookshop, a library and an art centre!" I answer proudly, like it's my own shop.

"A what? How can it be all this at once?"

"Well, the two sisters who run this place first thought of having Miss Moon open a bookshop and Hazelnut an art centre, but they really wanted to work together so they just fused the two shops into one. And that's how this place came to life."

"Come on, we'll show you!" Honeysuckle says.

At first, as Wind looks around and only sees books everywhere, he seems a bit doubtful but I explain that the art centre is on the first floor. We're met upstairs by Hazelnut who, as always, is very cheerful.

"Hello my friends!"

"Hello Hazelnut, we're bringing you someone new!" Honeysuckle announces proudly. She quickly became a regular at Dreams and has developed a great relationship with Hazelnut since I brought her here a few months ago.

"Really? Oh hello there!" she looks up at Wind, pretending she's only now noticing the giant bear behind the two tiny animals. "I didn't see you there!"

We laugh at this and right away I can see that Wind's feeling at ease despite the new environment.

"My friends told me you have a great art centre. How does it work exactly?"

She explains to him that you can buy art supplies and come to their workshop.

"Our next workshops are frame making ..."she stops to look for the pamphlet with the details. "Ah yes, here it is! So, yes, as I was saying, frame making, abstract painting with leaves and twigs, an introduction to watercolour, pottery, and knitting. We might also do one with beads next month. Oh and of course we have a sewing class."

Wind is impressed. "Waouh that's a lot!"

"Well it's over several months, so don't worry you'll have time to try different crafts if you're feeling curious. And you can leave all your supplies here and pop in anytime you want to do your thing."

"And they also have some exhibitions to show the students' artworks, it's so nice!" I add, suddenly remembering them.. I went to the first exhibition they had and it was so well organised. Buttercup's artworks looked so professional, displayed like that, with nice frames and little cards to indicate who the artist was.

"Oh that's amazing!" Wind is beaming and I'm so happy we brought him here. I just feel bad that we haven't done this sooner. Well, better late than never I guess.

I let him explore all that and go back downstairs. Honeysuckle goes to her reading corner while I offer Hazelnut my help. There's always some library books to tidy up or some new stock to take out of their boxes. We chat as we work and I tell her about our school project, my plans for the holidays and the latest book I've read. I'm so lucky to have a place like this to be with friends and books. If you add food, it's the ultimate recipe for happiness in my opinion.

Chapter 29

Grateday

We have two weeks of holidays ahead of us to celebrate Grateday. If you don't know what Grateday is, it is only the best holiday EVER! Ok, maybe I'm getting a bit too excited about this but it's true that I love this day. Basically it started as an occasion to celebrate our forest and thank our ancestors for creating our community but over the years, it has evolved and now we also use this time to thank the animals who help us in our daily lives and who are dear to us. There are no special rules to celebrate it and some families have their own traditions on top of the Woodland traditions, but the one we all share in common is that we're supposed to give something handmade to our friends and family. Or to anyone that you want to thank for helping you one way or another, like a teacher or a doctor. The gifts can be anything you want as long as you made it yourself: a small card, some cookies, a decorated frame, a poem, a favourite dish or even a song! Anything you can think of, as long as it says, "Thank you for being there for me".

The morning of Grateday is spent with your close family, exchanging gifts and stories about things you've done together. Then the whole forest comes together for a big picnic. It's the only time of the year when we are all together. We have to go to the very west edge of Woodland to fit in a big clearing (called Whimskle) since Kappa meadow is too small for all of us. There's a stream separating us from Woodbury, the forest next door, so it's the perfect place for a big event like this. Spacious and quiet.

Everyone brings a dish to share. Technically there's no need to bring too much since many of us love to give handmade dishes to our friends as Grateday gifts, but of course my parents can't help it and bring too much food every year. Now you understand why I love this holiday so much: lots of food everywhere for everyone, it's clearly the best day of the year! But honestly, I also really love the idea of thanking those who are dear to you. It's important to show them how much they mean to you by taking the time to make something yourself.

The celebration lasts all afternoon with food and fun things to do. You're also supposed to send your grateful list to the spirits of the Ancestors. A magical fire is lit by the Great Wizard (it smells like apple and cinnamon) and it stays on until nightfall, shining a nice warm light on us all. Once it's lit, you can go throw a list of everything you're grateful for in it, at anytime. You can write it on a simple piece of paper, decorate a nice roll of parchment, paint it, or wrap your list in a special box. It's all up to you! My family and I, we burn ours in a small wooden chest that's made by Roots, an old squirrel who has lived in the forest for a very long time. My parents always say it's important to give back to the community and that since Roots is a lonely animal without any family, it's nice to use this occasion to buy from his woodwork shop to help him. They always bring him some food, too, whenever they visit his shop. He has made some nice things for us over the years: a chest in my room, some shelves in the kitchen, our big outdoor table, and lots of furniture for the bakery. I love our annual visit there to buy our chests because it's a sign that Grateday is coming.

Our own family tradition is that we use oranges in all our Grateday dishes. Why oranges? Simply because my dad thought it was cute to use something the same colour as our squirrel family. Buttercup's parents make theirs with berries and nuts, and they make sure to cook them all together. Every year it's quite a sight to see the whole Dreamcreek family trying to fit in the kitchen, especially with Almond always jumping around everywhere. They often have to divide into two groups and have Almond work at the outside table to avoid any accidents.

Over the school break we have one week to get ready for the Grateday celebration and then, we'll have one week after that before school starts again. Most animals spend the second week travelling, visiting family members living far away, or simply exploring new places. My parents usually take this week off from working in the bakery but this year they said they'd rather wait until I'm done with my school year to avoid distracting me. I would have loved the distraction, to be honest, but at least I won't be spending it alone since all my best friends are staying here too. Wind is going to see some cousins but apparently he'll only be gone the first week and Honeysuckle told me it's too much work for her parents to travel with all her brothers and sisters.

I use my first week of holidays to make sure all my gifts are ready when Grateday comes. I may be a quiet squirrel but I have a lot of animals to thank. Are you ready for the longest gifts list you've ever seen in your life? Yes I'm talking about a list longer than the animals with prickles!

So here's what I made this year:

For my parents I made a big frame to hang in the bakery with a picture of us three making funny faces. I decorated the whole frame with paint, little shiny stones that I find at Dreams and some slices of dried oranges. I also baked them some orange muffins, which was tricky because I had to do it without their help while they were at work.

For Buttercup, I wrote down some of my stories in a little book. He's always asking me to write them down somewhere so I took some time to do this just for him.

I asked Tulip for help to make Almond's gift because I sewed her a bag that would be easy for her to carry when she's running around the forest. She often goes running for hours and forgets to take food with her.

I made a fruit tart for Uncle Basil and Auntie Dahlia, and I have a batch of orange-flavoured chocolate for Tulip, Apricot and Violet.

Handmade bookmarks for Honeysuckle and the Baileys.

I made Wind a wooden chest so he could keep all his crafts and supplies in it at Dreams. He's still keeping this a secret from his parents so it's better if he can leave everything there, not at home. I had to go to Roots' workshop to make this and it was such a great experience. I've never made anything with wood before and I was a bit scared of messing it up but he explained everything so well and I'm really happy with the result. I also painted his name on it to make it really personal.

Mrs Winter will be gone for the whole break so I'll give her a "thank you for being the best teacher" card when we go back to school.

And for Miss Moon and Hazelnut, I baked their favourite cookies (with my parent's help).

So, as you can imagine this first week of preparation was very busy! The trickiest part is making all these gifts without the recipients seeing me. And knowing who to ask help from. I think it's important to ask for other's advice as it's not a weakness to admit you don't know everything! Plus you can also offer your own help when it's needed. Although I don't know how my big appetite (for food and for books) can help others.

So I spent my whole week going back and forth between our home, Dreams, and Sweet Treat while trying to keep some time for myself to read by the lake. My nightly meet-ups under the stars with Almond and Buttercup have been really funny because we all want to talk about the gifts we're preparing without revealing the surprises we're making for each other. There are a lot of sudden silences and awkward giggles.

No matter how much I love preparing for Grateday, nothing beats waking up on Grateday morning. It even feels like the air has a unique kind of smell! Oh wait, actually it's not in my head, there is a different kind of smell because my parents made our special Grateday breakfast and the air is filled with this delicious orange smell that we only get once a year. I stretch and climb down our tree with a big smile as I see my parents setting our morning table a bit farther away than our usual one. Even though we share the kitchen space with the Dreamcreeks and we eat together very often, this is the only day when we make sure we all have our own family time. So we let them have the big tables and we set a smaller table for the three of us a bit farther away.

"Happy Grateday!" I tell them as soon as I reach them.

"Happy Grateday honey!" they both reply and we all come together in a tight hug. This is my absolute favourite moment of the year, this one right here. My parents and I kiss and hug a lot but this one hug, shared together is a special one. I always close my eyes for it, rejoicing in the warm feeling and sugary smell that comes from both of them. When we let go, we always tell each other a heartfelt "thank you for being here". It may sound simple but it means so much. We smile at each other before my mum asks, "Who's hungry?"

I laugh at this and jump up and down on the spot, drooling at the sight of all the food they've already brought on the table.

"Mmm ... everything looks delicious! But you should have waited for me to help you set everything up."

"We didn't want to wake you up sweetie," she says.

"But it's ok, you can help us tidy up after," my dad winks at me.

We spend hours eating our special breakfast slowly. We take our time, eating while exchanging family stories, playing guessing games and exchanging gifts. I'm glad to see that they love my frame and the cupcakes I made them. But they give me the best gift: they made me a scrapbook with pictures of me as a cute baby and tons of little anecdotes about me as a tiny squirrel, about my birth, my first steps, the time I learned how to read. They even included some pictures of me with my best friends when we were little (well, smaller that we are now!) playing outside the bakery and near the lake.

"And we left a lot of space so you can add pictures of your new friends and your new adventures," my mum says, all snuggled up against my dad.

"It's perfect, I love it so much! Thank you!"

We finish our morning with another one of our family traditions: every year on Grateday we spend some time reading aloud to each other. We always pick up a new story for this occasion and this year my dad chose a book called Fortunately the Milk by a man called Neil Gaiman. Judging by his picture on the cover, he has a lot of black hair that looks very fluffy. I don't know if it's as fluffy as my tail but my dad says he writes great books.

We spend an hour taking turns reading it and all three of us have so much fun with it! It's the story of a dad who has a lot of adventures (with aliens, dinosaurs, pirates, time travel...) while he's out to get some milk for his children. My parents and I all love to make the voices, so it's hilarious to see everyone's version of the same characters. Once we're done reading, I tell Dad that he picked a great book. I'll have to remember to check if I can find some of Neil Gaiman's other books at Dreams.

"Ok," my mum says as she yawns and stretches her paws in the air, "Time to tidy up and get ready for the Celebration!"

We tidy up the food, the book and our gifts, and meet up with the Dreamcreek family in the kitchen. With a little magic the dishes and leftovers are quickly cleaned and we start to pack our baskets to bring over to the Celebration. There's some planning to do since we have to bring over a lot of food and gifts. Thankfully we have a little four wheeled trolley that we can use for these kinds of occasions. As usual my parents are bringing too much food but it's never wasted since the leftovers will be given to the hospital for the sick animals. We're also bringing a big pot of hot cocoa which will stay at the perfect temperature all day thanks to magic!

I have wrapped all my gifts in nice rice paper so no one will be able to peek at their gifts on our way there. Once everything is ready to go, we all head to Whimskle clearing together, talking about our morning on the way.

"What did your parents give you, Applesauce?" Violet asks me.

"A great photo album. I'll show it to you once we're there, I took it with me in my bag. What about you guys? What did your parents make for you?"

They all take turns talking about the gifts they exchanged with their parents. There are so many of them that it's a bit hard to keep track of who offered what to who but in the end they are all very happy with what they got. Even though we live next to each other, we always wait to be at the Celebration to exchange our gifts. It makes it more special.

When we arrive at the clearing I see the big cotton banner

hanging between the trees, saying "Be grateful for what others have given you, smile at what you have and be there for the ones who need you".

And just below, a smaller banner saying, "Happy Grateday!"

Chapter 30
The celebration

O nce at Whimskle, I help my parents bring the food to the main area, which has several tables of different sizes where all the food is set. The whole clearing is filled with chairs, benches, logs, cushions and blankets on the grass. There are even some hammocks between the trees for those who want to rest after lunch. Since the Celebration goes on until night time, everyone usually eats small portions throughout the entire event, instead of having one regular sized lunch and dinner. I love this idea and how relaxed this day is. Once the food is set, my friends and I go to look for a place to sit together. We don't have to look for long because Almond has been running around as soon as we arrived, trying to find the perfect place for us all.

"Come over there, we can put the blankets under this big oak tree."

"Great idea!"

Almond always knows how to find the best spots to hide, sit or relax! We set down two big blankets on the grass and install some fluffy cushions for everyone. For now it's just me, Buttercup, and his sisters but it will evolve. The girls will go and spend some time with their own friends. Tulip made a lot of friends when she was at school and even more after she graduated. She's so talented at making clothes and accessories, she's met a lot of animals interested in her work in the forest and beyond. And of course Wind and Honeysuckle will join me once they arrive, and I guess we'll also see Almond and Buttercup's friends from school. Like I said, it's very relaxed, everyone can come and go without stress.

Once we're all seated, Almond immediately screams "Gift time!" We all laugh at her enthusiasm and take out the presents we made for each other.

"Who wants to start?" Buttercup asks. Every year it's the same organisational problem since there are six of us with a present to give to five others. Everyone starts to talk at the same time with their ideas until Apricot comes to the rescue!

"Since I'm the eldest, this year I thought of a plan!"

We all look at her with curiosity and see her place a glass jar in the middle of our circle.

"I've written all the combinations of possible pairs in our group on pieces of paper, so we can go one by one, without wondering who's supposed to go next."

She picks one piece of folded paper from the jar and continues "For example, this piece of paper says 'Almond and Buttercup' so that means they can go ahead and exchange their gifts first. What do you think?"

She may be the eldest but she's not bossy and always makes sure we're all on board with her ideas. Everyone seems happy with this plan. So simple and effective, I wonder why we didn't think about it before! The Dreamcreek siblings exchanged gifts with their parents in the morning but waited for the Celebration to give their presents to each other. So we start with Almond and Buttercup, and I smile at the cuteness of Almond's gift for her brother. She made him a little hedgehog out of a pinecone and sticks. She used some cut pieces of wood to make his tiny paws and she even painted a grey mark on one of his wooden ears. It's so adorable and quite remarkable for someone like Almond who, in general, can't stay still long enough to make crafts.

"Thank you, I love it!!"

"It looks just like you Buttercup!" The sisters joke and we all laugh.

In exchange, Buttercup made her a watercolour portrait and she loves it so much that she's speechless. It's really pretty indeed and he managed to capture her unique spirit.

We go on, picking the next names in the jar one-by-one and the gifts are all as thoughtful as those first ones. Violet has baked everyone their favourite dishes, which is so personal I don't even know what to say. She acts like it's nothing but I know it must have been time consuming to cook like this for us all.

I'm the first one to receive my gift from Apricot and she hands it to me with an apologetic face. "Sorry, you know I'm not great at making gifts."

"Don't be silly, I'm sure it's great!"

I open it quickly and find a nice wooden frame with a picture of us all that her dad took a few months ago. She decorated mine with tiny pinecones glued all around and used some magic to make them shine with a special light. It looks like there are some tiny fireflies all around the pinecones.

"It's so pretty, I love it, Apricot! How did you do all that?" I ask her, still impressed.

"Oh it's not much," she replies modestly. "I collected some pinecones, cleaned and polished them, and used magic to reduce them to fit on the frame."

"Those are real pinecones?"

She nods. They look so neat and tiny I thought they were just from the craft store. But no of course, Apricot made those with magic. She's so good at magic, she uses it for everything.

"This light spell is one you'll learn in the Flower class. But wait, you haven't seen the best part of it yet," she says, now proud of herself. She gets closer to me and presses the cute orange gem on the bottom part of the frame, in the middle. I just assumed it was a decoration and didn't realise it had a purpose. As soon as she presses it, a new picture appears in the frame and everyone in our little group is impressed.

"You can store up to fifty pictures in it. Next time I'll work on a way to set it so it can change pictures on its own at regular intervals but for now you'll have to press the button to do it yourself."

"Waouh, that's impressive and so pretty!"

Even though Apricot claims not to be a crafty hedgehog she still took the time to make all our frames unique by choosing different decorations for each of us. For her sister Tulip, for example, she glued some tiny objects related to fashion and sewing. There are some bits of pretty fabric, cute buttons and the whole frame is surrounded by a measuring tape.

Tulip has made everyone a scarf, each one made with wool in the recipient's favourite colour. So when I start unwrapping her gift I'm really surprised to find that I'm not getting a scarf! I look at her surprised and she smiles at me.

"I think you'll find this useful for your reading sessions by the lake," she explains as she gestures to me to keep unwrapping it. I do and that's when I find the softest blanket ever. On one side it's all orange with a soft fabric but she tells me to turn it over and I gasp because the other side is a patchwork. It's covered with squares of fabric, all representing things I love: my family, my friends, books, pies, cookies and Woodland!

"And look," she adds, "I magicked it so when you pull on the cord here it will wrap on itself and become lighter without you having to enchant it again."

"Waouh!" I turn to Buttercup and tell him, "It's so perfect I think your sister might steal your spot as my best friend!"

We all laugh but Buttercup just answers with a smile, "Well, in that case, I guess I can keep the gift I made you?"

"No, no, no I want to see it!"

But I still have to wait my turn to see what gift he made me for Grateday. Before I get to open his present, the cards we draw tell me to open Violet's gift. She has made me a chocolate tart and, just like her sisters, she loves the chocolates and cards I made for her. I knew it was easy to please the Dreamcreek sisters with chocolates but I was afraid they wouldn't turn out as well as my parents'. But judging by their faces I think they taste good so I'm relieved.

Then I give Almond her bag, which she loves and tries on right away. In exchange, she has made me a squirrel out of pinecones and pipe cleaners. She painted the pinecone orange to match my colour, used the pipe cleaners for my paws and soft pom-poms for my face with funny googly eyes. To make my soft tail, she has used another pipe cleaner as the foundation and covered it with the sof orange feathers with a hint of grey in the middle.

"Look at how she did my tail," I show the group. "It's so fluffy!"

"Sorry I couldn't get your grey mark well."

"Are you kidding? You did a great job!"

And everyone agrees with me!

All those gifts are really great but I can't wait to give Buttercup his and at last the jar is empty except for the last paper with "Buttercup- Applesauce" on it. Finally!

I hand him his gift and explain, "You're always asking me to write them down, so here they are, just for you."

And he understands right away when he sees the notebook. I didn't have a title so I simply named it *Stories, by Applesauce.*

"Oh thank you Applesauce! How did you remember them all? It's amazing!"

It seems I have a good memory when it comes to stories: the ones I read and the ones I tell. I wish I had the same ability to remember things my parents tell me. Buttercup hands me his gift and of course it's beautiful. It's another watercolour painting, like the one he did of his sisters. Mine is a bit more detailed though.

He's painted me with a pile of books, all curled up and reading in my favourite spot near the lake. And in the background he's painted a wreath made of autumn leaves, pinecones, and acorns because he knows it's my favourite season. Cold enough to warm up with a nice hot drink but not too cold that it's really annoying. And he added a quote from Anne of Green Gables, "I'm so glad I live in a world where there are Octobers".

"So am I still your best friend?" Buttercup asks me with a mischievous smile.

"Of course you are! But honestly, all these gifts were amazing. I'm really touched," and I add a heartfelt "Thank you everyone!" to our small group. These presents are worth so much to me, I can't wait to find a place for them at home.

Chapter 31
Magical fire

We're all busy packing our gifts away and, just when I think this day can't get any better, I see Honeysuckle looking for us. I call her name and she waves her family goodbye. She joins our circle just as Almond, Apricot and Violet leave to find their other friends and Buttercup goes off to explore. Tulip explains that since her friends will only be there a bit later, she's going to nap before they arrive. After all the food we ate, I totally understand this, I could use a nap too! But instead I welcome my friend.

"Hey, how are you?"

"Good! And you? Have you eaten already? "she asks me.

"Yes, we have."

"Argh, I wanted to arrive early but it's always a mess to leave the house with all my brothers and sisters. I hope there's still some food left at least."

I laugh at this. "Of course there is, don't worry! There's always plenty of food to last the whole day. I'll come with you and get some more food for me."

"Really? You don't mind eating again?"

"Don't you know who you're talking to?" I answer with a fake offended expression that makes her laugh.

"Yes, sorry! Ok let's get some food then, I'm starving!"

She drops her bag next to mine on the blanket and we head over to the buffet part of the Celebration. Honeysuckle is surprised by how big it is.

"I had no idea it would be so big! And I didn't realise the whole forest would be there too, it's incredible."

"Oh yeah I forgot that it's your first Grateday! What do you think?"

"I love it! It's so nice to see everyone gather together like this, eating and exchanging gifts. I saw a lot of friends exchanging theirs when I was looking for you. Did you get yours already?"

"Yep! We did it with my parents this morning, and we just finished with Buttercup and his sisters."

As we fill our bowls with food, I tell her what gifts I received. I see some dishes have been added since my first lunch, so I help myself to them.

"Waouh, what a lot of gifts you got! I'm glad I don't have too many friends yet because I couldn't have made that many gifts," she laughs awkwardly and I reassure her.

"Oh don't worry about it. It's not about the gifts, it's the thought that counts."

"I didn't really know what to make. For you it was easy but for the rest, I made a lot of cards and … well, I hope it's enough?"

"Of course it is!"

Once our plates are full we go back to our spot and eat in silence, listening to the sound of the other animals around us. I love being with Honeysuckle because, just like Buttercup, she never minds silence. We can have a great time talking together but she can also appreciate silence. Once we're done with our food I'm excited to give her her gift.

"You say you're always losing them so here…" I hand her the collection of bookmarks I made her, all wrapped up in colourful gift paper.

"Oh it's lovely!" She looks at them one by one and reads the quotes I calligraphed on them. "And you picked quotes from my favourite books? Oh it's perfect, I love it so much! Thank you!"

She gives me a quick hug and hands me a small package wrapped nicely.

"Sorry it's not much but I hope you find it useful."

I open her package all excited and I'm a bit puzzled at first when I see a notebook. It's quite a simple one, but sturdy and I'm trying to understand what she meant by "useful" when she tells me to turn it around and to look inside. When I see the title I finally understand. On the cover it says "All the books I've read." She wrote it delicately with some black paint and under it, painted a pile of books with another one lying open on the side.

"Waouh did you paint those?" I ask her.

"Yes, it's not my specialty but I didn't know how to turn this into a handmade gift so I tried my best to decorate the cover. Oh and the pages inside too."

I open the notebook and I'm surprised to see that she has added some book related doodles on the bottom of every page. A feather here, a bookshelf there, and some simple drawings of characters we love. I spot Paddington, Willy Wonka's golden ticket, Anne Shirley's house ... I also notice that she has divided the notebook into two parts with a handmade cardboard tab.

"See, it's so you can write down the books you've already read in this part and the ones you want to read in the second part."

"Oh that's brilliant! It's a great idea and a perfect way for me to keep track of all the books I want to read. Thanks, I really love it!"

Once we've exchanged our gifts, we lie down on the blanket, chatting about our favourite memories with our family and things that happened to us when we were younger. Once the conversation dies a bit, I lie there thinking about how nice it is to be here with the light breeze, the smell of food around us and the knowledge that I have so many kind animals in my life. I doze off for a short time before being woken up by some noise. I open my eyes to see Dahlia and Basil stop by to give me my gift (a bag of nut cake bars) and I hand them the orange cake I made for them. Later, while Honeysuckle is busy eating a second serving of apple pie, I see the Moon sisters pass by us and call them over to give them the cookies I made for them.

"Have you been to the game area yet?" Hazelnut asks us.

"No, what game area?" asks Honeysuckle, surprised.

I tell her that there are some game booths and even a small concert area in the north corner of the Celebration.

"Really? Oh great! Let's go have a look!"

We say goodbye to the sisters, and leave all our food and gifts on our blanket. Once there, we meet up again with Buttercup and Almond, and spend two hours playing games like bean bag toss, apple bobbing and pick-a-duck. Sometimes, when we are between games, we go to listen to the local artists playing music on the stage nearby. There's a rotation of bands singing their own songs and animals of all ages playing instruments. Some are even using magic to play music. We also chat with the neighbours and school friends we meet. Smore is having lots of fun at the apple bobbing booth, Jasmin is killing it at the ring toss area, and Paprika and Parsnip are racing with Almond a bit farther away.

Once the sun is setting down and we've had our dinner, I take my wooden chest to go give my thanks to our Ancestors.

"Do you want to come and do it with me?" I ask my friends.

Almond has already given thanks to her ancestors but Honeysuckle and Buttercup agree to tag along. I know Buttercup likes to write his list on a nice roll of parchment and I see that Honeysuckle has written hers on a postcard.

"Is it okay like that?" she asks me, a bit worried. "I was not sure what to write mine on."

"Yes, don't worry, it's perfect. As long as you write what you're grateful for and burn it in the Ancestors' fire, that's all that matters."

We walk up the hill to reach the special fire the Great Wizard lit earlier and I smile at the beautiful sight in front of me. A lot of us love to wait for night time to burn their list so they can meet around the fire with a drink. I go first to reassure Honeysuckle and show her how simple it is. I approach the fire, close my eyes and say, "Ancestors, I present to you the joys, big or small of my life. I'm thankful for them and for all the deeds others have done for me."

As I toss my list in the fire, a purple flame sparkles to let me know it has been received. This year I had a lot to be thankful for, between the school, my friends (old and new), my parents and Berry. I always like to add little details for the Ancestors and make my list as personal as possible.

Once I'm done I step back and go wait for my friends on a log a bit farther away. Not so close that I bother the animals waiting for their turn, but close enough to feel the nice warmth emanating from the fire.

Just as I'm thinking that I should have brought some hot drinks for us to drink around the fire, I see my parents arrive on the hill with their wagon behind them. They go around offering cups of their amazing hot chocolate to everyone sitting on the hill. Everyone is delighted by this gift but no one seems surprised by their kindness. By the time my two friends are done burning their list, my mum comes to our little group and hands us three mugs. Between the familiar smell of the chocolate and the heat of the cup, it's the perfect way to end this day. And as I drink my cocoa, I think what a lucky squirrel I am: an amazing family and great friends! What else could I ask for?

Chapter 32

An unexpected encounter

Once the Grateday celebrations are behind us we still have a week off school and, even though I'd like to do nothing but read and eat all day, I remember that I have to think of an idea for my Special Project! Today I'm hoping to get inspired by rereading my spell book and all the notes I took since I started Woodland Academy. I'm trying to imagine what I could do to improve the lives of those around me but all my ideas seem useless or already exist. It takes me a while to reread all this but having Tulip's blanket to cuddle under gives me some courage. After spending the morning like this in my room, I go down to make myself a quick lunch with the leftovers from the Grateday food we received as gifts yesterday. By chance I spot Buttercup coming back from his morning stroll just before I enter the kitchen.

"Hey, are you hungry? I was about to have lunch."

"Sure, I was coming home to eat too. I'll make us some tea," he offers, as I start to gather a bit of everything on a tray for us to bring outside. Buttercup's parents left a small fire near the eating area before leaving for work this morning so we won't get cold. Once we have a selection of food on the table, we start eating and talking about our morning. After he tells me that he met Bloom and Bean during his walk I explain to him that I started my research for our project.

"What about you? Do you have any ideas yet?"

He shakes his head, his mouth full and says, "No, nothing yet. With all the preparation for Grateday, I didn't have time to really think about it. So, did rereading your notes help you?"

"No, I still got nothing," I admit, a bit disappointed.

"Maybe we should ask our parents," Buttercup suggests.

"To do our work?" I ask, shocked.

"No," he smiles a bit, "but we could ask them what their projects were. It might give us ideas."

"Oh yes, that's a good idea. I've never asked them."

We chat a bit more and just as we're tidying up and ready to take everything back to the kitchen, Honeysuckle arrives with a big smile.

"Hey guys! How are you?"

"Great and you? Do you want something to eat? We just finished but we can put something together for you if you want," Buttercup offers her. He's such a kind friend.

"Oh, no, thank you, I ate so much yesterday I think I'm still digesting."

We both laugh. "Yes, we know the feeling! What have you been doing?"

"Nothing yet. I was hoping to sleep in but my youngest brother was awake very early, so I took care of him to let my parents sleep. And then there were some chores to do. I only just managed to escape now and was planning on going to read by the lake. You want to join me?" she asks us.

"Sure! Buttercup?"

'Great idea! I'll grab my new easel so I can paint by the lake, it should inspire me."

We quickly pack up our trolley with books, two blankets, a snack, some drinks and Buttercup's painting supplies, then get going. On our way Buttercup asks Honeysuckle if she has any ideas for her school project but she only gives us a mysterious answer.

"Maybe ..." she says.

Buttercup and I look at each other, puzzled.

"Can you tell us what it is?" I ask.

She stops on the road to think about it, wiggling her long white ears and her tiny nose.

"No, not yet."

"Why? Is it a secret?" I joke.

"For now, yes, "she replies, all serious.

"Really?" I'm so surprised, it's not like her to keep secrets. I'm a bit bothered by this and ask her why.

"Is it secret because you think it's a terrible idea or because you're afraid we're going to steal it?"

"No, of course I'm not scared of that. No, it's a secret because ..." She pauses for dramatic effect, "First, I think it'll be better if you are still surprised on the presentation day. And second, I'm not actually sure I'm allowed to do it so I'd rather not have you involved in all this if it turns out to be ..."

Another long pause. I think she's enjoying the drama a bit too much, "... illegal!"

She finishes this last bit with an exaggerated whisper, like someone might be spying on us.

"Illegal? What are you talking about? What kind of project is that?" I ask all excited, curious and frustrated at the same time.

"You'll see," she just adds with a wink just as we arrive near the lake, at our favourite spot. I try to ask her more questions but Buttercup says it's useless.

"She won't tell us anything for now. Besides, it could be fun if it's a surprise!"

Argh I hate it when my best friend is right!

"Come on, sit down and stop being all moody."

Honeysuckle laughs as we place our blankets on the ground. As usual, we quickly get lost in our books and Buttercup in his painting. All is quiet until, out of nowhere Buttercup jumps on us and tells us to hide. Hide? Why? This could only mean one thing: humans!

We quickly hide our books, our art supplies and our bodies between the tree and the water so they can't see us. We stay very silent, waiting for them to pass and leave. I hear their footsteps getting louder, closer and closer to us, and I can tell from their voices that there are only two of them. I think they sound like adults but it's tough for me to hear the difference between young and old humans. They're so close now that we start to hear bits of their conversation. I love to listen to human conversations because they give me ideas for my nightly stories.

"Look at this, it's so beautiful out there, isn't it?" says Human Number One and I have to agree with him.

"It is! I love coming here! Especially in this weather, it's perfect. A bit chilly but not too cold yet. It's the perfect time to have a stroll in the woods and go home to a hot tea."

"Oh yeah I know! And today we get to go home, and snuggle under the blanket with our new books! It's the definition of a perfect Sunday!"

Books? Snuggle under a blanket to read? Oh I know what they mean and I agree with whoever is talking. If I was not scared of humans I'd go to them and have a nice chat about books. Well, IF I was not afraid of them, AND IF they could understand animals AND IF they could accept that animals can do way more things than humans realise. Ok, maybe that's too many "if's.

"I still can't believe someone put this free library in the forest. It's brilliant! I've read online about boxes that allow people to exchange books but I've never seen one before. We'll have to remember to come back to put new books in exchange next time. I always have some to give away."

"Really? Oh, I have such a hard time letting go of my books. I don't know how you do it," Human number two replies.

"Well, obviously I don't give away my favourite books, only the ones I don't want to reread. I think it's ok to pass them on to someone else who could enjoy them."

"Oh yeah, I never thought about it like that."

"And there are always books that I don't like. Remember that book that everyone was talking about last year but was ..."

They're getting too far for me to hear the rest now. As usual, we wait a bit more before coming out of our hiding place. Once we do, we set all our things back on the ground but I can't help thinking about the conversation I just heard. They were talking about a library and a box to exchange books. I must look like I'm daydreaming because Buttercup asks me if I'm ok.

"What? Oh yes, I ..." I mumble, still lost in my thoughts. "I was thinking about the humans."

"They were too big for my taste as usual," Buttercup jokes. "It scares me how they walk on their two legs like this, looking so tall compared to us."

It's true that he doesn't like humans very much. Honeysuckle, on the other hand, doesn't seem to mind them, even though she's only seen a few of them since she moved to Woodland.

"I don't know, I like them. I think they're funny looking with their big heads and long arms hanging along their body like ... like two snakes with fingers," she says.

"Big heads?" I ask her, half laughing.

"Yeah, compared to us their heads look ginormous," She jokes as she settles down, trying to find her previous reading position again.

"Anyway, I was thinking about their conversation. They were talking about a library. They seemed to say it was here, in the woods. Do you think that's possible?"

"Well, I saw them carrying a few books so I guess they did go to a library."

"You did?"

"Yes I couldn't help myself and had a peak."

"Honeysuckle! You're supposed to be careful around humans, you know? My parents always say it's best not to look at them."

"Why? Do they have dangerous X-ray vision or shoot missiles?" she jokes, while imitating laser beams shooting out of her own eyes with her tiny paws.

"No but you never know how they'll treat you. I know they are fine in books but here in the woods you always have to be careful. They could ..."

"They could what?"

"I don't know. Come and pet you maybe?" I suggest. "I honestly don't know but you have to be careful."

"Well, it's fine. They can come and pet me, I won't mind!" she replies with an overconfident smile while lying down and reopening her book.

I try to go back to my own reading but my thoughts keep going back to this library the humans were discussing. I'm wondering if it's possible for a library to exist outdoors and I'm trying to picture what it would look like. Five minutes pass in silence as we're lost in our activities and our thoughts. Then Honeysuckle sits up and asks us cheerfully, "Should we go and check it out?"

"Check what out?"

"This library thing they were talking about," she replies, like it's totally obvious.

"What? Now?"

"Yes now! Why? Do you have something else planned for today?"

"No but …" I'm trying to think of a reason not to go exploring an unknown part of the forest on a whim like this.

"But we can't go today, we have the trolley with us!" Buttercup finishes for me.

I look at him and thank him with a smile. He must have guessed I wouldn't be comfortable with a last minute plan like this, even if it's with my closest friends.

"Oh yeah," Honeysuckle's face falls as she realises he's right. "You're right, it wouldn't be convenient."

"But we can plan it for another day though!" Buttercup offers, looking at me with a tentative smile.

He's right, we could try later. "Another day" is fine because it can be anytime in the future, no pressure. It gives me the feeling that I could do it while actually staying safe and sound at home. I admit I'm very curious about this library and the notion of free books. I mean, just the notion of books, free or not, is exciting! But I'm also very nervous about exploring unknown territory.

"Yes! Let's do that, let's go tomorrow!" Honeysuckle decides.

"Tomorrow? What? Why? Don't you think it's a bit too early?" I ask, panicked.

"I didn't say we should go at sunrise silly!" she teases me.

"What? Sunrise? I-" Oh, I finally get her joke. "No, I mean … I'm not sure we should go."

"Come on, live a little! Aren't you bored of always staying here and only getting your books from Dreams?"

"No!" I answer faithfully. Who could ever be bored of our forest or of Dreams?

"Ok. Then, aren't you curious at least?"

"Yes" I admit. "But are we sure it's safe to go? We don't even know where it is..."

"Applesauce, come on, it's fine!"she says, full of confidence. "You know, the world is bigger than Woodland forest! I used to live outside, I know my way around. Trust me! Besides, remember what Mrs Winter said. That our magic needs to live and that we need to experience new things in order to be inspired. I'm sure it will be a great way to find inspiration for our projects! None of you have any ideas so far, right?"

We both nod.

"Yeah, I don't have anything yet," I admit.

"And maybe we can plan some snacks and make a day out of it! Oh! It could be so fun! What do you think? Come on guys, say yes! There will be books and food! You can't say no!"

Honeysuckle's big smile and very excited expression are very hard to resist and make me cave. I finally agree to go and "live a little" as she said.

"Well if you tempt me with the promise of books and food, of course I'm in!" I reply with a smile.

"Speaking of food," I say standing up, "I need to go home and prepare some dinner for tonight. My parents must have been busy today so I want to make sure they have nothing to do when they come home from work."

I start packing and Buttercup follows my lead.

"I'll come with you, I need to do some reading about my project. I feel bad for not working on it today."

"I think I'll stay here a bit longer," Honeysuckle says. "I'll see you tomorrow and we can plan our trip!"

"Great! See you Honeysuckle!"

Chapter 33
A plan is formed

As I imagined, my parents come back from the bakery exhausted. After spending the week preparing all the food and handmade gifts for Grateday, it's a bit tough for them to go back to work right away. They're used to having this week off but since they preferred to postpone our annual trip until I'm done with my first year of school, they had to go back without any rest. And as usual they helped so much at the Celebration yesterday, I don't think they had time to unwind much. They can't help themselves, they always go around assisting everyone, making sure everything's okay, and handing out drinks and snacks to the Woodland residents.

"But you see, honey, we know so many local families through the shop and it's hard not to offer a little something to our faithful customers!" Mum explained to me one time. "Since we can't go and make gifts for all our acquaintances, serving drinks and snack food like this is our way to say thank you to everyone."

On the other hand, when I see how full the kitchen always gets after Grateday, I know that their kindness does not go unnoticed. Our table and counters are covered with tins of biscuits, bottles of alcohol and cards made just for them. They are so loved in the forest. Miss Palmer always makes them some jam and I can tell you, it never lasts long. Especially spread on my dad's bread, yummy!

I'm happy to welcome them with dinner all ready to go if it makes their day a bit easier. The smile on their faces when they see the food waiting for them on the table says it all.

"Oh sweetie, that's so nice of you!" My mum comes to hug me as soon as she sees it.

"It's ok, it's not much Mum. I just made a salad and a pumpkin soup."

"Not much? You made my favourite soup!"

I laugh at this, "Mum, every soup is your favourite!"

My Dad smiles at this and tells me as he comes to hug me, "It's the best thing with your mum, she's so easy to please!"

The Dreamcreek family usually eats earlier than us, so dinner is just the three of us, with our little magic fire burning next to the table to keep us warm. We eat quietly together and talk about our day but I decide not to tell them about our encounter with the humans and the library story. My mum is a cheerful squirrel but she gets easily scared when we talk about humans. She says they're not reliable. Of course I'm not talking about you, reader, I'm sure you're nice. It's just my mum's opinion, not mine!

After our quiet dinner, Buttercup meets me in the kitchen to prepare our evening drinks and we go to our secret fort to meet Almond. I haven't seen her at all today so we catch up and tell her about our close encounter with the humans.

"Humans? Really? Oh I haven't seen any in a long time!" she says, all excited by our story. It's surprising since she's the one in our group who should fear humans the most, after losing both her parents to hunters but she doesn't see life like this. She never stereotypes humans as "the bad guys" or "scary." I asked her about it one time and she told me something touching.

"You know, the way I see it, I think it's not about humans versus animals or if they are good or scary. I think there are good humans like there are good animals. But there are also some awful ones in both groups. No side is perfect. My parents had the misfortune to encounter dangerous humans but it doesn't mean they are all like that. And think about those books you read. Those writers can't be in the scary category if they wrote your favourite books, can they? I think life is just a mix of both, whether you walk on two legs, have four paws or no paws at all."

Just as we're recounting the human's conversation about the library, Honeysuckle jumps into our story. And I mean, she literally jumps into it because she enters our fort suddenly with a hop and finishes Buttercup's sentence for him.

"And then I jumped on the humans and scared them away!"she lies to Almond.

"What? Really?" Almond asks, obviously surprised. She's cute, she trusts her friends so much that she believes anything we tell her. We laugh and tell her that, no, that's not how the encounter ended.

"Oh, way less dramatic then" she says once we tell her the real story.

"Hey Honeysuckle, what are you doing here?" I ask her. And now that I think about it, how did she find us here? She's never been to one of our nightly meetings.

"Oh, I came to tell you something and your parents told me you guys were here."

We all look at her, waiting, wondering what was so important that she came all this way to tell us at night, but she makes us wait by slowly nibbling on a biscuit.

"Come on, tell us your story!" I finally cave. "We're dying to know! What has happened to you since we saw you this afternoon?"

She gives us a wicked smile, finishes her biscuit and finally tells us.

"Well, after you left I couldn't help thinking about this library thing."

Same, I think.

"So ... I went to try to find it! "she announces, so proud of herself.

"What? You went alone? Why?" Buttercup asks.

"Waouh!" Almond says in an admiring voice.

I'm so confused that I don't say anything. She went there alone? Without planning anything? How? My small nervous squirrel brain can't picture that she wanted to go so she simply went. If I have to do something out of my comfort zone I usually have to plan and think about it for days before it's even an option.

"Well, I thought it would be easier for us to find it tomorrow if

I already knew exactly where it is."

Tomorrow? Did we say we were going there tomorrow? Are we really doing this?

"So tell us! Did you find it? What is it exactly? Is it far from the lake?"

Now I can't stop the questions from flowing out of my mouth. She laughs at my enthusiasm and replies in order.

"So, yes, I did find it. What is it?" She settles down comfortably on one of our cushions to think a bit. "Well, it's a big wooden box with a door and a roof."

"A roof? Why?"

"Applesauce, let her finish!" Buttercup tells me, smiling at my impatience.

"Yeah, there's a roof but I don't think there's a purpose for it, it's just there to look like a human house. And there's a door to protect the books but it's a glass door so you can see the books from outside. And there's a wooden sign explaining how it works-"

"How ..." I start to ask but remember to just wait for her explanation. "Sorry, I'm too excited about this."

"So the sign says that the books are here for free and that you can take as many as you want. You don't have to put a new book back in exchange but the main idea is to have a rotation so it's never empty. You can exchange one book for another one, or more, if you want. It also says that you can bring new books later and ... what else? Oh yes, you can also bring back the books you borrowed after reading them or you can keep them. And that's it, basically. Seems pretty simple."

Indeed it seems simple. I love this idea and I wonder who put the box there.

"Is it far? Where is it in Woodland?"

As soon as I ask my last question I see Honeysuckle's expression change.

"Well, about that ... It's not exactly in Woodland. It's a bit farther."

"How much farther?"

"I don't know ..." she's fidgeting with the corner of the blanket under us, "I didn't time my trip but I think it was called Black Shadow Forest. Does it ring any bells for you? It was written on the box. Black Shadow Small Library or something like that."

"Black Shadow? Are you crazy?"

"What? Why? Is it haunted or something?" she jokes.

Buttercup, Almond and I all look at each other. Buttercup explains the story to her with a low and serious voice.

"Well, no, it's not haunted ... I mean, probably not. But there are lots of stories about this forest, so no one dares to go there."

"Stories? What kind of stories? "she asks, half amused, half curious.

"Mmmm, there's the one about the bear who went there to hibernate and never woke up."

"What? He died?"

"No, he just never woke up from hibernation. Legend says he's still there."

"Yes. Actually, that's why local bears don't hibernate anymore. They're so scared they might wind up staying in an eternal sleep, they stopped doing it years ago," Almond adds.

"What? But that's ridiculous!" Honeysuckle cries. "It's just a story."

"Well, next time you see Wind, ask him about the bear of Black Shadow Forest and you'll see his reaction."

"There's also the tale of the silent badger. The story says that he went through the Black Shadow Forest and when he came out, he couldn't speak anymore."

We all nod at this story that we've heard many times.

"Oh and there was the weird story about the invisible lion!"

"A lion? Here? No, that has to be made up!" Honeysuckle exclaims loudly at this. "There's no way it's true."

"Yeah, I'm not sure about this one either to be honest ..." Buttercup says.

"But there's the story of Miss Pamplemousse, you know the Flower class teacher? No one knows how a hen came to live in the forest. And all alone."

"No one has ever asked her?"

"Well, that's the thing, she doesn't know herself. She says she has no memories of coming to Woodland Forest. Some say it's because she went through the Black Shadow Forest and it took her memories away."

We're all silent for a beat until Honeysuckle says, "Honestly, I think those are just stories made up by adults to scare kids and prevent them from going too far outside our forest."

I think about it and look at my friends, trying to guess what they're thinking.

"Mmm, yeah all of those stories do seem strange," Almond starts.

"Yes, they all sound so exaggerated that they're probably fake," Buttercup continues.

"But what about Miss Pamplemousse? Her story is still weird, isn't it?" I ask them. "I'm not a fan of scary stories but I still think it's strange. How did she get here without even remembering it?"

"Mmm I don't know, maybe she's faking it because she's ashamed of her past," Honeysuckle starts slowly and keeps going, suddenly very excited about her theories. "Or *maybe* she's under police protection! She helped them catch the mean fox in her old farm and they had to send her away for her own protection ..."

"Protection from what? From who?" Buttercup asks, laughing at this idea.

"From the other foxes of course!" She answers like it's obvious and we should have thought about this before. "Maybe there's a whole mafia gang of foxes that are after her and she's hiding here, pretending to be a nice teacher when actually she's a badass who put the chief of the thiefs, the famous Dark Tail, behind bars."

We all laugh at her crazy story but keep on imagining other improbable reasons why Miss Pamplemousse ended up living here, each theory crazier than the one before. Another theory of ours is that she used to be a famous rock star in a big city but the fame became too much for her so she decided to run away and hide where no one would ever know who she was! We go on like this for a bit until Almond starts yawning and we realise how late it is. We pack everything up and agree to meet tomorrow to go see the Black Shadow library.

A few hours ago I wouldn't have agreed to go there but after all the funny stories we've told each other, I don't feel that scared by this mysterious forest anymore.

"What time?" Almond asks Honeysuckle, since it was her idea.

"Mmm, I'll have to help my parents in the morning so maybe we can go after lunch?"

We all agree to meet by the lake after lunch and wave Honeysuckle good night before going back home.

Chapter 34
Preparations

Since we're only meeting after lunch, I plan to spend some time at "Dreams" this morning to look for information about Black Shadow forest. Once our parents leave for work, Buttercup and I are alone in the kitchen tidying up breakfast. When I share my plan with him, he agrees to come too.

"Great, I want to keep working on my new painting."

"Ok let me grab my bag so I can pack some food and we can go."

"Are you packing a sandwich? I thought we'd eat at the bakery."

"Oh yes, of course we'll eat there but I want to take some things with us, just to be sure ..."

"Like what?" he asks, curious.

"Well, first, I'm obviously packing some food and water for us all."

"Of course! You wouldn't be Applesauce if you weren't planning this carefully!" he winks at me.

"And I think it could be a good idea to take some invisibility potion with us too, you know, just in case. Or do you think I'm overreacting?"

"Actually, I think you're right, it's safer to take it and not use it. We never know what we'll find there. I mean, I don't think Black Shadow Forest is really haunted but still, it can't hurt to be cautious. There are more humans over there than we're used to."

I'm glad my friend approves of my idea!

"Also, I'm wondering if I should take a book to put in the library in exchange for what we'll take."

"I was thinking the same. If you don't mind carrying mine in your bag, I'm taking some books to leave there. Is there a book you don't want to keep in your collection?"

"Mmm, I'm sure I can find one or two that I didn't like enough to reread, yes."

"Ok, you go grab your bag and I'll pack us a snack."

"Great! Don't forget to pack something for Honeysuckle and Almond too."

I run out of the kitchen and up my tree to get my bag ready. I start by grabbing a bottle of invisibility potion first, thanking Mrs Winter in my head for making us prepare some in advance "just in case", as she said. Then I take a look at my bookshelf, trying to find a book or two to take with me to the Black Shadow Library. (Should I call it the BSL? Maybe not, it sounds more like a mysterious disease than a bookworm paradise.)

I usually organise my books in different categories: my favourites, the ones to be read, and the ones I have already read but won't read again. I select two from the last group and pack them in the backpack Tulip made for me for last year's Grateday. It's a bit bigger than the pouch I usually carry around the forest, so it's perfect for today's excursion. I use Berry and some magic to make them lighter and smaller to fit in my bag. I love how easily I have become used to carrying Berry with me at all times and to casting spells without having to think too much about it. I look around my cosy little room and before I get down, I grab my scarf and a small first aid pouch with some healing potions we made in class. Just in case.

I meet Buttercup back in the kitchen just as he's finishing packing two boxes of food.

"Are you ready?" I ask him.

"If you can grab the water bottle behind you on the counter, yes, I'll be good to go!"

"Great!" I put all this in my bag and Buttercup notices the scarf

I tied up on one strap of my backpack.

"Why did you take your scarf? Are you afraid to be cold?"

"Well, maybe, who knows? Maybe the weather is very different in Black Shadow Forest."

"Really? You know it's not that far from here?"

"Mmm, we don't know how close it is. Honeysuckle didn't check any distance or time so I'd rather be safe than be cold."

Buttercup laughs at my cautious nature and adds, "I don't think you'll need it but if it can make you feel better, fine!"

"Oh you laugh now but when it's so cold that we see polar bears and penguins, I'm sure you'll want a piece of my scarf too!"

I joke around and spend the time until we reach "Dreams" making up funny stories about what mysterious animals and monsters we could meet over there.

"Maybe there'll be an Ice Queen whose only weakness is that she can't stand the sight of books."

"Great, then I'm in luck if I meet this evil queen with you. You'll just have to open your bag and attack her with your books."

"Yes!" I say. "And I'll become the new hero of Black Shadow Forest because I'll be the first to defeat her. She's been terrorising the forest for decades, icing everything around her, making it impossible for food to grow and scaring everyone around..."

I stop to take a heroic pose with my paws on my sides and a serious look on my face, "Until the brave Applesauce came to save them all with his books!"

Buttercup is laughing so hard at my silly stories that he's having a hard time breathing properly. When he finally catches his breath he says, "You should really write all your stories down."

"I did, it was your Grateday gift!"

"No, not just for me, to share with others. Don't keep those stories in your head."

Once at Dreams, both Miss Moon and Hazelnut are very busy with customers, library users and a knitting workshop. They don't have time for us so I have to look for the books about Black Shadow Forest on my own while Buttercup goes upstairs to work on his painting. I spend so much time trying to find one book mentioning the forest, that by the time Buttercup comes back downstairs, with some paint on him and a satisfied expression, I only have three books to show him. I let out a big sigh as I drop them on the table and he sits down next to me.

"Pff, I can't believe that's all I found! I wish I could already master the searching spell like Hazelnut, it's so useful."

It's basically a spell that looks through all the books around you for the key words that interest you. So, for example, you could use it to find all the books talking about how amazing squirrels are and here you go! Well, ok to be honest, you wouldn't get a result that precise, but it would bring you all the books with the word "squirrel" in it at least. And as you get better at magic, you can refine your search and add more details to make it more efficient. But we'll only learn this spell after the holidays.

"Ok, let's have a look, maybe we'll find something useful," Buttercup says, even though he doesn't sound so hopeful.

I look at him and smile, shaking my head, "I'll look and you go clean yourself. If you get paint on the books you might not be allowed here again."

I am in a better mood already. Buttercup has this effect on me somehow.

I look through the first book and sadly it doesn't take long. The only books I find are human geography books that describe where Black Shadow Forest is located and what kind of animals, plants and mushrooms you can find there.

"So? What did you find?" Buttercup asks me once he's cleaned up and I tell him quickly about the few lines I've just read.

"Well at least we learned one thing!" he exclaims like we just discovered something big.

"What?"

"No polar bears!" he cries a bit too loudly.

I laugh at his excitement and at the funny face he made when he said this, but we get a few "shhhh..."s from other readers around us. We go through the other two books quietly together but they pretty much say the same basic facts. Nothing about the forest being haunted, mysterious disappearances or curious beasts. And no polar bear or Evil Ice Queen either! It's almost disappointing.

In the end I don't know if I'm more upset about not finding

much information about this mysterious forest or mad that our beloved Woodland Forest is mentioned even less in these books.

"How dare they not say more about our great forest? There's so much to say!"

"Like what?" Buttercup asks quietly, flipping through the third book again just to make sure we didn't miss a thing.

"Well, first, obviously our bakery!" my friend smiles at this, and I go on, "This place, the school. And they could talk about how amazing the animals here are ..."

Another amused expression from my friend.

"Well, yeah but obviously humans know nothing about us so they just see it as a simple forest."

"Yeah I guess you're right!" I sigh and after a short pause Buttercup suggests something.

"Maybe you could write your own guide about it!"

My own guide? That's ... an idea! I guess I could do it. There is so much to say about Woodland and I still have a few days of holidays left. I don't say much but I'll have to think about it. But for now, my stomach is rumbling so it can only mean one thing: lunch time!

"Let's go eat, it will make me feel better!"

"Yes, I'm starving too!"

We tidy up the books and hurry next door to eat before our big adventure.

Chapter 35

A story from the past

The bakery is really quiet when we enter it but that doesn't stop my parents from being very busy, as usual. There's soothing music in the background and I see some familiar faces enjoying their coffee and pastries with a book or a magazine. There's also a couple sharing a piece of cake while playing a card game but apart from these few customers, the place is rather empty, which is to be expected since many animals leave Woodland for the second Grateday week.

"Oh hello, my sweet boys!" my mum welcomes us warmly from behind the counter. She seems to be cleaning something, with bags and boxes all around her.

"Hi Mum! Can we get some lunch before we go meet Almond and Honeysuckle?"

"You're here for lunch? "she asks, all surprised, and looks at the clock to check the time. "I can't believe it's lunch time already! I thought it was still so early."

"It's because you work too much, dear!" my dad tells her as he enters the room from the kitchen with a tray of freshly baked buns. "Come on, let's take a break with the kids."

Thankfully my mum agrees and even lets him bring some food and drinks for all of us. I hate seeing her like this, when she can't stop working and forgets to take care of herself. Buttercup and I help my dad bring everything over, and in a flash we're all set with nice sandwiches, carrot and cucumber sticks, and glasses of fresh lemonade.

"Thanks darling!" my mum says. "Ah, it's so nice to sit down a bit."

She sighs, clearly tired from her busy morning.

"I thought you were supposed to have a quiet week after Grateday because so many customers are away?" Buttercup asks my parents. My dad immediately chuckles around his mouthful of sandwich.

"Well, yes, we were supposed to but Rose couldn't help herself. She wanted to deep clean the bakery while it's so quiet, so we spent the morning emptying cupboards, checking our stock, cleaning, and planning the next few months' specials."

"Mum, you should rest more!" I tell her after taking a sip of lemonade.

"Argh, it's fine we'll rest tomorrow, don't worry!"

We all laugh at this, knowing that there's little chance my mum will manage to spend the next day without getting busy. There's always something for her to do, a project to take care of, something to clean or organise.

"Anyway, what are you boys up to?" she asks us.

"We're going to go for a walk, to get some inspiration for our school project," I answer quickly, trying to sound totally casual. I don't mention where we're going because I'm scared my parents will say no if I do, and now I'm too curious about this mysterious library to be told I can't go. I'm still a bit nervous about Black Shadow Forest but my curiosity is getting the better of me.

"Oh that's a good idea! Fresh air is always good for inspiration."

"Where are you going?" my dad asks us.

Why does he want to know? Does he suspect something? I don't know what to say? Lie? I don't know how to do that! Tell the truth? Impossible, the whole plan would fall apart. Can I phrase this in a way where I'd tell the truth without really telling the truth. I'm starting to panic and worrying that my parents will notice and know I'm lying. Oh no, what to do?

"Oh, we're just going by the lake," Buttercup answers simply, with his most trustworthy smile. How can he do that so easily? And suddenly I see him subtly change the subject, trying to stir the conversation away from our afternoon's plans.

"Oh! I just realised that you and Auntie Rose never told us about your school projects? We're trying to ask the more experienced wizards and witches around us what their projects were so we can get inspiration from them."

"That's a great idea, Buttercup!" my dad approves with a big smile.

"As long as you don't copy other animals' work, of course," my mum adds, always worrying about teaching us the right values.

"Of course!" I answer. "So what were your projects?"

I realise that even I don't know.

My mum finishes her sandwich and, after a sip of lemonade, starts her story.

"Well," she says, "it may not be surprising but both our projects were related to food!"

We both laugh, clearly not surprised by this.

"But what you may not know," she continues, "is that our projects helped us meet and fall in love."

"Really? Waouh! Tell us!"

Buttercup and I are all ears and my mum has this little smile that tells me she's remembering something dear to her.

"Well, during our first year, your dad and I didn't know each other yet."

"What? But you were in the same class, weren't you?"

"Yes, we knew each other but we weren't friends. We mostly had different circles of friends. Or, I should say, I had a lot of friends but a certain someone here," she gestures toward my dad with a cheeky smile, "didn't really meddle with the rest of the class."

What? My dad was a loner? It's funny how I never stopped to imagine what my parents were like when they were younger. I just always saw them as they are now, being married, with their unique dynamic, always cooking together and having so many friends in Woodland. I never thought of their lives before they had me or before they opened the bakery.

"You should have seen him, he was just so cute, going everywhere with his nose stuck in a book. And so brilliant in class! Oh he was so good and so quick to master the spells!"

My dad blushes as much as it's possible for a squirrel to blush at that compliment.

"It seemed like everyday he was reading a new book-"

"- no, come on, not everyday," my dad interrupts, smiling.

"Oh almost! But you see, he looked so serious that I didn't dare to talk to him."

"Until Project Day came along and we realised we actually had so much in common!" my dad adds.

"So, on that day I went first. My project was quite simple: I enchanted a set of containers so they could keep your food and drink warm for you as long as you wanted. It was a challenge because I had to think of all the different sizes and shapes of the containers animals might need to store their food. I knew I wouldn't need to use these things much since I was learning magic but I wanted to make them for my parents and other animals I knew who couldn't cast spells."

"That's what made me fall in love with her," my dad adds with a warm smile, looking at her like she's the most amazing squirrel in the world.

"What?" I ask, lost in their story.

"The fact that she went through so much trouble, and was such a perfectionist about finding all the different shapes for the containers and all that, when her project was not even for her but for others. She really made this to help her community."

Now it's my mum's turn to blush a bit.

"What about you Dad? What was your project?"

"Well, mine was more selfish than hers. Even back then, I loved to make bread but I wanted to find a way to make the rising period easier. I thought it was a hassle to find the perfect spot to keep the dough warm enough every time. Sometimes it would get windy and it didn't rise properly or the temperatures would drop and everything was ruined. It was driving me crazy so I made a special box that would stay warm all the time no matter the weather."

"What? But that's the box you're using today, isn't it? The proofing box?"

"Yes it is!" my mum answers, obviously proud of him.

"Of course, I made some upgrades over the years as I became a better wizard but yes, that's how it started."

"So when I saw that his project was also related to food and how brilliant it was, it gave me the courage to talk to him," my mum explains. "And once we started we couldn't stop! We walked home together that day, talking about nothing but food and cooking. We quickly became best friends, I introduced him to my friends and he seduced them all with his amazing food. You should have seen him, always bringing some treats to share with the teacher and the class. Then, after graduation we quickly got married, opened the bakery and had you. And all because of bread, can you imagine?"

"Waouh, that's a great story!" I say and Buttercup agrees, adding that he's so glad they finally talked to each other thanks to their projects. "Otherwise I would never have had my best friend!"

We were so lost in their story that we didn't pay attention to the time until I suddenly saw the clock on the wall. "Oh shoot, we have to go! Honeysuckle and Almond will be waiting for us!"

I tidy up our trays while Buttercup quickly buys some food for Almond (in case she hasn't eaten lunch yet). My parents rarely let him pay for food because "he's like family" but once in a while he manages to convince them. I kiss my parents goodbye and we leave the bakery in a hurry, excited and ready to go explore.

Chapter 36
The first surprise

We arrive at our usual meeting point by the lake at the same time as Almond and Honeysuckle. "Yeah perfect timing!" I shout happily. "I think this is the power of friendship, making us all arrive at the same time!"

"Or it's simply the power of punctuality," remarks Honeysuckle with a smirk.

I stick my tongue at her and we all laugh.

"What are we waiting for?" asks Almond, running in circles around us. "Let's go!"

We start walking together along the lake, in a straight line with Almond at one end and Buttercup at the other.

"Oh, I'm so excited!!" I cry out. I can't contain my excitement, especially now that we're out of earshot from my parents. Even Berry is vibrating in its holder!

"Well for someone who was so scared about exploring yesterday, you seem to be the most excited of us all now!" Honeysuckle laughs.

"Why are you so excited about this library when you already have Dreams?" Buttercup asks me.

"I don't know, I think it's more the idea of a human library than the library itself. I'm curious to see what they read, what books they put in there to exchange."

"But you already read books written by humans."

It's true, although some of our books were written by residents of Woodland and other forests.

"I don't know, it's exciting to me!"

"But then, anything related to books is exciting to you," teases Almond.

"Aren't you guys excited too?" I ask them. "I thought we all wanted this? To explore ..."

"Oh yes I am!" says Almond, always full of enthusiasm. "I don't care much about the library, but I'm excited to see how it looks outside Woodland and if there are better places to run."

Better than Woodland? Is Almond going crazy?

Buttercup says he wants to use this trip to get some inspiration for our project.

"And even if I don't find any ideas, it's fine, it's still nice to see new things."

Honeysuckle is hopping up and down and can't hide how happy she is.

"Oh I'm so excited to do this, to get out of Woodland for a while!"

We all laugh and chat, imagining what it looks like outside our forest.

"Maybe it doesn't look different at all," Buttercup suggests.

"Well, that would be rather disappointing, wouldn't it?" Honeysuckle answers.

And after walking all around the lake for a while, we reach the famous border line that we've all been told never to cross. Technically it's not really visible but we all know it's there because our parents told us and because of a small wooden sign up in a tree that indicates "This is the end of Woodland Forest. We hope you had a magical time with us!" I have never noticed that it's painted with colourful flowers all around the writing. Now that I'm practising magic, I also realise that it's been enchanted.

"Oh yeah, you're right, it glows, I never noticed it before!" Buttercup says, surprised.

"Ok, are you guys ready?" Honeysuckle asks us, clearly enjoying being the one who started this whole trip.

We all look at the sign and cross the invisible line at the same time. Once on the other side, we look at each other, wondering silently if we will feel any difference.

Honeysuckle laughs at our reaction, "Don't worry, you won't grow an extra pair of whiskers just by taking an extra step outside your precious forest. Come on guys, let's go, it's this way!"

We all relax a bit and follow her lead. At first the path beyond the border seems pretty much the same as it was in Woodland, and we exchange jokes for the next ten minutes or so, but slowly I start to see a difference in the kind of trees we see, the rare animals we meet or the way the grass is more brown than green with a lot of broken tree branches on the ground. The more we walk, the more we see a bigger human presence here than at home, with wooden signs indicating the next trekking trail and some resting areas with wooden tables and benches.

The first strange thing that I notice is a plastic bottle near one of the benches, which I assume is an unfortunate accident since there's a big trash can just next to it. And then, as we keep walking, I realise that even the air smells a bit different here. And not in a good way. It doesn't smell like fresh baked bread or pine trees. It smells like something rotten. I'm not the only one who notices it because I see Buttercup and Almond stop and suddenly smell the ground around us. They both have a great sense of smell and our group has become silent. I'm wondering what's going on.

"You smell that too?" I ask my friends.

They both nod and without realising it, we start walking toward the smell to find out what it is, with only Honeysuckle staying behind us on the main path.

"Guys, the library is this way, what are you doing?" she asks us, gesturing to the road ahead with her small paws.

"Just a second, we want to see what smells so bad," Almond tells her.

After walking behind a bush, we finally spot a small pond and we're so shocked by the state it's in that none of us speak for a minute. Buttercup finds his words first.

"What's this? What ... what happened here?"

I look at the state of the pond again and I'm as lost as he is.

"I don't know, it's awful." I just say, my heart heavy at the sight in front of us.

Instead of a clean pond like the ones we're used to, we see a waterbody half covered with rubbish. There are plastic bags filled with water floating on the surface like sick jellyfishes, bottles of all sizes, with and without caps. Some are filled with water, some with some strange brown coloured drinks still inside, and some with their labels floating around. There are even old bike tires, big metal containers, paper hamburger wrappers, cardboard boxes, straws ...

Everything that should be in a bin and nothing that you'd expect to see in a forest.

"How is it possible? Did a garbage truck fall in the pond?" asks Almond quietly.

"No, it's not an accident," answers Honeysuckle quietly behind us. We were so shocked that I didn't hear her join us. "I've seen this before where I used to live. This is the creation of humans."

"What? They did this?"

"Yes. Not all humans are like that, but some treat nature like a giant trash can."

"How dare they do that to the forest?" Buttercup asks angrier than I've ever seen him. "How dare they treat those woods like it belongs to them? They have no right! Oh I'm so mad!"

I want to calm my friend down but I'm boiling inside too. I can't believe there are people who think they can pollute nature like this without worrying what it would do to the animals in the pond or to the forest itself. It's disgusting! I don't know what to do or say but I see Buttercup take a deep breath before speaking to our group.

"We have to do something, we can't leave the place like that. There are animals living inside this pond and all around, we have to help them."

We all agree and start to think of the best way to do it.

"Argh, I wish we already knew how to move bigger objects but the big trash can there is too big and too far for us to bring over."

"Anyway it's attached to the ground."

"Then we have to think the other way. If we can't bring the bin near the pond, we need to take all that trash to the bin."

"But how? It's going to take hours if we do it like this, one by one."

"Guys, we're witches and wizards, aren't we?" Honeysuckle finally says. "So let's do this our way. Grab your Magicol and let's get to work!"

We don't lose a minute and form a line, magically taking the objects from the water to make them reach the bin. Almond is the first in line, getting the objects out of the pond, then Honeysuckle passes them on to me and I finally pass them to Buttercup, who dunks them in the bin. It takes us a good thirty minutes but magic really helps us go faster. In the end, the only thing left is the bike tire and since it's a bit too heavy for us to lift with a spell, we conjure some wind to push it back to the bank where Almond grabs it and drags it all the way to the trash can.

Once we have cleaned the pond of all the unwelcome objects, we go to check the water to see if the animals in it are fine. The surface still looks dirty so we try to come up with a solution to clean it.

"Is there a potion we could use?" Honeysuckle asks.

"I have some in my bag" I say, "but I don't think any of them will be of any use. So far we have only learned how to heal physical problems in living bodies. We have nothing to purify water."

We keep thinking for a while when Buttercup finally comes up with a solution.

"We could take out some of the dirty water and conjure up some clean water to take its place. It's not perfect but it will help a bit. We'll have to come back later with some Woodland doctors though, to check on those animals and clean the water properly."

We agree even though we all know it means telling grown ups the truth about us leaving Woodland. I'm nervous just thinking about it but for now I'm trying to focus on the state of this pond.

"Ok let's do this!"

We warn the fishes, the frogs, the newts, the turtles and all the bugs about what we're going to do so they can all stay on the other part of the pond while we act.

"Someone grab the metal container that we put in the bin and enlarge it with magic. We need a place to put the dirty water. And this way we'll be able to check if any tiny animals came with the water too."

Soon the container is next to us, bigger than it was in the water and we all get to work, reaching for our Magicol and casting the same spell in unison to go quicker. We lift the water from the surface into the container. We're careful not to take too much water out since it's just a temporary relief solution. Once it's done we conjure clean water to fill the place again. After checking the container for any sign of animals, Almond drops it back next to the trashcan.

Before leaving we all go to check up on the pond's residents and promise them that we'll come back with more help soon. They're all so quiet, I'm not sure if it's because they're so grateful they don't know what to say, or because they're scared of us. Maybe we look very big to them. Without hearing of their voices, we start to leave but the biggest of the turtles finally comes to the edge of the pond to thank us. We're so surprised by his deep voice that we all jump a little but once we're past our shock, we listen to what he has to say.

"I'm sorry we were all so quiet but we've grown so used to living like this that we never imagined anyone would help us. We've tried to clean it up ourselves but we're so small it was not really useful. And we've never seen Magical animals before, so we were really surprised by your little group. But please know that we're all really grateful for your help. You're all so kind."

Once we're back on the main road, we're all silent for a minute or two. We're all so shocked by what we've seen that we don't know what to say.

"We're so used to seeing Woodland so clean, I never imagined it could be that dirty elsewhere. Especially that close to us," I say first. Occasionally we get some trash left by humans but nothing like that.

"Yeah it's crazy to think what humans did to this place," Honeysuckle adds.

Buttercup is very silent, his face so sad that Almond tries to cheer her brother up.

"I know it really sucks but we should focus on the fact that we helped those animals. And now that we know there's a problem here, we can tell others and come back to help and think of a solution."

"Oh I'm going to think of a solution for sure!" Buttercup finally says, his face determined. "Actually I'm thankful that we came here. Honeysuckle, you were saying that we could use this outing to get ideas for our school project and it's definitely going to inspire mine. I don't know what yet, but I'm going to work on a way to make sure this never happens again."

Chapter 37

Peppermint

We keep walking on the same path for a bit until we reach a fork in the road with several signs showing us where we are and indicating our options. In the middle, there's a rough map showing some hiking trails all marked with different colours.

"I've read about this. Humans who love to hike plan walks with different routes." Honeysuckle explains.

"What do the colours mean?" Almond asks her.

"I think they show the difference in difficulty. You see the blue trail is quite short, then the green one goes a bit farther. Look, the kilometres are written here. And the red one is much longer and I'm pretty sure it goes uphill too so you'd need more experience to walk it."

Ok, so all the hiking trails are on the left road. And then there are several wooden signs pointing to the right path with names like *Moonlight Farm, Black Manor, and The Nirvana, the zen retreat that helps you leave your worries in the city.* Underneath all these signs is a smaller one that seems more recent, indicating *The Black Shadow Tiny Library,* and a smaller text under it explaining *Open all day long for book lovers of any age.* On top of all the signs, we can see a bigger one stating *You're now entering Black Shadow Forest, don't worry it's not haunted!*

"Waouh, so it's really named Black Shadow Forest?" I say. I think I almost hoped this place didn't really exist because the name still creeps me out a bit.

"Yes! So should we get going?" asks Honeysuckle with a big mischievous smile. "Unless you'd rather go on a hike instead of going to see the books?"

Her joke helps me relax. "Yes you know me so well, I'll easily give up books for the promise of a good hike in unknown territory. Especially in a place named Black Shadow Forest!"

We all laugh at this and finally enter the famous forest. Once inside, we pause for a second, probably all thinking the forest will suddenly become dark and very misty.

"No, nothing's different!" jokes Buttercup, who seems to understand what we were all thinking.

As we all walk together, Almond wonders out loud what the Black Manor and the Zen Retreat could be.

"Black Manor sounds like the name of a very haunted house if you ask me."

"No, stop it! Don't spook me even more!" I say half scared, half joking.

We're so noisy with our jokes and theories about what those places really are, that we almost don't hear the cry at first. With her great hearing, Almond hears it first and makes us stop in our tracks.

"Did you hear that?"

"Hear what?"

"I- I think I heard someone crying."

We all look around us and once we're all quiet, I hear it too. It's faint but there's a noise coming from deeper in the forest.

"It sounds like a baby," Almond adds.

"A baby? Well its parents are probably with it then!" Honeysuckle suggests.

"No, I don't think so. The sound is too muffled and there's no voice nearby trying to soothe it. I think we should go and check, just to be sure."

We all agree, even though I'm scared at the idea of going off the main path into the trees, in a forest with such a creepy name.

"Stay close to each other or we'll get lost," Buttercup advises us.

We approach the edge of the trees, listening carefully, to find out in which direction we should head in. Thankfully, since it's the middle of the afternoon, there's still light filtering through the trees even though it's way less open here than in Woodland. I guess with a name like this, it would be weird to have a very open forest with lots of light. We walk slowly among the trees, focusing on the sound that's closer and closer now.

"Hello? Is there someone there?" Almond calls out.

At first we only hear the same muffled crying sound but after asking a second time we hear a soft, "Here, please help me. I'm hurt."

Almond immediately rushes toward the voice, telling us to stay there.

"I'll be back, just wait for me."

Obviously worried for our friend and this crying animal, we don't listen and follow her, rushing to stay together. We arrive where the trees are a bit more scarce and we see it right away. It's a young raccoon, lying down on a tree stump, obviously exhausted, eyes only half open. I'm not sure if it's hurt but it's obviously very weak. Almond is next to it in a flash, lifting its head very softly.

"Hey, we're the ones who were calling. Are you hurt? What happened to you?" I know she's worried but she still manages to ask all these questions in a reassuring tone, making sure not to add more stress to the situation.

"I- I'm fine but I'm not feeling well, I haven't eaten since yesterday-"

I don't wait for more details and run with my bag, emptying it all on the ground and offering the snack I had prepared to the baby raccoon.

"Here, take it. There are some berries, nuts, carrots ..."

It doesn't hesitate and eats silently for a bit while we're looking at it, waiting to hear more about its situation. When it's done eating, I offer it our water bottle and it drinks everything in one go. Once it realises what it's done, it feels guilty and apologises for drinking it all.

"It's fine, don't worry, we can magic some more if we need to."

And Almond does refill the bottle instantly, her paw on her

Magicol so fast I'm honestly impressed. She's usually good at performing magic but I've noticed that she's even better when she wants to help others.

"What's your name?" Buttercup asks the racoon.

"Peppermint. What about you? And how did you do that magic water trick?"

He looks better now and we introduce ourselves before he tells us his own story.

"I tried to steal some food from the vegetable farm close by, but the humans were too scary, they had electric fences to protect everything. I didn't want to risk it, especially alone.'

Now that he says that, I realise that he is indeed alone, like Almond assumed.

"Where are your parents?"

He takes a deep breath and explains to us that he used to live in a nice forest days away from here, but that the old man living near them was not happy with animals coming on his property.

"He kept chasing all of us away until one day he had enough and came outside with his big gun and ..."

Peppermint doesn't need to describe what happened to his family, we understand right away.

"My parents barely had time to tell me to run away and to jump in front of me to protect me when he shot at us. They sacrificed themselves to save my life."

Without realising it, at those words we all move a bit closer to him and Almond and I quickly put a paw on his shoulder. I want to comfort this poor baby and make his pain go away.

"I've been running for days, I've been so scared all alone like this. I ate what I could find on the way but I hurt my rear paw yesterday and since then, I just walked too slowly to find any water. I didn't catch any food either and grew weak. I'm so happy you guys found me, you're my guardian angels."

We all smile, my heart hurting for this poor raccoon who lost his parents and has been lost in the woods for days.

"You said you hurt yourself?" Buttercup asks with his soft and warm voice. "Can you show us where? We can help you."

Peppermint shows us his left rear paw, all bloody.

"The blood is all dried now but it hurts badly. I don't know how

I'm going to walk, I think it's broken."

"Don't worry we have what you need!" Almond says with a reassuring smile and I reach for my first aid pouch. I pick two bottles and explain to Peppermint what they are.

"This one will clean up your cut and the blood. And this one," I pause for a little dramatic effect, "will fix your broken bone!"

He looks at me like I'm insane, "You're joking? It's not possible!"

We explain to him that we're witches and wizards from Woodland Forest.

"Waouh, I heard about magic but I thought it was just a bunch of stories."

"Just watch this."

And we demonstrate to him directly how true those stories are. The first potion cleans up all the blood, the dirt and the cut. He looks at his clean paw in surprise, then when Almond uses the second potion on him, we all watch his reaction since we can't see the results ourselves. We see his little eyes opening wide with amazement.

"Try to move your paw now."

He keeps staring at it, completely stunned and finally says, "But … I can't feel the pain anymore, how is it possible?"

He slowly moves his paw and finally tries to stand up on his two hind legs. We all smile at his happy expression when he realises he's really healed. But suddenly his smile turns back into a frown and he starts crying, leaving all of us lost. Oh no, what's going on? I look at my friends trying to understand.

"I'm sorry, I'm just so grateful that you found me but I'm also very tired and sad … and …" he tries to keep explaining himself through more sobs, "and I don't know what I'm going to do. I have nowhere to go …"

He stops talking and falls down on the tree stump, his shoulders shaking.

"You really have no one left back home?"

Peppermint only shakes his head no, his whiskers and fur all dirty from the days he just spent lost in the woods.

My friends and I look at each other and we all know what we're going to say.

225

"It's ok, don't worry, you can come back with us to Woodland."

"Really?" he asks with his eyes full of tears. "You mean it?"

"Of course! And I'm sure we'll find someone to take care of you there."

Peppermint dries his tears and Almond explains her plan.

"I'll take him back to Woodland now. I can put him on my back so he can rest a bit."

"Should we go with you?" Honeysuckle offers.

"No, it's fine. You three go on and have fun at the library. You'll tell me all about it tonight."

I'm torn between my curiosity for books and my desire to make sure Peppermint is fine but Almond reassures me.

"It'll be easier like this, I'll go faster and you can go have some fun."

Before they leave us, I give Almond some of our food in case Peppermint gets hungry again.

"Do you want the potions and water too?"

"No, don't worry, if we need water I'll magic some and Peppermint is not hurt anymore. I'll bring him to the hospital to have him checked as soon as we arrive back home."

Poor Peppermint is so exhausted that he's asleep on Almond's back before we even have a chance to say goodbye.

Chapter 38
The tiny library

After finding our way back to the main dirt path, we keep walking toward the library. The three of us are a bit shaken by our meeting with this poor orphan baby and we talk about how lucky it was that we found him.

"I really hope he'll be ok."

"Well his paw seemed fine thanks to your potion," Honeysuckle says to reassure me.

"Yeah I know, I mean ... I hope he'll recover from such a traumatic experience. Losing his parents like this must be awful."

"I'm sure he'll be fine because he won't be alone. He'll have Almond and all of us to help him. Look how well Almond did when she arrived in our family," Buttercup smiles at me reassuringly.

"Why? What happened to her?" Honeysuckle asks us. "I figured something happened to her parents but I never dared to ask her."

We tell her the story of how Almond lost her parents and how Dahlia and Basil took care of her, adopting her as their own without hesitation. It makes Honeysuckle very emotional to hear the full story and she just says quietly, "I'm sure Peppermint will be fine. We'll find a new family to adopt him like yours did with Almond."

I nod, imagining what it would be like to have this sweet and brave raccoon in my own family.

We keep walking and Honeysuckle tries to lift up our spirits by telling us we're very close now.

"Waouh, I can't believe you went that far all on your own yesterday! You're so brave!"

"Brave or irresponsible?" she asks, and we all laugh at this remark.

"Yeah, not sure," Buttercup says, "But it's fine, nothing bad happened to you so, in the end I guess it was ok for you to go explore yesterday."

I don't add the fact that, after meeting Peppermint hurt in the forest I'm not so sure it was that safe for her to travel alone like she did. But Honeysuckle quickly ends this conversation about safety by pointing us to the object of our trip.

"Look, it's just here!" she shouts.

Books, finally something good! Oh I'm so excited!

We all smile at each other and run up to the wooden box that we spot just a bit farther away. And it's just as Honeysuckle described it to us last night, even better! Just like she said, it's a big wooden box with a glass door that displays the books and protects them from the weather. The whole thing actually looks like one of the cupboards we have in our kitchen at home. It seems sturdy and it's taller than I imagined.

Luckily there's a big tree stump right next to the library. We can use it to see the library in detail since it's too high for us all to see in, especially without Almond to carry us on her back. It's probably from a tree broken in a storm since it's cut unevenly and higher than a regular stump. The wood of the library box is painted red all around, and inside, behind the glass door we can see books of all sizes and types.

On the side I notice a framed sign painted in black, attached to the library with some text.

"Oh what does it say?"

I get closer to read it.

"It explains the origin of the library."

It says:

The Black Shadow Tiny Library

Why have a library in the middle of the forest? Why not? My husband and I are both bookworms and we've been inspired by all the little libraries we've seen during our recent travels. When we moved to the manor up the road, we wanted to create something to show that Black Shadow Forest and its manor are not only fun places to come and scare your friends around Halloween, but that there are people living here too. We want to show that you can find more to enjoy about this forest than its creepy name. There's a nice organic farm just up the road, the Nirvana Retreat, and we're working on transforming the manor into a bed and breakfast. Our house is always full of books so we thought why not share some with the people passing through?

How does it work?

The books that you see here are all free to take home. You can bring them back after reading them or keep them and add some of yours later on. You're very welcome to borrow even if you have nothing to put in exchange right now. No pressure!

The goal is to keep this library alive and make sure it's never empty. Tell your friends. Let's all try to bring some life back into Black Shadow Forest.

There's just one rule: read and have a good time!

We hope you enjoy our little library!

Eva and Rob

And I notice an extra note at the bottom.

Feel free to contact us by mail (b.shadowlibrary@gmail.co.uk) or come directly to the manor if you have questions or simply want to chat about books or the forest. We always have coffee ready!

It also says we can scan a QR code (whatever that is) to get more details about the upcoming bed and breakfast at the manor. I wonder if this code thing is some kind of magic because it doesn't look like a language at all, it's a black square with lots of irregular black shapes in it. It seems very strange to me.

I'm lost in my thoughts wondering about this mysterious code thingy when Buttercup asks us, "What's Halloween?"

I explain to him what I've learned about it through the novels I've read.

"Oh, so people scare each other on purpose?" he asks, surprised.

"Yep, apparently."

"Humans are really funny!"

"Ok, so let's see what books they have!" I exclaim.

There are maybe thirty-forty books inside and we look at them with the door closed. We have to tilt our heads to the side to read the titles on the spines and I'm really surprised by the diversity of the books offered. There are several books about babies and pregnancy. Apparently humans need instructions to learn to take care of their own babies. That's surprising! I'll have to ask Mum and Dad if they ever read a book about raising a baby squirrel. I'm not sure I'll borrow those but I admit I'm curious to have a look to see how they manage to grow tiny humans inside them. There's also a few books about diets, like *The No Carbs Diet, Say Goodbye to Your Extra Kilos* and one called *New Year New You: How to Lose Weight After the Holidays and Get Back in Shape with Minimum Effort.*

"What are all those diet books?" I ask my friends. "Why would anyone want to lose weight? That's crazy! Just the thought of it makes me hungry!"

Buttercup and Honeysuckle laugh at this and we keep looking at the books offered. Some seem to be about the lives of famous people (well, I assume they're famous if people wrote about them) like a man called Steve Jobs and a Michael Jackson who's wearing a very shiny glove on the book cover. I also see titles that teach you how to learn new skills and some relating big historical events. Ah, I also notice some tourist guides: Canada, Japan, Spain but nothing about our forest. I really need to do something about that!

"I wonder why those guide books have years on them ..."

"Maybe they change the names of their cities every year so they need to let tourists know?" Honeysuckle jokes.

"Oh, look! It's this Harry wizard boy!" I say when I spot one of his books on the top shelf. "Mango told me about it."

I take a closer look through the glass door but notice the number on the spine,"Oh no, it says it's the third book."

"Maybe there's the first one, let's see ..." Buttercup says and he's right, quickly we spot the first title of this series. It's called Harry Potter and the Philosopher's Stone.

After looking at the titles we finally open the door and spend some time browsing through the books that might interest us, sitting on the ground. I don't know how long we spend here looking at them but Buttercup finally tells us that we should pick one or two and get going before we get spotted by humans. Honeysuckle and I are lost in our books but we agree reluctantly.

"What are you going to pick?" he asks us. "I'll take this one."

He shows us a big book about art, Artists that Changed the World.

Honeysuckle seems to hesitate between several books so she explains, "I like all of these three books but I only brought one book to put in exchange so I'm not sure it's ok to take more than I give."

"Don't worry," Buttercup tells her, "I'm giving away more books than I'm taking, so in the end it'll be a fair trade."

"Really? Oh thanks!"

So she ends up taking three books, A Wrinkle in Time, Pippi Longstocking and I have to ask her the name of the last one because it's so long I can't read it properly.

"It's called Narnia, the Lion, the Witch and the Wardrobe. It seems really exciting!"

That's a funny title in my opinion but I recognise the light in her eyes of someone impatient to discover a new world.

"What about you Applesauce?"

The choice was tough but I show them my final selection.

"Harry Potter and this one, Matilda. Look, it's from the same author who wrote Charlie and the Chocolate Factory!"

Now that we're happy with the books we have picked, we put the rest back and use our magic to change the size of the ones we brought before placing them inside. After reducing the size and weight of the ones we'll be taking home, I notice that Buttercup looks worried.

"What is it?" I ask him.

"I know we're allowed to do this and that we even gave some of ours in exchange but it feels so strange to borrow these books without asking anyone's approval, you know like at Dreams. It looks like we're stealing."

"We're not stealing Buttercup," Honeysuckle reassures him, confident as ever.

"Ok, let's go home then!" I say, once the books are all packed safely in my backpack. But I see Honeysuckle's expression and I know she has something else in mind.

Chapter 39

Moonlight farm

What do you have in mind?" I ask her.

"Don't you guys want to go and have a look a bit farther?"

"How much farther?" asks Buttercup suspiciously, with his tiny eyes squinted at her.

"Just to the end of this road. Here, look, we can hear some noises. I think that's the farm that was indicated on the road signs and mentioned on the message left by the library's creators. I want to see what a farm looks like," she explains with a giant smile, the kind that clearly says, "please, please, please, just say yes!"

But Buttercup is not sure we should, "It may be dangerous ..."

"Don't worry we are so small, they won't see us," I say.

I don't know if it's because Honeysuckle sounds so sure of herself or because I'm so excited after finding the tiny library, but for once I'm the one to agree without too much hesitation. I want to see how humans live too!

As we reach the end of the dirt path, we start hearing more noises on top of the chirping of the birds. We slow down to get a better understanding of where we're going. We look ahead and Honeysuckle gestures to us to keep going but to be quiet now.

"I think the farm is just over there."

To be safe, we leave the main road to hide among the trees and keep walking until we finally see it. There, just behind a small hill is the organic farm, and from up there the view is amazing.

"Waouh! I never imagined it could be so pretty," I say.

"What? The farm?"

"All of it! I mean, outside Woodland. I always assumed our forest was the only ... Well, no, not the only beautiful place out there but ..." I search for my words. "I mean, I read about a lot of places but I never really stopped to think that it could be that pretty this close to us. I always assumed you had to travel to far away countries to see truly beautiful areas but this farm here, it's simple and still, so pretty. I love it."

They look at me in silence and simply nod, understanding what I mean.

"Yeah, there's beauty in little things and in things you never thought about before," Buttercup says.

Past the mount of green grass we're standing on, it's like life has reclaimed its right after the darkness left by Humans in the rest of Black Shadow Forest.

It's green everywhere: on the ground, in the trees and bushes surrounding the farm, and also all around the building itself. It's almost hard to see the boundary between the farm and the rest of the forest because of the abundance of greenery everywhere. The humans have decorated the whole farm with plants and flowers in pots of all sizes, at the door, on window sills, and hanging from the porch. There are also different bushes everywhere, bringing so much colour to the house. I remember from all my readings that this kind of small house is actually called a cottage. I love the word cottage, it's so cute!

"Do you think it's still part of Black Shadow Forest?" I ask my friends.

"Yes, it was on the map we saw earlier, wasn't it?"

It's sad to think that Black Shadow has a bad reputation based on how dark a small portion of it is because the rest is absolutely gorgeous and full of life. And even the darkest part that we walked through was not bad. I'm sure its residents love it because it's theirs. And also, now I can definitely confirm that it is not haunted.

"There's so much green, I love it."

The cottage is surrounded by very well organised rows of fruits and vegetables, bringing even more colour to the landscape. Even from far away, we can see lots of green with spots of orange, red and green under the leaves.

The funny thing is that the forest seems to end just after the cottage, with suddenly way less trees and only fields going on and on forever. Past the cottage it's just rows and rows of wheat with big machines here and there to take care of the production. Even from far away, those machines seem huge and scary to an animal my size.

"Do you want to get a closer look?" Honeysuckle asks and I agree right away.

"Ok but we have to stay discreet. Remember, we're not in Woodland, there are some humans here and we're basically on their territory."

"Their territory?" I ask a bit too loudly, surprised at how strongly I feel about this. "I don't think humans grow in the forest. They're not born here, they came and took our lands. It's ours."

"I know, but you know what I mean."

We agree to approach the farm cautiously, keeping a low profile under long grass or running to hide behind flowers and shrubs. There's a nice wooden sign hanging at the entrance, telling us that Moonlight Farm sells organic food and that they also have The Best Cider in England. I should show this to my Dad, proving to him that others have no problem claiming they're the best and that they should do the same with their bakery.

We're so close to the farm now that we can hear the sounds coming from inside the house through the open windows. There's some chattering and I'm imagining a few people in the kitchen, judging by the sounds of utensils and running water.

Then I smell so many amazing things at once that it's overwhelming. I detect the delicious perfumes of fresh mint, lettuce leaves and strawberries, but I also get the smell of chocolate coming from the kitchen. Probably a cake, still warm, waiting to be eaten. Maybe they need help eating it? I feel myself move forward but right away Buttercup grabs me and whispers to me in a sort of menacing tone (well, as menacing as my best friend can be), "Applesauce, no! You can't go there and take their food!"

"Look! People are coming!" Honeysuckle says, showing us a man and his daughter arriving by another road. I have no idea how old the child can be because to me human children all look so big but she has nice red hair like this Anne girl whose books I love. I smile at the thought and pay more attention to how they're both dressed. So many clothes and accessories!

She's wearing a yellow raincoat with a big scarf to protect her from the wind, blue pants and again some yellow rain boots. Does she like yellow or is it a human habit to wear yellow in the woods? I'll have to look it up. Her dad is quite funny looking too with very bushy black hair, a greyish beard and only black clothes. So I guess no, not all humans wear yellow in the woods. Just as they enter the farm, I hear the dad ask his daughter what she feels like buying today.

"Strawberries for sure! You know they're Mum's favourites! We also need some eggs."

"Yes," the dad agrees. "And we'll get some lettuce, theirs are so much better than the ones at the supermarket!"

They disappear inside and suddenly I notice that Honeysuckle is eyeing the rows of carrots intensely and I see her taking a few steps toward the farm.

"Honeysuckle ... what are you doing?"

"I'm going in!" she announces proudly like she's challenging someone.

"What? Are you insane?" Buttercup says, trying to grab her before she does something stupid but it's too late. She jumps away quickly and we're stuck, wondering what to do.

"Should we go after her?"

"No, it's too dangerous" objects my friend.

"But she might need help."

"We'll be more visible if we go after her. She has a better chance of being invisible alone. Whatever her plan is ..."

We both look intently, wondering what went through her mind to go so close to humans. Is she just trying to get close to the low wall separating the cottage from the road? Oh no, she stops behind the wall, has a look and skips on top of it, using a wooden crate as a step.

"She's going in the garden? She's nuts!"

We stay put, hidden, and watch our friend navigate between the rows of fruits and vegetables but just as she reaches the carrots, we see humans enter the vegetable patch. I recognise the man and the little girl, and I guess they're accompanied by the owner of the farm, a tall woman with very long braided hair, who is taking them to select their products.

Just as Honeysuckle is grabbing a small carrot with her paws, we see the three humans getting closer to her. What will they do if they find her here? I'm trying very hard not to think of what happened to Peppermint's parents when they were chased away by humans but Buttercup senses my fear and puts his paw on mine. Even Berry is vibrating a bit and I feel it's reassuring warmth against my skin.

"Come on, get out of there," I can't help whispering to Honeysuckle even though I'm way too far for her to hear me.

The humans are now almost in the same row as our friend, then the little girl is distracted by a noise coming from the chicken's coop a few meters away.

"Oh don't be scared, it's the chickens fighting again!" explains the woman, laughing slightly. "They always do. I'll have to reorganise their living arrangements because they're plucking the feathers from one of the hens, always picking on her."

"Oh no, that's so mean!" the little girl cries out.

Thankfully this incident was enough to let Honeysuckle grab the small carrot between her teeth and cross the garden in a flash, before jumping over the wall again to make her way back to us. I breathe again, then I hear the man ask the owner, "Oh I didn't know you also had rabbits?"

Oh no, he saw Honeysuckle!

"Rabbits?" She spots Honeysuckle just as she disappears from her garden. "Oh no, it's not mine. It must come from the woods. But it's strange, they rarely come this far."

That seems to be enough for the dad to drop the subject but just as I see Honeysuckle climb back up to our hiding place, I notice the little girl is still looking around, searching for her.

As soon as Honeysuckle is back with us we run away back to the road where we came from. Once there, we stop, and both

Buttercup and I ask her what she was thinking.

"Are you crazy? They could have caught you!"

"Relax, they didn't! Did you see how I got this carrot like a pro?"

She's so proud of herself but I'm honestly a bit mad at her. I'm glad we saw some humans and all, but we were so scared for her and she doesn't even seem to see what the big deal is.

Buttercup and I are both silent after this, trying to get our heads around what just happened. We agree we should take a small break on the side of the road before walking home, to drink some water and catch our breath. I wish I still had some of the food I gave to Almond and Peppermint because I could use some comfort food right now. I tell Buttercup this and Honeysuckle offers me her carrot. I don't like to be mean but I can't help my voice betraying my emotions.

"No, I don't want your carrot."

She doesn't understand that a carrot isn't going to make me feel better right now. I wanted something sweet. She doesn't understand how scared we were for her and how dangerous what she did was. And as if I need more confirmation that she really doesn't get it, she even adds, "Do you guys want to see -"

We don't let her finish her offer and just say, "No!"

Buttercup simply adds, "Let's go home, it's getting late."

He starts walking along the trees. Honeysuckle nods but instead of following him, she goes back in the middle of the main dirt path. She's silent, her head hanging low and I think she finally understands that we're not happy with her.

Just as I finish packing our water bottle back in my bag, I hear her yell and see her being picked up in the hands of the little girl, who lets out a happy exclamation, "Daddy!! Look Daddy, I got the baby rabbit! Can I take it back home?"

Chapter 40
Double Troubles

At that moment I seem to freeze completely and am incapable of doing anything. What's happening? For a short bit, my body doesn't react and from the side of the road I see the girl running excitedly back to her dad with Honeysuckle in her arms.

"Daddy, look how pretty it is! Can I take it as a pet? You promised me I could get one, remember?"

The dad seems to think about it for a second and smiles at her daughter's excited face.

"I did tell you that, yes it's true. I thought we could get it from the pet shop, but I guess it wouldn't hurt to take this one."

"Yeah!! Thank you, Daddy!" she cries, jumping up and down with our friend in her arms.

Take Honeysuckle home? As a pet? What are they talking about? Am I dreaming? It can't be real, can it? My thoughts finally catch up and my body wakes up from this moment of shock. I quickly slide my bag on my back and call for Buttercup. Where is he? I look ahead and spot him not far from Honeysuckle but hidden by the trees by the road. I run toward him, my bag jumping up and down behind me.

"We have to go help her!" I tell him before turning to yell at the two humans as loud as I can, "Stop it! Put her back down! She's not a pet, she's our friend!"

But Buttercup grabs me before I can go on the road next to them.

"Shhh!!"

He reminds me that it's pointless to try to talk to humans since they can't hear us. They will only hear our animal noises but won't understand what we're saying.

"Besides, we'll be more useful to her if we stay invisible. Imagine if they try to catch us too, then we'll all be lost."

Oh yeah, he's right. I wouldn't be surprised if that awful girl suddenly decided she also wanted a pet hedgehog. I can't lose my friends, I need to focus!

"Great thinking! So what do we do?"

We stop to come up with a plan while keeping an eye on Honeysuckle to make sure we don't lose track of her. Hopefully the road is a straight line so there's little chance they'll go somewhere else. I try to focus by tuning off the noise, especially the girl's non-stop talking.

"I think it's a boy rabbit. I'll call him Bunny!"

Bunny? What? No! I want to yell at her that her name is Honeysuckle. I'm panicking, wondering how two small animals like us can overpower two big humans like them. It seems hopeless until I feel something buzzing against me. It's not painful, it feels more like a tickle. It's Berry, trying to communicate with me in its wand holder. Of course! Magic, we can use magic!

"Ok, quick, quick!" I look at Buttercup. "Let's think of some spells that could help her. What do we know? What can we do?"

Changing the colour of an object won't help her. I can make objects hot but I can't make Honeysuckle hot. And how would this help? She'll get so hot that they'll drop her? No, focus, focus!! I shake my head and we keep walking along the road, still following them. Argh, why can't I make fire yet? It would have been the perfect way to scare them. Oh! I know! We can make water and wind! I have an idea and share my plan with Buttercup as quickly as I can, speaking softly to not draw attention to us.

"Come on, hurry up! In position!"

Now that we know what to do, we start to run behind the humans on the road while shouting at Honeysuckle, "We have a plan, don't worry!"

It's a good thing humans can't understand us, otherwise it wouldn't be wise to yell that we have a plan to defeat them. But they keep on walking all focused on Honeysuckle so we're safe. My best friend and I don't lose time and start to put my plan into actions. We run as close as possible to them and while Buttercup conjures a big gust of wind to twirl all around the dad and the girl, I grab my wand and do my best to scare them by lifting all the small objects on the forest's ground. Together, with our two spells combined, we make a sort of whirlpool of small rocks, twigs, pinecones, acorns, dead leaves, nuts and we hope for the best. It seems to get their attention immediately. The sudden wind and this big cloud of objects flying in the air around them start to scare the two humans.

"Dad, what's happening?" The little girl is yelling, starting to panic.

They stop walking and I can see her losing her grip on Honeysuckle but it's not enough, she's still holding our friend. Now that she has more freedom of movement Honeysuckle lets her head out of the girl's grip to see what we're doing and tries to shake her way out but she still needs help. We have to do something else to force the girl to let her go.

"It's not enough!" yells Buttercup, still focussed on his spell.

"What do we do now?" I ask him, and now I'm really starting to panic. What if they really take my friend away? We can't let that happen, we just can't.

"Keep going with your magic, I have an idea!" he tells me. As he lets go of his spell the wind stops blowing, so now it's just me lifting rocks and pinecones in the air. Way less impressive without the wind for sure. I wonder what his plan is but I can't look at him without risking breaking my own spell. I have to stay focussed and keep the humans scared in some way. I simply sense Buttercup going behind me and taking something from my backpack. I hear the pop of a potion bottle opening and I finally understand. He's drinking the invisibility potion! I don't really see how it's going to help though.

He doesn't lose time and just after turning himself invisible, he uses his acorn to transform some rocks lying all around us into big boulders. Then he magically organises them so they provide him with some steps to jump on top of the dad's head. I can't see Buttercup but I know he's there because the man suddenly stops walking and lets out a big yell, wondering what's happening. I guess that's not everyday you take a stroll in the woods and end up with an invisible hedgehog on your head. I see him try to get rid of whatever just landed on his hair but every time he tries to grab my friend, he obviously screams from the pain. And knowing Buttercup I'm sure he's making sure to expose his spines as much as possible.

"What is it? Annabelle, what's this? What's on my head?"

She looks so shocked by what she sees (or doesn't see) that she doesn't answer right away. He asks her again, his face torn between the pain and the frustration of not knowing what's on him. Then the girl finally answers him, "There's nothing on your head, Dad! Nothing!"

She seems more scared now, wondering if her dad is imagining things or if there's a ghost around.

He's more confused than ever, "No, there's definitely something. I feel it, it's gripping my hair very tightly. Check again!"

And just then, Buttercup starts making some creepy sounds like he really is a ghost. Of course it scares the humans even more and the dad is now trying to get rid of this unexpected guest without using his hands. He attempts to knock Buttercup off his head with his jacket sleeves and I would laugh if I was not that scared right now.

Finally he kneels down to let his daughter check closely and as she does, she lets go of Honeysuckle. The girl is so surprised by the invisible threat on her dad's head that she doesn't even seem to realise that she let her new pet go. She's just screaming, "Dad there's nothing, I swear! Oh my god, Daddy I'm scared!"

Honeysuckle is finally free but instead of hiding from the two humans who scared her so much, she immediately brings something to my attention.

"Applesauce, we need to help Buttercup now!"

Oh no, I didn't think about this! What if they hurt him while trying to get rid of him? We need a distraction. Luckily I don't need to think, Honeysuckle just yells at me "water and wind!" and I get what she wants in a second. I cast a wind spell and she conjures the biggest water spout she can. The combination of wind and water is amazing (especially since we're in the middle of a forest), and it's enough to create the distraction needed for Buttercup to escape without harm.

Since he's still invisible, he lets us know as soon as he's back on the ground and the three of us immediately run as fast as we can out of sight. We use the fact that the humans are still distracted and scared by what we did to them and we go hide among the trees. My friends stay on the ground but I quickly climb up a tree trunk to check if the humans are leaving. I don't think they will try to find Honeysuckle again, but I'd like to be sure. I'm hidden by some branches and leaves but I can still see and hear them.

They've stopped screaming but are still shaking and the dad keeps touching his head over and over again to make sure his nightmare is over. They are hugging each other so tight, you would think they had just been attacked by the most vicious beasts. To think it was actually just three small animals like us makes me smile. But I won't feel entirely better until I see them go far away from us.

They finally let go of each other, look around and the dad says, "I think it's gone", patting his head one more time to make sure.

His daughter nods and asks, "What was that? The wind, the water, the rocks flying off the floor ... It was like ...,"she hesitates a brief second on the word but finally says it, "magic."

The dad's expression suddenly turns dark and he immediately answers, "Don't be silly, there's no such thing as magic! Let's go home."

He grabs her hand and they walk quickly out of the path and hopefully out of our lives!

Chapter 41

Lost in the woods

I wait until I'm sure they're definitely gone before going back down the tree to reassure my friends.

"They're gone, we really scared them away! Well, especially you Buttercup!"

"No, it was a joint effort," he replies modestly.

"They must have thought Black Shadow Forest was truly haunted."

Buttercup and I start laughing but Honeysuckle suddenly starts crying instead.

"Guys ... I ..." She's sobbing, trying to get some words out. "I was so scared when she grabbed me. And I ... I can't believe you saved me, you risked your lives for me ... I was so scared I didn't even think of doing magic, I was just petrified in her arms but you two were so brave ... Thank you!"

"Did you think we'd have left you and gone home?" I ask her with a choked laugh.

She simply hugs us both and this time it's my turn to say, "Let's go home. It's late."

We start walking back on the main road and we all stay quiet for a long time. I think we're all so shaken by what just happened that we don't have anything to say. And it's fine, silence can be good too. We actually go faster like this. Well, we do until we don't anymore.

"Guys ..." Honeysuckle is the first to break our long silence, looking all around us as we stop walking. "Where are we? I don't recognise this road at all."

Oh no, she's right ... we're lost. Lost in Black Shadow Forest! It may not really be haunted but if we get lost in it, it will definitely feel like it is. Especially now that it's getting darker. With everything that happened since we left Woodland, it must now be the end of the afternoon already. And we have no map, nothing to help us and no way of contacting our parents.

"Oh we're lost, aren't we?" I say it out loud this time.

"It's ok, don't panic!" Buttercup reassures us.

"We're going to get eaten by some kind of monster or kidnapped by humans again."

"Applesauce, I just told you not to panic!" Buttercup repeats.

"I'm not ... Yes, ok I am panicking!" I admit. But come on, what kind of day is this?

"Ok, let's be sensible," Buttercup tells us. "We went back from the farm to the library then we walked all the way back on the same path. We even saw the signs at the cross in the road ..."

"Did we take the wrong path after that?" Honeysuckle wonders.

"No, I know we didn't," I say, "because I remember seeing the picnic area where we cleaned the pond. I saw the tables from the corner of my eye."

"You're sure?"

"Yeah, yeah, I'm sure, because I remember seeing a sign telling people not to litter and wondered if it meant those humans couldn't read."

"Maybe, it was a different one."

"No, no, it was the one we cleaned, I saw our overflowing garbage bin from the road."

"Ok, it's a good sign then. It means we're not far from the border then!" Buttercup says.

Oh yeah, he's right, we can't be far then.

"Let's think!" Honeysuckle says, looking around us, trying to find a familiar spot. But suddenly I feel Berry shiver against me. It's a new kind of sensation, not its usual vibration. I've never felt it like that before: it's not warm like when it's trying to reassure me.

This time, it's more like a buzz and it feels like it's trying to pull me away. I take my wand in my paw and focus my attention on it.

"Applesauce, what are you doing? Did you see something?"

"Shh, wait. I think ..."

I stop talking to focus on Berry only. I close my eyes and try to connect with my magic and my wand as much as possible. I feel the buzzing getting stronger in my paw.

"What's happening?" Honeysuckle whispers to Buttercup.

I don't pay attention to them and stay focused on the link between Berry and I.

What is it?

My wand doesn't talk back but I can feel its answer. It seems to say This way. I try to visualise what "this way" means but in the end, I understand that the answer is simpler than I thought. I slowly open my paw face up and let my wand rest on it, still vibrating, like a pulse.

"Look!" I tell my friends. "It's showing us the way."

And it really is! It's shaking slightly in a direction on our right. So the Great Wizard was right! On our first day, she said our Magicol could help us find our way if we got lost.

"Are you sure?" Honeysuckle asks, dubious.

"Yes, trust me. Or trust our magic."

They both look at each other and have the same idea of reaching for their own Magicol. Judging by the look on their faces I imagine they're feeling the same reaction with their stone and acorn as I do with Berry.

"Let's go!"

We nod, and as we walk in the direction indicated by our three Magicol, we quickly reach a part of the forest that we recognise from earlier.

"It works, it's this way!"

But as soon as we start rejoicing, we hear voices a bit farther away, and we look at each other, scared by the idea of meeting humans again. I grab my friends to run and hide, but Buttercup stops me.

"No, stay here and listen!"

I look at him worried, wondering if he's being the foolish one for once.

"What?" I whisper but he shushes me again and then I hear it.

"-sauce! Buttercup! Honeysuckle!" I hear some faint voices calling our names.

"Where are you?" another voice screams.

"Oh I really hope they're not hurt somewhere …"

This time the voice is closer and I clearly recognise it as my mum's.

"Mum? Mum! We're here!" I yell out loud even though I'm not really sure where she is.

I look around, and as soon as I see a hint of orange in the trees ahead, I run toward her and jump into her arms.

"Mum! Oh I'm so relieved to see you!"

"Me too, my sweet pumpkin, me too," she says, hugging me so tight that her voice is barely audible. "Oh we've been so worried, you have no idea!"

We? When I finally let go of her, I realise that she is with Basil and Mrs Wildsong, Honeysuckle's mum. Soon everyone is hugging everyone and once our parents are all relieved to see us in one piece, it's finally time to answer the big question I've been dreading to hear.

"Where were you?" Basil asks, looking at all of us.

"We went to explore Black Shadow Forest to see their library," Honeysuckle explains in a small voice.

"The library? What are you talking about? How far did you go?" His voice is very high and I don't know if he's more surprised or angry at us.

"Too far," Buttercup simply answers him. "We went too far, we're sorry, Dad, we shouldn't have. We won't …"

I see my mum eye the other adults and I'm not sure if her look means, "Let's be nice with our kids" or "Let's wait until we're home to yell at them and punish them for the rest of their lives."

I guess my parents could easily do this by taking away all of my books or forbid me from going to Dreams. Oh no, they wouldn't do that, would they? Just imagining a life without books is making me sweat, but my mum finally talks to the whole group.

"Ok, you must be tired and hungry, let's take you home. We'll have time to talk later."

Oh no, that means I could still get this punishment later on!

We all stay quiet for the first few minutes, and I quickly realise that in the end we were never really lost. Well, we were, but we were not far from our original path. Just as I see the border leading us to Woodland I let out a sigh of relief at the familiar sight of my dear forest. Oh! How happy I am to be back home.

Once on the other side of the invisible line, I ask my mum how they knew where we were.

"Almond came back to the bakery with little Peppermint, asking for our help to bring him to the hospital."

"Oh, how is he?"

"He seemed fine but Almond wanted to make sure he was not hurt so we agreed to have Doctor Peanut examine him just to be safe. Once at the hospital, Almond finally confessed about what you four were up to. When we saw how late it was and realised you were still not back, we came to look for you."

"Where's Dad?" I dare to ask timidly.

"He had to stay behind to close the bakery in a hurry. Thankfully Violet was there too, so she took care of everything while he went to warn Dahlia and Basil, and I went to tell Mr and Mrs Wildsong that you were missing. In the end, we agreed that Basil, Mrs Wildsong and I would go look for you while your dad and Dahlia stayed at the hospital to look after Peppermint and Almond, who was quite shaken by your adventures. And Mr Wildsong stayed home to take care of his other children of course."

Once at the lake we part ways with Honeysuckle and her mum and make our way home with Buttercup and his dad. As we reach our home, I see Apricot and Tulip run toward us, obviously worried. Basil tells the two sisters to go to the hospital to let the others know that we're back and safe, and to check if they need anything for Peppermint or Almond. We watch them go and my mum turns toward Buttercup and I to ask us if we're hungry. We both answer with a silent nod and she tells us to take a seat while she prepares something for us.

If it was not my mum I would be scared of her silence but she's not the type to yell, even though, in this case I think she should. What we did was really stupid. Buttercup is sitting next to me as silent as I am and we welcome our bowl of pumpkin soup with gratitude.

Once we're done eating, his dad and my mum sit opposite us on the bench. Basil coughs a little and finally says, "Kids, I ... I don't know what to say. You two and Almond are usually so quiet that we have never had to deal with this kind of situation before," he pauses. "I admit that I don't really know how to handle this, how to ... punish you and be mad at you. We're simply not used to doing that."

I would laugh at his confession if I wasn't feeling so guilty.

"I think first, I'm trying to understand why you did it," he says.

Both our parents look at us, their faces so worried.

I look at my best friend. What do we say? Should we tell the truth, that it was Honeysuckle's idea to go see the tiny library? It doesn't feel right to sell her out like this though. I see that Buttercup is as torn by this as I am and I finally take the decision to talk.

"We ... we were by the lake yesterday and we heard some humans talking about a library in the woods. We got curious and we wanted to see it by ourselves."

It is the truth and it doesn't put the blame on Honeysuckle.

Buttercup goes on.

"And also, we thought it would be a good experience to give us ideas for our school projects. We wanted to see the world outside and learn from real life observations," he says.

His dad sighs and asks, "And did you learn anything? Did your outing help you?"

Buttercup looks at me again and then back at his dad and says, "Yes, it did."

It did? I can see his dad is as surprised as I am by this. He didn't tell me anything about this on our way home this afternoon.

"Really?" my mum asks him.

"Yes. Seeing the world past the border showed me how polluted the forest could get because of humans and I think I'm going to work on this for my project."

Basil nods. "But it doesn't -"

"I know, I know, it doesn't excuse what we did."

"No, it doesn't."

"We're really sorry!"

"We are," I add to his apologies.

"You four were very irresponsible to leave the forest like this." Now it's my mum's turn to talk. "Especially without telling anyone. You could have asked us to bring you there."

We nod.

"Do you understand how serious it could have been? You got lost but it could have been worse, you could have been hurt by humans," she says.

I need to make sure our parents never learn how bad things did get with Honeysuckle and that little girl who almost took her away from us.

"Come on, it's time to sleep. You two must be so tired."

Once in our tree, my mum prepares my bed so it's all cosy and ready for me to slip in it once I'm done washing my face and paws with the basin of water we keep up there. Once I'm all snuggled up in my bed with my mum sitting so close to me, I feel a mix of shame for what we did and the remaining fear of seeing our friend being kidnapped and then getting lost in the woods. All these emotions hit me at once and I start crying in her arms.

"Oh Mum, I was so scared of getting lost and of ..." I pause, but decide to go on and confess everything, "... losing Honeysuckle."

I tell her the truth about the farm, the girl and how we got our friend back safely.

"I was so scared. I'm so sorry, we'll never do anything like that again. I swear."

My mum looks very worried when she hears the rest of our adventures and, after telling me again how irresponsible it was for us to go there, she says, "You have to be careful out there. As soon as humans are near, you need to be on your guard, always. Even here in Woodland. I know you feel safe here but humans can still hurt you."

She gives me a kiss and dries my tears before adding in a whisper, "Also, don't tell anyone I said this but I'm proud of you for going with your first aid kit and your invisibility potion. It was smart of you to think like that and it really saved you and your friends."

She makes me move to the right side of the bed so she can snuggle next to me and hug me tighter under the blanket.

"And I'm glad that you were able to heal Peppermint."

Suddenly I think about something.

"Mum ... I know what we did was stupid and all but ..."

"What? What is it?"

"Well, if it wasn't for our adventures, Peppermint would still be alone in the woods. Who knows what could have happened to him without our help?"

I'm not bragging, I'm just thinking about how his fate could have been very different without our chance encounter in those woods.

"Mum, what's going to happen to him? Who will take care of him?"

She hugs me a bit closer and I hear her sigh. I know that sigh, it's the one she lets out when she's concerned about something.

"I don't know honey, I ... I need to talk with your dad and neighbours to see what can be done for him. But for now, it's time to sleep."

With her arms around me, she starts scratching my right ear and before I have time to realise it I'm falling asleep, warm and feeling safe. I'm home.

Chapter 42
Surprise and apologies

The next morning I wake up feeling lost, wondering where I am, before hearing the familiar sounds of my family and friends. I stretch and get up, wondering how my parents will treat me after yesterday's debacle. I say hello to my friends already sitting at the big table outside and enter the kitchen, half worried and half starving.

"Good morning Dad" I say in a small voice. I guess I should apologise to him since I didn't get a chance to see him last night. But before I get a chance to say another word, he rushes toward me and hugs me so tight I can barely breathe.

"Dad..." I try to say, my voice all muted by his weight, "you're crushing me!"

"Oh, sorry!" he quickly lets go and I see that his eyes are all watery. "I know I should be mad at you for being so reckless but, I'm so relieved that nothing happened to you four that I can't be."

He dries his eyes with the tea towel that's on his shoulder. (A habit he's always had because of all the baking he does.) He's not mad at me but I still feel the need to apologise to him.

"I'm so sorry, Dad."

He simply smiles at me in response and hands me a plate with some nice raisin toast and a selection of fruits.

"Go sit down, I'll bring you some milk."

I thank him with a kiss and as I turn to leave the kitchen I ask him where Mum is. He looks up at the wooden clock on the wall and says, with a little smile, "Oh she went to see Peppermint, she should be here soon."

OK, I don't know what that smile was, but I guess I'll find out soon enough.

As I sit down at the table with Tulip, Apricot, Buttercup and Violet, the girls all look at me and all start talking at once. Apricot is praising Buttercup and me for our use of magic in the face of danger. Violet wants to know how to get to this farm. And Tulip keeps telling us how impressed she is that we managed to sneak out of Woodland like that. I'm not sure it's a good thing to hear them praise us when we did something so stupid, but there's no time to say anything because suddenly we see Almond run toward us and cry, "They're coming!"

I don't know who's coming but she looks really excited! Even my dad comes out of the kitchen to join us. I turn around in my seat and see Dahlia, Basil and my mum pushing Peppermint in the red wagon we usually use to carry our stuff to the lake. Someone put some blankets and small pillows in it, so it now looks like a bed on wheels.

"Peppermint!" I cry out as soon as I spot him! I leave my breakfast and run to him.

"Don't crowd him!" Dahlia tells me gently.

"Why? Is he still hurt?" I ask, suddenly worried. I guess someone would have told me if there was a problem with him. But then, I just woke up.

"No, he's fine but Doctor Peanut said he needs to rest."

"I'm fine, I swear. I ..." Peppermint hesitates, looking so tiny in the wagon, surrounded by so many layers of blankets. "I could have walked. Really, there was no need for all this," he says, gesturing toward his stroller-substitute.

"Nonsense, it was nothing and you do need the rest. Better feel safe ..."

"... than sorry!" We all finish in unison before bursting into laughter. Dahlia looks at us, stunned by our reaction.

"How did you know I was going to say that?"

"Mum, you always say that! It could be your middle name: Dahlia Better-feel-safe-than-sorry Dreamcreek," Violet jokes and hugs her mum, who then relaxes a bit.

"Ok, I suppose I could be a bit less nervous. How do you feel, Peppermint?" she asks.

"Good!" he assures all of us. Still a bit unsure about what he can do in this new environment, he asks Dahlia and my mum, "can I get down from the trolley now? Please? I swear I'm feeling great!"

My mum smiles and nods. Peppermint grabs the edge of his temporary bed and gets down in a flash. Once on the ground, he falls like his paw is broken and I see our mums rush to him in a flash. But I caught his little wink in my direction just before he fell, and I laugh as soon as I hear him exclaim, "Got you!"

Dahlia is so surprised by his joke that she doesn't understand it right away.

"Relax Mum, he was just having a laugh!" Apricot tells her.

And before we see it coming, she starts to laugh very loudly.

"Oh you're a cheeky one! I think we're going to be really busy with you around, won't we, Rose?" she asks, turning toward my mum, who has a knowing smile.

Around? Does that mean he's going to stay in Woodland? I look at my parents and I notice that my dad has his arm around my mum, looking very serious, like he has a big announcement.

"Well, we have something to tell you all," my dad starts as he goes to stand next to Peppermint. "Peppermint will be joining our little family."

He pauses to look at me and I hear Peppermint add, "If that's ok with you, Applesauce?"

What? Join us? I look at him and my parents, wondering who to look at.

"Really? I'm getting a baby brother?" I ask them, my eyes all teary now.

My mum comes to me and asks again, her voice all quiet, "is that ok with you? We talked all night about who could look after him but your dad and I thought we could be the ones. Be his new family. What do you think?"

I'm so overwhelmed by emotions I can barely talk. I just nod, my vision all blurry and kneel on the ground to hug Peppermint.

"Welcome to our family."

Everyone is all emotional at this announcement and after many hugs and "congratulations", my dad finally convinces everyone to sit down to celebrate this great news with some food and coffee.

"Especially coffee!" I hear him say. "The night was long."

And that's how we spend the next hour: welcoming my new brother, asking him questions, feeding him and telling him too many things about us. I see my mum relieved when Peppermint eats their bread and pastries with such an appetite, and Tulip leans into my ear to tell me, "I think he'll fit right in!"

When Peppermint is busy telling Apricot, Tulip and Violet how we saved his life for the tenth time, I ask my parents if he'll be able to go to Woodland Academy too.

"He will, yes, but not right now. We want to give him some time to get used to his new life, and cope with the fact that he lost his parents. I know he seems happy now but we can never forget what happened to him and that it will affect him emotionally. And anyway, he can't start the class midway through the year."

There's so much noise that I'm surprised when I hear someone ask from behind, "What's going on? What are you celebrating?"

I know that voice! I turn around and I'm so happy to see Honeysuckle.

"Hi! Come in, take a seat." I look around for a place for her to sit but with our two families squished around the big table, it's obviously already full.

"Are you sure? I don't want to intrude," she says.

"Of course!" my dad exclaims. "If there's room for eleven, there's room for twelve!"

I like his logic!

"We'll make some space for you," he adds and at that moment I see him exchange a funny look with Basil like they're on to something.

They both grab their Magicol as fast as they can and gesture toward the bench nearest to them. Suddenly the one I'm sitting on gets longer on my side and a short instant later the same thing happens with the other bench. Basil jumps, fists his tiny hedgehog paw in the air and cries, "Ah ah I won!"

My dad admits defeat and we all burst out laughing at their childish game. Honeysuckle looks at me confused and I explain to her that those two have been best friends since their Academy years, and that they love to challenge each other to see which one can cast a spell first. My friend sits down next to me and just as she asks us what we're celebrating, she finally spots Peppermint hidden between Almond and my mum.

"Oh Peppermint, you're here!"

He immediately waves at her with a big smile. "Honeysuckle right?"

"I'm so glad you're out of the hospital! Are you feeling better?"

"Yes!" he replies with a mouthful.

I can't help myself and tell her, "And we have some great news: Peppermint is going to live with us now!"

"What? Waouh, that's so nice!"

"Yes I'm getting a new brother, can you believe it?" I say, a bit too loudly. "Sorry, I'm just so excited," I confess.

"Well we are all very happy to welcome you Peppermint," my mum tells him.

"And I'm so grateful that you welcomed me like this."

"Do you want something to eat Honeysuckle? We still have some brioche," my dad offers her.

She accepts his offer (who would say no to his famous homemade brioche? No one, that's who!) but before he gets a chance to go back in the kitchen to fetch the dish, she says out loud, "But first, I want to say something to you all."

"Oh what is it? Did you get in trouble last night?" I ask her, worried about her parents' reaction.

"No, it's not about me, don't worry. They were angry but I think they were mostly disappointed in me."

She goes to stand at the end of the table and looks at everyone.

"That's why I came here. To apologise."

"It's ok, it was not your fault–" Buttercup tries to reassure her.

"You're very kind, Buttercup but we know it was. It was my idea to go there in the first place. I asked you to trust me and you did, but in the end we could all have been hurt or lost. I put my friends in danger just because I wanted some adventures. I was overconfident, but the truth is, I had no idea what I was doing. And when we were in danger you three were the real heroes. You're the ones that saved me from those humans ...," she says to Buttercup and I.

"...and you're the ones who saved Peppermint and knew what to do," she adds, looking at Almond and me this time. "You were also the ones who talked about cleaning the pond when I just wanted to keep walking. I was selfish and was only trying to have fun and impress you guys."

She pauses, and takes a deep breath like she's looking to inhale some courage in the air.

"I'm really sorry and I'd understand if you didn't want to be my friends anymore or if your parents didn't let you hang out with me."

She doesn't cry, not really, but her voice sounds very choked, like she's about to.

I stand up and put my paw on hers, "Apologies accepted, of course."

She smiles and from close I can see her eyes all big with the tears she's trying not to spill. She nods, like a silent thank you between us before looking at Almond, Buttercup and our parents. No one talks for a bit and for a moment I worry what their answer will be. My dad wouldn't forbid us to be friends after offering her some brioche, would he? Finally it's my mum who talks first.

"Honeysuckle, what you did was indeed ..." she searches for the word, "overconfident."

Basil hums his approval at this.

"But, it takes a lot of courage to apologise and to take full responsibility like you just did! Of course, you're still welcome in our families," she says.

I see Honeysuckle let out a big sigh of relief.

"Plus," my mum adds, "someone wise told me that without your little adventure, no one would have been there to take care of our little Peppermint so we want to thank you."

"So you're thanking me for ... being reckless?" Honeysuckle asks, surprised.

My mum laughs, "Yes, in a way I guess I am."

Honeysuckle stays to share this special breakfast with us and as I look around me, I know I want to remember this moment for the rest of my life. We're all together, laughing, without the stress of yesterday and with the joy of welcoming Peppermint.

Chapter 43
Little brother

O nce our long breakfast is finished, we all tidy up and Honeysuckle tells us she has to go back home.

"My parents didn't yell much, but I have a lot of chores to do to show how sorry I am for my behaviour."

"Sorry. I hope it won't be too hard."

It's not much but I know I can't offer her more.

"It's fine, I deserve it. What are your plans for this afternoon?" she asks.

"Mmmm, I don't know. With everything going on I didn't really have time to think about it."

Suddenly, I feel a small raccoon paw slide in mine and Peppermint offers an idea.

"You could show me around?"

He looks up at me with his cute whiskers and adorable face. I'm sure he'll be naughty and drive me crazy at times, but I'm so happy to have him as a brother. In a way, I'm almost looking forward to all this as it means I get to have him in our family.

"Great idea!" I reply.

"What's a great idea?" Buttercup asks, as he joins our little group.

"I'm going to show Peppermint around Woodland. You want to

come?"

"Sure! I have some work to do for my project but I suppose it can wait until tomorrow, we still have a few days before school starts again."

"School? Is that where you learned magic?" Peppermint asks us.

"Yeah it is. We'll tell you all about it today."

"Ok, I have to go. Have fun!" Honeysuckle waves us goodbye.

Almond decides to join us too, so the three of us take my new brother (Oh, I still can't believe I have a brother now!) to explore our forest.

"Are you sure you don't want to take the trolley?" Tulip teases Peppermint before we leave.

"No, no, no!"

Peppermint declines her offer so fast that we all laugh and Buttercup tells her to stop it, "or Mum will make us take it".

"Don't worry, I'll stay home with her to keep her busy. We need to find a spot for Peppermint's bed and I'm sure I can convince her to help me make him a new blanket …"

She winks at Peppermint like it's a joke, but I can tell she's really happy to do her best to welcome him.

"OK, off we go!"

We spend the next few hours showing Peppermint his new home, leaving nothing out, from the supermarket to the best paths, introducing him to every animal we meet on the way.

"This is my new little brother!" I tell them proudly.

Most of the animals are surprised by this sudden addition to our family (and by the small detail that he's not a squirrel) but after some explanation, they understand. I'm dying to show him the Academy but we don't really dare to enter when school's out, so we just show it to him from the outside, telling him how it works and what we've learned so far in our first few months. I promise to bring him back next week to introduce him to our class.

"Ok, what's next?" Almond asks the group.

"Mmmm, he already knows the hospital so I think we can skip that."

They all agree.

"So I think the last things on the list are…"

I pretend I don't already know where I want to take him next, which makes Buttercup and Almond laugh. Peppermint is waiting quietly.

"... the two best places in Woodland!" I announce with pride.

"Oh, what are they?" he asks, all curious.

"Come on, it's this way. We'll explain to you on the way there."

We walk together towards Sweet Treat taking turns explaining to him what we love best about our family bakery and Dreams.

"My favourite thing at Dreams is the craft corner upstairs. At Sweat Treat it's your mum and Dad's lemonade and of course the carrot pie!" replies Buttercup.

"For me, it's the hot chocolate and those little cookies!" Almond answers.

"And you?" Peppermint asks me.

"The books and the food!" I answer, without hesitation.

He laughs and I explain in more detail.

"Well you see, I love the books but also the atmosphere over there. Being with the Moon sisters, talking about books, spending hours reading. And it's the same for the bakery, it's not just the food that I love, it's how I feel when I'm there. Even though I visit it basically every day, I still love opening the door and being welcomed by all the delicious smells of breads and tarts. And even when my parents ... sorry, I mean our parents" I correct myself embarrassed, "are really tired, they always have a big smile for us. It's my second home."

"It sounds amazing!" he says.

"It is. Look! There it is. There's our bakery and Dreams is just behind, hidden by all those bushy trees and shrubberies."

We decide to start with the library and finish with a snack. Even though I came here only yesterday morning before we left for Black Shadow Forest, with everything that's happened to us in the meantime, I feel like it's been days since I've seen Hazelnut and Miss Moon. As usual, Hazelnut welcomes us with enthusiasm (actually, maybe with a bit too much enthusiasm in a place that's supposed to be quiet).

"Hey! How are my three musketeers? Oh, who's this? A new friend of yours?"

Peppermint is a bit shy at first, intimidated by all this space, the twinkling lights, the number of residents lounging around and maybe also by Hazelnut herself.

"No, this is not a friend, this is actually my brother."

Hazelnut, faithful to her unflappable nature, doesn't even flinch at this announcement.

"Oh, ok," she replies with a big smile.

She accepts what I say, as if I'd just said, "I'm returning this book." We laugh at her reaction and once her sister joins us, we settle down and tell them the story of how Peppermint came into our lives. They're both very welcoming and he seems to relax around them as we explain. I don't want to stay too long and overwhelm him though, so I excuse ourselves by saying that we need to go see our parents.

"So, what did you think?" Buttercup asks my brother quietly once we're outside.

"It's amazing. I ... I ... have never lived in a community. It was just my mum, my dad and me before, so this is all so new to me."

"I can imagine. Tell us if it's a bit too much. We have time, we'll be back, it's fine, ok?"

Buttercup eyes me discreetly and I nod. I think we both notice it's getting too much and that Peppermint is getting tired.

We quickly arrive at the bakery and our welcome is even warmer than usual. I know it's due to the tiny raccoon accompanying us and I can now see how genuinely happy my parents are to have Peppermint. I guess I have always been too busy being an only child to realise that maybe they wanted another baby after me. It's crazy to think that Peppermint has only been my brother for a few hours because this already seems so natural to me. Mum asks us all if we want a cup of their homemade hot cocoa.

"I don't know actually, I've never had any," Peppermint admits, a bit shyly.

"Well, let's find out! Just sit there and I'll bring it to you."

"And I'll bring the new cookies I made this morning," my dad says, proudly displaying his raccoon-shaped cookies.

"You made those just for me?" Peppermint asks in a low voice.

Dad nods. "Of course, to welcome you into the family."

"So you really don't mind that I'm not a squirrel?"

Almond doesn't let me or my parents reply, he answers for us.

"Psst, I don't know if you noticed but I don't look quite like my brother and sisters either."

She winks and adds, "and it's fine like that. Family is not always related to blood. It's made up of those who are here to take care of you."

I can see everyone is getting very emotional about this so I create a diversion by serving the mugs of hot chocolate.

"Ready to try it out?" I ask my baby brother.

He nods, takes his first sip and his reaction is priceless. He closes his eyes, hums his approval and licks his whiskers, all brown now. He takes a second and a third sip and I say, "I think he likes chocolate!"

We all laugh and let him try his raccoon cookies while we tell my parents what we've shown him so far. But suddenly, in the middle of Almond's sentence, I see my mum stand up and rush to Peppermint's chair to hold him in her arms. He has fallen asleep - halfway through his second cookie - so fast, I don't know how my mum managed to see it and react so quickly. She must have superpowers, Mum powers!

"I think this morning has already involved a lot of emotions and a lot of walking on his tiny paws. I think it's best if you take him home to rest," Mum says with a fond smile while patting him on the back gently.

She grabs the half eaten cookie that's still in his paw and rocks him back and forth slowly. Almond offers to carry him home on her back like yesterday.

"Thanks, dear!"

She transfers Peppermint onto Almond's back and packs some cookies for us before we leave.

Buttercup announces that he'll go back to Dreams to paint for a bit.

"Do you want me to look for some books about raccoons?" he asks me.

Oh, that's a good idea. I haven't thought about that.

"Yes please! Also, I think it will be great to talk with some of the local raccoon families to get some direct information about how to care for the little ones too."

"Ok, see you later!"

Almond and I make our way home, chatting softly and walking slowly, trying not to wake Peppermint, my eyes always on him, making sure he doesn't fall.

"Thanks for carrying him," I tell her.

"No problem. I was so scared when we found him last night."

"Me too, it was so ... so strange seeing an animal hurt by humans in real life. I mean, I know your story and I know it does happen but seeing him all hurt and without his parents was very hard."

"I'm so glad he's part of your family, I think your parents made the perfect choice!" she says.

Once home, we settle Peppermint in a quiet corner for him to sleep and have a good rest. As promised, Tulip and Dahlia have prepared a comfortable bed for him with covers and cushions, and I spot them working on a new blanket.

"Was he ok? Did something happen to him?" Dahlia asks us, worried, when she sees us return so quietly.

"No, no, don't worry. He's fine. It was just a lot for him to take in and I think he's still tired from the last few days' events."

Once I know he doesn't need me anymore, I go back to my room. After setting my bag aside all day, I finally succumb to the temptation and take out the two books I got yesterday. I look at both titles and decide to see what's so special about this wizard boy. I've heard Mango and Maple talk about this Harry Potter before, so I'm curious to see why he's so famous among humans.

I spend the next hour and a half reading it and it is such a good book! This poor orphan boy with no one to love him and take care of him discovers that he's a wizard and suddenly goes to this magical school called Hogwarts. It seems much bigger than our Academy but I'm loving all the details about it: the Houses, the points systems, this Quidditch game. Everything sounds like so much fun there! And there are some wizards doing dark magic? We don't have anything like this here. Oh, I wish I could spend the rest of the day reading it and learn more about Harry and his new friends. To be honest the only thing that pulls me out of it is hearing Peppermint wake up and call for me.

"I'm here! I'm coming!" I quickly rush down our tree to meet him by his temporary bed, his eyes still sleepy.

"What happened?" he asks, rubbing his eyes. "One minute we were at the bakery and the next I woke up here."

He looks so confused. I explain how he fell asleep mid cookie and how we brought him home to have a nap. Once he has some water in him, we go to run around and play with Tulip and Almond. We have a blast playing hide and seek, and showing him some magic.

After dinner, as I'm packing for our usual nightly meeting I smile when I realise I now need to add an extra mug so that Peppermint can join us.

"Where are we going?" he asks us all surprised when he sees us pack our basket.

"Not far, you'll see."

We all walk to our hidden fort and let him in.

"Do you prefer hot chocolate or tea?" Buttercup asks Peppermint. "We have both tonight."

"Hot chocolate!" he answers without hesitation. "I really like it!"

We all giggle at his new found love for chocolate. Of course he does.

We stay quiet for a bit, watching the stars and drinking. Finally we explain to our new member that each time we come here we take turns saying something we're grateful for or something that made us happy today.

"You can also add something you're proud of," adds Almond. "You can say anything you want as long as it's positive!"

"I'll start!" I announce. "Easy one today: I'm grateful that we weren't eaten, hurt or lost!"

We all laugh at this and Buttercup takes the second turn.

"I'm glad that in all this mess we found Peppermint, of course. And also that we managed to get some inspiration for our school project."

"Really, you did?" asks his sister, curious. She was not with us last night when he explained to our parents how our adventure inspired him.

"Yes. I'm not sure what or how I'll do it exactly but I'm going to work on something that'll help keep the forest clean from the human's trash."

"And I think I was also inspired by our trip. I want to create a system to exchange books like they did in the Black Shadow Forest but with some magic involved," I add. "What about you, Almond? Any ideas yet?"

She nods but tells us it's a secret for now since it needs some planning and research.

"As for me ... I'm grateful to have a family of hedgehogs to look after me. I miss my parents everyday but I'm so happy to know that at least I'm not alone, with you guys and my new adopted family here. I imagine many animals and humans out there have no one to laugh with, to cuddle, or to simply look at the stars together at night. I feel sad for all the animals who have no hedgehog to look after them."

"Ok, well, I guess the thing I'm grateful for tonight is very similar, sorry," Peppermint giggles a bit before going on. "I'm so grateful that you all disobeyed your parents because without you I'd still be lost in the forest. And I'm grateful that you adopted me in your family and circle of friends. I owe you all so much."

I grab his paw in mine and squeeze two times to let him know I'm here and that he's not alone anymore. It's something my parents often do to let me quietly know that they love me, and I don't think they'll mind if I use their technique on my brother. I'm sure he's going to need a lot of love.

Chapter 44

A mystery solved

The next morning starts with a funny surprise. Well, two actually. The first one is that my parents invited Honeysuckle for breakfast and the second one comes a bit later. We're all enjoying our breakfast with our friend, chatting and having fun, with Peppermint sitting next to me, when just as we're finishing, we see Mum arrive with Miss Pamplemousse, the level II class teacher. Being a hen, she kind of stands out in Woodland and the way she walks always makes me smile: like she's dancing to a song only she can hear. They approach the big table and I go kiss my mum. I haven't seen her yet, since she left for the bakery before I woke up.

"Hey, honey," she gives me a kiss between my ears before doing the same to Peppermint. "Hey sweetie, did you sleep well?"

He nods and compliments the bread we just had for breakfast.

"Ah, actually it's Violet who made this one yesterday afternoon. Do you want a slice?" she asks Miss Pamplemousse.

"Oh no thank you Rose, you're so kind. I don't eat much in the morning."

She turns toward us and says in a quiet tone, "Hello children."

"Hello Miss Pamplemousse. What are you doing here?" asks Tulip.

My mum seems to know why she's here and retreats to the

kitchen while Miss Pamplemousse answers.

"Well," she starts slowly and I realise she looks agitated. I tend to forget that adults and teachers can be nervous too. In a way, I find it reassuring.

"I came to tell you my story. Your mum was just telling me about your little adventure in Black Shadow Forest," she looks at us all now, "and I think it's time I come clean about it."

Come clean about it? I nudge Honeysuckle on the side with a smile. Oh we're finally going to see if all our crazy theories are true.

"First, I'm sorry you felt so scared in this forest. It's not haunted and there's no more danger there than here." We wait for her to continue. "Ok, so do you want to know the truth about how I ended up living in Woodland Forest?"

We all nod, and I'm thinking that we don't have a choice anyway, even if we didn't want to know.

"Well, I simply got lost. It's that simple. You see, I lived at the same farm from the time I was a chick and one day I got bored of always seeing the same feathers around me. I was fed up with all the humans coming in and out of our hen coop to take our eggs, and all the children screaming when they were going to pick fruit in the orchard. Every day was the same as the one before.

"I had enough, and decided to go and explore for a bit, just to have a look. I left the farm and had a nice stroll around, in the forest nearby. I could see this big forest from the farm so I thought it was so close that it would be very easy to come back home when I was done exploring. But I was daydreaming, singing to myself and not paying attention to where I was going. And once I wanted to go home, I realised that I didn't know how to go back to the farm. I was completely lost with no one to show me the way. So I kept walking for a long time and ended up here, in Woodland."

"You never tried to find your way back later? You didn't ask for help?" Almond asks her.

"Well, for a long time I was so ashamed of what I had done so I never told anyone. I just pretended I couldn't remember where I came from." She pauses for a second before adding, "but you see, with time, this forest became more my home than the farm ever was, so I stopped thinking about it and I simply put my old life in the past."

"But how come you never tried to deny those rumours about you and the Black Shadow Forest?" Honeysuckle asks, shocked.

"Mmm ... it was a convenient way to keep kids from exploring too much so I let everyone believe what they wanted. It was safer that way."

"Safer? But you just said there's no actual danger in Black Shadow Forest?"

"Yes but I've always been scared of someone else going there to explore and getting lost outside Woodland like I was. And it would be awful not to be able to find your way back to our forest, don't you think?"

She's right, I can't imagine one of us getting lost and never finding our way back to our beloved forest. We all nod silently in agreement.

Honeysuckle says, "Thank you for telling us. Now, I can guarantee you something: I'll never complain about Woodland being boring ever again! After almost being kidnapped, I think I've had my share of adventures for a lifetime, thank you very much!"

We all burst out laughing at this remark and she adds, "Also, I think I'm not so fond of humans anymore. I'll be fine seeing them from afar from now on but there's no need for me to go study them or their houses."

"Great decision!" Miss Pamplemousse says, before telling us she has a busy day ahead and disappearing in a flash.

Once she's gone, my mum comes back from the kitchen to check what our plans for the day are. Almond is gone before she can answer her, which is very peculiar even for her. Buttercup and I both plan to go to Dreams to study a bit.

"For your school project?"

"Yes, and I have something else I'd like to work on too. I'll show you later," I tell her.

"Ok, what about you Peppermint? Girls?" she asks Apricot, Tulip and Violet.

Violet plans to stay here to try a new recipe but reassures Mum that she'll stop by the bakery later to help out.

Tulip is going to the fabric shop to work on a banner for the school's Special Project day. Even though she has already graduated, she still helps the Academy from time to time.

Apricot says she's going to stay home and relax before going to see some friends. She really wants to enjoy this last week of holidays before going back to school. Since it's her last year I can imagine she has a lot to study.

"I think I'll come with you to Dreams! I want to explore it more and maybe try to paint," Peppermint says.

"Ok, have fun! I'm going back to the bakery. I just came with Miss Pamplemousse so she could talk to you about all this mystery."

"Bye Mum!"

I pack my Harry Potter book and some school notes, check that I have Berry in my wand carrier. Then we head off quickly together, Peppermint, Buttercup and I. Once at Dreams, I allow myself thirty minutes to read a bit before starting to work on my school project. In the end though, I'm so lost in Harry's adventures that I end up reading for an hour. Oops! When I go upstairs to check on my brother, I'm happy to see Hazelnut teaching him some basic watercolour techniques. I'm relieved to see he's having a good time and that he seems more at ease here than yesterday.

I go back down to the ground floor, select some books and get started on my work on one of the free tables. It's so early that the library is still very quiet, so it's a perfect time for me to concentrate. I'll admit, right now my school project is more of a concept than anything else but the main idea is to recreate the library system we saw in Black Shadow Forest here in Woodland. I plan to have several library boxes scattered all around our forest, and I want to use magic to connect them and send books from one box to the other. Also, I'd like readers to be able to fetch books from the nearest box to their house without having to move. It would help animals who can't move very much, are sick or are too busy, like Honeysuckle's parents who are always surrounded by their small children.

Maybe some users could have their own box at home to send books through? I have to think about this. Ideally, I'd also love to create some sort of catalogue system that'll keep automatically track of all the books in circulation, but this will probably require a level of magic I don't have yet. It's fine, just like Mrs Winter and my father, I can add alterations later as I get better at magic. I remember Mrs Winter telling us that the Great Wizard is here to help with projects that need to project magic in a large zone of the forest, so I'll have to see how to contact her.

Once in a while I check on Buttercup, who is also busy going through some spellbooks and taking notes. Just like me, he's scribbling ideas on how to make his project work. After one hour working on this, I put all those books back on their shelves and go outside to get some fresh air and stretch my paws before I start to work on my new personal project. Buttercup sees me leave and follows me.

"Hey, you need a break too?"

"Yes, I've worked so much that I can't read my own handwriting anymore," he explains. "I think I'm going to go and paint for a bit before studying some more. What about you? Did you find the information you needed?"

"Yes, I've made good progress. So far I'm happy with what I've got. But I also think I need a break now. Actually ..." I hesitate to tell him about my new project but if I don't tell my best friend then I can't tell anyone and that's just crazy. "... I'm planning on writing something."

"Oh! A new story?"

"No, not this time. After our research into Black Shadow Forest the other day, I started thinking and I want to write my own guide."

"About Black Shadow Forest?" he asks, surprised.

"No, I don't know enough about it. No, about our forest. I want to write a guide about Woodland. And..." I pause, not sure if it's a stupid idea or not, "At first the idea was to write it just for us animals here, but now I'm kinda of tempted to write it for human children as well."

"Really? For humans? Waouh! But why children? I thought you would hate them after what happened to Honeysuckle," he says, half joking, half curious.

"Because I think adults wouldn't believe any of it. But the kids have a power their parents don't have. They can dream and imagine. Didn't you see the difference between the reactions of the little girl and her dad when we attacked them with magic? The girl immediately asked if it was some kind of magic and right away her dad told her it was nonsense, that magic doesn't exist."

"Mmm ... Yes, that's true. The adults don't seem to be able to imagine things that they can't see."

"So what do you think? Do you think it's a good idea?" I ask him, a bit anxious, stroking my tail to soothe my nerves. I like my plan but still, having my best friend's opinion is very important.

"If anyone could write a great guide to Woodland Forest, it's you Applesauce! I'm sure it'll be great."

Relief flows through me. I suspected I would have my best friend's support but it's always good to confirm it.

"And even if it's bad, it's fine. No one will be hurt just because I wrote a book, right?" I add with a big smile.

"Exactly, that's the spirit!"

Buttercup goes back inside to paint. After a quick stop at the bakery for a nice tea and a quick biscotti (I couldn't say no to my mum, she insisted!), I head back to Dreams. My parents ask me to send Peppermint over for a snack too. I tell them that he's busy painting but promise to pass on their message.

Chapter 45

A helping paw

After letting my little brother know that he can pop up to the bakery anytime he wants for a snack, I start to look for books that'll help me with my research. I pile so many of them up so high on the library desk that Miss Moon chuckles when she walks by.

"I didn't even see you behind all those books! It looks like you've built yourself a fort!"

I smile at this idea.

"Well, a fort made of books would be the best kind, wouldn't it?"

"For sure. What are you reading? Is it for your school project?"

"No, I did work on my project earlier but now I'm ..." I hesitate for just a second.

"Oh, is it a secret?" she whispers.

"Actually no, I can tell you. Just, don't make fun of me, please?" I ask her in a small voice.

"Oh, Applesauce, when have I ever made fun of you?"

"Never, I know, I'm sorry!" I add sheepishly. "Ok, I'll tell you."

And I start explaining my idea to her and why I came up with it.

"Oh that's exciting! And that's a really good idea!"

"You think so?"

I knew Buttercup would love the idea but he's kind of biased since we're best friends and all. Having an adult I admire so much telling me she likes it too is a great boost for me.

"Oh yes!" She has a big smile and this little look on her face, like she has a secret she's about to share. "Wait, I'll show you something!"

She rushes out behind the library's counter and, after looking through drawers for a long minute, she comes back carrying a big file that she hands to me.

"Here, look."

I pull it closer on the table to see clearly what this is about and I gasp.

The file's cover says Woodland in beautiful calligraphy, the letters adorned with delicate drawings of flowers, leaves and vines. And at the bottom I see A Comprehensive Guide by E. Moon written in the same pretty handwriting. I wonder what the "E" stands for.

"What? You too?"

She smiles, nods and sits down next to me to show me the content of the folder.

"Yes, I also had this idea of writing a guide about our forest. But, like many things, it just stayed an idea."

"But you did some research!" I cry, indicating all the notes and drawings I see in front of us.

"Yes, I started researching and thinking about what I could write. I took lots of notes and I even asked the older animals of the forest if they had some stories to share. I managed to get some interesting tales from the Great Wizard, Mr Pinecone, Root and Doctor Peanut, who've all been here for a long time. I even got some extracts from Mr Blythe's diary."

"His diary? Isn't that a bit too personal?" I ask, shocked.

"Oh no, it was not a personal journal. It was more about the forest. He used to write about everything going on around here: who was born, who had just arrived, what celebrations they had ... He was maybe a bit too serious about it at times. He even recorded which residents were practising magic, enrolled at the Academy ..."

"Why?"

"Who knows? I know it makes him look a bit extreme but to

be honest, I think he just liked making lists. He was so lonely for a long time, I think it kept him busy."

I look at some of her notes and I'm amazed by all the information she has already gathered.

"Waouh, is this ...? No, it can't be ..."

"Yes, it's the Great Wizard before she became the Great Wizard. During her own school days."

It's an old painting of the Great Wizard when she was still learning magic, like me. It's easy to forget that, at some point, even adults had to learn what they know now.

"By the way, is there a reason why she's called the Great Wizard and not the Great Witch?" I ask Miss Moon out of the blue. It's been bothering me since I started school but I never asked anyone about it.

"Oh well ... the main reason is that no one wants to change old Woodland traditions older than some of our trees. Everyone said that it was the title and that we shouldn't go around changing it just because of her. The thing is, she's the first female Great Wizard, they were all males before her. And to tell you the truth, I think all those old crusty wizards thought she would never last and would give her title back in a month. But she never did. She showed them how good she was and earned their respect."

"But isn't that bothering her? She could ask to change it now."

"I don't know, I never asked her actually."

I'll have to tell all this to Honeysuckle, I'm sure she'll find it interesting and infuriating.

"Anyway, if you think my notes can help you, they're yours," Miss Moon says as she stands up. "I have to go, I have lots of books to resize and put back on the shelves."

"Do you want some help?" I offer.

"No, no, I'll be fine, don't worry." She starts to go but comes back to add, "Oh by the way, your baby brother is so cute! He seemed to have a good time painting with Hazelnut when I saw them earlier. How are you dealing with all this?"

"Oh I'm loving it!" I answer honestly. "It's funny because he has only really just arrived in my life, so it should feel very peculiar, but actually it already feels quite natural."

"Good, I'm sure he'll be happy with your family."

"I hope so too. I'll do my best to make sure he does anyway."

"I'm sure you will! Ok, have fun with the guide!"

"Yes, and thank you so much for all your notes, they are really going to help me a lot!"

"No problem!"

I spend the next hour checking which books I'll really use. I'm dying to read Miss Moon's folder first, but I think it's best to start by eliminating the resources I won't need to move faster. Since many of the books I selected contain only a snippet of information that I need, I simply copy the passage I'm interested in into my notebook before putting those books to the side, in the "I won't need you" pile. Working like this really helps me see clearly which books I'll keep and I manage to get rid of a dozen useless ones, either containing nothing or not enough. Once I'm done, my new pile only has three titles left. Magic, a History is all about our Woodland magic and was written a long time ago by a certain Professor Whiskers. The two other books are from the human world: Myths and Legends: a Complete History of Magic Through Time in Europe and Magic in the Forests Around You. A guide to English Folklore.

I'll borrow these three books so I can work on them at home. I tidy up all my unwanted books quickly and when I finally sit down with Miss Moon's folder I feel like I have received a special treat. Or like an explorer discovering an ancient hidden treasure in the deep jungle. For now, I simply look at everything she has collected and organise them by theme: personal stories from residents, basic facts, and the notes from Mr Blythe's diary. I also need a new pile just for all the information she has collected from the Great Wizard because it's a lot! I make a note in my notebook to check with her whether I can use all this in my book. I wouldn't want to do it without her permission.

I also love all the artwork she's collected because they really reflect the history of Woodland. There are paintings of our forest, showing some places getting greener with time and the Academy's location moving around. Some local artists have also painted scenes from the annual Grateday celebrations, as well as some family pictures. I recognise some of them by their names. There's also a bunch of small cards and flyers announcing local events like the opening of our hospital.

I feel my heart squeeze with pride when I spot a drawing of my parents at the opening of their bakery. It's just a drawing but they're beaming in it. I wonder who the artist was. It was drawn on a light cardboard postcard, and at the top it says "BIG OPENING!" with lots of little details about Sweet Treat all around. Just as I'm feeling very emotional looking at this memory, I see Peppermint coming down the stairs from the corner of my eye.

"Hey, what are you doing?" he whispers to me as he gets to my table.

"Oh perfect timing! Come here, I have to show you something!"

I gesture to him to sit next to me and show him the postcard.

"Is that your mum and dad?" he asks.

Technically it's our mum and dad now but I don't say anything. I guess it must be hard for him to get used to this new dynamic. I imagine it must be difficult for him to call two animals he didn't even know just a few days ago by such intimate names. He lost his parents so recently and I would never want him to feel like he's replacing them by adopting this new family. I understand that it's way easier for me to start calling him my brother.

I tell him all about my guidebook idea and Miss Moon's notes.

"Waouh, that's amazing! Can I read it when you're done since I know nothing about Woodland? Well, not much anyway."

"Of course! It makes me want to write it even more, knowing it will help you settle."

"But, there's a small problem ..." he adds, looking a bit ashamed to admit it.

"What is it?"

"Well, I can't read. There were no books where we were living and my parents never taught me."

Oh, I feel bad for not even considering this as a possibility.

"Don't worry, I'll teach you!"

"Really?"

"Yes. Look, we can even go and select some books to work on right now if you want. I'm pretty sure there are some we can use. Actually," I stop to think about it, "I have an idea! Why don't you go to the bakery, have a snack and I'll look for those books. So when you come back we can start working on it."

"But weren't you working on your guide?"

"Oh no, it's fine. I've worked on it for a while now so I can easily stop and teach my little brother to read. Besides, once you know how to read I'll be able to share my favourite books with you so that's a big motivation for me too, you know."

Chapter 46
Almond's secret

Peppermint goes have his snack and for a brief moment I wonder if I should join him to get one too. The snack I had earlier barely counted ... No, no, no, I need to focus on helping him instead of thinking about food! Like my best friend always says, "Think with your brain, not your belly Applesauce!"

Instead, I go ask Miss Moon for the best books on how to teach someone to read. I remember that my mum taught me herself, but I don't remember what books she used back then. Miss Moon quickly hands me a selection of books, and as soon as I see the one with the red cover and the drawing of a tree, I recognise it as the reader I learned on! I suddenly see myself at home, all little, with Mum by my side teaching me how to read each sound and how to combine them together. She spent a lot of time teaching me like this after coming home from the bakery. She must have been so tired but she was so excited to teach me that it motivated me to learn even more. She was so patient with me and used to finish each lesson by giving me cookies with milk.

It's so funny how memory can work sometimes: just seeing (or smelling) something and suddenly all those moments rush back to you. I can still hear her tell me, "Learning to read will open a new world to you Applesauce, the world of words and stories. You'll go on adventures, meet new friends, learn new things ...There's nothing like reading!"

And she was right, it did open a new world to me! Once I knew how to read I never stopped and now I'm hoping to give the same gift to Peppermint.

Peppermint and I start our lessons today and the rest of my Grateday holidays follow on in a similar way. Every day I teach my brother to read, study for my Special Project and read the books I borrowed for my guide. Oh, and I even find time to finish the first Harry Potter! I love it so much that I end up devouring the last chapters late one night in bed with my lamp (powered by magic!). It is fascinating to read a story with human wizards and witches, and see the differences and similarities between my world and this fictional one. (I find it so funny that humans don't believe magic is real.) I also really love meeting all those brave characters and I really want to read the rest of this series. I'll need to check with Mango and Maple if they have them, or see if Miss Moon can order the rest for the library.

Every day, Peppermint, Buttercup and I go to Dreams to read, study or paint and it takes me some time to realise that we haven't seen Almond much since our big adventure in Black Shadow Forest. Obviously we do see her at home, she doesn't disappear completely, but during the day we have no idea where she is. I'm so busy with my two projects and teaching Peppermint how to read, that at first, I don't notice. Then Buttercup asks me if I know where Almond is and I notice he seems really worried.

"Oh, I just assumed she was spending time with the Rumble as usual."

"I thought so too but I met Paprika the other day and when she asked me about Almond, I realised that she hasn't seen her in a while either."

"Oh that's strange."

"And the other funny thing is that my dad goes missing too," Buttercup adds, perplexed.

"Really? Mmm, maybe they're doing something together then."

"Yeah but it must be a secret because they're not telling any of us. I asked my sisters, they don't know a thing about it either, and when I tried asking my mum she pretended she was too busy to talk to me."

"Very weird indeed!"

The good thing is we don't have to wait too long to solve this new mystery because, on the Sunday before school starts again, Almond finally confesses the truth during our weekly potluck lunch. By now most of our neighbours are back from their Grateday trip and Honeysuckle is here with her family too. Almond waits until Buttercup, Honeysuckle, Peppermint and I are all together to tell us.

"Hey, I have something to tell you all ..."

"Is it related to where you've been those last few days?" Buttercup asks with his best big brother tone.

"Yes it is. How did you know?"

We all laugh and Buttercup goes on, "Well, you and Dad have been gone every day, no one knows where you go and Mum doesn't want to tell me anything either. So I'm guessing it's something fishy."

"Actually, it's not fishy at all. It's for my school project."

Oh, that's ... surprising!

"I've been going outside the forest, patrolling the area to see if I can find other hurt animals like Peppermint."

"Outside Woodland?" I ask, incredulous.

"What? Are you crazy?" Honeysuckle asks at the same time.

"Didn't you learn anything from our crazy adventure?" This question comes from Buttercup, and he seems torn between anger and fear for his sister.

Almond doesn't lose her nerves though and answers us calmly.

"Yes, outside Woodland, and no, I'm not crazy." And then she looks at her brother to tell him, "Yes, I did learn something during our adventure. I learned that we're very fortunate to have a safe life here, and to be surrounded by our forest and our ancestors' magic. But that's not the case for everyone and we can help so many animals if we put our heads together to think of a solution. We can make sure that what happened to Peppermint doesn't happen again. He was all alone in the woods with no magic but also no means to contact anyone to help him. So that's my project. I want to work on a device that will allow animals to contact each other in case of emergency.

"Even outside emergency situations I think we could use it to help animals who are lonely, even here in Woodland. There are some elderly animals who have no family to spend time with or who are too sick to go anywhere. With a device like mine, they could send a signal saying they need a bit of company."

"But why did you go outside? It's so dangerous, Almond!" her brother goes on, clearly still worried about her safety.

"Don't worry I was always invisible and with Dad on my back. We left the forest to get an idea of the distance we need to cover before we reach the places with lots of humans. We made a map of all the places that need protection and surveillance around Woodland. Most of the time, we only need to cover areas that are a few kilometres wide.

"And while we were doing this, we actually met some animals in need, who were lost or simply alone. We managed to send two birds back to their own forests, and to heal a badger and a rabbit who went exploring but injured themselves and were too hurt to find their way back home. We even welcomed a wild boar who was on an adventure, trying to see the ocean. After we explained to him that there was no ocean for hundreds of kilometres, he agreed to come live in Woodland. Well, he said it might be a pit stop before he goes on with his travels."

There's a silence among us, so Almond finally asks her brother, "So, are you still mad at me?"

"How could I be mad at you for doing something so kind? As long as you're safe I'm fine with your plan!" Buttercup admits.

"Peppermint, what do you think?" My brother doesn't answer her with words, he simply goes to hug her.

"I'm glad you like my project!" she says, hugging him back.

After a short silence, Honeysuckle asks Almond, "But, aren't you afraid of not getting your project approved? I know we're not graded but will the school allow it?"

"What do you mean?" I ask my friend. "Her idea is great!"

"Yeah, yeah, of course it's an amazing idea but I'm guessing you'll have to ask for help for some of the magic. Aren't we supposed to use only the magic we know?"

"I know, I thought about it but in the end I decided that I don't mind. I'd rather have this project not approved and help animals in need."

Almond is really full of surprises. Listening to her amazing idea, I realise that even though we tend to see Almond as the wild one in our group, she has grown up a lot recently. She can actually be quite mature with her magic when she has a goal in mind.

Chapter 47

Surprises & achievements

O nce the Grateday break is over, school starts again and the weeks until the big Presentation Day pass really fast. After a dry winter, the weather in Woodland gets warmer as the weeks go by and I'm blown away when I realise that the big day is almost there! It's insane to think that a few months ago we couldn't do any magic at all and now we're about to do our big presentation in front of the whole school.

We've read and studied our spells and potions books in their entirety, and with time we've all learned how to have more control of our magic and how to be more connected to our Magicol. Even Wind has mastered his spells like a natural. Mrs Winter was really impressed by his transformation when we came back from our Grateday holiday. She even took me aside one day to question me about it.

"Applesauce, have you noticed something different in Wind's behaviour over the last few weeks? Since he came back from the break, he's been smiling more, he's not messing up his potions, and he's even mastering his spells really quickly now. He's almost as good as ..."

She doesn't finish her comparison and I know why. Our

Academy puts a big emphasis on not grading students and not judging who is the best. It's all about celebrating our differences and our individual strengths. I personally like this. I think it stops a sense of competition developing between classmates, so I'm glad she doesn't finish her sentence.

"Do you know what happened to him? I'm really glad to see him improve of course, I'm just so surprised by the difference in just a few weeks."

I smile at her reaction and offer her my opinion.

"I think it's because he's happier outside of school now."

"How so?"

"Well, at the beginning of the holidays I brought him to Dreams and since then he's been so much happier."

"Why? Does he love to read too?"

"No, it's because of the art centre upstairs. He's been there almost everyday since he came back from his trip. Buttercup says he's always there painting or doing workshops."

I explain that he was not allowed to express his creativity at home because of his dad and that going to Dreams really changed him.

"So I guess school has been easier for him once he started feeling better in his head," I add.

"Then I have to congratulate you on being such a good friend to him! It seems that you did him a big favour."

I feel myself blush as I have a hard time accepting compliments. What I did was not much but I'm glad to see it had a big impact on Wind.

"So, do you think you're ready for your project?"

"I think I am, yes."

"Great, I can't wait to see what you came up with next Friday!"

I don't confess to her that, even though I did work hard on my school project, writing my Woodland guide has been taking me so much more time. But I'm almost done with this too and I'm really happy with the result. I actually interviewed Mrs Winter and other school teachers to add some of their own stories in it. I decided to have a section of the book for little stories like theirs, like a collection of memories. Some only wrote a small paragraph while others had few pages to share, but all their contributions were great to me because I love how unique they make the book.

When school started again, I quickly introduced Peppermint to my teacher and classmates and since then, he's been really impatient to start class too. Going to the Academy next year was a big motivation for him to learn how to read. He was a really fast learner and knew how to read alone in a month. He's so eager to learn magic that I regularly see him peek at my spell book. We told him to be patient, that he'll be in class before he knows it but still, he just loves to look at this book. He says he wants to prepare himself to be "the best wizard possible."

I'm biassed since he's my brother but honestly I'm so proud of him! In just a few months, he has really settled down to life in Woodland and he's even made his own friends on top of mine. Everyone around us is crazy about him because he was so small when we found him but he has grown a lot since then. He's not a baby anymore, and he's reading every chance he gets. I think that lately he's even been reading more than me since he's home all day while I have to go to school, and spend the rest of my time on my Special Project and my guide. He has also learned a lot from Buttercup and the Moon sisters at the craft centre. At first he was mainly painting but lately he likes to create objects with mosaic squares. Before that, he had a phase when he was really into pottery but it didn't last. It's all fun, he's exploring and growing up so fast.

I celebrated my birthday a few weeks ago and my parents really surprised me for this one. I finally understood why Miss Moon has never responded to any of my numerous requests to order the Harry Potter books that I wanted to read so badly. As usual we celebrated it at home, with the Dreamcreek family, with a simple lunch and a delicious cake. As my parents were cutting the cake, one by one my friends brought me a wrapped gift, each with a mischievous smile. Each gift had a similar shape so I easily assumed they were books but as I opened the first two presents, I started to laugh. Each package contained a different Harry Potter book: the six remaining books in the series and a play that's supposed to conclude the whole story. All of it thanks to my parents who relayed my wish to everyone around us.

"So now you can finally keep reading them," my mum whispers

in my ear as she gives me my slice of cake. "Sorry we had to trick you like this, I just thought it would make a great birthday gift."

And on top of all the books, I also received some amazing handmade gifts: Buttercup made me a wooden book stand so I can read while eating. Peppermint made me a paper bookmark with the outline of an open book on it and Tulip made me a pumpkin-scented candle.

"It's my first time making a candle, so I hope it'll smell good."

To top everything off, the birthday table was covered with chocolate frogs that Violet had made just for this occasion. Apricot enchanted them so they could jump just like in Harry Potter.

It was truly a magical birthday, in every sense of the word.

The day before we have to present our Special Project, Honeysuckle comes to see me at Dreams while I'm working on my guide. She sits down next to me. I push all my notes and my pile of books on the side to make some space for her but she doesn't even open her bag.

"Hey! How are you? Not too worried for tomorrow?" she asks me quietly.

"Hi! You know what? Strangely, I'm feeling quite relaxed about the school project."

"Really? You, the master of stressing over everything?" she nudges me on the side.

"Oh I'm way better than I used to be, believe me. You didn't know me before we started at the Academy but I was so nervous back then. I mean, more than I am now. I think magic helped me deal with my stress."

"So, you're really not stressed?" she asks again, surprised.

"Well, no. I don't know if it's because I kept myself so busy writing my little book and looking after Peppermint, but I feel like my project is good and ready to show to the teachers. What about you?"

"Ah ah ah, no, I won't tell you, it's a ..."

"... secret, yeah I know!" I finish for her.

It's been like this for weeks, she keeps insisting on keeping her project a secret from anyone. At first I was a bit hurt by this secrecy but now I'm just waiting patiently for her presentation.

"Still busy writing your guide then?"

"Yes, I'm almost done. I'm just fact-checking some last details because I heard different stories from different residents."

"Oh really? Like what?"

"Well for example, here ..." I show her a page of my notepad with notes from last week, "I have Mr White, who told me we started using magic here in Woodland in 1984. But Miss O'Hara, you know the nice rabbit who works at the supermarket, told me it went as far back as 1920. And don't get me started on the origins of the Academy because so far I've heard every version of 'Oh I remember very well when the Academy opened, it was in...' and then they all told me a different year. So obviously I had to go back to the headmaster himself to get the final word but he's so busy it took me some time to get confirmation on this."

"Waouh! Was it like that for everything?" Honeysuckle asks surprised. I laugh and tell her that for the most part yes, that's how it went.

"So, in the end, I think it took me more time to fact-check everything than it took to gather the information in the first place."

"You're brave, I'd have given up a long time ago!"

I show her some of my recent progress and she reads through some pages while I keep working on it.

"So what do you plan on doing with it once you're done?"

"First I want to give the original to Dreams and then I plan on making copies to share around."

"How do you do that?"

"What? Make copies? Mmm, I was curious about that and checked in our school book but there was nothing in it about a spell or potion to duplicate objects. So I went to check The Big Book of Woodland Magic at the library and found a spell to do it."

"A spell that we don't learn at school? I didn't know it was possible, I thought you were supposed to leave the Academy knowing everything?"

"I thought so too but this book contains extra spells and potions that an old witch wrote down to share thirty years ago. She explains that she learned some of them during her travels to other magical places, and that she created some new spells herself."

"Waouh! So how does this spell work?"

I explain to her how I'll have to copy each page one by one by visualising its content and then assemble everything together to bind it as a book.

"Can't you just copy the whole book in one go?"

"One day, yes, I guess I'll be able to do that directly, but first I'll have to be patient."

"And where will you put those copies?"

"I was thinking about asking Mango and Maple to leave some behind them when they travel, but I'd also like to leave a copy or two in the Black Shadow Forest library."

"What? You want to go back there? You're crazy! I won't let you do that, I'll tell your parents if I need to!" My friend is suddenly so agitated and serious that I believe she would sell me out to my parents without hesitation. Which is reassuring in a way I guess?

"Oh no, don't worry my parents won't allow me to go back there alone either. Not for now anyway. They said I could go back alone when I can master more advanced magic. But in the meantime, I can go with them. They said I just have to ask.

I remember how my mum had calmly reassured me when I told her about my plans for the guide, "We understand your desire to see more of the world, we've been there too. But you're still too young to do it alone. Just ask us and we'll be happy to take you there."

I snap out of my reverie and return to the present.

"Anyway, you don't have to worry, it's going to take me some time to make those copies," I tell Honeysuckle.

Honeysuckle nods reassured.

"Ok, well, I'll let you work, I'm going home. See you tomorrow at school for the big day?" she asks me with a big smile.

"Yes! Will you finally let us know what your project is or will you keep it a secret from the teachers too?" I tease her.

She laughs as she grabs her bag and waves me goodbye.

Once I'm alone again, I spend hours working on all the last details that need to be double checked. Then I reread what I wrote and move some pages here and there. And finally, after weeks of writing this guide and one final reread, I'm done! I finished it! I'm so excited and proud of myself that I can't help yelling a bit too loud, "I did it!"

After some hard stares from those around me, I add a quiet "Yahoo!" for myself. Even Berry is celebrating with me, vibrating against me in its pouch!

I can't believe I managed to write it all and finish it before my big presentation tomorrow. I really worked hard on writing this book and I can't wait to show it to everyone. I look around and I'm a bit upset to realise that neither Miss Moon or Hazelnut are here to see this moment. They must be in the storage area or busy with customers upstairs. It's a pity, I was really hoping to show it to them right away. With no one here, I guess there's nothing for me to do but pack my bag. But just as I'm almost done packing, I hear them enter through the back door, laughing at something Hazelnut just said.

"Oh you're still here, Applesauce? You're really working hard on this book, aren't you?"

"Actually," I start, grabbing the final book in my paws, "I'm ... I'm done. I just finished it."

"What? Really?" Hazelnut exclaims really loudly.

This time though no one dares to give her "the look" to tell her to keep quiet. I guess when you're the owner of the library no one can shush you. She jumps toward me, grabbing the guide from my paws with such enthusiasm that I can't help giggling. Her sister seems equally happy to hear my news, even if, as usual, she shows it in a more subtle way. She approaches me slowly and gives me a quick hug.

"Oh I'm so proud of you my dear!"

Her voice is soft but her kind words mean so much to me.

"So am I!" cries Hazelnut. "Oh we should celebrate! We have to!"

I laugh and tell them that they don't even know if my book is good.

"Maybe we should wait until you've read it to celebrate," I suggest.

"Nonsense! I'm sure it's great!" Hazelnut simply declares.

"Besides," adds Miss Moon, "even if this guide of yours turns out to be a big pile of poo, we're still proud of you for finishing it!"

I laugh at this and joke, "Yeah, congrats to me for writing a bad book!"

"No, but I'm serious Applesauce! You managed to finish what, years ago, was only an idea to me. So many animals say they will do something, start a project and give up halfway. Many even give up before they ever really get started. So no matter what, you can be proud of yourself for working hard on this project. It's an accomplishment to finish. We'll close the shop a bit earlier and join you at the bakery in a second."

Once alone outside, I stop and smile about what they just said. I finally see their logic and agree that I should be proud of my achievement. My parents are so excited by my big news that we end up celebrating with tea and a strawberry tart to share between the five of us.

The Moon sisters, my parents and I talk about the pictures and stories that I have collated in my guide until it's time to close the bakery. We wave the Moon sisters goodbye and go home together. They tell me again how proud they are of me for writing this book and what kind of cakes they baked for tomorrow's celebration lunch. Just like our first day of school, we'll have a big picnic all together to celebrate the end of the school year and the presentation of the projects. By the time we get home, I'm tired but my belly is already rumbling as I think about all the food!

Chapter 48
The big day

The big day is here, it's finally Presentation Day! We've studied magic for months and now it's finally time to show our friends, families and teachers what project we have created with our new knowledge. As soon as I wake up, I get down our tree quickly, say hi to everyone and when I meet my mum in the kitchen, I let her hug me a while longer than usual.

"Hi Mum! How are you?"

"Oh hello sweetie. I'm fine, I'm fine, but how are you? Not too nervous?"

She's asking less questions than usual so I know she's stressed. She usually talks non stop but when something is on her mind she gets silent. Well, silent compared to her norm. I know she's worried about me so I put her at ease right away.

"Don't worry Mum, I'm fine."

"Really?" she asks, playing nervously with the nearest jar on the counter.

"Really. I'm a bit nervous but it's more because I'll have to talk in public than because of the project itself. I'm actually more curious to see the others' projects than worried about mine."

"Oh great, that's nice to hear!" She lets out a sigh of relief. "I mean, I know you said you were confident about it before, but sometimes once the big day is here, we're not so sure anymore so I wanted to check that you really are feeling fine."

"Totally fine!" I tell her once more with a reassuring smile.

"Ok go outside get your breakfast then! I'm almost done packing all your food for the picnic."

"You need help?"

"No, no, don't be silly, go eat it's more important! A full belly for a clear mind!"

I smile at her logic, thank her with a quick kiss and get out while I hear her talk to herself, "Ok so the apple pie and the carrot cake in this basket and the chocolate muffins in there ..."

Breakfast is a quick and quiet event today. Not because Almond, Buttercup and I are nervous, but because we're all going over our notes one last time. Peppermint is on his second bowl of nuts and dried fruits, his nose stuck in a new book. Once we're done eating, we leave for school ahead of our families.

"We'll see you there in an hour!" Buttercup calls out to his parents as we go.

The walk to school is quick and relaxed. My best friends and I talk about how fast our first year has gone by and what we loved most about this time. Once at the Academy, we're told to wait for directions in our classroom, and we say hello to our friends while we wait for Mrs Winter to arrive. My usual group gathers together quickly: Buttercup, Honeysuckle, Almond and Wind. I try to make sure Wind is not too stressed by the presentation but he assures me that he's fine. Well, he has certainly come a long way since the day I bumped into him, trying to run away from school!

"I'm nervous but not because of the presentation itself. Well, not really. My parents are coming to the presentation today and my dad said that, depending on my performance, he'll allow me to go to an art summer camp."

"Waouh, that's great news!"

"It's nice to see that he's warmed up to your love of art, isn't it?"

"Yes, it's a big progress for sure! I mean compared to 'I'll never let a son of mine waste his time on something as useless as painting'," Wind says. imitating his dad's deep voice. Then he adds, in his own voice, "But I'm still nervous. What if he says no? Oh I hope he'll let me go. And what if he says yes but the art camp is too hard for me?"

"How can an art camp be too hard?" Honeysuckle asks, chuckling.

"Well, I don't know. Imagine I arrive there and all the other students are amazing. Maybe on the first day there's a test where the teachers ask us to "Draw an apple! Draw a tree! Draw a deer!" and the ones who can't draw it get kicked out."

"Why would they kick students out?" Almond asks him.

"I don't know, maybe they don't want to waste their time."

Ok so maybe I talked too fast when I said Wind was doing better with his stress.

"Wind, stop! You're panicking for nothing." Honeysuckle shouts at him.

"Calm down, ok?" she adds, calmly this time.

Wind takes a deep breath and I try my best to reassure my friend.

"First, you don't know if your dad is going to say yes or no and, secondly, if you go to art camp, I'm sure there won't be any kind of crazy tests like that and no one will be kicked out. It's a place to learn, not to make fun of students."

With some more reassuring words from all of us, Wind manages to calm down just in time for Mrs Winter's arrival.

"Hello everybody!" she says as she enters our outdoor classroom.

We all stop chatting and welcome her in return.

"No need to sit down, we'll get going right away. Just like on our first day, the presentation will be held at the Kappa meadow since we need space to accommodate your families. Plus, some of your projects can take some space. Before we go I just want to explain that once we get there you'll have to wait for your turn. Your families will be watching in a special area and you'll wait in a separate one. We've already put your names on the designated benches to make it easier for you to find your place. We will call you one by one based on the demonstration order. Once everyone is done with their project presentation, there'll be a speech by Mr Pinecone and a small awards ceremony to celebrate the end of your first year. Now if there are no questions, we can go."

Of course there's a question because Plum always has a question about everything. I think Mrs Winter was expecting it though because she immediately turns her head toward Plum's raised paw.

"Yes Plum?"

"What kind of awards? I thought we were not going to be graded on our performances."

"Oh no, don't worry! They're the fun kind of awards. Nothing to take too seriously," Mrs Winter answers with a wink.

From the look on Plum's face, I can see that she doesn't share the idea that awards can be fun. If it was up to her, we'd be graded all the time and we'd receive serious awards.

"Ok time to go, follow me!"

We all know the way to Kappa meadow by now and walk there with no problem, exchanging jokes or singing songs all along. Once there, we all follow Mrs Winter's explanations and take our place on the benches already placed there for us. I end up sitting between Plum and Bean, and after months at school together we all know our classmates well. I'm not best friends with everyone but I've come to know them well enough to have an easy chat with them while waiting. Plum is a bit tricky because she tends to answer to you in a sort of aggressive tone even when you're super nice to her. But I now know it's not personal, it's just her personality.

Once we've all settled down, I look around us and see that the benches for the parents and teachers are placed at a 90 degree angle from ours, so the student presenting can address both sides easily. In the middle is the presentation zone that Mr Pinecone is now entering. He walks slowly, making the fact that he's so big even scarier. Once he reaches the wooden podium set up in the middle, he looks down at his notes and magically amplifies his voice so he can be heard by all before starting his speech. Well, he is trying to be heard over the hubbub of the crowd.

"Welcome, welcome everyone! I am Mr Pinecone, the current headmaster of ..."

After some confused murmurs from the crowd, Mr Pinecone double-checks his notes and realises that he's using the speech from the beginning of the school year. He tries to switch it to the correct one, hoping no one has noticed but of course we all did. There are some giggles among us and even among the parents. Only Plum is throwing everyone a disapproving look, as if to say, "We shouldn't make fun of the headmaster!" Finally, Mr Pinecone clears his throat and starts again like nothing happened.

"Parents, students, teachers, welcome! As you know, today marks the last day of our school year and, as is customary, we're celebrating by asking the Seed class students to demonstrate what they have learned through a special project. Ideally the project should help others, but it can be anything. We're here to celebrate, not to judge or grade these assignments. As long as it's an original project, we'll be proud to watch. The students will come here one by one, and Mrs Winter, the Great Wizard and I will stand nearby in case there are any problems."

"Any problems? What kind of problems?" I hear Wind ask our classmates a bit too loudly.

I guess Mr Pinecone heard him all the way over on his podium because he immediately adds, "But do not worry, in all these years we never had an animal lose an ear or a paw due to a badly executed project."

I hear Wind's loud sigh of relief but Mr Pinecone adds, "Well, we did have some burnt whiskers once but I'm sure it won't happen again today."

"What? Burnt whiskers?" asks Wind, very loudly this time.

"Shhhh ..." Plum shushes him. It's her typical way of letting you know that it's time to be serious and stop interrupting the headmaster. Mr Pinecone ignores this interruption and goes on.

"After all the students are done with their projects, we'll have a fun awards presentation and then of course it will be time for our traditional end of the year picnic."

He gathers his notes and nods towards Mrs Winter.

"I will now let Mrs Winter introduce her students."

He gets down from the podium and I see our teacher take his place with the list of names in front of her, ready to go.

"Thank you Mr Pinecone. Students, I will call your names one by one. We have arranged your seats in the order that you'll be called, so make sure you are ready to go before your friend has finished. If your project calls for you to use some extra objects, please gather everything ahead of time to be ready for your turn. It's nicer for everybody if things go smoothly. But most importantly, remember this: relax! Take a deep breath and remember that it's just a presentation. It's fine if you stutter or if your project is not perfect. It won't be the end of the world. And if you're worried about talking in front of us, remember that you know almost everyone here. They are your classmates and their families. We're all a big family in Woodland and no one will judge you. Don't be nervous, be proud! Show us what you've learned and ... ," she adds with a smile in her voice, "show your parents how great your teacher was!"

All the parents and students laugh at this and with that we're all relaxed when she calls the first name, "Breeze!"

Breeze flies to the podium and starts to talk to the small crowd.

"Hello, my name is Breeze and I'm going to show you my school project. Those who know me, know how much my brother and I love to sing. We can't help it, we sing all the time."

There are giggles among the parents, as well as the students, who know the twins. I smile, remembering how they were initially planning on doing one project for both of them. They think so much alike that we had to remind them that it was one project for each student, not each family.

"So, to make the lives of those around us easier and to make sure we don't lose our friends we ... I mean, I, came up with this."

We all wait to see what she's going to show us. Is it an object? I don't see anything from here. Maybe it's because Breeze is so small. Ah, I see her put her right wing on her acorn and it looks like she's singing but I can't hear anything. I look around and see that everyone is as confused as me. Breeze takes her wing off her acorn and talks again in the mic.

"Did you hear me sing?"

I don't want to hurt her feelings by saying no, so I do nothing and wait for her explanation. Everyone is shaking their heads no and Breeze smiles at this.

"Well, that's because of my *Breezie Bubble!* I created a soundproof bubble to surround me whenever I want to sing without disturbing those around me."

That's actually a great idea! I start to listen to her explanation of how she did it but my classmates are a bit noisy, so it's hard to understand everything. I'll have to ask her later.

Then it's Smore's turn. He's walking to the podium with a small bag in his big bear's paws. After introducing himself, he opens his bag and extracts some stones that he lays in his open palm for everyone to see.

"I'm sure you're all thinking that these look like ordinary stones but this is my project, I call it Warm Paws. You simply need to hold these special stones and activate them by saying 'Brrr, I'm cold!' They will start heating up immediately to warm you up."

"Very clever Smore!" Mrs Winter says. "Can you tell us how this idea came to you?"

"Well, I'm always ... I mean, I have a friend who's always cold despite being a big animal, and I wanted to help him ... I mean her!" he stutters, trying to cover his small lie.

"That's very thoughtful of you!" Mrs Winter replies with a little smile.

Everyone in the class knows that Smore is always cold. He's not as massive as Mr Pinecone but he's big, bigger than Wind, and he's always complaining that he's cold or that he might be cold. All year long, he's often been seen wearing a scarf "just to make sure I don't get a cold!"

I remember Honeysuckle asked him "what about the animals with no paws?" when he told us the name he had chosen for his project, and he got really upset, declaring, "It's my project, I can name it whatever I want!"

The good thing with Smore is that he never stays upset for long and that he's not scary at all despite his size. He's really more like a big marshmallow: he looks tough from the outside but he's very soft on the inside.

Chapter 49

Our turns

Caramel and Bloom come after Smore but I'm most excited to see what Wind came up with. Just like Honeysuckle, he was quite secretive about his project and didn't tell us much. He only hinted that it would be very helpful for our group so I'm really excited to see what it is. I catch his eye on his way to the podium to encourage him and I hear Almond cry a big, "You can do it!" to cheer him up.

"Before I talk about my project, I want to say something about my process. Months ago when we were assigned this project, my initial idea was to create something to help students stay awake in class."

Parents and students laugh and Mrs Winter pretends to be offended with a little "Oh really?"

"Well, by 'students', I mean me. But thankfully my friends helped me realise something important: I was not falling asleep because the class was boring but because I was not happy. And because of this my magic was suffering. But the same friends helped me find a way to feel better through art. So I wanted to create something that will benefit them and that's how I came up with this."

He turns slightly to show his right ear to the parents' side, but from our side it's hard to see what he's showing. It looks like one of those earpieces humans use to talk on their phone without holding it. I've seen them wear those while passing through the woods and I wonder how Wind got one.

"This is the *Talkie Talkie*. Basically, it's a communication system to help animals talk easily, whatever their size. As I said, I'm lucky to have found great friends here, but they are all ... quite small compared to me so it's not always easy for us to understand each other. But with the Talkie Talkie now it will be!"

He goes on to explain how he magicked it and that he made several headset versions to fit different animals' heads. It's really impressive!

"And my hope is to work further on this idea and maybe develop some sort of telephone like humans use to facilitate communication with animals living far in the forest."

His project is a big success and gets lots of applause. I see him blush a bit under his fur but he deserves it, it's such a great idea! And he's right, it's going to help us so much!

Almond follows just after him and arrives at the podium with a bunch of acorns attached to strings, like the necklaces used for Magicol.

"This is called The Help & Care Acorn. When Mrs Winter assigned us this project, she told us to be inspired by our experiences and that's what I did. When my friends and I got lost outside Woodland, we were lucky to find Peppermint before something really bad happened to him. He was injured and all alone, and that inspired me. I knew I needed to do something to make sure it wouldn't happen to other animals."

She explains to the crowd what she told us last time. How the acorns will be placed in various places inside and outside our forest and how they will be filled with magic to make sure they can be used by anyone, whether they practise magic or not.

"My plan is to help injured or lost animals outside Woodland but the acorns could also be here for any animals who may need our help here in Woodland. It could be for something serious like a medical emergency but also for social calls. Some of our residents have no family and would be happy with some simple visits. We could even put a system in place so youngsters go and play some board games with them regularly."

"And who will receive the signal when someone presses the buttons?" Mrs Winter asks Almond kindly.

"For now, I have designed each acorn to be linked to a receiving one, with a flashing light to let us know that someone needs help. I obviously can't deal with all of them alone so I hope we can organise a system, where volunteers are responsible for one acorn each. But I'm sure that with some help from more experienced wizards and witches we can think of something better for the long term."

Mrs Winter and Almond discuss this idea for a minute or two, and the Great Wizard even promises to start working on it tonight.

"Almond, this is a very good idea and I have to say I'm impressed by you! I'm sure it's going to help a lot of animals in need," our teacher compliments her.

"Although, to be honest, I had to ask my father's help to explore and research the area ... I just wanted to be honest about it."

"It's perfectly fine to ask for help, Almond. Especially for a project so selfless. Never hesitate to ask for help if you need it!"

Almond gets back to her seat to let Nutmeg and then Echo follow with their presentations. Once they are done, it's my best friend's turn and I'm so impatient for him to show his brilliant project to everyone. I've seen him practise it and it's absolutely PERFECT! He walks slowly to the podium carrying a black garbage bag behind him. He starts directly by asking the audience a question.

"What's the biggest problem in our forest?"

(When he asked me the same question weeks ago, I admit my answer was "Not enough chocolate" and this was not the answer he was expecting.)

"Well, I should say outside Woodland to be more precise. You see, some time ago my friends and I left the forest to explore a bit farther than we usually do and I learned something important that day. Humans are simply ... disgusting!"

A lot of parents and teachers seem to agree with him.

"I mean, not all of them of course. I'm sure there are some nice ones somewhere but, to be honest, what we saw made me very angry. There was trash everywhere, it was unbelievable! But I realised that, instead of us going there to clean their mess regularly, we should teach them a lesson. Let me show you."

He walks up to a garbage bin that was set on purpose by Mrs Winter and empties all his trash from his garbage bag on the ground. A collection of plastic cups, burger wrappers, bottles, tissues lie there. Buttercup touches his Magicol, casts his Whisper and I see the light travel from his acorn to the pile of garbage until all the trash flies into the bin. The parents applaud and he goes back to the podium to explain the rest.

"My spell will work directly on the ground. Of course, I could simply put a spell on our surroundings so that everything will fly directly in a trash can but I really want to educate those dirty humans. That's why my spell will make sure any trash left by humans in Woodland and around, will jump back into their bags or their pockets."

"What if they're not carrying anything?" asks a curious parent.

"Well, in their face!" he answers, with his tiny fist in the air.

Buttercup is not the kind of hedgehog to get mad easily but when it comes to our planet and our forest you shouldn't mess with him!

"Enough is enough! If they don't like getting trash in their faces then they shouldn't throw theirs in ours. It's our home and even though we are small, we don't have to stay silent. We have to fight back!"

Everyone cheers for him and he adds that since it will take him some time to enchant so much land, he will gladly accept some help. Just like with Almond's project, many animals volunteer and some even add their own suggestions.

"We could even make their trash bigger? How about their phones smaller? That will teach them!"

Ideas fly back and forth for a minute until Mrs Winter asks Buttercup, "And what's the name of your project Buttercup?"

"Oh! I call it *Dirty Pigs*" he explains with a cute coy expression

At that, all the parents and students laugh and cheer him on some more. I'm yelling louder than everyone to show how proud I am of my best friend. If there's an award for the most popular project I think he'd win it without a doubt!

After Buttercup, it's Dean's turn to present his fashion-themed project, then Rain and Plum, before my name is finally called. I take a deep breath and remind myself that I have nothing to fear.

I know everyone in front of me, I'm not afraid, I'll be fine! But just in case I get nervous, I still decide to lock my gaze on my family. I locate them easily. Peppermint is sitting between our parents, waving at me with a little flag he made yesterday. Even if I do poorly with my presentation, at least I have the comfort of knowing I have the best little brother! And just as I leave my seat I also hear Almond and Buttercup cheer for me. The best brother and the best friends in the world!

I take my place behind the wooden podium, stroke my tail very briefly, take a deep breath and start my presentation.

"For a lot of bookworms in Woodland, it's not easy to get new books to read. Of course we have Dreams but I know that many animals are too busy or too old to go there. So, in association with the Moon sisters, I'm creating the Books in Tree project to help bring books to everyone.

"Basically, the idea is that we'll have boxes in different parts of the forest where you'll always find a selection of books, donated by the library. I also want to use the boxes as an opportunity to recycle books to encourage a continuous cycle. Once you're done with a book that you don't want to keep, you simply put it in the nearest box and it becomes part of this new magic moving library. I connected each box so that books can travel from one to another. It's not much yet but I'll work on ways to improve it as I learn more magic, like creating an index system to keep track of all the books available in real time. I also used the water repellent spell to protect the boxes from the rain."

I demonstrate with the two prototypes I made, already lying on the floor, by transferring a book from box A to box B.

"I know it doesn't require a lot of magic but I'm sure this small project can help others. Sometimes small things can have a big impact!"

I see a lot of smiles from other small animals but also from some bears and wolves.

"Don't worry Applesauce, we don't ask you to use the most magic, we just want to see if you can put your learning to good use for our community. Because, you see," Mrs Winter now speaks to the whole class, "this is not only about what you've learned this year, but also about the fact that you'll use your magic for good.

And I'm sure that no matter your age or your size you can all do something big if you put your mind to it." She turns back to me, "Thank you Applesauce, that's a very nice project and I'm sure I'll have some books to give to your library."

As I leave the podium to go back to my seat, I hear applause and a specially loud "Yahoo!" from my brother and my mum. Now that I'm done, I can watch the remaining students and relax. And I'm lucky because after Bean and Sidney, it's my friend Honeysuckle who wraps up all the presentations and, knowing her, I'm sure it's going to be something special! All these weeks, she's been very secretive about it, always practising in secret. The only thing I've seen her do that seemed connected to her project was moving objects with her Magicol. I'm impatient to finally see what it was all about.

"Hello, my name is Honeysuckle. My family and I are quite new in this forest since we moved before the beginning of the school year but I have to say, it's been a very nice year among you all. You all gave us a warm welcome and I was glad to quickly make some great friends."

She turns towards the students' benches and waves her little white paw at us. I wave back all excited and proud to be in her speech. She turns back and continues in a more serious tone.

"But I have to admit that when I started at the Academy something kind of surprised me."

She pauses for effect before explaining.

"I'm talking of course about the fact that it is called 'Academy for Wizards' with no mention of witches, even though they're allowed there and make up a good percentage of the number of students. I know it seems like it's not important but you know, for weeks it has been bothering me. I kept asking myself why we were not included in the name of the school if it was indeed open to all. I've even asked the headmaster and to be honest, he didn't know either. Well, he didn't know or he didn't want to discuss it, I don't know."

She shrugs innocently and pauses just long enough to make the headmaster uncomfortable. Even from my place I can see him fidget in his seat.

"I could have stopped there but when Mrs Winter told us about this end of the year project, I knew what to do!"

She turns to the left with her Magicol stone in her right paw, and focuses on a pile of tree branches that have been prepared for her. She starts to lift them and arrange them mid air to form letters, then words.

"Wait a second, I'll make it bigger so everyone can see."

Once enchanted, the words are big enough so that I can read them from my seat. It says "Woodland Academy for Wizards of all Ages and Sizes."

"So you see, that represents the school sign as it is now. Well, should I say, as it was until this morning. Because I went and changed it just before the ceremony. Now it looks like this!"

She makes new branches fly from the ground and moves those already in the sky, so it now reads "Woodland Academy for Wizards and Witches of all Ages and Sizes".

With the letters that big we all see what she did right away and the reaction is immediate. There's a big silence! Some female animals in the crowd start to clap shyly then quickly the cheers get louder as everyone joins in, family, students and even the teachers. The only one not clapping with enthusiasm is the headmaster. Before the unanimous crowd reaction, he seemed to wonder if he should reprimand Honeysuckle but he soon realises that he doesn't have a choice but to join in. Telling her off now in front of the whole school and the families would look terrible. And it gets even worse for him when Honeysuckle adds with a mischievous smile, "I actually wondered if I should put witches first since our Great Wizard is female ... "

The crowd becomes silent again and I'm curious to see how this will turn out. I should have brought a snack, there's so much excitement! The Great Wizard immediately cheers louder at this and walks toward Honeysuckle to join her at the podium.

"What's happening?" I ask in a loud whisper to my neighbour. Everyone else seems to wonder the same question and to be on the hedge of their seats. Once she reaches the podium, I see the Great Wizard wink at Honeysuckle before turning toward the public.

"Well, I didn't expect this day to offer so many surprises but

I have to say I totally agree with this idea to add some female representation to the name of this grand school!" she starts to say.

Honeysuckle smiles at this and I'm sure she's glad to have at least this approval.

"Just like Honeysuckle, I also think that there is no reason why wizards should come before witches, but I think we could perhaps have a vote among the school teachers and students to decide on that later."

Poor headmaster is looking really gloomy now and I see Honeysuckle laugh softly at this proposition.

"In the meantime, I would like to announce that from now on I want to be called the Great Witch! There's no reason I should be named the Great Wizard since I'm not one!"

"What? But the law?" asks the headmaster loudly.

"The law? What law?" replies the Great Witch.

"I mean the ... the tradition. You can't suddenly change your name like this. It has always been like this, animals will be confused and ..."

The Great Witch interrupts him quickly but does it with a smile so it doesn't look aggressive which I think makes it even more powerful.

"Yes, it has always been like this, but it doesn't mean that it can't be changed, does it? Imagine if we never changed anything just because it has always been done that way."

Mr Pinecone is speechless.

"And, as for your other concern, we can ask everyone what they think right away."

Again, he's left with nothing to say. He tries to argue that there's no need to rush this and suggests that they organise a proper poll later but the Great Witch doesn't reply to this. The crowd even starts to chant that they want to vote now.

"OK, so let's see ..." She drums her paws on the podium and says, "Raise your paws if you won't be confused by the fact that I won't be called the Great Wizard anymore."

In a flash, parents, students and teachers are raising their paws, tails or wings unanimously. Everyone is here to support her choice.

"Well, I think that's settled then!" she declares, looking at the headmaster.

"Thank you Honeysuckle for starting this conversation," the Great Witch tells her. And she adds, "I never really liked this Great Wizard name anyway" with a wink.

Honeysuckle is overjoyed and goes back to her seat with the biggest smile I've ever seen.

Chapter 50

Awards and Feast

From what Mrs Winter told us, once we're all done with our projects, the ceremony is supposed to close with a speech from the headmaster and her awards presentation. Then we can finally share the end of the year feast with our families and friends.

Once Honeysuckle is back with us, Mrs Winter and Mr Pinecone make their way toward the podium. Mr Pinecone seems to be completely lost in thoughts while Mrs Winter is walking slightly ahead of him to clean up the mess left by some of our projects (some puddles of water and piles of leaves and twigs). By the time our headmaster reaches the podium it's all clean and she gestures to him to go on. He gives her a small nod and after retrieving a piece of paper from his waistcoat pocket, he starts his speech.

"Thank you Mrs Winter for cleaning all this for me, I really appreciate it."

She looks up at those kind words, obviously surprised by those. He pauses, looks at his speech in front of him but folds it up and puts it back in his pocket, shaking his head. That's strange, doesn't he need it?

"I had prepared my usual speech but I think this year I won't need it."

I hear others whisper in the crowd, everyone clearly as surprised as I am.

"I ... Well, first I need to start by saying congratulations to all of our students who showed us their projects. Another year has gone by and I'm always surprised by our new students' ideas. We saw some very interesting ideas and I personally loved the projects that were created to help others. There's nothing more important than being there for other animals. I also love that your ideas," he says, turning toward the students' bench, his eyes fixed on Honeysuckle, "helped inspire us who have already graduated. I admit, I didn't think this day would be so educational for me."

He pauses again, hesitating.

"I know, I can give the impression that I'm an old bear, not easy to talk to. And I look like I don't like changes ... Well, it's true, I don't. I'm a bear of habit. If I can be honest with you, I love to have my breakfast at the same time everyday, and have my little routines at home."

We all smile and I giggle picturing Mr Pinecone with his morning juice and his slippers waiting for him at home.

"But I'm also a headmaster and I want what's best for my students. Miss Honeysuckle's project made me realise that we could indeed do better for our witches here and I'm sure you all have other ideas. I believe we can work on ways to improve life at the Academy, so I have decided to hold regular meetings for anyone who'd like to talk about issues they face at school, or suggestions they have to improve our current system. I'm not saying I'll accept every idea but at least I'll be open to listen to them all. So don't hesitate to join the New Academy Committee. We'll organise all this and give you all the details later but for now, I'm leaving the podium to Mrs Winter who is dying to present the awards to her students. And I'm sure everyone is impatient for lunch, so I'll finish now."

Everyone cheers for him as he leaves. I think we were all very surprised by his speech. I hear my classmates around me comment "Great idea!", "Honeysuckle it's all thanks to you!", and "Waouh who knew he could be so open?"

Who knew indeed?

The crowd goes silent quickly though because, like he said, it's time for our special awards and we're all excited about them!

"Thank you Mr Pinecone for this touching speech. I support

314

this great initiative to form the New Academy Committee and I'm sure we'll see great changes in the near future. But now, let's be serious because it's time for me to present the end of the year Absolutely Amazing Awards!"

She says those last words extra loudly, almost like she's singing. She takes a brief pause and smiles, before asking us, "Seed class, are you ready?"

We all cheer loudly and Mrs Winter starts right away with the first award.

"Let's start then! The first prize is for the best singing voice."

Everyone laughs because there's clearly no suspense there. In fact, just as she's about to announce the winner, everyone in the class shouts a combination of "Breeze!"and "Echo!" at the same time. Mrs Winter laughs at our enthusiasm but declares that there can only be one winner for the Absolutely Amazing Award.

"So this award goes to Breeze!"

Echo cheers loudly for his sister and right away our teacher continues with the award for the most cheerful student.

"And this one goes to Echo!"

We all clap and agree with these first two choices.

Then comes the award for the most artistic paws and I'm so glad when Wind gets it. He's beaming as he goes to the podium to receive it. He waves to his parents and almost trips on his way back to his seat but I'm so happy to see him so excited.

Bean gets the "Outstanding Organiser" award and Honeysuckle receives "Best Problem Solver" just after.

"We had some hesitations about the next one because several of you were fit to receive it, but in the end we decided to hand the "Sharing and Caring" award to Almond."

I jump up and down on my seat and cheer loudly for my friend because she really deserves it. Her project, plus her precious help in our rescue mission for Peppermint, is the proof that she was well chosen.

Next to me, Plum receives the "Most Likely to Become Headmaster" award and she seems really proud of it. I laugh when I'm called for mine: "Speedy Reader"

Mrs Winter hands it to me with a pat on the shoulder and a

"great job on your first year, Applesauce!"

The awards are made of wood and shaped like opening seeds with the title written on it. I recognise Root's woodcarving style immediately. It's really pretty and I can't wait to put it on my bookshelf at home. Names are called and one by one everyone in the class gets a special prize.

Once the last award is handed out (to Dean for being the "Fashion Expert") Mrs Winter makes her final announcement.

"The projects have been presented, the awards have been given. Seed class, your first school year is officially over! We can now all feast and celebrate!"

She nods toward us and at those words, we all grab some blue powder from the jar she handed to us earlier and throw it in the air above us. Mrs Winter waves her stone toward the big cloud of magic dust and it explodes in the sky like fireworks.

We read "Congratulations!" in the sky and the whole message stays in the air for a short moment before disappearing in a bigger explosion. I expect it to fall down on our heads but it just vanishes completely. We all cheer and everyone around me is giddy with excitement and relief now that we're done with our first year. I rush to go meet with my friends and congratulate them on their projects and awards.

"We're done, yahoo!" Almond cries loudly, jumping up and down to celebrate.

Everyone in our little group starts to congratulate Honeysuckle on her project.

"It was so sneaky, I loved it!" I tell her.

"Such a great idea! A simple use of magic to do something big!" Buttercup says.

"Honestly, sorry guys, but I think it was my favourite project!" Almond adds. "Your projects were all amazing but you can't compete with Honeysuckle's!"

"Are you insane?" Honeysuckle asks her, shocked. "Your project was so brilliant! I just moved some twigs but yours is going to help animals in need."

"Yes, but yours helped to start something big and ..."

Wind uses his big size to interrupt them and settle their friendly argument.

"You know what? All our projects were great!" The girls laugh, agree, and Wind continues "So no need to fight over this. Let's celebrate instead because I'm starving!"

We don't need any convincing and follow him to meet up with our families. The teachers and parents (Magicals and Non-Magicals) are already setting everything up for the big feast. I think we're not the only ones impatient to start eating. Whether they practise magic or not, everyone comes together, getting rid of the podium, pushing the benches away on the side, and setting several big blankets on the green grass while the rest are unpacking the food. Just like on our first day, everyone brought some dishes to share and we'll have a simple picnic on the ground.

We grab some baskets and bags to help unpack and quickly everything is ready. Small groups form here and there, and after receiving our parents' congratulations (mine gave me a big hug), my friends and I find a spot to eat together while the adults form their own group a bit farther away. Of course Peppermint joins us. He came rushing toward us as soon as possible. He's so excited by this special day, and keeps talking about all the things he loved. It's "Oh did you see Plum's project?" here and "Did you see how Caramel did this? It was so amazing!" there. He's so cute.

"Oh I forgot the juice! Who wants some carrot juice?" Honeysuckle asks us, getting up again.

"I do, thanks!" Almond asks.

"Who wants some cucumber sticks?"

Everyone sits down on the blanket with their own selection of food but we quickly start sharing bits and pieces here and there. It's very natural now and I love how easy it has been to become friends with them. Honeysuckle comes back to the blanket and as I look around our small group I smile at how many things have changed since I started Woodland Academy (for Witches and Wizards!)

I met Wind by accident, became great friends with Honeysuckle, got lost in the woods, fought with some crazy humans to protect my friend, found a brother, wrote a whole book, read many more, and oh yes, this little detail, I learned magic!

"Waouh, I still can't believe the first year is over," I sigh to

Buttercup who's next to me, nibbling his nut mix.

"I know! It went so fast!" he grabs a cashew nut and adds with a wink, "but you know what the good news is?"

I shake my head, wondering if he's talking about some pies or some cookies I haven't seen on the big table.

"The good news is that we still have so much to learn!"

I smile at this. It's true. I was so focused on how fast those first months at the Academy went by that I didn't stop to think about what's still ahead of us. There are still so many potions and spells to learn. Maybe new friends to make too. I hope there will be less scary adventures in unknown woods. Although, now that I think about that, if we hadn't taken that risk that day exploring the woods, then we would have never have found Peppermint, seen how humans live, discovered how dirty some parts of the woods were, and I probably wouldn't have written my book. And I did learn a lot while writing my guide, about our forest and about magic.

I also believe it showed me how important it is to keep our history and our magic alive. So many things tend to get lost with time. We forget and get confused about who did what first, how things used to be, what our traditions are. That's why writing this book was so important to me and why it was great for me to tell you, dear reader, our story. I've done my part, now we need YOU to keep the magic alive! Share this story with anyone who still believes in the power of potions, spells and enchantments. The more you talk about us and our little forest, the more people will start believing in magic again. And I think the world would be a nicer place if more people believed in magic, don't you think?

So that's your mission: BELIEVE in us, believe in magic and never forget. Share our names and our stories with your friends, parents, cousins, teachers ... Tell them that magic is real and that it's not only for fairy tales and novels.

And if they don't believe you, keep us in your heart and think about us when you feel lonely or when you can't fall asleep.

Maybe we'll meet again for new adventures, who knows? In the meantime, I realise that my plate is empty and I still have some space for dessert! What should I get? A slice of apple pie or some chocolate chip cookies? Or maybe both?

-THE END-

Acknowledgments

When the idea of Woodland Academy came to me in 2017, I had no idea that it would take over my life like it has. What started as a small idea in the shower was supposed to be a short story for my kids. But at one point my characters became so alive to me that they told me to forget the other novel I was working on and to focus on them. I tried to work on both for a while but in the end, I'm glad they won the argument.

Writing this book has been a real adventure and those characters were my companions through years of chronic pain. My health has been getting worse and worse over the years but somehow, I always knew I would finish this story because it was so alive in my head. I had times when I didn't touch it for months (because of my pain or because of Covid and the sudden surprise of having to homeschool my children!) but every time I went back to Woodland it always felt natural, like I was with friends. Writing is hard but one of my favourite things was seeing characters come to life under my eyes, like I had no control over them. It was a truly magical experience to see them being born like that. I'm glad I never gave up because even if it took me years I still did it!

I wrote this story for my sons and they were the biggest inspiration for the main characters. Applesauce is a mix of Ewan and myself but also has the appetite of my youngest son. But Ulysse has so much energy that I couldn't have only one character for him so I see him in Buttercup (who loves to recycle) and Almond (who's always running around and overexcited!). Even my husband inspired Sprout with his love for baking and his infinite kindness.

Some places or character names were also inspired by real life, and all the books mentioned are real, except one.

This story took years to write so I have some people to thank.

First I'd like to thank you for reading this book! I know how precious time is and I'm honoured that you took the time to be with Applesauce and Buttercup.

Then I'd like to thank my friend Maria for her friendship over the last few years. Whether it is during our hours-long meetings or viaour daily texts, your support means a lot. No one else can get my Jane Austen memes or can fangirl as much as I do.

Thank you Cion for making my life easier, I don't know what I'll do without you.

This book wouldn't be what it is without Christine's invaluable help, as she worked hard on editing it. Thank you for your neighbourly friendship when our kids were babies and for coming to my rescue with this other kind of baby.

Thank you to all the coffee shops in Hong Kong where I wrote for hours: Zaks, Starbucks and Pacific Coffee. I lost count of how many coffees I went through to write this book!

Thank you to my late grandmother for putting books in my hands when I was living in a world without stories.

I'd also like to thank all the authors that inspired me and helped me go through those last few years of chronic illness. Their books helped me feel better when my body was in daily pain and to me, that is a true gift.

Thank you to:

Mackenzi Lee, for the Grand Tour and the imperfect Monty. You'll never know how much comfort it brings me to reread your books.

Rainbow Rowell, for creating my favourite vampire and inspiring me with your magic.

Chris Colfer, for the never ending trip to the land of stories.

Becky Albertalli, for Simon, Reid and so many wonderful characters.

Cassandra Clare, for creating one of my favourite characters, Will.

And a special thank you to Neil Gaiman for showing me that it's okay if it takes you years to write a book. Reading Coraline really helped me let go of my guilt.

And most importantly, the biggest thank you to my three men!

To Ewan and Ulysse for being the best thing that happened to me. You'll never understand how much I love you but now you'll be able to say, "My mum wrote a book for me!"

To Greg, for being the most amazing Sprout to my Rose. I still can't believe how lucky I am to share my life with you! Thank you for taking care of me throughout my years of daily pain: for the food you make me, the takeaways you pick up for me, and all the times you let me choose a movie just to cheer me up a bit.

Everyday when I write down what I'm grateful for, you three are at the top of my list. Always.

Maëva

About the author

Maëva loves to travel and has lived in Asia (Japan, Singapore and Hong Kong) for 15 years (and counting). She has a husband who still makes her laugh after 20 years and two boys who keep her (very) busy.

When she's not writing about squirrels and hedgehogs, she's reading, painting or rewatching a favourite movie. She enjoys simple things like drinking a nice cup of tea or eating a good apple pie (with vanilla ice cream!).

Her favourite superheroes inspire her to keep fighting her illness.

Woodland Academy is her first novel.

You can contact her by mail: contact@maevadraws.com

Or follow her on Instagram: @maeva.writes

If you loved spending time in Woodland, please take a few minutes to leave a positive review on Amazon. Reviews make it easier for readers to find self-published books so your help would be really appreciated!

Thank you,
Maëva

Lightning Source UK Ltd.
Milton Keynes UK
UKHW022027060922
408432UK00009B/2218